For Hele

The Author: Robert William:

I was raised in the ., ... an area known as the Black C __.y, un the outskirts of Birmingham. My parents were shopkeepers. They had strong beliefs in education, self-reliance and hard work. Resulting from such a positive upbringing I was the only one in my family to go to university. I studied Medicine at St Bartholomew's Hospital Medical School, 'Barts.' Following that I trained at Moorfields Eye Hospital in London, then St George's Hospital, London, until being appointed Consultant Ophthalmic Surgeon in Worthing and Chichester when I was thirty two. I remained in West Sussex practicing as a Consultant Ophthalmologist for ten years in the NHS, then for a further fifteen years in full time private practice.

In my fifties I moved to Ireland with my wonderful Irish wife. Here I have been involved in renovating dilapidated houses.

The Book: 'Love and Vengeance'

If you get one millionth of the pleasure from reading this book that I have received from writing it, then you will have a very good read. It is a yarn of crime and romance.

With only one exception all characters are entirely fictional. I have not met Rebecca, but I would like to. I am neither Marcus nor Luke, but I would like to be. One of those may surprise you, especially as the only feature that I have in common with either of them is with the other. The only true-life character is Toby; the giveaway is that I have kept his actual name. The descriptions of him and of most of his actions are factually correct. Only his involvement in a fight is fictional. You may recognise the city but a little lateral thinking is needed.

The Plot

Rebecca arrives in a new post. She has been unlucky in

love and feels side-lined in her career. Her disenchantment increases when she faces misogyny and corruption at work. Following an attack on her in the street the sequence of events is distorted and she is unjustly arrested. This precipitates further major problems in her profession.

Then she is surprised by an unexpected change in her career.

Even better, following the uplift in her work, Rebecca at last finds love again. Unfortunately, unknown to her, the handsome and charismatic man that she has fallen for is a serial abductor, torturer and murderer.

CHAPTER 1:
REBECCA: ARRIVAL

The doors opened with a sigh. Alighting from the train only required a short step down to the worn flagstone of the platform. I walked a little way forwards and then I stopped. I turned around and then I looked around. What I saw made me feel that I had not only stepped down a hundred millimetres but that I had also stepped back more than a hundred years. This station is frozen in time. Everything looks Victorian. All is timeworn, old but well maintained and in good condition. The vintage waiting room, the wooden signal box with its outside steps, the trimmed bushes to the rear of the platform; they all belong in a black and white film.

During my journey the carriages had been nearly empty but here, on the station, all is totally deserted. The train seemed to hesitate, as if it had stopped unwontedly. No one went and no one came, the platform is bare. Someone unseen in a rear carriage cleared his throat. Then the dusty silence reclaimed the day.

I felt the heat of the afternoon. Today the weather is reminiscent of late June, not the usual conditions for late October. Our Indian Summer is continuing. The morning haze has burnt off. It is already twenty-two degrees, not a record, but it feels hot after a cool September. It truly feels like summer. No air is moving and small insects are whirring.

The train gave a small jolt as if finally preparing to move, reluctantly. As I am clearly in the past I half expected a crashing of doors as they are swung shut by a whiskery man in a dark blue hat as he blows a whistle. Surely there would follow a hiss of steam then the clackity-clack of bogeys bouncing across the gaps where the ends of the rails do not join. Instead there came a near inaudible thud of automatic doors sliding shut, their rubber edges softly touching. Then I heard a quiet electronic whine accompanied by a deep rumble of smooth metal wheels on smooth modern track.

I watched the train depart, marvelling that it is a mere two hours since I had caught it at Paddington and that it has transported me to an alternative world. Back there I had passed a fleet of serpentine rolling stock arranged in row after row, their chisel fronted engines on their geometric, straight parallel, tracks. I had stood on polished, modern, white stone; I had faced endless facades of glass ticket barriers; I had walked under huge stainless tubes holding aloft glaring signs as the Tannoys incomprehensibly blared and crackled. The tall cast-iron, Victorian roof supports were indeed there and were clearly visible but they went largely ,unseen, their massive beauty undetected by most in the busy crowd of scurrying passengers, their pasty faces back lit by handheld 'phone screens.

Here the Victorian iron is prominent; its curlicues could be touched with the aid of only a step-ladder. It is similarly unseen other than by me, this time because I am the only one present. The roof is of old wood. An old white-painted return from its trackside edge has carved, pointed ends to its ancient planks which hang down over the edge of the platform. The tracks, only two pairs here, are curved, set in age-old brown stones and are open to the sky. There are smells of timber and dust. Can I smell coal-smoke? Is it ingrained in the old yellow bricks of the buildings or is it merely a mental suggestion?

At first, after the train had departed, the silence continued absolute. Then a blackbird gave an unseasonable, late song. I cannot see him. There are only high, lonely cloudlets visible in the fair sky. He must also be fooled into thinking that it is June.

Finally I realised that I actually have to move, sometime, preferably today. There is no exit visible from this platform. At the far end is a white wooden bridge to the opposite side of the tracks. I looked across and saw a disused but well maintained station house and an old ticket office. Again, they are wooden, again they are white painted. The exit and entrance doors are marked alongside. I half expected the doors to swing open and a group of fresh-faced Tommys in their scratchy brown uniforms to emerge, their girls long-frocked and weeping as the young men, mostly in reality only boys, loudly proclaim that they "will be back by Christmas." To the other side of the doors from the original ticket office there is a modern ticket-machine making the station itself appear even more anachronistic. No, it is not the station that is incongruous, it is the grey metal dispenser with its stainless credit card port that is out of time. Einstein used to say, "the station is leaving the train." It is the frame of reference which counts. Here it is the modern ticket machine, and I suppose my track suit, that are in the wrong time.

Then I spotted that I am not alone. In the shadows, in front of the gables of the station house, there is an old man and an even more aged little white dog. They are both staring at me, transfixed, as if to say, "a passenger. How extraordinary, a passenger, here, on a Sunday afternoon." I realised with a start that he is watering the geraniums. I had noticed them but I had discounted them, disbelieving my eyes. I had assumed that I had been hallucinating. I had indeed noticed them but I had not dared to consider that they may be real. That would simply not be possible on a twenty-first century mainline railway station platform.

There are in fact hanging baskets, actual baskets containing real plants. There are thick tresses of blood red trailing geraniums. It is not a fantasy, they are truly here.

The disbelieving man looked at the equally incredulous me. We both nodded acknowledgement and each noted the others' bafflement. Finally I felt released to walk. I reached down for my luggage thankful that I had only a holdall, my lovely Dad having supervised the removers on Friday whilst I concluded a few files in my previous job.

I walked up the stairs and across the bridge.

As I moved above the tracks I thought of how I came to be here. The Bear, as my then boss was always called when he was out of earshot, had called me into his office and suggested that I apply for another job, assuring me that the application was a mere formality. When The Bear makes a suggestion a wise person leaps to their feet, salutes, and rushes out to action it. Rupert Lightman is called The Bear for a very good reason and it is nothing to do with his forename. I had sat stone still, astonished. I have to admit to myself that I was also very disappointed, even hurt. After the overwhelming success of my last assignment, which had been widely reported in the press though my role had to remain secret, I had hoped for promotion. It could also be argued that career advancement would be further and appropriate compensation, in addition to the money I had received, for the injuries that I had sustained. As I then sat there, in his suddenly claustrophobic enormous office, I could see that The Bear wanted to say more. He internally wrestled with himself but did not elaborate, something made him keep his own council. Eventually, wisely, I thanked him for his "suggestion" and left to take it. Technically it is a sideways move. In reality it is a demotion. Perhaps the death that resulted from my last role is too much of an embarrassment and I have to be put out to grass.

I must get back to London. I must not be trapped in this backwater. More, I must achieve the promotion that I so desire. I will try here for a year. I will work hard and re-build my reputation. I had not thought that it needed rebuilding but I was clearly wrong. If after a year I remain side-lined then I will return to my previous career in forensic psychology. I will undertake the research work that I had been offered after completing my Doctorate. It will hurt, I love my early second career, but I will not spend my days in a rut.

As I crossed the bridge it shook, creaked and wobbled so much that I also questioned if I would make the other side. With a degree of relief at having survived the crossing I started down the worn wooden treads to the opposite platform and exit. As I descended the sun's heat again hit my face and made me remember another sunny Sunday a little over two years ago. When, on that day, John had opened the door to leave the sun he let into the frigid atmosphere in our house was then warm on my tears. He never returned. The pull of his sick daughter was greater than that of our love, greater for him that is. I think about him every day but even more so when it is sunny.

Thankfully I reached the up-line platform intact, physically intact that is. Now hearing a drip-drip from the well-watered hanging baskets as well as the confused blackbird's late song, nodding again to the mystified man and his perplexed pooch, I finally exited the station.

Immediately I detected that it is a good job that I had already decided to walk to my new home. There is not a taxi in sight. In fact there is no form of conveyance whatsoever; no cars on the car park; no bus nor bicycle; not even, as I had begun to anticipate, a pony and trap. I started to cross the car park but paused in the centre to look back at the station façade. It is much more modern on this side. It is art deco. Naturally, in keeping with all of the trackside woodwork, it is painted white. Here the hanging baskets of red geraniums have been supplanted by fluted pots of white lilies. They are resplendent. There are dark stains on the side and at the base of the pots where water is still dripping away. They have also been recently watered and they are well cared for.

As I started to move on a contemporary sound came to my ears. That is contemporary as in being in existence for a mere fifty years. I heard the irritating rumble of hard plastic wheels on the tarmac. Skateboarders are approaching. Five of them swept onto the carpark. Spotting me the tall leader swerved towards me and the others followed. I am five feet ten inches, relatively tall for a woman, but he towers over me. As he approached I can see that he is in his twenties, far too old for a skateboard. His whole demeanour is that of a loser, a man among boys. Even his skateboard is an old fashioned wooden one. The sidekicks are teenagers, roughly my height. The leader swooped around me several times in tight circles forcing me to stop walking. I cannot decide if he is trying to be impressive or intimidating. He is failing whichever it is.

He whooped as he circled me and finally stopped directly in front with his acolytes in formation, two either side. He is lanky, pale and wears a ragged polyester shirt. I wrinkled my nose, he should wash more often. The boys are young, impressionable. They look fresh-faced and decent. Their only problem is that they should choose better role models. After leering at me for a while he finally spoke in a nasal whine, 'woo-hoo, a blond girlie. We do like blonds don't we men.' I don't see any "girlies," I have to acknowledge that I am thirty now. I guess that he is trying to be both misogynistic and demeaning. There are certainly no men around but I chose not to point this out. They brayed at each other like excited donkeys. I think that something was meant to be amusing. 'Why don't you come with me and have a good time, girlie?' More donkey noises followed.

I tilted my head and looked at him but said nothing. I stood stoke still. In his actions, in his early decay, I can see his determination to avoid self-improvement. In my eyes he is devoid of the least manliness.

As I was about to push past him, ignoring him, I heard a voice behind me. I hesitated and I turned to see that the old man had come out behind me and was waving his stick at them and trying to shout. 'Jason, leave the woman alone. Push off home. I have had enough of you pestering women and girls around here. Push off now. You should also leave the young girls alone when they are catching the train to school. Stop pestering them. I have had enough of your antics.' They were good words but his voice is so weak I could barely make them out. His kindly but determined face is a breath away from a crumbling ruin. He started to fall; I am too far away to catch him. Thankfully he repositioned his stick finding the ground in time and he remained as near to vertical as he seems able to achieve; that is a good twenty degrees off. The dog yapped, more accurately yipped, but he is so decrepit that he had to sit down to do so. He cannot stand up and bark simultaneously. Anyway, I am grateful for the added security of such effective backup; moral if not physical. I am after all a lone woman confronted by five men; well, five males.

Jason, as I now gather he is called, sniggered and shouted, 'shut up you stupid old fool.'

More hee-haws came from the children, all five of them are children. Eventually they realised that not only am I silent and unmoving, I am staring at them. They all suddenly looked less cocksure. They do not yet realise that the old man's words carried information that makes this confrontation far more to me than just something between Jason and I. There is more here to redress than any affront to me. The younger ones seemed about to leave but froze as the lanky leader said, 'Wot youse starin at darlin?' He is clearly trying to be dominant but I detected uncertainty in his voice. I could easily face him down but as the old man has said that he terrorises young girls I think he needs a lesson in manners. Further he should not have spoken to the old guy in that way. This now silent staring is a pivotal moment. I can see that Jason has not even a hazy prescience as to how this may unfold.

Ignoring his appalling diction and poor grammar I chose to reply. They were taken aback to hear my clear authoritative voice which contained menace, not fear. 'I am considering my options.' More false woo-hoos came from Jason. The others are now losing their bottle. 'Option one is to kick you in the balls.'

He shouted in derision at this and feigning mock terror he stepped back and stamping on one end of his skateboard which flicked it up. The board spun in the air and he caught it with one hand on each end. Then he held it in front of himself, in a mock defensive posture, across his groin with his arms locked. He turned to face the two on his right for more childish chortling as he waved the board around pretending to fear a kick. If only he knew.

He then held the board still, only for a fleeting moment but that was sufficient. In fact it was perfect. Not only is the skate board now at an ideal height but he is also looking away. I spun around and with a roundhouse kick split the board in two. The sharp crack silenced them but I was back in position, feet on the ground, smiling serenely before they had even fully comprehended what had happened.

His mouth gaped and then he realised what had just transpired. With a sullen stupid expression he looked down at the remnants, one half in each hand, then his gaze fell lower still to the splinters of wood on the ground. Surprise and anger raged across his features along with unease and a fear of losing what he had mistakenly believed to be his control. He saw a need to assert himself but is clearly uncertain as to how to achieve that. Eventually he stammered, 'you have damaged my property. I could call the police.' He started to try to look determined. The others look ready to run.

'You should have allowed me to present option two.' I took out and held up my warrant card. 'I am the police. Option two is to arrest you.' A laugh which morphed into a hacking cough came from behind me accompanied by a mirthful yap.

Lanky pest looked over me and repeated, 'you can shut up you stupid old fool.' Jason really has no insight whatsoever

Now the gloves are off. I leaned towards him and snarled, but quietly, so that the decent old man could not hear my profanity. 'Fuck off now before I do both.' They all immediately and correctly read my demeanour. I looked at the skateboard to emphasise my skills. The lads turned and sped off on their boards not waiting for Jason who pathetically ran behind calling for them to wait.

I walked back to the man and his dog. I said, 'thanks for speaking up.' He grimaced, ruefully shaking his head. He knows that he could not have physically helped me. 'No, I mean it, it is a great boon when people speak out and support our work.' I paused to ensure that he registered what I said and then I asked, 'you said they are regular pests, do you know them, where they are from?'

'Only the tall older one is a regular, the others vary, he brings along whichever impressionable child he can find. I don't know where he lives but he works in the pizza takeaway in East Street, just below the Langley Pub.'

I took out one of my cards with my name and mobile number and, passing it to him, said, 'if you see him causing any more trouble please call me and I will ask a couple of burly uniforms to have a gentle chat with him. They can wedge him in the rear of a squad car and advise on the pros and cons of pestering women and girls.'

He brightened and chortled at that, 'I think you have advised him sufficiently this afternoon.' Taking my card he read out, 'Detective Inspector Rebecca Fletcher. You must know my neighbour, Barbara, the WPC.'

I shook my head, 'not yet, tomorrow is my first day working in this city.'

'I think that you have already made a good start. Look out for Barbara, she works full time at the Police Station and also is the carer for her poor crippled Mum. Sometimes I look in when she is at work; so do others, but the brunt falls on Barbara.' He looked me up and down and said, matter of fact, not in a salacious manner, 'I am sure that a woman as beautiful as you has a following of tall, dark, handsome men. Barbara is lovely but does not get out, she has not the time. A boyfriend would, I am sure, be a great comfort for her. Spare her one if you can.' This could have been demeaning but was said with such concern and affection that I felt for the lonely, burdened Barbara.

I have found out more about Barbara than is appropriate as her superior officer. I have also found out that we have at least one thing in common. In the time since John left me I have been more like a nun than a single, young woman in London.

I deflected the awkward turn in the conversation. 'The station is lovely, do you look after it.'

'I do my best.'

'The geraniums are beautiful. I have never seen such

abundant flowers before. How do you achieve that?'

He glowed with pride. 'It is all in the compost. There is a secret ingredient. I cannot tell you what it is as you would then have to arrest me.'

Whilst struggling to think what could possibly be illegal in compost I continued, 'the whole station is lovely. You keep it well.'

With his chest puffed out he added, 'I was the last station master until I was replaced by a machine that is mostly out of order. Some of the older drivers remember me and we have a natter when they are waiting for the signals to change. Anyway, I must get home or my wife will think I am chatting up strange women.' He put my card in his pocket and started to stagger off. After a few steps he hesitated, he turned and then called back to me, 'try to ignore Brutus and the harm he causes for many of the PCs. Most officers in your station are good people.'

Brutus, who the hell is Brutus? Clearly he is not good and it is implied that he is senior. I very much hope that he will not be an impediment to my plans to excel and to escape.

I called after him, 'I will. Thanks again for your support.' He did not turn but waved his stick and walked on, now more sprightly, now with a mere ten degrees of list.

I picked up my bag and started on my way to my new home. The route, which I had already looked up on Google, will take me down East Street, past the Langley pub and the pizza takeaway. If lanky pest Jason is there I will give him a wave to show him that I know where he works.

My first day has not even started and already I have been involved in an altercation. I had anticipated in this quiet cathedral city a mundane diet of domestics and rounding up yobs with a little drugs and prostitution every couple of months to spice up the work. At least this time I have neither shot anyone nor been shot myself; not yet anyway.

As I exited the car park the sun shining on my face again recalled the past, this time a happy memory. It was early on a sunny Sunday morning more than twenty-two years ago. I would have been roughly eight. I was holding the hand of my sister, Julia, who would have been six. Mom and Dad had been late getting up and were flushed with happiness. In retrospect I can now guess why. They were dancing in the kitchen to music from their past as Julia and I looked on with joy and amazement. Mom was wearing only a skimpy nighty and Dad had a towel wrapped around him. I was filled with delight at their happiness and with horror as Mom's nighty was riding up and Dad's towel was slipping down. The demanding beat of Jefferson Airplane filled the house and Grace Slick's clear, insistent voice rang out.

'If the truth turns out to be lies,

And all the joy within you dies,

Don't you want somebody to love,

Don't you need somebody to love,

Wouldn't you love somebody to love.'

As I shouldered my holdall and pushed through the heat restarting my solitary walk I thought, "Yes Grace, I do, I would."

As I stepped out of the car park all was again so quiet and deserted that I began to suspect that I had dreamed the last ten minutes. I looked back over my shoulder. The geraniums are there, the flakes of skateboard are on the tarmac. It was not a dream.

CHAPTER 2:
LUKE: RULES ONE AND TWO

I heaved myself up on to the top of the wall. I disturbed a few fallen leaves, they fluttered down. I lay still and flat across the top, quiet, fearful. I cautiously looked down to scrutinise the dreary yard. There was the faint breath of a dry hot breeze on my neck, the only part of me exposed. This is the hottest October that I can remember. As it is Sunday I have at least been able to take it easy during the day. Actual relaxation had been out of the question, given what I have to do this evening. I fully realise that it is not only the heat of this Indian summer, nor my almost total covering of clothes, that is making me perspire so heavily. It is my mounting anxiety.

I paused a little longer on top of the wall, partly to let my heart settle, partly to reconnoitre further. Given our precipitous action I have to ensure that we have not overlooked any other security apparatus. During our brief reconnaissance during the week we had not even spotted the fairly obvious camera until the last moment. That close encounter with what would have been a disastrous mistake has rattled me, to say nothing of the size of the man that I have to deal with.

At least, admittedly again at the last moment, I had thankfully found out that the shop was unusually planned to be shut yesterday. There was a local Saturday competition he was attending. He had put a small notice on the door saying that he would open this afternoon and evening instead. Our original plan was to deal with him on Saturday evening. If we had turned up then he would simply not have been here. We were forced to change the day at the last minute. That further near mistake is not in keeping with our usual meticulous planning. I then hurriedly cancelled my Monday lectures as having to deal with him overnight, even though we will drop him back near here tomorrow before daybreak, I will be in no condition to work. We had discussed postponing this action but the clear and urgent need is overwhelming.

In spite of the heat I felt myself now sweating profusely. Again I thought that this is not because of the clothing and other items that I have to wear, it is my mounting panic. Even so, I must do this. I have to deal with the exigency faced. However I also fully realise that I am untrained for it. Worse, it is simply not me, not my personality, not my skill set. Compounding this I am flouting Rule One. As one of the two authors who made this rule, literally hand-written by me as we did not want to risk a digital trail, it now seems particularly stupid to violate it. We had discussed tonight's challenge yet again whilst driving here. It had sounded a reasonable exception to make on this occasion, once only, given the extreme circumstances. That was before I peered over the top, preparing to commit myself, facing what I have to do now. I am beginning to suspect that rather than taking a reasonable necessary risk we are being reckless. In future we should decide whether or not to proceed when at the site, not when sitting with a gin and tonic, feeling righteous anger and a faux false confidence. I have slithered into foolhardiness, no, more, insanity. Rule One, Maximise surveillance, Minimise risk. We have broken this. We are acting precipitously without good surveillance.

Our reasoning then being that the danger of further and more extreme violence by him is obviously high. At the time, quietly discussing it whilst seated in comfortable armchairs, it was a good decision. That was then. The problem is this is now and I am preparing to roll over the wall.

I froze, startled, as a door opened to the rear of the adjacent shop. A babble of Chinese voices split the air. There is an accompanying pungent smell of the cheap fat used in the take-away which mingles with the reek of the overflowing untended drains. That would have convinced me never to eat there. That is had I not already decided that on seeing the rats as I first pulled myself up here.

I must move, soon, preferably tonight. Breaking the rule is making me hesitate. The purpose of it is to enable our work to continue. Even if one of those whom we are trying to protect is injured or killed, by our failure to act in time; this has to be balanced against the certainty that, if we are stopped due to us not following the rules, then many others will suffer. Utilitarian thinking demands we follow the rules. Emotional distractions led us to break one tonight, hopefully only one. Why him; why did we choose to break the rule for such a big, vicious bastard who is potentially more than usually dangerous to handle? We cannot afford to make mistakes. If caught, either by the police or by one of the brutes, we will have no defence, legal or physical.

I prepared to lower myself into the yard. As virtually all of my skin is covered most likely I will not trigger the PIR and floodlight the yard, exposing myself to the camera which almost certainly feeds to where he is now standing, counting his money, locking up. Even so I extended the metal pole, with the denim bag dangling from the end. I reached out and slipped the bag over the detector. With a rope I lowered my kitbag eight feet down to the dirty yard floor, then myself, transferring my weight from my hands, still desperately trying to maintain a grip on the slippery top, sliding my feet down the wall, taking my weight slowly onto my soft soled sneakers. I silently landed.

Looking cautiously around I gave thanks that the floodlight has not come on, the rear door has not opened. I cannot see any sign that I have been detected, yet. I noticed that I have disturbed some moss on top of the wall; that should not matter. He will certainly know that I came over the top, that will be the least of his concerns, and no one else will either notice or care.

I am now at my most vulnerable, cornered in the yard. Our decision to take him this way, not our usual manner of taking them in the street, now seems impetuous. What were we thinking of in our haste? I feel a hollow dread of what will happen if he comes out now.

The clocks went back last week and though it is still only early evening it is nearly dark. In spite of this and being dressed in black I kept to the side shadows and hesitatingly approached the rear door. From our drive-by a few minutes ago I know that his shop is still brightly lit but the door to the rear store room was then closed, hopefully it still is. Now, through the glass panel in the rear door to this yard, I can see that room remains in darkness. To enable ready access to the shed here, outside, where it appears he keeps more stock, I had guessed that the back door now in front of me, the door between the rear room and this yard, will not be locked. With my gloved hand, while still looking through the clear panel, I tried the handle.

A dog barked. I froze and then smiled, more grimaced, to myself. The bark had been a long way away, not here. I tried the handle. At least one assumption had been correct, the door opened but the hinges gave a loud creak. With the noise my shoulders tightened, I stood stock still and waited. Every second, every noise only serves to further unnerve me. The internal communicating door thankfully remained closed.

Cautiously I inspected the room. In the gloom, I can see racks of fishing rods, high stacks of tackle baskets, shelves of reels and rails of waterproof clothing. The centre of the room is clear but all of the walls are stacked high with the fishing paraphernalia that he sells.

I put my kitbag on the floor and unclipped my Taser. As I moved to the door to the front of the shop a small red light winked on above it. Shit, he has CCTV in here as well. That there would not be a camera in here was another wrong assumption, which is yet another mistake. Thankfully the lights have not come on. The security system may be defective. There again it may be infra-red.

I lunged forward to the side of the door and under the camera praying that I had not been seen. I have to presume that it is linked to one of the screens I had noted next to the till when I had looked through the front window yesterday evening. For such a small shop I had jumped to the conclusion that all the feeds would only be from the external cameras that we had noted. Now that seems more like wishful thinking than a sensible plan. Rule One has been shattered. By now he will have locked the front door for the evening and be tidying up the shop. Hopefully he is nowhere near the screens. I pressed myself against a rack of rods and prepared to wait for five long minutes. When I am sure that he is following his usual routine, when I hear him at the counter, I will quickly step through and Taser him.

Almost immediately the door exploded open and smashed into the wall narrowly missing my shoulder. There was a deafening crash and bits of plaster flew off the wall, hitting me in the face. He hurtled through heading directly for where I had been standing moments before when the camera had winked. If I had not lunged for the wall he would have delivered such a shoulder charge that I would have been immediately and totally incapacitated. Instead, not making contact with me, he was surprised and unbalanced. He stumbled and then he collided with the shelves of fishing baskets just beyond where I had been. They all, along with some shelving, fell over on top of him, ensnaring him. He wildly thrashed around to disentangle himself. He sprang up and turned cat like snarling in my direction.

I am tall, fit and, though lean, I am strong. Despite this I do not have a chance in a brawl. He is as tall as me, out of shape but burly. More importantly he is a street fighter, raised in a rough area. I am not, I was not. I am corned, out gunned, in an impossible situation. There can only be one outcome.

He is now facing me but appears to be having difficulty seeing, I realised that he is still dazzled by the shop lights which are shining through the door adjacent to me as it hangs off its hinges. Whereas my eyes are dark adapted, I am dressed in black and I remain in the shadows. I have only one option and barely one chance. I raised the Taser.

He caught a reflection of light from the doorway which glinted on the metal of the Taser. With lightning speed he swatted it out of my hand. Shit, I had not even seen him move. He may be fat but he is astonishingly fast. Again he charged. This time he caught me in the chest and smashed me back against the wall, pushing me further away from the door and I was propelled into his stock. As the fishing rods fell all around distracting him I managed to slip from under his arms and to one side. Made stupid by my panic I had managed to step straight into the small dim pool of light coming from the doorway. He can now see me clearly.

Foolishly I tried a punch to his head. Even as my fist was moving through the air I realised the futility of it, me trying to punch a roughneck. Even if it connects I doubt he will even notice it. I should have tried to run for the back door, not that I would have had a hope in hell of reaching it.

Not only did he easily block the punch he then used my arm and momentum to pull me into him, his powerful arms then wrapped me in a headlock that I had no way of escaping. He wriggled, shifting his grip, and took a firm lock on my neck. I tried to knee him but he effortlessly pulled me sideways off balance. I am completely immobilised, my face is squashed into his sweaty armpit. I should be frightened of suffocation yet, as the soft well-mannered man I am, I find myself more disgusted by his feral stench. Instead of breaking my neck, which he could easily do and which I now feared, he grabbed my ear and viciously twisted and pulled it. He clearly expected this to be hideously painful for me and that my whole head should have been pulled back which should have at least disabled me, if not killed me.

To his astonishment not only did my ear come off in his hand but so did the whole of my scalp, my face and my neck. He looked at them, dangling in his hands, dumbfounded. As my head had come out of the latex disguise that I had been wearing he was suddenly pulling on only a few ounces of mask and not my whole body weight. He had not been expecting this. The theatrical mask is good enough to fool people when I am driving. In this dark room with only a shaft of light from the door he had no hope of spotting that my face had been a mask. He looked in astonishment at my real face now clearly caught in the one shaft of light. To my horror I saw a flash of recognition in his eyes. We have never met but strangers often recognise me as my department, along with photos of me, is often in the local news.

Distracted by this, still off balance and moving he stumbled backwards. He caught his heels on my kitbag. He then fell over crashing into a rail of full length waterproofs with built in waders. They fell across him and his efforts to throw them away led to him becoming more entangled.

I have one more chance. Thankfully my fear then gave me strength and speed instead of indecision and paralysis.

I threw myself across the room and picked up the Taser. By the time that I had correctly gripped it and turned to face him he was already rearing up towards me. This time he is pulling a long knife from a sheath on his belt. His face is contorted with rage.

He is too close; if the darts are not sufficiently separated it will not work well. I fired; it was all that I could do. It is a police issue Taser with the full 50,000 volts and I kept my finger down for much longer than a well-trained officer would have. As I fired he lunged and I braced myself for the blow or the knife

He collapsed to the floor mere inches from me, the knife narrowly missing my leg as he hit the tiles. He lay sprawled face down in the now only clear central area. He jerked for a while and then he lay still.

I dare not stop to take a breath. Time is now not on my side, I have to complete two actions before the Taser wears off and he is able to move again. He should be out for at least five minutes, possibly fifteen, but I am not dealing with a normal human here. He is closer to a wild animal. I do not know how long I have, possibly not long enough. When I have endlessly practised in my warehouse I can complete both of the tasks now required in ninety seconds but tonight I am not in the easiest circumstances. My reflexive fight or flight response, which saved me moments before, has already degenerated into jelly like wobbling. Also I have to subdue more than a practise mannequin.

I reached into my kitbag and took out the slim metal tube. I slipped out the pre-loaded syringe and I can see that it is thankfully undamaged. I plunged the ready attached needle into his buttock. Pressing the plunger hard, with a level of desperation, I gave the full dose of Ketamine. No half measures with him, no more mistakes tonight. That should act in three minutes. The high dose carries the slight possibility of killing him. So what, his vicious behaviour carries a much higher chance of him killing not only another but in addition she is innocent. There is no presumption of innocence for this creep. There is a preponderance of evidence against him. Usually the hands of the police are tied and they have my full sympathy for the frustrations they face. Unusually, with this one, a senior officer called Meadows has been completely incompetent. I have to do his job and Meadows should lose it.

Then I took out Gaffer tape and put several turns around his ankles and wrists and a strip across his mouth. With him I doubt that this will hold when he is fully awake but hopefully it will for a short time whilst his is still weakened and disorientated from the drug and Taser. In readiness for them wearing off I took out heavy duty cable ties and further bound his hands and feet. From my kit bag I then extricated a mountain-rescue style collapsible stretcher that I have modified. I unfolded it, clipped it together and added my own addition of wheels to one end. I rolled him on to it and wrapped several tie-down ratchet straps around his legs, arms, chest and head. I pulled them firmly into the cleats. Testing them I thought that they are strong enough to hold a gorilla, which is fortunate, for tonight they have to.

Then an additional unanticipated danger; I have to step into the brightly lit shop and hope that no one is looking through the window, I had not prepared for doing that. My original plan had been to Taser him as he stood behind the partition between the shop floor and the doorway to this rear room. Now I have to step through the brightly lit area to reach the till. Worse, I then have to stretch up to reach the security camera hard drive which, thankfully, I had already spotted during the outside surveillance. Unfortunately it is high, above the monitors. I peeked around the door and then around the edge of the partition in front of it. All appears clear, no window shoppers or late customers preparing to hammer on the door for an emergency supply of maggots. I quickly stepped in and with one determined pull I tore away the hard drive from the CCTV, backed into the store room and tucked it under one of the straps around the stretcher.

Three minutes, he remains completely unconscious. Picking up my mask and kitbag I also secured them under a strap and taking out my burner 'phone I sent the prewritten text, {ready}.

I picked up one end of the stretcher and wheeled him out to the yard, this set up enables me to more easily handle the weight and, as important, it is silent. I deliberately left my makeshift bag over the external CCTV; it is only the sewn over end of one leg of Tesco jeans and completely unidentifiable. Without doubt, with what has happened tonight, with what I now unexpectedly and unwontedly have to do, the police will be in this yard someday soon. I mentally rechecked that I have not left behind anything else. With one exception the police are not even aware of our other previous actions; they will not have anything else to go on even if they are able to make a connection between this shit and the even worse one of a year ago. That would be a considerable stretch. I think, I hope, that we are safe. That is with the one proviso that is now inevitable; enact Rule Two which has been occasioned by fouling up on Rule One.

I waited mere seconds by the yard door; the text came in, {outside}. I pulled back the bolts and leaned into the alleyway. The van is immediately in front of me with the sliding door already open, only inches away. We had already noted that luckily the yard door opens inwards which allowed Sam to closely line up the yard and van doors.

There is only a narrow gap between the van side and the wall, it is nearly impossible to see down the small service road especially as we previously disabled the streetlights. Even so, even with Sam checking before texting, now was the second dangerous time, will we be seen?

The stretcher effortlessly, silently, slipped over the rubber roller in the van doorway. I stepped in behind it and pulled the door quietly shut on its well-greased track. The panel under our research apparatus is already open. I slid him through with my kit-bag and face mask. Then I unclipped the door roller and threw that in as well. The panel slid down. Anyone looking in the van would not be aware of him hidden there, only a close inspection would reveal the compartment.

I stepped forward into the passenger seat and whilst driving away Sam looked at my unmasked face and simply asked, 'did he see your face?' I nodded yes. No other response is required. We both know that Rule Two has to be enacted. Now looking very concerned Sam continued shakily, 'we must slow down. There can be no more mistakes, after tonight no more killing.'

I softly replied, 'no, we must simply get better. You know, even more than me, how vital this work is.' Keeping my own council I also thought, "I can live with more deaths. I would even welcome more deaths."

After fifteen silent minutes we reached the farm, I unlocked the gates and then relocked them behind us once the van was through. I repeated the same with the warehouse doors.

As soon as the van was securely inside I opened the side door, then the secret panel and I slid out the stretcher. To my astonishment he is beginning to come around, he is breathing through his nose with some difficulty and saliva is coming from under the tape across his mouth. Sam and I looked at each other, we had written it together, Rule Two, "there must be no chance whatsoever of either of us being identified, even if that requires lethal action." It is my duty to now action it.

Sam returned to the van. We reversed the entry procedure, locking one set of doors before opening the others so any passing vehicle cannot see in. Sam is to take the van back to the university car-park while I finish here. Normally I would have been collected in the morning and we would drop off the chastened and broken man near his home. We would simply roll him drugged and loosely bound out of the side door. He would then be able to wriggle out of his bindings and stagger home thoroughly broken. Not tonight, I will simply cycle home. He will remain here.

I had taken off my black gloves during the short drive here, if anyone had looked through the van window and seen me wearing them on a balmy night whilst inside the van it would have looked suspicious. Now I slipped on a latex glove and then pinched his nose. His eyes opened and he tried to thrash around but the bonds held firm. Still futilely trying to release his bindings he stared at me with loathing and anger. I crushed his nose harder and spoke to him; there is no need to worry about covering my face or using my voice modulator tonight. He will never be able to identify me.

'This is for all the years that you have beaten your wife. I know that you have hospitalised her on several occasions and the worst beating you inflicted on her was only recently. I know that your viciousness is increasing. You will never hit her again. She will never need to fear you again. Tonight you are going to die.' The look in his eyes changed to fear and just as they started to close it morphed into terror.

After a few minutes he stopped struggling. I held his nose closed along with his mouth covered by the Gaffer tape for a total of eight minutes. Rule Two, "there must be no chance whatsoever of either of us being identified". We had known of the implications when writing it. I had had to do this once before, to kill our first, though deliberately, in a different manner and for different risks. It seems a little easier this time. Deep inside I realise that I even found it satisfying. As with all of the others; the usual corporal but non-fatal punishment; the results and knowing that I am addressing such a need are so satisfying. It even goes some of the way to expunging my own previous failure, my oversight.

Now I must undertake the disposal. I swept into action with a practiced grace. My movements seem to flow. I have rehearsed with pigs and of course this is the second human body that I have had to deal with.

With the understandable and inevitable exception of the first we had planned that none of them would die, hopefully. We had also fully accepted that in some circumstances death may occur as a result of side effects, complications, or, as tonight, for our security. Not planned, not wanted but necessary, and, with the more we do the more likely it becomes. For some of them, probably for this one, it is most likely the only safe outcome for their victims. No one will cry for this one, not for any of them.

I took off the ties and with him still on the stretcher I wheeled him outside. Standing next to the line of pre-dug pits I looked across to the one, now filled in, where Robin lies. Or I should say where the well composted remains are. The tree that I planted there above him is growing remarkably strongly.

I desperately hope that our usual treatments will permanently stop the other abusers. I have a foreboding that the effect may wear off with time. It would be safer to kill them all but Sam would need some persuading to agree to that. No doubt that would also lead to our crusade reaching police and public awareness. Some flaky psychologist would make excuses for their disgusting behaviour and turn them into the victims. If they saw at first hand the damage to the true victims, the women, then perhaps even the naïve pseudo-liberals would see the need we are addressing. While the police remain hamstrung our work is both moral and essential. Grudgingly I have to admit to myself that we should try not to kill them as if our work becomes known it will be made more difficult. If we do not remain under the radar we will be compromised.

CHAPTER 3:
REBECCA,
UNEXPECTED END

We were both dispirited as we trudged in the damp, half dark, through the sink estate, up a crumbling path between discarded cheap toys to a house that is desperately in need of repair. The streetscape on both sides of us was recently built, it is prematurely grubby, the concrete houses resembling the worst of the Stalinist era mistakes. They are evidence of the continuing failure and lack of imagination of city architects and planners. For me it is the dreg end of my first day in my new post. My worst first day ever.

It had started with me meeting my new boss for the first time. In my assessment I had been interviewed solely by his superior from head office as he had been absent, called away to some emergency, now I suspect deliberately so. Naively I had anticipated being invited to his office for a welcoming chat before today's, all-station, morning briefing; then to be personally introduced by him to the whole team. But no, my appointment could not possibly interfere with his late start on Mondays.

The kindly Sergeant Bender is technically only the Desk Sergeant but he clearly runs the station. He obviously commands the deepest respect of all of the junior officers. He welcomed me warmly. He stepped in. He did his best. He stood up and introduced me to the fine team as we waited for god and his close associates to deign to arrive.

When the boss, Meadows, finally appeared he completely ignored me and he then proceeded to strut around, browbeating and disparaging the others. Even his appearance is underwhelming. He is slender but with a saggy paunch. From his sparse, receding rust coloured hair, down past his rumpled jacket and creased trousers, to his scuffed brown shoes, he shrieks his repugnant core. His face is narrow, freckled, and his thin, pointy nose is framed by close set eyes with a slight squint so it is uncertain where the focus of his attention is. His habit of looking sideways combining with his squint makes his whole appearance and demeanour portray consummate insincerity. He is clearly incompetent. Worse, he was rude me, his new 2IC, in front of the team. I am tough enough to handle that but it will take all of my strength to deal with his bullying of all the more junior members, particularly the women.

Now, at the other end of a dull day, as we approached the battered, dismal house, I noticed a broken bathroom cabinet on the uncut grass adjacent to the path. I caught sight of myself in the cracked mirror and it this made me consider how my appearance may affect the treatment that I am bracing myself for; not only in my work, which I have grown used to, but now, also, from the boss and his acolytes who stand out from the rest of the team like bad teeth. At 5' 10" I am tall for a woman and being slim and athletic that is good, so far anyway. Then the problems start; soft blond curls, pale blue eyes and a delicate bone structure. My features may be marvellous for advertising cosmetics. They are not so good for facing down dinosaurs on the team or for the occasions that I am called upon to intimidate people as part of my job, the infrequent occasions when I play "bad cop.". However there is some advantage to be had from my looks, at work that is, and they are often helpful in more social events.

Occasionally I use, should I say misuse, my countenance. Playing the dumb blond can wrong foot some stupid men before I surprise them with a coup de gras as I arrest or charge them. That always gives me a sense of satisfaction. There, in the mirror, at last I can see a smile flicker across my face. It is possibly my first of the day.

This morning, at my first station meeting here, my first day on the job, other than from Sergeant Bender's necessarily brief, informal, introduction, there had been no induction for me. There was not even any comment from Meadows other than, 'we don't waste time with that PC crap here do we boys. Real men don't need it.' This was followed by sycophantic cackles from a few toadies in their poorly fitting, cheap suits, standing either side of him, arrogantly glaring at the rest of us who they clearly consider to be secondary beings. After this comment silence had echoed through the rest of the room.

Then I had been packed off to make demeaning routine calls, to deal with issues below my new role, including this one. His instruction was, 'you're a woman, you can deal with this silly domestic.' He had paired me with Julian, denigrating him as 'the geek.' No doubt he had been chosen as my bag carrier as he is one of the most junior members. The reasoning, if it can be so glorified, was clearly, "why waste someone experienced on a useless woman?"

That strategy from Meadows has at least has backfired. It may come back to bite him on the bum. I think Julian and I will work well together, I am seeing more resources in him every minute. He has a wicked sense of humour and the personal strength to tease me. The bloody cheek of the man, he is ribbing someone considerably his superior on his first day with them. However I can see that he is doing it kindly and respectfully. I would not admit it to him but I am enjoying it. In the last six hours we have already forged a bond, I feel it is the beginning of a trustworthy relationship. I looked at him out of the corner of my eye as I raised my hand to knock on the peeling front door, its bell hanging uselessly by its cord. With his height, blond hair, blue eyes and chiselled features; he could be my slightly older brother.

He is a big, muscular man. With his hi viz jacket and the medieval looking equipment hanging from his belt he looks intimidating. He resembles a Viking. That could come in handy in any confrontations. His bearing is softened by his expression which is that of a kind, sensitive man. There is a trace of sorrow in his eyes.

I can't place his accent but I suspect shires, country; it is well-educated and modified by travel. He is immaculately groomed and mannered. I suspect that he has means far beyond his current role. I guess that he is a few years older than me, mid-thirties. He has only recently started work on the force, only a few months ago. He is undertaking his compulsory stint in uniform as part of his fast-track detective training. So he must have had another career before. I wonder what that was. I guess that it had been professional and well paid. What has precipitated his change? He caught me appraising him and smiled. I have caught him regarding me with the same intention several times. We are getting the measure of each other. We are finding mutual approval.

As my fingers firmly rapped on the cheap, plastic door Julian grudgingly muttered, 'the worst thing is that The Troop is probably correct.'

'Julian, are you referring to our superior and the men who were at the front with him during this morning's briefing? Also, by "troop" do you mean as in a group of monkeys?' I tried to scowl but his description of the boss and his coterie of crawlers was unerring. I failed to prevent myself from grinning. The branding of them is perfect.

'Yes to both, ma'am.'

'I am your superior officer and I have clearly indicated that when it is the two of us together you must call me Rebecca and that at the station that you should refer to me as boss. Call me ma'am again and I will fully extend your baton and put it where the sun don't shine. Am I clear?' Again I tried and again I failed to scowl.

'Is that a threat or a promise ma'am?'

I elbowed him hard. I just had time to wipe the grin off my face as the door opened. Unfortunately, in general, " The Troop" would have been correct. A man missing for only twenty-four hours and a wife already panicking would almost certainly turn out to be a row or him voluntarily being off on a bender.

I was horrified by what confronted us. I sensed Julian tense. A cowed, strangely elongated, spidery woman hesitantly peered around the door. One glance shows that there is more going on here than we expected. Her face, already ravaged by the vicissitudes of life, is now overlain with additional, recent damage that is framed by poorly cut hair frizzed at the temples. My attention snapped away from our banter back to the job and it rocketed; it focussed on her obvious distress.

She saw Julian's uniform and a look of relief flooded across her pinched features. That was not expected. It was not the apprehension that we are usually greeted with when we call at the home of a missing person.

The summary we had been given said that she is 32, almost the same as me. I am often thought to be less than 30, I doubt that she would pass for less than 40. The poor woman looks broken, depleted. She is shabbily dressed in cheap clothes, the baby in her arms is crying as are the two toddlers behind her. One of the children is sitting alone,

under a table, sucking on an empty spoon. All that I can see
is overshadowed by her two shiners. Not only are both eyes
blackened but the bruises are clearly of different vintages.
The one around here left eye is the worst that I have ever
seen. There is another yellowing one on her left cheek. Now I
know two things about her husband, the second is that he is
right handed. I suspect that her relief on seeing us was that it
is not him returning. I felt Julian's tension soften and morph
into concern as he appraised her.

'Mrs. Sally James?' She nodded. I held up my warrant
card and said 'I am Detective Inspector Rebecca Fletcher, this
is Constable Julian Courtney. We understand that you are
concerned that your husband is missing.'

Gently shushing the children and softly stroking the
toddler's cheek she indicated that we follow her back in.
The room is clean and tidy but very poorly furnished. I had
the impression of someone doing her best under difficult
circumstances. She dealt with the children very tenderly but
I noticed that as she bent down to them her back is clearly
painful. The room smelt of children, a mixture of sickly food
and, like cows, a milky odour with, no matter how fastidious
the parents, a hint of excrement.

'I am sorry about the children crying. Brian did not
come home last night so today I have had no money to feed
them. They are hungry.' So that is why she is so concerned
and not jumping for joy at his absence.

I felt foolish for having thought that there is nothing
worse for a woman than being beaten at home. She has
reminded me of what I was clearly taught in training. There
is. I guess that two thoughts are roiling within her; please let
him return so I can feed the children; please may he be dead
in a ditch so that I will not be beaten again. As she looked at
Julian I looked her over again. Her washed out dress had been
inexpertly altered and only approximately conformed to her

bony frame. It still carries the stale air of the charity shop.

After we agreed to use first names, over the next couple of minutes Sally told us the scant details. He leaves at eight in the morning six days a week to his fishing tackle shop in a small street near to the river which majestically divides this old city. He comes back at six in the evening and gives her money for the next day, no more, one day at a time. On the seventh he rests, that is he goes fishing and boozing. Yesterday there had been an alteration in his schedule. His shop had been closed on Saturday, as he had been involved in a local fishing competition; instead he had opened for a few hours on the Sunday evening. He did not return from that.

Sally has no mobile 'phone and there is no 'phone in the house, I presume that either she is not allowed one or cannot afford one. She borrowed a neighbour's 'phone several times during today to call him but he is not answering. She does not know any of his friends; they always meet at the shop and go out from there. She did not even know where he drinks, saying "he likes to keep his own friends." She was unwittingly but eloquently telling us that she is excluded. Sally said that she has "no friends," which I guess means that she is not allowed any, but 'the old lady next door is kind'. Though he is obviously a brute the last 24 hours actions are equally obviously completely out of character.

She had told us that he used an upstairs room as an office and kept all of his personal items there but it is locked and that she does not have a key. Julian said, 'I carry a set of keys, do you mind if we have a look?' I raised my eyebrows at him, a set of keys to every door in the land?

'OK, I will have to stay down here to look after the children. It is first on the right at the top of the stairs.' She hesitated and then she continued with fear in her voice, 'when he comes back please be sure to tell him it was you who went in, not me.'

We went to the door and before I could say anything Julian bent down, scoffed at the lock, took a set of picks out of his pocket and opened it immediately. I have seen locks picked before but never as quickly as that, even simple ones. He grinned at my wide eyed stare and shrugged.

There was nothing of note in the tiny, tatty room. No 'phone, no computer, just piles of receipts for fishing tackle supplies. The walls are covered with photos of a few scrawny looking fish being held up by a huge bloke who has more equipment than I would have thought would be necessary for a trawler, let alone to catch a tiddler. Either the men around him are all small or the charming Brian James is colossal. He is as big as the poor innocent fish are tiny. The images are of a brute of a man, flabby but with an aura of menace about him.

Julian whispered, 'I don't want to be sexist but I think it would be better if you went downstairs to address the other issue whilst I poke around here for something on lover-boy.'

I replied, 'I don't want to be sexist but I agree. A woman will do a much better job down there than a galumphing chap.' He grinned and held the door open pretending to bow and scrape to me as I went through and back down the threadbare stairs.

It took me a while to persuade her even to admit that she is regularly beaten. A week before it had been so bad that she had to be taken to casualty where, of course, he played the doting husband and refused to leave her side. Only when the consultant came in and insisted that he waited outside had she told the doctors that she had not actually fallen downstairs. She had pleaded with them not to report it for the sake of the children. A very lovely pharmacist had come in and had given her powerful painkillers. Sally said warmly how kind the pharmacist had been, how strongly she had assured Sally that all would soon be better. I thought it inappropriate to give false hope. The analgesics are clearly helping but we both know that this will be be only for this episode, not the next time. She was wringing my hand and begging me not to report the abuse when Julian came downstairs.

Julian held up the 'photo of the big man looking ridiculous with the little fish and he asked, 'is this Brian.' She nodded. 'May we take it?' She nodded again. Glancing at me he flicked his eyes towards the door with a "nothing more to do here look." I also nodded and he continued, 'we will do all we can to find him soon.' Under a bus I hoped to myself. 'In the meantime I will make sure that the family liaison officer calls tomorrow morning and she will ensure you are looked after until he comes back.' Julian gave me a "god help her then glance." He had clearly intuited that I had got nowhere. As we were leaving he stepped back and took two twenty pound notes out of his pocket. Pressing them into her hand he softly whispered, 'the corner shop is still open, why don't you pop out and get some food for the children.' She tried to refuse saying it was too much but he waved her away saying that the FFO, the Family Finance Officer, would reimburse him in the morning. A flicker of a smile crossed his face. I guess that not only is he comforting her but he is enjoying his own doubletalk.

Her face crumpled and was suddenly immersed in grateful tears as she clenched the proffered notes. They may be merely a few drinks to us but they are as manna from heaven to her. I left in fear of what is to come for her; whatever happens next.

We almost fell back into the car and we simultaneously slumped back into the seats. Together we said 'oh fuck.' Clearly he feels as impotent as I do. We can look for the missing scumbag but we cannot help her. My duty is to look for a man that I would prefer to remain lost; to search for a person whose mere existence makes the world more degraded, more profane.

I reached into my pocket and gave him a twenty saying, 'pay me back when you get reimbursed by the FFO. Also could you tell me sometime, not now, what an FFO is? I have never heard of one.'

Grinning, now widely, he said, 'shall we take a stroll by the shop? It will need to be in our time. It is the clocking off hour and our great leader will never agree to overtime for anyone not in The Troop.'

'I am fine, it will be a welcome break from unpacking but,' I indicated his wedding ring, 'surely you have better things to do.'

His kind, cheery face collapsed. Breaking our gaze he said, 'Lucy died two years ago, leukaemia. There is no one at home. I have nothing better to do.'

We sat in a still silence for a few moments. Now I know where his sadness comes from. His arose at the same time as mine. Around the time that my John was walking out his Lucy was dying. Then I put my hand on his arm, I squeezed with a complicity that I saw he did not miss. My face deliberately showing my empathy I said, 'my unpacking can wait, there is no one at home for me either. Let's go fishing. You never know we may catch a shark.' Giving me a "thank you" nod he started the car and we drove off.

We went down to a part of the city I had not seen before and he described the set up on the way. We were heading to a small parade of shops on a side street leading off a major road as it approached the new bridge over the river. The very bridge that I had walked over this morning. I had not spotted this shabby little street as my attention had then been taken by the sharply contrasting magnificent cathedral, above me and then on my right, grandly looking down from its elevated position on a hill. In fact will be no more than half a mile from our station, which is on the same road, a little further from the river.

On this side of the river is an old quay which he said previously had some warehouses alongside. They have now been demolished and a new residential, shopping and office development is being constructed. There is a linear park along both sides of the river as it flows through the town. The narrow park, in reality a wide walkway, extends from the cathedral, near us next to the new bridge, along to the old bridge, that is the centuries old bridge, nestled under the castle a mile downstream. I had discovered that when walking out from my house yesterday evening. My front door opens on to a road immediately alongside the park on the opposite side of the river. Julian told me that at this end of the park, and only on this side, the path continues a couple of miles upstream to a weir. In the opposite direction, beyond the old bridge, which is roughly a mile from us know, paths continue another mile downstream on both sides to another new road bridge. The route in both directions passes through housing and then light industrial and office areas but apparently is a delightful path from which you can only see river and trees and, indeed, you are quickly in countryside.

Looking at me with his infuriating, knowing smile Julian said that it was a good place to do my training. I had the distinct impression that he knows what I do and that it is not simply jogging. At this he pulled up outside a brightly lit shop in the middle of the run-down side street. It is wedged between "Blinds and Curtains" and the "City Wok." Though bright the shop is poorly kept and its sign read "F SHI G TACKL ." As we stepped out of the car I resolved to challenge Julian on what he knows about me, and even more importantly how he knows it, another time.

We tried the shop door which was firmly locked. As we peered through the windows a grey, aging man in an equally washed out grey work jacket came out of the curtains shop next door. As he locked up he told us that Brian had not been in all day and that he had not opened today was most unusual, 'fust time eva if youse ask me.' We asked if there is another entrance. He indicated a narrow alleyway on the other side of his shop and said we could get down there to the service road behind and that there is a rear entrance. However he added that the rear door is kept locked and that the wall is high.

We thanked him and made our way to the rear. The service road is in darkness and Julian pointed to the street lamps being recently vandalised, the broken Perspex still litters the road. We tried the handle. The rear door is indeed locked. The keyhole is rusted and Julian cannot pick this one. Julian cupped his hands ready to give me a lift up. When I pointed out that scaling walls was his job he retorted by questioning my desire to lift someone his size.

He effortlessly lifted me until my shoulders were above the wall. I immediately noticed that the moss on the top has recently been scraped off, exactly where I was about to cross. I passed that info back down to Julian.

I dropped down into the yard. The rear door is fastened but only by a small Yale lock, which would have lightly secured it if it had been pulled shut behind someone. The massive bolts are drawn. I let Julian in pointing out the bolts and he in turn pointed up, drawing my attention to a fabric cover over a CCTV camera.

We walked cautiously to the rear door of the building, all here is in darkness. Julian tried the door handle. The door opened with a loud creek of the hinges. As we stepped in the smell of age old damp assailed my nostrils. It was accompanied by more than a hint of body odour. Overlying both was a sweet, putrid aroma, new to me. Judging by the writhing plastic box, thankfully still upright on a shelf, this was of maggots. With the aid of my pen light I saw a light switch next to the door. I flicked it on and we saw chaos in the room. It is clearly a store room but rods, baskets and waders are all across the floor except for an oblong, clear area in the middle. I said to Julian, 'it is not all wrecked. Look the shelves and racks on two opposite sides are pulled over but on the other two walls they are tidy. It looks as if there has been a fight and they have crashed from one side to the other.'

He nodded appreciatively, he had not spotted that. Then with a jerk of realisation he added, 'and that gap in the middle looks Brian sized.' It does. Looking around, to my surprise, I cannot see any blood or teeth. We stepped through another door and found ourselves in the brightly lit shop. It is tatty, it is shabby. The lurid lures seem to indicate that the whole enterprise is a sham. There is a mobile 'phone and laptop on a shelf under the counter. Above the counter is a bank of four small screens for CCTV. Simultaneously we noted that the hard drive has been ripped out. We looked around Brian James's squalid kingdom. Other than the torn out CCTV there is no suggestion of foul play in the front.

We went back into the fight scene. Again, other than the wreckage, there is no obvious, helpful evidence as to what has happened to James or the other person or persons. Julian sadly opined, 'crime scenes are supposed to tell us something about the criminal. There is nothing here.'

Shaking my head I replied, 'yes there is. There are clear indications that he or they are very careful. If James has been taken it is by someone experienced. They may have form. We can start by looking at known violent men.'

Nodding; Julian added, 'I agree with what you did not say. Not she; most women, other than you that is, could not fell a man of that size. Nor could most men do so either for

41

that matter.' Again he is indicating, this time accidentally, that he knows more about me than I had anticipated. I will have to interrogate him, but not now. He continued, 'there is no blood or other fluid, a cudgel or gun cannot have been used. He, in fact possibly she, could have used a Taser.' Julian is clearly thinking aloud and he then added, 'no, again not she. A woman is unlikely to have been able to lift him; that is assuming he was incapacitated.'

Now shaking my head I pointed at the marks on the floor, clearly left by a pair of wheels. 'Julian, this is no chance robbery or fight. This presumed abduction has been carefully planned by a person well equipped and experienced. There is insufficient room in here for more than one assailant. Whoever has taken James had the skills and wherewithal to take down a huge man on, presumably his, own'

Julian said with a wide grin, 'so, it does not appear to resemble someone leaving after a row or going on a bender. I can't wait for tomorrow's meeting when The Troop finds out how wrong they all were.'

Smiling I said that I would call it in, that I will ask for the area to be sealed off by duty uniforms tonight and that I will ask forensics to attend here in the morning. As we left I reflected on how our unpaid half-hour overtime has transformed our day. I caught Julian's eye and we exchanged looks of delightful anticipation of the schadenfreude, which we will both indubitably revel in, at Meadow's discomfort during tomorrow's briefing. Meadows will then discover, not only that he was wrong in calling this "a silly domestic," but that his attempted side-lining of Julian and me has spectacularly backfired on him.

CHAPTER 4: REBECCA – BUMBLING BRUTUS

I cannot remember being so angry before. After yesterday, the worst Monday of my second career; at ten am on a dismal Tuesday in October, I sat motionless in a cheap, plastic chair at the rear of the meeting room. My apparent calm is barely concealed rage. The clearly flawed and limited Troop filed out all kowtowing to Meadows. Detective Superintendent Alan Meadows, not troubling to hide a triumphant grin at finishing the meeting with a snide comment towards me, strutted at the front of the odious gang. I have never before come across such a loathsome man in the service, let alone reported to him. Most other officers in the room can see that I am puce with fury. I had come so close to lashing out; definitely verbally; possibly physically. My police training would not have prevented it. I gave thanks for the mental training that I have undertaken for my sport, it enables me to contain myself physically, as I struggled to maintain my composure whilst they left.

The Troop, being far too busy fawning, largely did not notice my wrath. Those that did looked at me with justifiable concern, they are very wary. Perhaps they are not all totally brainless; some at least have the prescience to detect and to be watchful of my rage.

On the other hand, as I sit in this station containing too few professionals in a crumbling infrastructure, I am already beginning to appreciate that, other than his Troop, the majority of the team in this station are a decent professional group that he does deserve to command. The good guys quietly left looking sombre; several nodded at me or gave complicit smiles. With a jolt I realised that Meadow's foul behaviour has the potential to weld the rest of us together. This may prove useful. Though a battle with the boss raises the spectre of disruption for me and for the honourable majority here, as I find myself silently vowing to end this disgraceful conduct, conflict seems inevitable.

Eventually it was just the two of us who sat in the remaining stillness.

Julian said, 'if it is any consolation that is not the worst that has happened and today is not the worst that you will feel. You will reach a point where you want to scream at him.' I looked at Julian with puzzlement. Initially I had thought that he was trying to console me but these are not soothing words. With an empathetic grimace he continued, 'you then realise that there is nothing that you can do so this enables you to enter a Zen state. Brutus does what Brutus does. Let it wash over you.' I gave an incredulous sarcastic laugh at this. I know that I cannot consider such a response and I very much doubt that Julian could either. Julian continued, 'sorry, I am being serious.' I looked back in horror.

Then, finally, I realised; under normal circumstances I would have instantly detected it. I must be careful; I must not let rage cloud my mind and slow me down. With this Julian's words came to the front of my mind. He had referred to the obnoxious DS Meadows as "Brutus." Meadows must be the one that the old man in the railway station had been referring to when he advised, "try to ignore Brutus and the harm that he causes for many of the PCs." From my point of view that was sage advice, given by an old man who I instantly respected. It has been seconded by a junior officer who is undoubtedly dynamite. I cannot take it. It is my duty as a senior officer to stand up for the juniors. Sod that I thought, stop trying to fool yourself Rebecca; you cannot ignore it and you do not want to ignore it. You are a resourceful woman but stepping away from a justified confrontation on behalf of others in need is not in your skill set.

This had been only my second station meeting here. It had started; or rather it had not started; extremely badly. Meadows had postponed the morning briefing without notice and we all had to sit around twiddling our thumbs for two hours. Julian had disappeared but most of us could only shuffle paper. It was a staggering waste of resources that are already so over stretched. Never before had I even heard of, let alone been involved in, a briefing being so delayed. The whole purpose of them is to organise and get on with the day's work. Usually if the Super cannot attend then the deputy is expected to step in. I was categorically ordered not to; I guess he aims to undermine my role.

When he finally graced us with his presence he sat in high, plush chair, itself set on a podium. He resembled a poorly dressed, uninspiring emperor. The Troop were then plainly portrayed. Six of them, all male of course, were arrayed about him on smaller but still comfortable chairs. They fawned to Brutus and condescendingly smirked at the fifty or so of us other officers. We faced them from our tacky, tiny, red stools across the hot, airless, cavernous meeting room which, as in most of the rooms here, is painted in a nauseous yellow gloss.

Meadows indicated that each of his pets should report in turn. They each gave a meaningless summary of work in hand. The only new information imparted was that all had been the recipient of a charisma bypass. Then Meadows berated and ridiculed most of the juniors in front of him. He blamed them for any shortcomings in the stations results. He had no qualms whatsoever, not even a fleeting hesitation, about abusing his position and wielding his rank as a weapon. Finally he addressed me, not directly of course, a member of the Troop was asked to report on what I had filed yesterday evening. When Brutus heard that I suspected foul play in the case of Brian James, possibly abduction, he was initially speechless revealing that he does not read the reports sent in.

Then he roared with false laughter. The troop joined in shaking their heads in complicit mockery. Recovering, pretending to that is, he continued, 'DI Fowler, I thought that you were a detective.' More hollow laughter, initiated by him and quickly taken up by the Troop, followed this mockery. I am uncertain which would be more insulting, either him deliberately calling me by the incorrect name or him not knowing. Obviously pleased by the reception from his gaggle he continued, 'clearly I was wrong. Even I am from time to time.' Some of the sycophants shook their heads and one said that such an unimaginable occurrence had not been seen in all his years here. Smugly Meadows resumed, 'he got pissed. God knows he is married so he needs to from time to time. He fell about in his shop and now he is sleeping it off somewhere.' More guffaws had then reverberated amongst the Troop. Their nickname is spot on, they closely resemble preening monkeys.

'Sir,' I had sneered in the most condescending tone that I could manage, a few hands had gone to faces, no doubt to cover smirks, 'staggering drunks do not usually cover the CCTV cameras, remove the hard drive and then carefully close both the back door to the shop and the rear door to the yard.' Yet more hands had been raised to hide mouths. Several coughs covered what were probably suppressed laughs.

Brutus had looked thunderous. He had been completely wrong footed. One of the Troop went bright red, no doubt it was him who had quickly briefed Meadows and he had forgotten the most important part. Recovering; seeing his intentions in pairing me with Julian had been thwarted; realising, even though he is a patriarchal dullard he does retain a glimmer of insight, that he has lost face; trying to hide his stupidity with aggression; Meadows barked out, 'well have a quick look if you must. But we are busy here; don't go wasting time chasing reindeer.'

Sotto voce Julian said, 'Rainbows. Prick.'

One of the young WPC's overheard and could not stifle a laugh. Meadows rounded on her and shouted, 'and what are you tittering at, girlie.' I could not believe my ears. Girlie, does he think that he is back in the era of the "Life on Mars" series? He had stood stepped back, his already nasty face contorted into a cruel grin. The Troop had leapt to their feet alongside him. Then, cupping his hands in front of his chest, he jiggled them as if playing with huge breasts. 'Tittering, gedditt lads?' They all snorted and aping him they similarly started jiggling their smutty hands in front of their chests as they all marched out. I had been uncertain if it was intentional but they walked in time, almost in a goosestep. All of them seemed to think that, not only was such disgraceful behaviour permissible, but also they could conduct it with impunity; without fear of being reported and disciplined.

The WPC who had laughed, who has enormous breasts, looked distraught. She started to flee the room. The still cackling Troop had sneered at her as they exited. All the good guys remaining in their seats graciously looked away from her. As she had passed me, as I sat rigid at the rear, I gently took her arm and I had whispered, 'I wish my figure was half as lovely as yours.' She had smiled her thanks through her tears and then fled for the ladies. It had been a lie, a bit more of a curve for me would be good, but I would hate to have breasts as large as hers.

I sat for an interminable age mulling over the supposed meeting. Julian remained quiet beside me. In spite of his advice I had the distinct impression that he is also seething. As we continued sitting something else came to my mind. I pondered on the moniker given to Meadows. I asked Julian, 'Brutus?'

'Apparently he achieved his obviously undeserved promotion by stabbing everyone else in the back.' Finally a smile came to me. Seeing this he continued in a sombre tone, 'sorry, but I am still being serious. There is something else that I should warn you about.' I sat up and looked at him intently. 'You are no doubt wondering how and why he is still here? How on earth can he get away with such vicious behaviour as well as being a useless leader and hopeless detective. Many of us have discussed making formal complaints. After some digging we found out that this was undertaken in the past. The only outcome was that the complainants were all kicked out of the service. There is something welding the Troop together. If you criticise one all round on you and form a near irresistible force. I do not know what it is but it is certainly more, much more, than the usual silly handshake brigade.'

I looked at him closely, showing my appreciation and understanding of his warning and concern. I am shocked at having such an open and frank conversation with a much more junior officer on only my second day. I realised that yesterday, in one day, we had assessed each other's personality and worth. Then we had quickly formed a close bond. Whatever happens he will have my full support. I have no doubt that is reciprocated. Not such a bad new job after all.

The moment passed and I asked, 'you disappeared before the meeting, anything interesting?'

'Unfortunately it is only a little interesting. Forensics are overrun and I popped down to see if they would let me have a look at the computer and 'phone we found in the shop last night.' I raised my eyebrows at the irregularity of this even though it had not surprised me in the least; I am getting to know this unconventional copper. Seeing my look he shrugged, 'I have certain skills, they often ask me to lend a hand. The computer showed nothing of note other than that he watches a lot of hard-core violent porn. No surprise there. Otherwise it has only shop accounts, a Facebook group of a lot of large, fat men with copious, expensive equipment saving our fine country by clearing the rivers of vicious looking tiddlers. There were searches and links regarding far right but just legal groups and chat rooms. Other than confirming that he is a nasty individual there is nothing of help.'

'Given the hard porn I am surprised that there was not a password.'

'Oh there was. It delayed me about as long as it took to get past as his door lock did.' I burst out laughing and shook my head with admiration. From now on I thought that I knew that nothing would surprise me about this man. He immediately proved me wrong.

'Rebecca, there is something else I must tell you. I hope it does not destroy our work together before it even gets underway. I didn't know when to tell you this but as it has some overlap with what I have just said about accessing his computer I feel that I should enlighten you straight away.'

What is coming now?

'I know Rebecca. I know what happened in the Met. I

know what you did.'

I nearly fell off my chair. That is classified.

'It is an honour to work for you Rebecca. When I found out that you were coming here I looked you up, as I do with everyone. When I discovered what you had done I was seriously impressed. When I was told last week that I was to be working directly with you I literally jumped with joy. It was Sergeant Bender who told me that I was to be with you, he is the older guy who really runs things here. He thought that I had gone mad.'

I cannot believe his flippancy. I almost shouted, 'how do you know. Who told you? That is supposed to be sealed and I and several others are at risk if people are blabbing.'

He had been expecting my anger and my alarm. He effortlessly shrugged them both off and continued as if we were discussing a football match. 'Don't worry, no one told me. It is deeply and securely hidden. In fact, the only thing that alerted me and what made me go digging is that it is so well hidden. By chance I spotted that which is so difficult to see, something not being there rather than something that is. Without inside knowledge no one would know that there is even anything to be sought let alone be able to open it. It was very satisfying to get in. It was quite a challenge, the longest time that it has ever taken me.'

Shit, he has hacked the Met. Visibly I maintained my composure, I think. Internally I was metaphorically rocked back on my heels. He has half admitted to an offence that, if discovered, would certainly have him thrown out of the force and most likely he would be clapped in jail. For now I will let it pass, I will pretend that I have not processed the implications. 'Julian, where on earth did you learn how to do this?'

'Before joining the service I was working in a

computer security firm advising banks and insurance companies on how to prevent being hacked. In fact I am still involved on a part time basis.' Then he quickly added, 'I have registered this with HR and all is above board.' He had the temerity to give a little smirk at this. His consultancy work may be above board but not his extended interests.

'I presume that to know how to prevent it you have to know how to do it.'

'Yes, and it is necessary to know more than the people trying to get in. Let me assure you that I have not and that I will never look at your personal records. Other than your service record I only know of your sporting achievements as they were in your file. I guess that you will join the club here and all will know them very soon.' With a grin he finished, 'know and fear that is.' Then as an afterthought, 'oh, of course, your qualifications and previous work were also on the service file.' He did not seem particularly impressed with them.

I sat still as I can see that there is more he wants to tell me but he is finding it difficult. If he can casually admit to hacking the Met what on earth is coming that even he finds difficult to say?

Eventually he spoke again. 'I cannot believe or understand why you have not been promoted. He looked at me but I did not respond. I want to see what he says. After a pregnant pause he continued in a conspiratorial, yet at the same time probing, tone, 'I am wondering if you are on another undercover mission.'

He is exploring whether or not I am her to investigate the Troop. He is considering, and I suspect hoping, that I am. 'The truth is, Julian, that I was disappointed not to be promoted. I do not know why not but I suspect that the Brass do not want to be seen to reward what happened.' He scoffed at this as I continued, 'I am only here as a DI. There is no subterfuge.' He looked crestfallen.

I am desperately trying to regain my composure, whilst trying take in all of this and to assess my own exposure to risk from hacking, all at the same time. I managed to multitask further and ask, 'these, er, skills of yours that you alluded to, can we put them to use in our work?' One thing is becoming crystal clear to me and it is allowing my pulse rate to start reducing; he is very good at this. To crack the Met he must be amazing. I trust him, I am sure that my previous activities will remain well hidden. My head is buzzing with trying to process all of this and to maintain our discussion.

'Oh yes, well you saw me pick the lock yesterday.'

'Berk, you know damn well what I mean.'

'Let's just say that from time to time I may be able to give snippets of information from ...er.. unknown sources. Unfortunately, as their provenance will therefore also be, let's stick with unknown, they will be inadmissible in court. That's the bad news. The good news is that they could guide us in pursuing other routes of an investigation which would be admissible. In the very unlikely event of our knowledge of the original information ever coming to light, if the source remains unknown to you then you have plausible deniability. I have it on good authority that the source is very, very careful not to be identified. Also, he or she can move undetected and also will remain untraceable.'

I gave Julian a wry smile but inwardly I resolved to up my game. It seems he is bringing more to our partnership than I can currently offer. I am not easy with that, it is the opposite of my usual experience. 'Ok, well back to today. Can you have a look through his 'phone and try calling his contacts?'

'Done. Nothing there was of any interest to us. There

were three calls yesterday from the old neighbour's number; at least they confirm what Sally said. Also he has recently received multiple texts on fishing arrangements and on drinking at a low life pub in town.'

'Surprise me, has anyone asked the local beat PCs to canvas the area?'

'Underway as we speak. The only reports so far confirm that the darling missing Brian is a complete shit. He regularly beats up Sally. All of the people that we have so far spoken to say that they hope never to see him again. There is an indication that his violence is increasing. Perhaps we, you or another female officer that is, should re-engage with Sally. I would be happier if we could get her into a refuge in case we have the misfortune of finding him in one piece.'

'Excellent. Would you stay here and use your charms to persuade a couple of others to help you trawl through the local CCTV? Sorry to be sexist but I will pick up on your suggestion and cajole a WPC to come with me to talk to Sally.'

'Not sexist ma'....boss, sensitive policing is my middle name.' I can see his supposed slip to say ma'am was not a slip at all. I am being wound up again.

'The three of us should meet back here in my office at 3.30 pm.'

'Three of us?'

'You, me and your insolence.' With an even bigger smile he went to the CCTV room.

I arrived back at the station a little early and found to my surprise Julian was already sitting in the little office that Sergeant Bender had commandeered for me. With a little start I asked, 'you can't have finished the CCTV already?'

'Yes we have, Barbara helped and she is superb. Very fast, very efficient and, as are so many here, underused and under appreciated by Brutus. What is more, we have something to show you on CCTV. She is going to join us here at 3.30.'

I nodded my understanding and added, 'Barbara?' As I asked him who Barbara is, he clearly thinks that I already know her, I wondered if it is the same Barbara that the old man spoke of, the lonely neighbour who looks after her mum.

A little surprised, Julian continued, 'sorry, given the morning's events I thought that you had already met her. Barbara Sturgis is the WPC who was cruelly treated during the briefing. By the way she thought that the sun shone out of your arse but don't worry, I have thoroughly disabused her of that.'

Before I could offer a suitable rejoinder I heard someone come to the doorway and speak to Julian. I cannot see who it is and they cannot see me as I am leaning against the side wall and I am effectively hidden behind the now open door. 'Hi Jules, it is all set up ready for when Tibs gets back.' She stepped in, it is Barbara. Spotting me there she blushed to the roots of her hair.

Before either of us could react Julian adroitly stood between us and said, 'thank you Barbara. You carry on down and we will be with you in a couple of minutes.' She leapt out of the room.

'Well, I note that I haven't been invited to call you Jules but I will do so from now on.'

'You remember what you said you would offer me if I call you ma'am, well I have the same response to people who call me Jules. I let her get away with it today as she had such a hard time this morning.'

At last, I thought, a useful weapon, 'a deal, you don't call me ma'am and I won't call you Jules.'

'Absolutely, I agree.'

'Now, the other issue, please explain.'

'No other issue, all is good.' For the first time he could not look me in the eye.

'Hand me your baton for the aforementioned use or tell me all about Barbara referring to me as Tibs. It sounds like a bloody cat. It is your choice.' I held out my hand for the weapon.

'OK, OK, I give in but please, I am only the messenger, don't shoot me. After the briefing earlier, I use the word briefing loosely, the lads spent some time in the changing room discussing the behaviour of Brutus and your response. They came up with two nicknames. A new one for Brutus, which is not to be used in polite company; and Tibs which is now being used for you.' He paused, then he continued, 'great, now let's go and look at the CCTV.' I gesticulated for him to pass the baton to me, 'OK, OK, I surrender yet again. It stands for Tough, Intelligent, Beautiful and Sexy.' He ran for the door shouting over his shoulder, 'see you in the CCTV room.'

I stood back for a moment and thought what a bloody awful acronym. However, I could not help but feel complimented, perhaps even a smidgen smug.

When I joined them downstairs I could immediately see that Julian had obviously mollified Barbara. Though quiet she appears comfortable. As she was starting the machine Julian asked, 'you haven't told me about Sally James. From your demeanour when you came back I guess that the visit was not entirely successful.'

'Not a great success, she is clearly terrified of him. I think that given time we will persuade her to tell us more about the abuse and more importantly she may agree to report it. Until then we cannot help. Hopefully he will not turn up too quickly and we can have her to safety before then.' The silent, dark image started to slowly scroll across the screen.

Julian nodded acknowledgement at what I had told him and then, almost immediately, he said, 'here it is boss. Freeze there please Barbara.' As we peered at it he added, 'Barbara spotted this on the first take.' She justifiably looked proud. 'There, look, a grubby white van driving away from the area around the time that the lovely Brian's shop was due to close. Barbara has also seen it on some other cameras leading east out of town. I know that in itself a van is not suspicious but look at the occupants. You cannot see their faces but, as Barbara rightly pointed out, they are in black clothes not overalls.' She flushed again but this time with pride. Beyond that I can see that she is brimming with zeal. She is an excellent officer, competent and enthusiastic. Brutus does not deserve to command her.

Gazing at the screen I asked, 'can you read the number plate?' No one answered. I glanced up and saw that Julian was looking at Barbara. She was still examining the screen and had not spotted him studying her. She turned to see why he had not answered me and Julian gesticulated that she should do so.

'Er... yes..er..Ma'am.' She is not used to being involved, something else that I must correct. 'I can read it and if you don't mind I took the liberty of looking it up.' Don't mind, I thought, I felt like giving her a hug. 'It is registered to a Mr L. Cape. This is the number and his address. Believe it or not he lives right behind the station.' She handed me a well presented typed note.

Taking the paper I said, 'thanks Barbara and well done. It is a little early but we may catch him in. Let's walk around and have a chat with him now.' Julian and I stood and moved to the door, Barbara remained in her seat. Turning back to her I said, 'you too Barbara, after all you are the one who found him.'

I thought that she would be pleased but to my chagrin she twisted with anguish. I can see that instead of involving Barbara I have undoubtedly caused her to agonise over something. 'Oh ma'am, I would love to but I can't. I am only part time and I have to leave at 4. I can't be late as I have to be back in time to care for my mum. I do the evening turn.'

So, yes, she is the same Barbara. For the second time today I put my hand on her arm. 'Family must always come first. I will make sure that when we next go to interview someone earlier in the day we will take you. If this chap is not in now, that will mean the three of us,' I stressed the word three, 'will be going to see him in the morning.' She shone with pleasure.

We stood to leave. Whist Julian's back was towards her I spotted her regarding him with a hungry yearning. For the first time her mask slipped and I saw her sad loneliness. I felt for her, partly as I do not think Julian is ready for another relationship and she will be disappointed, partly as I so often feel the same myself.

As we walked towards the stairs Julian muttered, 'I was wrong, it does.'

'What was that Julian, you wrong, surely not? Tell me what is worrying you.'

'I said that it looks like a sunny evening.'

We are still in the basement.

CHAPTER 5:
REBECCA, FIRST
IMPRESSIONS

I can see that WPC Sturgis, Barbara, is bitterly disappointed. The three of us walked together up the concrete stairs; that is two walked with anticipation and the other trudged despondently. I tried not to look at either Barbara's crestfallen face or the vomit yellow wall paint beloved of station interior designers. Julian and I are going to interview the van driver whereas she has to return home to care for her mum. She is torn between two duties which are also desires, she wants to do both. She is so dejected as well. I can see that in addition to her being torn by this decision there is another underlying need. Is this because she wants to be there when I interview Cape or because she wants to be next to Julian? I risked a surreptitious glance back at her. There is no doubt, again it is both.

We stepped into the draughty main corridor and I walked shoulder to shoulder with Barbara towards the front door of the station. After a couple of steps I realised that she is looking at me oddly and that Julian has disappeared. I heard him call me from behind and I turned to see that he had been walking in the opposite direction.

'This way boss.' He looked bemused and I felt wrong footed. 'I guess that you do not know about the back door.'

No, I do not.

We walked out across the rear yard with some very old, probably supposedly temporary, prefabricated offices to my left and a high stone wall on the right. Rising above the wall I can see the roof of a large house beyond it. Presumably that is where we are headed. I tried to peer over but the wall is it too tall to allow me to inspect the house itself. There is certainly no need to drive to our destination; it could not be any closer. I have never before visited a potential suspect who lives closer to the station than where our unmarked police car is parked.

We continued out of the rear gate, which I now see is an alternative vehicle access to the station, then we walked along a short road with tiny but quaint, gentrified, alms houses on the left. On our right there is the very house that we are going to. Near to the station gate, presumably screening a courtyard to the house, there is another high wall. This one has a large secure door in it, opening to this little lane. At the far end of the road is the side wall of the house itself. We walked past it out into a city square.

I stopped dead, transfixed, as I took it all in. 'Julian, it is utterly beautiful.'

He looked around with pleasure, as if regarding the scene for the very first time, though he must have been here many times before. He is clearly a sensitive man. On three sides of the square there are low, two storey terraced houses in a selection of soft pastel colours. Each is double fronted with a picture perfect wooden front door. Window boxes adorn the top and bottom symmetrical windows either side of the door. There is a narrow road around all four sides of the square and in the centre is an immaculate lawn demarcated by box hedging. The grass is split into quadrants by limestone paving. At the centre where the two paths intersect, in a paved area with wooden benches around, there is a life size, white stone statue of a young woman. Her head is coyly bowed. Her long dress, held up on her right side by one delicate hand, ripples behind her.

The piece-de-resistance, though, is facing us. Looking down from a great height, situated at the opposite side from where we are standing, is an elegant, beautiful church. We are end on to the nave. Though the church is narrow it is unbelievably tall. The steeple gives the impression of reaching up to the clouds, or, I suppose the believers think it reaches to god. The tower, belfry, lantern and spire are all slender and seem stretched out; they are so delicate as to appear tenuous and insufficient to withstand the winter storms. It is highly decorated in a Gothic style with many additional subsidiary towers, spires and flying buttresses. Though imposing it is also soft, feminine. It gives the impression of being an integral part of the square. It says "look at me." It draws in the attention but it does not dominate.

Seeing me speechless Julian said, 'I surmise that you have not yet explored this part of the city.'

'No, I have not. So far I have only had time to start unpacking and to look out of my windows. I have moved into a house on the far bank. It is on the little road which has the narrow park on one side between my new home and the river. From my front door I can look over the top of the war memorial and across the river. I have a superb view of the stunning Cathedral a little to the right. Directly in front I can also see more spires which I suppose are the top of this church.' He nodded yes. 'With the city rising up on this side I cannot see the body of this church. As you know I only arrived here two days ago. On my one previous work day, and also today, I walked down the steep path through the park to the track alongside the river; I then followed it upstream a short way. That, along with you driving me to the James's house and the wife beater's shop, is the limit of my exploration. To get to the station I have crossed the river using the new road bridge. Then I follow the main road, with the cathedral on its embankment to my right, until I get to the front door of the station. I haven't entered the Cathedral yet but I have admired it. Nor have I had a chance to suss out this part of the city. I had no idea that this square was even here, let alone to be so impressive and beautiful.'

'Yes, here is one of my favourite areas of the city. I suggest a different route for you to take to walk to the station. It sounds as if you are in the centre of North Street; in one of those chic, terraced houses which look across the road to the railings where the park slopes steeply down to the river. The ones with polished floors and ragged walls, full of young, upwardly mobile professionals eating smashed avocados.'

His eyebrows are raised, he is teasing yet again with his envious description. He is also questioning. I nodded "yes" to where I am living. I allowed his ribbing at my luck in finding such a perfect location to go unacknowledged. Seeing that I am not going to rise to the bait he continued, 'instead of going right, walk a little to your left and you will find a steep path down to a footbridge.' I nodded again, I have spotted it. 'Walk over the bridge. As you cross over, if you look left between the hanging baskets, as well as the glorious view downstream to the castle you will see the ubiquitous padlocks signifying undying love. A couple of weeks ago I was called out to deal with a woman who was reported to be vandalising the bridge. When I arrived I found a very pregnant and very cross young lady trying to manipulate some bolt cutters and remove a padlock. With the tears and mascara in her eyes she was making a right mess of it.'

'What did you do? I hope that you did not arrest her.'

He gave me a deliberate, "of course not, idiot," look.

'I removed the padlock for her. It was engraved AM love RT forever. It looked almost brand new. I wanted to leave the bolt cutters there for use by most of the other lovers, a week or so after they sealed their everlasting adoration, but she took them back to her dad.'

'You wanted to leave the bolt cutters, so thoughtful, so romantic.'

Smiling down at me he said, 'anyway, cross the river and walk to the old market square where the seats and cafes are. On the far side you will see Market Slip, a cobbled passageway between and under the shops. Walk up there, cross the High Street, walk up the narrow cobbled street directly opposite where you exit Market Slip, and, voila, you arrive over there.' He pointed to the side of the church. 'The code to the rear door of the station yard is 1234.'

'You have to be kidding, on a police station?' He shrugged. 'Thanks for the directions. Now let's go and see our Mr Cape.'

I turned around to face the house for the first time and had yet another shock. The house is unlike any other in the square and, if possible, even more beautiful than its fellows. It is a house, no, it is a residence of extraordinary splendour. Sitting proudly on its own, in the corner of the square, with its garden extending behind the terrace to the left, it is much larger than the others. It appears massive as it is raised up a little with railings and a small garden in front. The house is as a child would draw. There are large sash windows to each side, a big, navy blue front door, three steps leading up to it and a stone arch over. There is a stone tiled roof slightly overhanging the smaller upper sash windows and a central chimney. To our left is an entrance to a paved drive with a small copse of trees to the side. Behind is the other side of the tall stone wall I saw before, the roof of our station is poking above it.

As we walked up to the door Julian mused, almost to himself, 'I always wondered who lived here. It is quite a contrast to Sally James's door that we knocked on last night.'

That saddened me. I tugged on the brass bell pull. There is no broken plastic button to push nor peeling paint to knock on here; poor woman. The door opened and then I had another shock. Another wonderful sight banished the thoughts of the black eyes that greeted me yesterday.

He is absolutely, drop dead, gorgeous. He is at least as tall as Julian, I guess 6' 1." Our Mr Cape, I presume it is him, he looks like one who would own such a house, is equally muscular, as well toned and as well-groomed as the Viking next to me. They could be clones other than their skin colour. I estimate Cape to be a little older than Julian. He is late thirties, maybe early forties, I guess. I seem to have lost the power of speech.

I scrabbled to assemble my thoughts and to give the standard introduction that I have fluently managed so often before. I was flummoxed by his disarmingly handsome Mediterranean appearance. He has light brown skin, intense dark brown eyes, strong features and a prominent slightly hooked nose. His thick wavy black hair is shoulder length. He is wearing a loose back linen shirt and immaculate black chinos with black sandals. Julian looks like a Norse God, Cape looks like a Greek God. He stood with an effortless, elegant pose. As he looked towards Julian I can see he has an aesthetic, studious profile.

Then something else took me by surprise. I held up my warrant card and seeing this, as he simultaneously took in Julian's uniform, a flash of fear crossed his previously smiling features. It was fleeting and quickly suppressed. Instantaneously the smile was back, but now tepid, mirthless. I am used to apprehension when people see my card, but not fear. I felt Julian tense a little. He had seen it as well.

'Mr Cape?' He nodded. He now covered the initial response with an unflinching gaze. It was soft and teasing but also deliberately intense. Instead of covering his first reaction it had the opposite effect. A grain of suspicion formed in my mind which was finally working again.

I gave my name and rank. I then similarly introduced Julian. I asked if he is the owner of a van and I gave the registration number. As he said with an intrigued smile, 'yes, guilty as charged,' there came a flurry of wind and fat rain drops spattered across us. He threw the door open, 'come in, come in, out of the rain.'

We stepped into a wide, light hallway. There is a plush, dark grey carpet. The walls, in marked contrast to those we have recently left, are a beautiful soft grey. They are covered with paintings of serious, stern looking men and women with alert, intelligent expressions. All are original oils. I recognised a couple of scientists, Lord Florey and Professor Chain. I asked, 'is this Florey and Chain?'

Julian stopped and looking closely at the artwork, he added, 'the developers of penicillin no less.'

Cape looked a little surprised and impressed, 'yes they are. Most people don't recognise them and have usually only heard of Fleming.' Looking at us somewhat carefully, even warily, he added, 'come in to the sitting room, make yourself comfortable.'

He opened a heavy wooden door to our right. As he ushered us through I noted a barely detectable hint of an exotic perfume lingering in the hall. I would expect nothing less from any woman who is with this man. He graciously waved us in.

Sitting room, my arse; this is a withdrawing room for an aristocrat. On the floor are overlapping oriental rugs.

Two large leather sofas face each other. Between them is a well-worn, somewhat incongruously battered, leather chair reposing in pride of place. It carries the air of being someone's favourite place to rest. The walls are panelled in a rich dark wood. They are lined with bookshelves. In the occasional book-free space there are picture frames but they do not frame pictures. Instead they display highly polished slices of different rocks, some speckled, some striped. Each specimen, I thought, "can a bit of rock be a specimen?" is lovingly presented, leather backed and illuminated with a curved brass picture light. Around the edges of the floor are glass topped display cabinets filled with mounted moths. Most are drab but some are astonishingly beautiful, I have never seen anything like them before. At one end is a magnificent, mahogany roll top desk.

The room could have been Victorian with the exception of a state of the art computer with three curved black screens sitting atop what is clearly a custom made mahogany table. I saw Julian eyeing the computing array with profound admiration.

The afternoon seems to linger here. The peace of the room; the background smell of wood smoke, wood and leather with, there it is again, a musky perfume. The hiss and pop from the fireplace; the late afternoon light filtering through the amber glass panels above the door; they all combine to enforce deep contemplation and conversation; here, frivolity would be unnecessary and unwelcome.

The rain has quickly stopped and now bright sun is streaming through the window which overlooks the Square with the white statue which is now shining and wet with rain. There had been no need to come in but I am very glad to have had the opportunity to see this room. Cape headed to the sofa on the left and waved us to the one on the right. Julian walked straight across to the leather chair, I suspect in order to surreptitiously observe Cape from the side whilst I am speaking to him.

As Julian sat down Cape said with alarm, 'sorry, no, not there. It may be a little grubby.' I looked around, the room is spotless. It was too late, Julian had sat. Cape said, 'sorry, it is just that ....'

Before he could complete what he was about to say a door closed outside and a soft, disembodied, female voice called out, 'I'm back.' This is a man's room but I had noticed the perfume and thought there must be a woman somewhere. There is a puzzling contradiction, no female influence in this room but a woman in the house.

Cape called back, 'I have visitors.' I, not we; that is intriguing.

'Wonderful, are they sexy and interesting?'

He looked straight into my eyes, holding my gaze he called back, 'yes, both.' I felt myself redden as I had been thinking exactly the same about him. I could not even look at Julian who I am sure has the perfect expression to torment me.

My embarrassment was short lived as then the door violently flew open and banged against the wall shaking the rocks in their frames. From the voice I had expected a slight woman to slide in gracefully, like a ballerina, not this violent, crashing entrance.

In fell a colossal black dog. He had obviously reared up to push on the handle with his paws and to open the door himself. He had hit the door so hard that it bounced off the wall and closed with a bang behind him. His front paws struck the ground with a thud which now shook the moths in their cabinets. He then lumbered slowly, with focussed deliberation, between Cape and me. He headed straight towards Julian. He looks like a black bear. If he even glances in my direction I will throw myself out of the window, even though it is closed. As he passed in front of me, not even deigning to acknowledge my presence, I dared to look at him. He is solid muscle with sleek, long hair. It is his head what transfixed me; it is huge with a long jaw full of savage white teeth. His nut coloured eyes stared ahead, firstly at Julian's eyes and then down towards his crotch, then swopping from one to the other. He lumbered forward with a slow, purposeful roll. I realised that I had stopped breathing. I saw that Julian had also.

Cape quickly said, 'ignore him. He is a big softie. Toby, come here.' Softie, shit, I would not like to meet his aggressive brother. We both breathed again as Toby abruptly changed direction and went to put his chin on Cape's knee for his head to be scratched. His eyes, however, did not leave Julian for a second. Cape resumed, speaking to Julian, 'he is staring at you because............' He did not finish as the door opened again, this time silently and slowly. What I had anticipated finally occurred. In glided a svelte woman.

She moved with grace but I also noted a slight limp. She was exactly as I had anticipated. Not pretty, as I have been told I am, but exotic and sexy. Though she is medium height as all the rest of us in the room are tall she appears smaller. She is dark skinned, darker than Cape who is dusky. I guess that she is of mixed race, possibly Indian and Caucasian. Her features are regular and delicate. The scar alongside her right eye does not spoil them, it adds to her air of mystery. It has been expertly sutured. It is healed but it looks relatively recent, I guess it is only a year or two old. Previously I have too often seen such irregular scars; there is no doubt that this one was made with broken glass. Her auburn hair is tied back in a tight bun, formal, old fashioned, yet simultaneously arrestingly sexy. Her clothing is unusual with a nod to the East. She has a loose black and scarlet top which is decorated with intricately worked gold trim and it has gold threads through it. A beautiful, clearly horribly expensive, off-white pashmina with gold tassels hangs down to her baggy black silk trousers. She carries an ebony walking stick with an intricately carved ivory handle; it is clearly both an antique and necessary, not simply an affectation. Even though she had to lean heavily on the stick her movements towards us were free and assured. She effortlessly carries her unconventional appearance. She exudes mystery and mastery.

Then, for the second time today, came the same surprise. As I stood and held out my warrant card and, again as Cape had, at the same time she took in Julian's uniform, a flash of fear crossed her green eyes. Again I as much felt as saw Julian tense. He had again seen it also. She equally quickly covered it and looking intently at my I.D., not risking further immediate eye contact, she firmly took my proffered hand. 'I am Detective Inspector Rebecca Fletcher, this is Constable Julian Courtney.'

As she shook my hand she said, 'Samantha Cape.'

She moved to Julian who stood to take her hand also. As she shook his hand he said, 'Mrs. Cape.'

To my surprise and Julian's consternation she loudly laughed and shook her head. 'Certainly not. Surely you do not think I would marry this lump and live in this den. He is my big, ugly brother. I live in the annex behind though for family unity we do have an intercommunicating door.' She moved to sit next to her brother as I thought, "ugly lump?", I can hardly take my eyes off him. She misinterpreted my stare, thank god. 'I can see what you are thinking; we do not look like brother and sister. We are actually half siblings, different Mums. We have another half-brother who looks like a slightly smaller version of you,' she nodded at Julian, 'Constable Courtney.' Most people when introduced to a policeman do not register his name the first time. That is most people, not her. She continued, 'we have three mothers and one father between us.' She paused and then, with a cheeky smirk, added, 'if you don't mind me saying you both look Scandinavian and very alike. You look more like brother and sister than we do. Are you?'

Giving thanks for the distraction from my unprofessional gawping at Cape I quickly replied, 'no to both Ms Cape.'

'Please, call me Sam.'

As we all started to sit she suddenly lunged forward and seized Julian's jacket. With surprising strength, in spite of their differing sizes, she pulled him up from his half sitting position whilst shouting, 'no, no, don't sit back.' We turned to see that Toby had stealthily moved on to the chair without us noticing. He is curled up and appears to be already fast asleep. 'Sorry, that is Toby's chair. I don't want you to get hairs on your uniform.' So that is why the brute had been eyeballing poor Julian. He didn't want to bite off Julian's balls; he only wanted his chair. He has for his canine delectation a large, soft, leather chair that would not look out of place in a Pall Mall club.

Cape said, 'my fault, that is what I was about to say when Sam came in.' Big as he is, Julian had looked comfortable in the large chair. There is barely room for the dog. On hearing this Toby opened his eyes and rolled on to his back putting up in the air paws the size of small shovels. Samantha bent down and scratched his stomach. A tail which is as long and as thick as my arm thwacked rhythmically against the chair back. We all sat on the sofas, police on one, the Cape's on the other. Cape started, 'I have not introduced myself properly, please call me Luke.'

In return I asked them to call us Rebecca and Julian. As I said this we all became aware of Julian, mouth gaping, staring at Luke. Julian managed to croak, 'are you Professor

Luke Cape?' Luke gave a hesitant, uncertain nod. Julian leapt up, strode over and grabbed Luke's hand again, now shaking it vigorously. 'I am delighted to meet you. You are the last on the Board that I wanted to trace. I have seen all the others. I have only been in this city for a few months. I was aware that you were here somewhere and I fully intended to look you up but have not yet had the opportunity. This is wonderful, most fortuitous.' We all gawped at him as if he was speaking Chinese. Seeing this Julian gave one of his naughty grins, now I know that something enigmatic is about to unfold. 'My name is on the Board in the Long Room, five below yours.'

As far as I am concerned he is still talking in gobbledegook but this galvanised Luke and Samantha. They leapt to their feet. Luke pumped Julian's hand and Samantha gave him a hug. When this love fest calmed down I had the temerity to ask, 'would one of you please translate?'

Luke looked at me, still distracted and delighted. He said, 'the translation is that Julian and I both captained the rowing team at our college in Cambridge.' So, that explains their physiques and their self-assuredness.

Samantha chipped in, 'I thought that I had seen you before. I was up a few years after big brother and we must have overlapped if you were five years behind him.'

Luke asked, 'I guess that you read criminal justice.'

Julian shook his head, 'no, policing was an afterthought. I read Computer Science. I then undertook a Doctorate in Forensic Computing in the States. Following that I worked in Computer Security for a while but finally I realised that I preferred to chase actual crooks rather than virtual ones. I enrolled on the fast track detective training a few months ago. We have to spend some time in uniform before progressing.' At last, something that I already knew, that he is on the fast track programme. Everything else was news to me.

Luke replied, 'so, there are three supposed doctors here. You and I are real ones. Samantha is a medical practitioner, a mere double bachelor, they like to call themselves doctor.' Samantha gave a resigned sarcastic, "ha ha," it is obviously not the first time that she has heard that.

Looking back at me, the cheeky grin returned, Julian said, 'no, four. Even though it was that second rate place, what's its name, yes, Oxford, that's it? In spite of being there I suppose we should count Rebecca and make it four.' Luke and Samantha looked at me as Julian continued, 'undergrad psychology, Doctorate forensic psychology.' The cocky bastard knows everything about me and I can only glean the occasional snippet about him.

We all sat back down. Toby rolled over and went back to sleep. I found it difficult to relax as I am sitting only feet from a wolf. I mentally chastised myself. "At least be honest with yourself, Rebecca." The reason I am not relaxing is not the dog, it is him. I cannot take my eyes off him. I tried, I am sure I am failing, to keep my expression professional but my true feelings are far more visceral. I found him staring back at me. His dark, brooding eyes convey and conjure thoughts alien to a police interview.

I was snapped back to reality as Samantha asked sharply, 'back to business, why are you here?' To call her manner direct, after the levity, would be an understatement. She was forceful to the point of being offensive. Is she simply rude or was the tone of this interjection due to her being anxious? I suspect the latter. Why?

I replied, 'we are investigating a missing person, possibly a violent abduction, which occurred on Sunday night down near the quay. A van registered to Luke was seen on CCTV to be in the vicinity. It appeared to have emerged from a service road where the abduction possibly occurred. There was a man and a woman in the cab; though they could not be not seen clearly enough to be identified. We wanted to ask if was you both in the van and, if so, had you noted anything unusual.' Julian wriggled a little. The truth is we want to ask if they had abducted Brian James, though, looking at them, I am struggling to find that likely.

She looked appalled and exclaimed, 'women are simply not safe these days.'

Julian followed up, 'actually it is a man, a large man, who is missing. We are making the presumption that it was abduction as there were signs of violence. Were you in the area at that time?'

Luke replied, 'definitely, yes, both of us. Sam was driving and I was the passenger. It is my research van and I was undertaking some preliminary measurements. My Chair is in Earth Sciences and as you see from the specimens around my chief interest is, or at least was, in rocks. Of late I have become interested in atmospheric pollution and its effect on moth populations. This is now taking over from my previous work as it is relevant to the move to clean air zones in cities. Whilst the press are fixated on nitrous dioxide the scientific community is realising that particles released from brakes are even more damaging, that is of course also relevant to the use of electric cars. The moth population seems very sensitive to such pollution. The van has a Skinner Moth Trap inside opening to the roof. Alongside that is a spectroscopic air pollution analyser.

Samantha cleared her throat and with a doting smile at her brother said, 'as you can see Luke is obsessed with this and gets evangelical. On subject if you please Luke.' In spite of her smile and a lame attempt at frivolity there is an icy undertone in her manner. The atmosphere in the room, though superficially congenial, is laced with a strange, uncertain emotion.

'Sorry, sorry, I do get carried away. Anyway this means

that Samantha and I tour the city and surrounding country areas looking for suitable sites. She drives so that I can make notes. I then return on another night with a couple of post-grads and we monitor through the night. Being parked up in the city at night does mean that we sometimes detect much more than moths. If you look in your records you will see that we have reported two crimes and stayed on the 'phone relaying the bad boys' activities to your station until your officers arrived.

Yes, we were there down by the quay two nights ago, for a short while. We looked at that service road. As it was a dark enclave I thought that it would be a suitable site for my investigation. When we arrived we found that the street lights had been vandalised. If they were to be repaired whilst we were monitoring, which we need to undertake on several occasions over a few weeks, it would negate all of the work. Whilst we were assessing the area I did not notice anything strange, did you Sam?' She shook her head. Luke continued, 'If you look ahead at your CCTV you will find that I returned there for much of the following night, on that occasion with two post grads. If access is allowed we will be back tomorrow.' This was directed at Julian.

Then Luke turned his chocolate brown eyes back on me and I felt my concentration slide. Again my thoughts should make me blush. I didn't. 'I noticed that you looking at some of my specimens before. They were all collected within a mile of here. Some are the same as ones we collected last night.'

I jumped, 'what, even the colourful ones.' Then I realised that there are two possible interpretations of his apparently throw away comments. Is he returning to something that he clearly loves or is he deliberately changing the subject?

'The pink and olive green one is the Elephant Hawk

moth. The one with white forewings with brown blotches and orange hind wings with blue spots outlined in black, is the Garden Tiger Moth. Beautiful, aren't they.' He looked straight into my eyes and I felt my insides melt. 'If you want to see the van I am afraid that it is not here, it is always parked at Hogwarts. You can view it there anytime.'

I thought that he was taking the mickey and I exclaimed, 'Hogwarts?'

Julian chipped in and addressed Luke, 'Rebecca has only been in the city a couple of days.' Then to me, 'if you leave the city going south there is a lovely stone wall on your right. Behind that is a university building. As it is in the Gothic style it is known locally as Hogwarts.' Then turning to Samantha he asked, 'do you practice as a specialist or as a G.P.?' It appeared to be meant as a polite comment to include her as the occupation of the other three present is clear. Getting to know Julian I think it more likely that he wants to bring her in, to get her talking and to see if we can glean anything useful.

'Neither. A fuller answer requires that I give you some background information. What you ask leads me to something that I was going to comment on before you left. It is completely irrelevant to your investigation. That is, Luke and I know it is irrelevant but you will undoubtedly have a different take on it. I presume that you will research us both and you will find out what I am about to say anyway. If we have appeared to have hidden these events from you then surely that would be judged suspicious.'

Luke chipped in, 'obviously I can surmise what is coming. I fully agree with what Sam has just said. I did not make any comment myself because I know she would not let you leave without informing you. More, it is for her to say, not me.'

Julian and I are rigid with attention and intrigue.

'The scar on my face and my limp are due to injuries. There are others that you cannot see. I am currently having physio as part of my recovery from recent knee surgery, the fourth such operation in nearly two years. Because of my rehabilitation for this, in the recent past because of treatment for other damage as well, I cannot practice medicine as such but I am very happy in a part time role in the hospital pharmacy working as a pharmacist. I do not have to see patients or undertake night work so it is easier to fit in. This is for background only; I am coming to the relevant part.

My injuries were not accidental. I suffered years of domestic abuse which almost two years ago culminated in a frenzied attack which left me comatose with multiple injuries. Thankfully all have healed well with the exception of severely torn knee ligaments which can be more troublesome than a broken leg. My then husband was charged and imprisoned for the abuse and particularly the last violent attack. Whilst he was incarcerated I divorced him. His name is, possibly was, Robin Newnham.'

Julian and I jolted a little at the "possibly was." What can that mean? As she spoke, about the abuse she had suffered, I felt both a softening in her previous brusque manner. This was accompanied by a subliminal interaction between her and Luke. I felt him warning her. What else is going on beneath this surface chat?

'The police acted promptly and well. He was arrested on the day of the attack. They, that is you, had not been able to act before as, out of fear, I had not reported the abuse and I had treated the injuries myself. As so often happens, it was hidden behind closed doors. Luke knew and was desperate to intervene but stupidly I would not allow him to do so. I was only too well aware that even if abuse is reported, mostly the man is not imprisoned, and this may precipitate a worsening of the violence. It is a Catch 22. Of course this escalation happened to me anyway. My criticism is not of the police service but of the criminal justice system which sentenced him to only one year in prison. Worse, he was released well before then.

Now, finally, you will hear the relevant part. On the day he was released he disappeared. No one, including his mother, has seen him since. I have no idea what happened to him but I do know that he doted on his mother and as he has not seen her my guess is that he is dead. As this is not certain I remain fearful that he may return which is why I have come to live in Luke's annex. Even with my protective big brother here if you come next door you will see that I live in a fortress.

So you are investigating a missing man and this has taken you to the home of a woman whose ex-husband is missing. More, she admits to being in the vicinity of your recent case. Roughly one year ago, when he disappeared, Luke and I were extensively investigated; clearly, understandably, we were suspects. Then, thankfully, we had good alibis. If it had been a usual night with the two of us sitting here reading, or, even more suspiciously, in the vicinity in a van with no independent witnesses, I think that we would still be suspects. I do not want to second guess you and I am not an amateur Sherlock Holmes but that must be the standard presumption.'

Julian and I sat back astounded. I had not realised that both of us had literally been sitting on the edge of our seats. I thanked her for her frankness and commiserated on the serious shortcomings of dealing with domestic abuse. I told her that during my time in the police, in only five years, the way it is dealt with has markedly improved but I agreed that there is still a long way to go. I also confided to her that I have had first hand dealings with several cases in which, in my judgement, the custodial sentence was sickeningly lenient. I did not refer to her comments that she presumes that we consider them to be suspects. That slipped by. We all fell quiet. The interview had come to a natural end.

We thanked them for their time. Julian and Luke promised to meet for a beer without committing to an actual arrangement. We had not made any remark regarding us inspecting the van. As we left Toby did not stir. Back in the soft, grey, airy hall Samantha held back a little. Luke quickly shook Julian's hand.

Then he took mine. He clasped it. He seemed to hold it for longer than usual. He is standing so close to me. In spite of the light in here the air feels muggy. Whilst holding my gaze as well as my hand he gently said, 'it has been lovely meeting you. I do hope that I will see you again.' I felt light headed as I stammered a bland reply.

Julian and I stepped into the square. The rain has passed and the lawn is bathed in a warm evening light. I suggested that we sit on one of the seats in the centre next to the statue. I deliberately chose the one facing the house we had left and motioned to Julian to join alongside me. Before speaking I again took in the wonderful, quintessentially English scene. To our left the sun is now low, going down behind thunderous clouds. There are long streaks of vivid orange between narrow breaks in the black cloud. The sun itself can be partially seen through one of the gaps and it bathes the square in a warm light.

Julian spoke first, quietly, as if confiding a secret. 'I guess that you wanted to sit here knowing they would see us. You are hoping to rattle their cage aren't you? I don't have to ask if you saw what I saw. You also know that I did not miss it. We held our breath at the same instant, twice, when we caught their fleeting look of fear.'

I nodded. It is only our second day together and

already we are working in concert. 'Yes to both. I can't see them looking out at us but if they are at the rear of the room I would not expect to be able to. With my warrant card and your uniform I would have expected a look of apprehension but the first reaction was, as you say, fear, for both of them.'

'Yes the uniform engenders disquiet in many people, but not in middle class intellectuals. Rarely fear in anyone; that is of course unless they are guilty.' I realised from his demeanour that he considers they are suspects. No, stronger, he thinks they are guilty, the motive presumably being linked with domestic abuse. Perhaps James has been despatched in return for a similar favour with Newnham. Julian had completely fooled me, no doubt the Capes as well. I had not picked up on his suspicions. He must be a formidable poker player.

'In addition to that, Julian, we were not with a woman whose husband is simply missing but one whose husband is missing following serious domestic abuse perpetrated on her by him. His disappearance has considerable overlap with that of the charming Brian James. Also, I would like to have a good look at their alibis. Even more, she could not handle a big man but he could. If one of them is involved then they both are as they had the same reaction to us.' Then with a teasing smile I turned to him and continued, 'I forgot. It can't possibly be him. Not only was he at Cambridge he was also captain of rowing.'

He smiled, rather sadly, and continued, ruefully, 'unfortunately that is not the case. I said that I had looked up the other captains on the board. I did not say where I found them. I tracked one down to Pentonville where he is being held for multiple armed robberies and another is under investigation for serious fraud, he is almost certainly guilty.'

I exploded with laughter. 'Which side are you on Julian? I have only known you for two days and already I have found one reason to arrest you.'

'Only one; and I thought you were a detective.' He had mimicked Brutus perfectly.

He was not finished. Now with his usual wide, cheeky smile back in place he added, 'but there is a far more important reason why it can't possibly be pretty boy.' I looked at him intrigued both by the possible reason and the soubriquet, whilst, due to his expression, bracing myself for yet more teasing. 'You have the hots for him. At one stage I thought you were going to sit on his lap. A smart detective would not make eyes at a crook.'

I tried to deny it. The problem is that what he said was true and my reddening face confirmed it. The only part not true is that I had not considered sitting on his lap. My thoughts had been far more carnal but I'll be damned if I will admit to that.

'It's no good trying to deny it, it was written all over your face. I am sure that you noticed that he was similarly smitten. At times it was like sitting between two fully charged Van de Graf generators. Your secret is safe with me but it is relevant to the investigation.' My eyes widened, surely he is not going to suggest that I may be partial because I fancied him. 'Please take that look off your face, of all people I would not think of you as being skewed in an investigation. I meant Samantha. She saw you lusting after each other. She could hardly miss it. She did not like it. My thinking is that she is fearful that her brother is likely to start seeing a detective who is not only stunning, both in detecting and being delectable, but also the very same sleuth is investigating what they have possibly been up to. That is more likely to be the issue than her being concerned for his honour.'

'Well, thank you for the compliments Julian, though as your senior officer I am not sure that you should have made one of them. Are we reading too much into a coincidence? I have the distinct feeling that you consider that we have solved the case and that it is now only a matter of finding a little of that pesky stuff called evidence before we arrest them both.'

'Possibly it is all coincidence. It would not be the only one. It is also happenstance that we were not only at university together but both captains in the same sport. There are remarkable odds against that. Coincidence is hardly evidence. On the other hand it should at least suggest that we look further. On the downside they are both wearing black today, admittedly her only partly but him completely. Perhaps being in black clothes in the van was more of a fashion statement than camouflage.'

'Yes to both. Possibly it is wishful thinking that in one of my first cases in my new job the first person I interview is the culprit. I know that it is as likely to be him as it is to be the hundredth person that we interview but emotionally it feels improbable that it is our first

There is nothing more we can do tonight. I am going to go home to finish my unpacking. I don't need to return to the station, I will follow your directions and walk across this lovely square. Tomorrow I will be in late as I have to undertake some admin in H.R. first. Perhaps you could take a look at the van, from the outside, no need to ask him to open it up yet. Why not take Barbara with you? Afterwards, if you both return to the station and start looking up Samantha's file I will meet you in the office.'

We said our goodbyes but as we parted I had a further thought. I am not certain that I should share it but he is very open with me and I should reciprocate. 'Julian,' he turned around to face me, 'when you see Barbara be aware that I am not the only female copper near here to have the hots for a tall handsome man.' His face showed that he had no idea.

'Though you wear a wedding ring my guess is that she knows that you have lost Lucy. If you are not ready for a relationship then may I suggest that you drop a few hints about that.' He looked very surprised, very thoughtful and very thankful; all at the same time. I had been unsure but now I am relieved to see that I have made the right call.

CHAPTER 6:
LUKE: WRATH

I watched them walk down the path. I cannot take my eyes off her athletic figure and her lovely bum. She walks like a cat. It is a sensual slide with ill-concealed power and control. To my surprise they started across the road towards the green. I had assumed that they would turn left towards the police station's rear entrance. I realised that Sam has not joined me in seeing them off; it is unlike her to be so discourteous. Then I remembered being surprised at Sam being sharp to the point of rudeness when speaking to them. She has had yet more physio today, perhaps it did not go well. I hope that her pain has not returned and is not underlying this curt manner. I reluctantly closed the door and returned to the sitting room.

Toby is curled on his seat. At first I could not see Sam. Then I realised that she is pressed flat against the side wall, rigid, staring out of the window opposite.

'Luke; get over here against the wall so that they cannot see us watching. Quick; stop faffing around.' What; I am not watching anything nor am I faffing. It is so unlike her to speak like this to anyone, let alone to me.

Then Sam hissed with a wrath that I have never seen before. 'The bitch, look, I knew that she would do that.' Through the window I can see that they are now sitting in the square looking towards the house. They seem at ease chatting in the late afternoon sun. The warm light is making her appear even more beautiful, more desirable. Their demeanour is friendly. I can see nothing to inspire such venom from Sam.

As I reluctantly left the window and joined Sam alongside the side wall she continued, 'she is trying to rattle us.' They are succeeding with you, I thought. Having realised how angry Sam is I figured it better to avoid a quip. I looked at her more closely, now with concern. She is quaking. For some reason Sam is angry but there is more going on. There is an underlying foreboding verging on panic. I guess that Sam is concerned at being questioned. She has not faced it before. When I killed Robin she was with me on the day but went in for more surgery the day after. The police only closely interrogated me and merely briefly spoke to Sam whilst she was recovering in hospital. Her being in pain and looking vulnerable hid the fact that she was capable of driving me when I disposed of his body.

I put my arms around her and spoke quietly. 'Sam; it was a routine check. We have a good alibi. There is no reason for them to suspect us. Even if they do there is no evidence which would incriminate us. I am sure that we are secure.' From here we can see them chatting next to the statue. I wish that I was sitting there. Though Rebecca is partly obscured by Julian looming over her, in my mind's eye I can still see her beautiful face. Her features are so delicate and soft. Her intense blue eyes and cupid-bow lips are framed by her blond curls. Even so I can see that it is a dangerous beauty. She has the intensity, the concentration and the power of a stalking lioness.

Sam turned her face towards me. Her façade has slipped. Firstly I saw her disbelief at what I had just said. Then her previous wrath dissipated as she glanced back out of the window and she saw the police are now facing each other, talking amiably, no longer looking towards my house, towards us. She started trembling. She shook in the same manner and with the same fear as she had when we were told that Robin was being released. Turning back and looking straight at me her face collapsed into being my baby sister. Now I finally saw the full extent of the fear underlying her behaviour, causing her wrath.

'Luke, please don't tell me that you have been taken in by her flirting with you, by that pretty little face and blond curls.' Sam's lovely soft mouth curled into a snarl as she said, "pretty little face." She looked into my eyes and gave an exasperated groan. 'Oh shit, you have been. Can't you see that neither of them are PC Plod. They are both as sharp as tacks, particularly her. You only saw her giving you "come hither" looks with those pale blue eyes. You did not see that when you were looking at the constable they were like ice and dissecting you. They both suspect us, him more so, but she is the dangerous one.' As I looked at her with incredulity she hardened again and snapped at me, 'oh for god's sake look at you. You are like a spotty teenager in love. Luke, snap out of it.'

It is now my turn to get cross. 'For two years you have been trying to persuade me to start seeing women again. Now, the first time that I feel attracted to one, the first time I can look at a woman again without those feelings flaring up, you slap me down.' As I said it I regretted the nasty tone that I had used. I had not been able to stop it and now I cannot take it back.

'Don't speak to me like that when I am trying to get you to see sense. She is leading you on. She has you by the cock and she will not hesitate to use her undoubted charms to interrogate you more effectively than any waterboarding.'

After this uncharacteristic attack she relented and took my hand. After a pause, now speaking softly, she said 'I am sorry. Let's be friends.' We leaned back against the wall together. 'They are a good team. There is nothing sexual between them but, boy, do they complement each other.' I nodded and to my surprise I felt a little relief at this. I had thought it possible they were an item. Now it appears more likely that she is unattached, certainly she does not wear a wedding ring. Sam's comment had had the effect of jolting assumptions, suggesting possibilities. I should have known better.

Sam immediately detected the direction of my thoughts. Now, again a little irked she said, 'Luke, since you were sixteen you have been able to have virtually any woman you wanted and god only knows you have taken full advantage of that. With you being unattached for the last couple of years, when I have accompanied you to the university functions, I have felt like hanging a sign on my back. For my protection it would say, "don't stab me, I am his sister." It is clear that the word has gone around that you do not have a current girlfriend and all those very sexy lecturers and post grads are practically throwing their knickers at you.' I smiled and shook my head but I can see the truth in what she has said. 'Don't try to laugh me off, I am not flattering you. It is simply the truth. If you are beginning to feel able to chase women again, or should I say not fending them off, then pick one of them. Not an obviously brilliant detective who has been charged with investigating the results of our activities. We know that what we are doing is moral, but, let's face it, it is illegal. It is so important that we are careful Luke. Not only for our freedom, but what we are doing is vital and we must not be stopped.'

Whilst Sam was saying this an understanding came to me. It was all true what Sam has said but now I see why I feel the way I do. My thoughts are on Rebecca, not the mission. Yet again my lovely little sister, who infuriatingly can read me like a book, caught my look. 'What is it?'

'You are of course absolutely right on all accounts. I am very attracted to her and a relationship with her could be dangerous. Apart from being beautiful and clever I see something else.' Sam looked at me with exasperation. I can see that she already knows. 'That which I fear; that which makes it impossible for me to see other women; I think that it would not happen with her.'

Sam gave a soft, indulgent laugh, 'you bloody idiot. You know damn well that with a wonderful man such as you it wouldn't happen with any woman. You are also right, it certainly wouldn't with her. That is assuming you want your head and cock to remain attached. Look, they are going.' I raised my head and saw Julian heading towards the station and Rebecca crossing the square. I can only think of them in forenames. Sam whispered what I was thinking, 'she is very beautiful. She looks and walks more like a model than a detective. Please be careful Luke.'

'Keep your friends close and your enemies closer.'

'Don't give me that crap Luke. You want her to be more than a friend and yet you have to see that she is an enemy. It's not just you. If you are caught then I am as well. It's not just us. What about the people that we are protecting?' She gave me a vexed stare and then calmed. Before I could reply she continued, 'I am sorry that I am being so cross. It's your life and I want you to be happy. I so much wish you would return to seeing women again. Even her if you promise to be careful.'

She hesitated and then she continued; now with her usual determination, 'I am not simply frightened by her. This visit has only compounded what I was feeling before I came home. Two strong emotions of me being already upset and my fear at seeing the police combined and took me by surprise. I am very upset by something that I saw at the refuge today. I know that what I am about to say is breaking rule 3. I know what you had to do to Brian James because we broke rule 1 was so difficult for you. I fear that what I am going to suggest may also create yet more problems from breaking our code yet again.'

"Rule 3; we do not undertake more than one intercession a month to minimise the chance of a pattern being spotted and thus exposing our activities." I fear for what is coming but I am pleased that Sam has not spotted that killing Brian James was easy for me. He deserved it, it was essential. I have no qualms; even so, surely I should feel a little contrition. 'What have you seen?'

'A young woman came in to the refuge with her two children. Not only has she been beaten by her husband but she was also viciously, anally raped. I persuaded her to allow me to examine her and what I found meant that I had to insist that she was immediately sent to A and E. Her anus has been badly torn and she must have surgery. I suspect that it may also involve the inner sphincter and if so, even when repaired, she is likely to be left incontinent. She will be in hospital for some time. At present the children are being kept at the refuge. As the mother is not there then that is possibly illegal without the father's permission as they are not being supervised by a family member. If he finds out where they are he will be able to collect them. It would be very difficult for the refuge to refuse to hand them to a parent without a court order which could not be obtained in time. If that happens then she will have to return to him or risk the safety of her children. We have to force him to stop attacking her again and from harming the children. We have to undertake this very soon.'

Sam is clearly distraught at what she has seen but I can see from her characteristic tic of biting her lower lip that there is more to come. I circled my hand in a "go on" gesture. 'Luke, it is not one of our rules but I have also done something that may make you cross. Before I tell you what, you must appreciate that I was very careful. You know that I would not take any unnecessary risks.'

Oh shit, I can see what is coming.

'Whilst I was examining her I asked about him in a very casual manner. She thought that I was making polite conversation. I found out where he works and that he usually undertakes an afternoon into the evening shift. I know where they live from the records. I looked him up on social media and quickly found an image of him.' She held up the smartphone we have under a false ID and pay-as you-go scheme. It is untraceable. We use it for all such research. In addition to deleting our searches after every action we throw the 'phone away every six months and the replacement is kept hidden outside when we are here at home.

I took the 'phone and said, 'he looks like a nasty, scrawny prat.' Sam dipped her head in agreement. 'Out with it, nothing you have said so far would concern me. What are you holding back?'

'On the way home I cycled out by their house. I saw him leave.'

I started to interrupt and she gently put a finger to my lips. 'Don't worry, my over protective, wonderful brother. Please don't blow a gasket when you hear that I also followed him to work.' Another press on the lips; this time accompanied by a little smile and a lift of her eyebrows. She can be so exasperating; she knows exactly how to get her own way with me. Sam flicked to the next photo on her 'phone and showed me the same guy walking up a residential road. At least it was taken from some way off. 'They live almost next to the little supermarket in the corner of those tatty shops grandly called the "Woods Centre." He works in the DIY store in the retail park off the ring road. To get there he walks up the main road. I cycled ahead and stopped in the petrol station for a Coke and a muffin, as an excuse to hang around.'

'Now I know that you are fibbing. You would never eat or drink those.'

'I pretended. They were foul and went straight in the bin. Again, don't panic. I kept under the cameras at the station, I was not recorded there, and there are none on the route he took. He walked past the petrol station and then turned between two houses and disappeared. I cycled after him and found that there is a small alley between the houses which I have never spotted before. It comes out opposite a Bridge Club in a residential road. Fifty meters down there it opens onto the ring road and he crossed over into the retail park.

Luke, where the alley opens into the road it is ideal. It is at a bend in the road. If I park there I will be able to see far down the road in either direction. If anyone does come they will not be able to see into the alley until they are almost next to it, the entrance is obscured by the bend. There are bushes there. You could lurk in them pretending to have a pee, Taser him when he is next to the van and he will practically fall in.'

I went to the sofa and sat down in astonishment. Toby picked up on my heavy collapse into the chair. He lifted his head, scrutinised us both, checked the room for threats and then went straight back to sleep. It is obvious that Sam has achieved in an hour's observation what normally takes us days and several visits to accomplish. 'The photo you have just shown me, that is where you are thinking of?' She indicated yes. 'Sam it sounds perfect. I will take a spin out there on the motorbike. It appears we need to get on with this one.' She gave anther nod. 'It seems precipitous but if we collected him it tomorrow afternoon I could perform the instruction tomorrow night. I can easily rearrange a couple of seminars booked for the following day and I will not have to go to the University. I know that you are then on duty but I could undertake the persuasion whilst you are at work and then we could return him when you have finished.'

'It would be great if you could check it out now. I consider that we have sufficient justification for breaking rule 3. Her need is urgent. I very much doubt that if we do undertake this one that it would ever be reported. He is one of those vicious little creeps who is also a devout coward. Ten minutes of your persuasion and he would sell his mother to stop any more. Even if he did it would help us if an alibi was needed as I will be on duty. Also that hard-nosed detective you fancy so much surely would not suspect us undertaking something only one day after her showing us clearly that we are under scrutiny. It would be perfect to have the bitch herself as part of our plan to allay suspicion.'

I ignored the comments about Rebecca. I can see that Sam is not really thinking that and has simply, unwittingly slipped into her previous manner. Sam's abject fear has been replaced by her more characteristic unwavering devotion to what we are doing. That is what is consuming her now. When she is like this her eyes become quite mesmerising. That we are breaking rule 3 is irrefutable but any resulting problems will not be insurmountable.

As I let the previous comments about Rebecca slide I considered the full picture and further implications. It is so uncharacteristic of Sam to speak, even to think, like that. Sam had been seriously perturbed by this combination of events. To be confronted with the results of a viscous attack; to have been planning a serious crime and to then return home to find a detective sitting in your home would discommode the strongest, even her. Rebecca is only doing her job, if anything I admire her as clearly being good at it. I caught myself and did not know whether to smile or grimace. I am thinking of her as Rebecca, not DI Fletcher.

Her brief but indelibly vivid visit seems stamped on my consciousness. I stepped out into the yard and wheeled my motorbike out of its garage.

....

....

As he walked up the alley I pretended to pee in the bushes. Sam gave the signal, a mere scratching of her ear, meaning that he is in position immediately behind me. A minor flick of her finger showed me that all is clear. I swivelled as he passed me and I Tasered him from behind. I caught him before he even hit the ground. From inside Sam slid the van door open and I bundled him through. She gave him an injection of Ketamine and then slipped back into the driver's seat whilst I strapped him to the stretcher. As I secured him we started to move off, less than twenty seconds from the start.

Sam drove the fifteen minutes to the farm. I unlocked the gate and relocked it behind as she drove in. I repeated the same at the warehouse.

I wheeled him out of the van checking the straps holding him onto the stretcher as he will be secured there for the next twenty four hours. Then I manoeuvred the stretcher next to the apparatus. By lifting first one end on, then the other, I can handle even large men on my own. This little runt is easy to move.

I fixed more ratchet straps over both him and the stretcher to secure him to the apparatus. I applied more gaffer tape applied to cover his mouth to silence his screaming. Yet more of it stuck over his eyes so that I cannot be seen. Then the absorbent pads pushed down his trousers front and back. So often they are incontinent, especially when the mark is applied.

He is already completely secured and yet only now

beginning to come round. I nodded at Sam to go to her car. We had previously left it inside the farm gate to enable her to go on duty. No speech will pass between us within his hearing. When he hears my voice it will only be through a modulator.

Sam silently left and I swung him out in readiness.

Then I waited for him to recover completely from the drug before I start. By this time tomorrow he will be broken. He will never hit a woman again.

CHAPTER 7: REBECCA, UNEXPECTED

Over a few weeks, as the dark days leading to Christmas slid by, a pleasing rhythm developed. This surprised me given some of the challenges in my new post. My relationship with Meadows is dire. His posturing at the morning briefings, the manner in which he treats the team, his misogynistic carping, the sniggering sycophants he holds close to him; they are all disgusting. They are reminiscent of policing from a bygone age.

Brutus ignores me as much as possible. The only contact we have results in him insisting that I undertake some basic police work far below my rank. His excuse is that it will familiarise me with the station and the city. The reality is that he intends it to be a demeaning humiliation. It has completely backfired on him, much to my delight. The only disappointment I have is that he does not have the insight to see this. After the danger and subterfuge of my undercover work in the Met it is a welcome break to reacquaint myself with basic policing. That is my first love in this job; I have always found it so satisfying. From time to time, to the astonishment and the delight of the station, I borrow and wear a WPC's uniform and go on foot patrol. Not only do I take pleasure in it there is the additional advantage, I cannot think of this without a frisson of schadenfreude, that it does in fact thoroughly familiarise me with the station and the city. By shear accident, certainly against his true wishes, Meadows was correct yet he is the loser. I have forged strong relationships with all of the team. Other than the Troop, they are a professional and a gratifying group to work alongside.

Though I am at pains to work with them all I do spend the majority of my time with Julian. Throughout my time in the service I have had excellent and rewarding working relationships with many of my fellow officers. My relationship with Julian is more than even the best of previous ones, it is outstanding. He is a superb policeman. He is also great fun. He teases me constantly but in such a good natured way it brings us closer. Beyond his excellent official work the additional snippets of information he provides, from his possibly illegally applied computer expertise, do help further. We are often ribbed in the mess by others saying that one of us is psychic as we appear to make connections from thin air. Julian has developed an algorithm to scan locally social media for the injudicious boasting that so many bad boys cannot restrain themselves from posting . The snippets it reveals enable us to focus our attention and we can then act like a laser guided missile. The only difficulty is in camouflaging the true origin of our insights. I do wrestle with the ethics of such snooping. I justify it by saying to myself that we do not act unless there is other evidence and we are only looking at what people have publically posted.

I should be more honest with myself. I have just implied to my own conscience that I often grapple with the moral foundations of what we are doing. The truth is that I have only thought about it once and then only for a few seconds. Julian and I are not trying to re-write the legal or moral rule book; we are bear hunting.

Mostly though, our success comes from the way Julian

and I work in concert. We think the same and at the same time. It seems as if we are indeed telepathic, as fellow officers say, we read each other's reactions so well. So far it has been mostly small, low level crimes that we have solved. Even so, with the whole team and in particular with Julian, I have made a series of satisfying arrests and the morale of the station is soaring. This is in spite of our dear leader.

Other than the chore of the morning briefings the station is ignoring the Troop. The awful moniker they fashioned for me on my second day, Tibs, has stuck and now it is openly used. Though the meaning has been largely forgotten it is said as a compliment and with affection. It seems a contradiction but I feel both proud and humbled to have been welcomed so completely by them.

Meadows, I can ignore but one thing eats at me. I think about it every day, especially when I walk to the station via the rear entrance. Julian also raises the subject frequently. It is obviously on his mind as well. Brian James, the abduction; our first case and the only one in which we have not made any progress at all; nada. He has vanished into thin air. Barbara has undertaken some follow up visits and has reported back that at least Sally is thriving. Door locks have been changed, barring orders have been obtained in his absence, injuries have healed and she is finally able to relax a little again. The best outcome would undoubtedly be for us to find him dead in a ditch. Only then will she be able to truly and completely rid herself of the fear.

Yes, the James' case often comes to my mind as I pass the lovely house behind the station as I walk in each morning. So does the occupant of the house. I see him frequently. Every day I run through the park and along the side of the river right in front of my own house. It is a lovely place where I can enjoy a demanding workout in glorious surroundings. Even now in winter, when the dank nights seem to fall at four in the afternoon, the park is attractive. With the majestic river flowing by, the old bridge and the castle both reflected in its still water; the whole scene is breath taking. Though I am in the middle of the city I can breathe the soft damp air and smell the wet leaves as I exercise.

Then there is the other advantage, Luke. I see him several times a week. He runs regularly as well. I notice all of the women openly stare and give him encouraging looks. They are clearly peeved that I am the only one that he stops to talk to. I have no doubt that he would ask me out, our attraction is clearly mutual, if it were not for her. His sister always joins him, her cycling next to him running. Toby always accompanies them. He seems to have taken a shine to me as he always comes up and rubs against me. How I wish that Luke would.

Perhaps Luke indeed would, were it not for Samantha. She stands next to him, tight lipped, looking like a Victorian maiden aunt chaperoning a young girl. Her only contribution to any conversation is to ask him to move on. Always she is either late or getting cold or there is some other lame excuse. She clearly dislikes me. At least Toby gives an excuse for a pause. I can speak to Luke, briefly, while scratching the dogs head. I do not have to bend down; his massive head comes up to my waist, so I can look his master in the eye while doing so. I feel the warmth of Luke's gaze and icicles form on the side where Samantha stands.

Thankfully Julian interrupted my reverie in my cubbyhole cum office. He asked if I wanted to accompany him on a call out; oh yes. We drove to casualty; they had telephoned to report an assault on a minor.

When we arrived, initially, we could not see any staff. We walked around the department. I hate these places. The air is astringent, the décor offensive, the lighting harsh and the noise is invasive. How people are supposed to get better in such an atmosphere I do not know, it is certainly not conducive to healing. Worse, it is not necessary. The ambiance could be reversed with a change of attitude which need not cost more. Surely the senior managers, nurses and consultants could, should, campaign to alter it.

Then we spotted a receptionist who said that the medical and nursing staff are in a lunchtime meeting and that it would soon finish. She suggested that we wait outside the door of the meeting room. As we went to sit one of the people inside looked through a glass panel in the wall and spotted Julian's uniform. She conferred with one of the others, then waved us in.

With a puzzled glance at each other, we opened the door and entered. There were roughly a dozen people there, varying ages, all but one in hospital scrubs. They had the air of being a team of doctors and nurses. I looked at the women in their ill-fitting, drab garb. I thought, "do they not have any self-respect? Can they not make even a smidgen of effort." If it is necessary to wear such clothing could they not take it home, pull out the sewing machine and persuade it to at least partially fit? Even a good ironing would help.

I felt an odd combination of being a little self-conscious of what I am wearing, yet, proud at the same time. I have to dress for many eventualities. Certainly I cannot wear high heels as beloved by coppers in films but that does not prevent me from being well dressed. My time is spent moving around, entering peoples' homes, ransacking warehouses. Often my work is undertaken outside in all weathers. Though it very rarely occurs, I also have to be prepared to chase a crook. My clothes need to cover all such circumstances. I also take every opportunity to walk or run during or between my daily tasks and this has to be accommodated as well. I have to dress accordingly, as this dreary group similarly need to, but, there is no need to be poorly turned out. I am careful to keep myself well presented. Today my Emporio Armani EA7, charcoal-grey, quilted track suit and matching trainers stand out. Several pairs of envious eyes took this in.

One of the group, the oldest one, also the only one in a suit and one of the few men present, grandly gesticulated that we sit in the corner. His manner made me feel that he wanted to hand us a pointy hat with "dunce" written on. He started, 'well, I see the police have finally arrived. No doubt you have come about young Timothy Breen who we were just discussing. As usual you are too late. His father has discharged him against medical advice.'

A little shocked at what he said and his pompous tone I looked more closely at him, biding my time to reply. He has an expensive suit and handmade leather shoes but he is fat with flopping jowls and there is a thick layer of dandruff on his shoulders. Though well dressed he has an air of limited personal hygiene and I would not be surprised that if I were a little closer he may smell musty. His whole demeanour, I now see that it extends to all in the room, is redolent of an unsympathetic era. Before I could prepare a suitable rejoinder he continued, 'what a waste of resources, constable,' he glared at Julian, 'bringing your secretary on a routine, minor call such as this.'

My first thought was " holy shit, this greasy looking creep must be the A and E Consultant, Dr Wynn-Davis. I have heard so much about him, most of it derisory. He is obviously another Meadows." The second emanation from my subconscious was unfortunately not modified by being thought through at all. Even as I realised this I also saw that, knowing me, I would most likely say it anyway no matter how much I overthink it. Later I will blame Julian. His teasing and irreverent manner encourages the worst in me, perhaps that should be the best.

As I stood I thought to myself, "sit down, don't prod the bear." As usual I failed to control my urges, though at least on this rare occasion I was not going to hit anyone. I strode over to him, fixing him with a stern look. He looked taken aback and the others looked aghast. It seemed they suspected that I was going to strike him. From the corner of my eye I spotted Julian grinning from ear to ear. I adopted a façade of ignorance. I grasped Wynn-Davis' hand and shook it theatrically, squeezing so hard that I saw him wince. 'Detective Inspector Fletcher at your service.... sir.' Heavy emphasis was placed on the sir. 'Using my well-honed detective skills I note that you are differently attired from the others present. I deduce that you are the unit administrator.'

For what seemed an age you could have heard a pin drop. He scowled and turned to an unhealthy looking puce colour. Several of the others looked down, their faces contorting as they suppressed laughs. A slim man with attractive boyish features, one of the few who looked good in his scrubs which actually appeared to fit him, leapt to his feet. Other than Wynn-Davis he looked to be a little older than most others present, in his mid-thirties I think. Though clearly self-effacing he carries an air of authority and has an almost military bearing. He firmly shook my hand. Now we are face to face I see him clearly. Though his features are ravaged by tiredness his gentle hazel eyes are twinkling. He knows that I know exactly who I have just addressed. He is very well presented. His clean, ironed and tailored scrubs show his lean frame well. The loose shirt gaped a little showing a tuft of brown hair. As I leaned toward him to take his hand I noticed his fresh, manly smell. There was a hint of fresh perspiration as if from a heavy shift but nothing stale, no false after-shave and certainly no antiseptic odour.

Wynn-Davis had not stirred though this but looks

thunderous.

The slim man spoke a little awkwardly; obviously he is trying to suppress a laugh at the same time. 'Good afternoon Detective Fletcher. I am Marcus Rice and this is Dr Wynn-Davis.' He turned his hand to indicate the still suffused, still mute, old git. 'We are the Consultants here in A and E.' Then a cheeky grin formed on his gentle features. 'So that you know that, like the police, we are a progressive unit, I will point out that we also have young blondes in positions of authority. May I introduce Mary Roberts, our nursing sister in charge of the department?' It was an edgy comment, close to being sexist, but his easy, familiar, manner prevented any such interpretation. I wondered; is he flattering me or the sister? He is rather tasty, I hope me.

He indicated to the other side of the group. A woman with dyed blonde hair, younger than me, waved, smiling. She may be pleasant but her figure resembles a barrel, her hair is lank and her uniform is at least three sizes too small. Christ, I hope he is not comparing her to me. He finished, 'please take a seat. There are so many of us I will ask the others to introduce themselves as they speak.'

As I sat I indicated to Julian that he should introduce himself. He stood and said, 'Julian Courtney. I am delighted to meet you all.' Julian's educated tone and public school accent clearly surprised them. Whilst Julian was saying this Wynn-Davis rudely strode out muttering that he had more important work to do. He walked as if he had a broom handle up his rear end. Julian caught my eye and wiggled his baton at me. I fought to suppress a laugh. Ever since our exchange on our first day together the expression, "put your baton where the sun don't shine," has become a regular part of our parlance. Marcus Rice spotted our unspoken communication. Judging by his wide grin behind his colleague's back, he not only understood but also agreed.

As Wynn-Davis left the atmosphere seemed to ease.

We chatted for a while about Timothy Breen. Though only twelve years of age he had been assaulted but thankfully his injuries are minor. He refused to tell the A and E staff what had happened but they suspected bullies on the estate where he lives. His father had taken him out against medical advice but, on the other hand, clearly caring for him. As he left the father had been heard to mutter under his breath that, "he would go and sort this out."

Julian and I left whilst they concluded their meeting.

Walking back towards the hospital entrance and our car we determined that Julian would drive out to the estate to defuse any further assaults. I told him that I would take a short break and then return to the station to catch up on paper work until he came back. The reward for so many gratifying arrests is a mountain of admin. He offered to drive me back to the station but I said that would take the opportunity for some exercise and jog the three miles back to the centre of the city.

Julian went off and I lingered by the entrance looking into the hospital cafeteria, considering whether or not to risk a hospital coffee. There was no smell of fresh coffee or an enticing bakery but inexplicably there was a stink of overcooked cabbage. I have no idea how they managed this as there was no cooked food on offer. As I stood there came a gentle tap on my shoulder. I turned to see the Consultant, Marcus Rice. He advised, 'don't go in there unless you want to see me professionally. The coffee is poisonous. I haven't seen any fatal cases, yet, but I do see many faces twisted in disgust.'

I smiled at him, subtly looking him up and down and again approving of what I saw. He has changed and is now wearing perfect smart-casual clothes. One glance was sufficient to appreciate his immaculate chinos, designer rugby shirt and a soft leather jacket, I had to restrain myself from leaning toward and stroking it. My smile intensified as I saw him looking at and admiring me. I am not sure if he is being deliberately obvious or if he is inexpert at hiding his thoughts. As I looked into his innocent eyes I thought, "definitely the latter." 'Thank you for your advice Doctor.' Then following with, I couldn't help the tease, 'I am impressed to see that you are such a strong advocate of the hospital facilities, particularly the catering department.'

He grinned, 'please, call me Marcus. I recommend the Cultural Café in the Market Square. In spite of the pretentious name their coffee is sublime and their chocolate chip cookies are to die for.' Then he deliberately, now openly, looked me up and down again. This time he did not make even a futile, amateurish attempt to hide it. He said admiringly, 'although, looking at how slim you are I guess you do not eat them.'

'I love them. I allow myself one a week. I will go there right now and indulge myself.' Christ girl, what are you up to? Was that a simple flirt or a blatant come on?

'I am going into town, may I join you?'

All too quickly I replied, 'Yes, that would be ......' What do I say, very nice would be crass, lovely will be too strong? '..............wonderful.' Bloody hell Rebecca, I thought, get a grip. If lovely is too strong then what the hell is wonderful?

He smiled like a little boy and suggested that we walk together to the car park, drive in separately so we have our cars for later, then meet in town. 'I am on foot. Julian has taken the car to go and see little Timothy's father.'

'Please come with me,' we are now walking out of the doors, 'I am on the Consultants' car park over there.' He pointed left.

'Thank you but I want to take the opportunity for some exercise. I will run in and meet you there.'

His eyebrows raised as he replied, 'OK, tell me what you want and I will get them in ready.'

I scoffed, 'you have to get your car off the car park. There is not much traffic at this time but you then have to cross three sets of traffic lights and a busy intersection to get there. Also, you then have to re-park. I will be there first, tell me what you want.'

He initially laughed but then he looked hard at me. 'You are not joking are you?' I shook my head. 'OK, how about a challenge? Whoever is last buys the coffee.'

'You're on.' I had noticed him squirming and looking down throughout this exchange. In fact it would have been difficult to miss it. I decided to tease him yet more. 'It is more your field than mine but may I be so bold as to practice some preventative medicine.' As he nodded, intrigued, I held up my left hand and splayed the fingers. 'No, there is no ring. I am not married. You are going to get a crick in your neck trying to find out on your own.' He laughed but blushed endearingly to the roots of his hair. 'To further demonstrate my formidable detecting powers I advise you that I have noticed that you are not wearing a wedding ring.'

He somewhat enigmatically countered, 'no, I am not wearing a wedding ring.' I had teased him enough. I let that pass unremarked.

I turned and sprinted for the road. The route he will have to drive takes him along roads that are fairly busy at all times. Even in this quite period he will not be able to drive quickly. All of the junctions always have queues. It is roughly three miles. If I exit the rear gate of the hospital grounds I will be on the ring road. A couple of hundred yards along there, where the bypass bridge crosses the river, there is a path down to the side of the river which joins with the path into town that I use for training. It is a shorter route. Within a short two miles I will meet the old bridge in the town centre. I can cross there, turn right to pass on the opposite side of the river from my house and that will take me into Market Square. I might just make it in time. As I went through the gate I dialled up the effort and set the maximum pace that I feel that I can sustain for two miles.

As I turned into Market Square I caught sight of him driving into the adjacent car park. It is fortunate that I spotted him as I did not previously know what he drives. It had been the vehicle that caught my eye. It was not what I would have expected him to have. If I had thought about it I would have guessed a nearly new, black, five series BMW. I would not have thought a rugged, old, long wheel base Land Rover. I approve. He even has the only acceptable colour for one, their classic green.

I ducked behind a couple of cars feeling like a naughty teenager. As I slipped into the café I gave the waitress, who was surprised at my surreptitious entrance, a conspiratorial wink. I quickly sat at a corner table. Seeing some old books available for customers to read I took a thick one, opened it half way through, put it page down on my lap and with my head back pretended that I had fallen asleep.

Seconds later the door opened and I heard him walk towards me. I thought that he would make a gentle "ahem." Instead he playfully kicked my foot and said, 'don't give me that crap, I saw you come in.' "Bugger," I thought, but I could not help laughing as I sat up straight. He continued, 'even if you did only just beat me I am still very impressed. I know the path along the river and that it is shorter. When I saw you head for the rear gate I knew you were going to go that way. Though a quicker route it is still at least a couple of miles. You certainly deserve a coffee and cookie.' At that my stomach gave a loud rumble. He laughed and said, 'I missed lunch as well. Can I buy you a late lunch instead?'

I ordered butternut squash blini with a goat's cheese

whip and salad. I had never before even heard of one and I was intrigued. Marcus had piri-piri chicken and salad. As soon as the order had been given he opened with, 'I insist you tell me what you and Julian were joking about, your little silent exchange, as Windbag left.' It was a kindly insistence accompanied by an intrigued smile.

'Surely you don't call your esteemed colleague Windbag?'

'I note that you did not ask who I was referring to.' He leaned in, so did I. As I smelt the leather of his gorgeous jacket, again I had to restrain myself from touching it. More likely I was restraining myself from touching what was under it. He whispered conspiratorially, 'go on.' I told him about the running joke that I have with Julian about batons and "where the sun don't shine." He roared with laughter so much the few others in the café turned to us smiling. They smiled at us as if to say, "look at that couple so obviously in love." Though not in love I do feel very warm towards him, it seems reciprocated. It certainly seems as if I have known him for more than an hour or so. As he recovered he spluttered, 'how long is the baton?' I told him 21 inches when extended. Shaking his head he said, 'no good for Windbag, not long enough. He needs the full broom stick.' Now looking a little despairing he continued, 'the perverse part of this is that he is actually a superb clinician. In spite of that, because of his behaviour, I can't wait for him to leave. He retires in three months. He is stupefied to know that his replacement is a woman and he is predicting that the department will collapse.'

When I had first entered I had been aware of the elegant surroundings. The café was beautifully decorated with floral wallpaper, being so old fashioned it gave a welcoming air. There were books scattered around and little flower arrangements on the tables. Here, unlike the grim hospital excuse for catering, there was a delicious smell of coffee and bread. When Marcus first sat down I had been aware of a gentle hum of the conversation at other tables. Through the crystal clear window with its etched pattern in the glass I had seen passers-by, a young woman was amazingly not on her mobile but holding and actually talking to her baby. An old man and a middle aged man in a sharp business suit exchanged jovial greetings as they passed each other. As Marcus spoke all of this evaporated.

The food arrived and conversation paused for a short while as we both started to eat. I had not realised how hungry I am and clearly he is as well. I told him that he had recommended a superb café and that the food is excellent.

When we had finished eating he asked what it was like for me working in the police, whether or not I face such misogyny as he sees with Windbag. I told him the full truth; that most of my colleagues are delightful, but I also told him about Meadows and the Troop. I added that it is worse still for me as not only is Meadows a useless policeman but he is also only in his 50's and I will not soon see the back of him as Marcus will with Windbag. I joked that unless I can find a reason to arrest him, then I am stuck.

I realised that we had both opened up to each other about sensitive problems with senior colleagues that would usually only be shared between close friends. There is no doubt that we are both finding a connection. It reminded me of when I first met Julian. This is however different. This has a strong sexual element.

I chanced an intimate comment. He looks exhausted and a little worn. I said to him that he looks tired and I asked if he is overworked due to the NHS money and staff shortages that we hear so much about on the news. To my surprise he snorted and suddenly looked cross. Looking back at me, softening, he said not to get him on his soapbox or I will be here all afternoon. When I pressed him he agreed to start on the proviso that I tell him to shut up as soon as I have had enough.

A couple of hours ago, after seeing him in a meeting in his scrubs, I would have expected the usual self-important whining that comes from the effete doctors that I see in the media. Over lunch I had already begun to re-appraise him, to correct my stereotyping. His way of sitting, walking and talking; his demeanour; even his car; it does not fit. As he is unconventional it did not surprise me when he started by obtusely saying that he had an army scholarship for medical school. It was not immediately apparent what that had to do with being tired now but I am sure all will soon be revealed. He continued by saying that after qualifying he had served in the Army for several years, longer than required by the scholarship. He apologised in advance for what he is going to say next. He is concerned that it may make him sound like a Colonel Blimp harrumphing over the top of his Torygraph, or worse still like Meadows.

He told me that he has had three tours in Afghanistan. Though this was after the official British withdrawal in 2014 I was surprised to hear that here was still a considerable presence there. As well as work in the British military hospitals he had also practiced in an Afghani hospital. Then he let rip. Both his ire and its direction astonished me. Now I understand why he started by detailing his military career. It is his firm opinion that what many people in the NHS require is a week or two's such experience. To see what it really means to be under stress. To see what can be done with less than ideal conditions. He said that he considers that there is sufficient money to do the well-established basic NHS work but much is wasted extending death, rather than prolonging life, and on expensive treatments of dubious or little benefit. He considers that there are sufficient staff numbers to achieve this, it is just that many are spending time and undertaking useless, expensive treatments and moaning rather than pulling their weight on the effective routine work. He added that, in his opinion, if all staff, particularly the consultants and senior nurses, took ownership, made and implemented effective plans rather than looking for scapegoats and portraying themselves as victims, then many difficulties would be eased. He revealed that he is currently so tired as he has to do Windbag's work as well as his own. Further, in addition to the medical work, he has to spend hours listening to drivel, mainly in Consultants' meetings, sometimes from his own staff. He is working to implement such policies in his department and the dumpy Mary Roberts is apparently surprisingly effective. Windbag doesn't interfere and the incoming woman replacing him is has similar attitudes to Marcus and Mary. Though Marcus is clearly knackered he remains optimistic.

After this mini explosion he relaxed and smiled at me, he carried on talking about his department but on a different subject. He said that he had observed me appraising some of the staff in the meeting. He agrees with my obvious assessment that they eat as many cookies in a week as I do in a year. He finished by combining the two themes, partly light-heartedly, partly sadly, saying that if they spent more time with patients and less time moaning over coffee and cookies it would be better for all, especially them. As with the silent exchange regarding the baton with Julian, Marcus has again accurately divined my thoughts. He seems to be able to effortlessly interpret some clues, such as this, but to be charmingly naïve when it comes to more intimate ones. I hope that the others in the meeting had not so correctly interpreted my impression of them.

The subject naturally changed. There was no need to discuss his problems further. It was clear that we are in accord and there is overlap between some of his difficulties and what I face at work. As we chatted on it transpired that, like me, he had previously been in London though he moved here six months ago. We had even lived near to each other and knew the same pubs. I joked that we may have even been in one at the same time. He looked straight into my eyes and said dogmatically, 'certainly not. I would not have forgotten.' As he said that, clearly meaning it, I felt as if my heart stood still for a few beats. A yearning spread through me. It was so powerful that I suspect even the guileless Marcus spotted it. I would have blushed if he had known where it had started.

As with Julian I see a sadness about him. Clearly he is committed to the NHS and finds at least some of his colleagues satisfactory. There is more, I am sure. Perhaps, again like me, he has left more in London than a job.

We lingered over our coffee. Conversation flowed effortlessly. When we came to leave I was astonished to find that we had been there for more than two hours. He commented on this, obviously also happy with it, saying that he would leave a very generous tip in return. We walked outside. He is going left back to his car and I am going right, back to the station. I am wondering what I should tell Julian as he will no doubt be intrigued by my uncharacteristic absence.

We stood, side by side, in front of the café. Each of us seemed reluctant to say good bye. An unspoken question hung between us.

Finally, Marcus turned to me, cleared his throat and diffidently said, 'I have really enjoyed seeing you. Can I see you again, for a date that is?' He smiled sheepishly at both what he is asking and his clearly deliberate use of the old fashioned term, date.

'What, you want another date?' I stressed the "another." He looked quizzical so I continued, 'we have had a long lunch and an intimate chat. Surely that counts as a date?'

He laughed yet again. I love his easy, sad laugh. I did not have to say yes, my response is obvious, so much for me trying to appear cool. He suggested Saturday, two days' time, and an Italian restaurant, Nuncios, opposite the castle gate. I had seen the entrance but I did not know the restaurant. He explained that the small entrance is deceptive. There is a passage down which opens to four cellars. He said that it is very smart; and, again with a gentle smile he added, very romantic. I coyly said that I could make it. He can see that I cannot wait.

As we were finally going to pull ourselves apart he asked, 'if this was a date, can I kiss you goodbye?'

'I suppose, but only if you keep your hands to yourself.' He pecked me on the cheek. Looking sternly at him I said, 'cancel, Saturday, I am not coming.' He can see that I am joking and raised an eyebrow to ask what I meant. 'I am not going to waste my time with a man who calls that a kiss.' A relieved grin came across his face. He pulled me towards him and gave me a warm kiss on the lips. He leaned back still holding me. We looked at each other for a long while. I thought "in for a penny." I pulled him back towards me and kissed him in return. It has been nearly two years since I last kissed like this. It is wonderful.

We finally parted; our hands still on each other's shoulders. We heard clapping to one side. We turned to find the two waitresses outside of the cafe door and the people at tables in the windows are looking out. All are clapping.

One waitress called out, 'we have been expecting that since the moment you sat down. What took you so long?'

....

....

The two days until our dinner together passed by in a haze of work and me looking forward in anticipation, and, to my great surprise, also with considerable apprehension. It is unheard of for me to be phased by anything, well, it now appears almost anything. I do not really know him. I do not know the restaurant and in recent times I have not been used to going out with men. All that added up to the typically female, but uncharacteristic for me, agonising over what to wear. The last year spent in trainers and track suits has been easy. I Googled the restaurant. I can see it is very smart; bloody hell, very expensive as well. Assessing both him and the restaurant I decided that for once I had to dress up. With yet more surprise I found that I am also looking forward to that.

He had telephoned last night and we had arranged to meet in the restaurant. In the café we had discussed where we both lived. Where we are going to is only half a mile from me and he lives another half mile further on. Chivalrously he wanted to collect me at home. I am not ready for that. As lovely as he is it will be some time before I can again invite a man into my home. I still feel the need for a sanctuary. The fact that we live in opposite directions from the restaurant was a good excuse, I had insisted that we meet at Nuncio's. Even though I went through the untrue practical reasons for that being the better option he was not happy but relented.

Arriving at the restaurant door I checked myself in the mirrors on either side. They are guilt framed and ornate. Ostensibly they are there to decorate the heavy, grand door but no doubt also for women to do exactly what I found myself doing. I have to admit that I am looking good. All I can see in the mirror is my black, suede trimmed, herringbone coat and soft, black leather, knee length boots. I pulled the coat collar a little apart to check for the hundredth time my textured charcoal and black box jacket and off-white silk blouse. I adjusted the wide collar of the blouse so that it sat high and symmetrical. I went to fasten up another button thinking I am too exposed. With a little grin at myself I took my hand away, leaving the buttons as they are. I wanted to check my pleated black midi skirt but without taking off the coat that is impossible.

I turned the massive iron handle. With the oak door and its large black iron fittings I had expected it to be heavy. Perfectly balanced it silently and easily swung open. I stepped through. I found my breathing to be irregular and fast. Good god, am I really nervous? I deliberately took a couple of slower breaths. After the cold December air outside I was hit with warmth and the mixed aromas of great food, wine and lots of garlic. I walked the few stone steps down and opened the internal, frosted glass door into the cellar restaurant.

I stopped in shock as I stood in the door way. On the net it looked smart. In reality it is sumptuous. The cellar is surprisingly tall and large. Well-spaced round tables with immaculate white linen are nearly full of people. The ostentatious chandeliers, oil paintings, again with ornate gilded frames, all combine to an air of magnificence. This is most certainly not, "popping out for a quick spaghetti." A couple of waiters in immaculate tuxedos looked up, the older one hurried over. As he did so in the far corner I spotted Marcus beginning to stand, he has seen me. He is wearing a beautiful black linen suit and an immaculate open neck white shirt. We will match. If I look half as good as him I will look very good.

The waiter reached me. I can see by his demeanour that he must be the head one. As he reached for my coat he said, 'tu devi essere Rebecca. Come ha dottore sei molto bella.' All I understood was my name. How does he know who I am? As he put my coat over his arm and ushered me towards Marcus he said, 'bellissimo, bellissimo.'

Marcus took my hand and kissed me on the cheek. My knees threatened to give way. He said quietly, 'I know it is not your preferred option but only a peck on the cheek in here if you don't mind.' Then he leaned forward and whispered in my ear, 'you look absolutely stunning.' I thanked him and went to sit down, only then realising that the maître d' is still standing next to me. He is looking at me, no, staring. The usual disdain is absent. He said again, 'bellissimo, bellissimo.' He walked off, it appeared a little reluctantly and we both sat.

I looked at Marcus who had a cheeky grin, 'OK, I don't speak Italian, what did he say?'

'I don't speak Italian either but I am pretty sure that bellissimo means beautiful. He is not wrong.' I felt myself colour a little, he continued, 'I am not trying to embarrass or flatter you. It is simply true. You are beautiful. Not only in the elegant clothes you are wearing tonight but also you did so in the tracksuit you wore two days ago. I could not help but notice though that it was a designer tracksuit.'

'Why thank you. I have to say you are a dashing date.' He laughed at my deliberate repetition of outmoded terms. 'The head waiter used my name. I have never seen him before. How did he know who I am?'

'You surprise me detective. I would have thought that you would have deduced that. Obviously I described you to him when I came in.'

Now with a combination of alarm and intrigue I fixed him with a look and demanded, 'what did you say? How did you describe me?'

He shook his head indicating that he will not tell me. I pressed and he again refused, now smiling even more broadly. At this the Head Waiter came back with the menus. I looked at his name badge and said, 'Stephano, this supposed gentleman here described something to you that made me instantly recognisable. Please tell me what he said as he refuses to elaborate.' He shook his head apologetically.

'Stephano, you must tell me.' Now both of the men started to shake their heads in a "no, no" gesture with conspiratorial, boyish smiles at each other. I am not going to let this go. 'Stephano, do you want me to make a scene in this demure restaurant?' Stephano gave Marcus a "surely she will not look." Marcus returned an, "actually, it is possible, look," and shrugged.

Stephano reluctantly said, 'Doctor Rice told me to look out for the ravishing, slim, athletic, woman with soft blond curls and blackbird egg blue eyes. His description was perfect. I had no doubt who you were.' He looked me up and down, repeated, 'bellissimo,' left the menus and went to the adjacent table.

Sitting back speechless I looked towards Marcus who said, 'now you know what I think. I could not have got through the next few minutes without telling you anyway.'

The food was sublime. We shared an antipasti Nuncio, cured Italian meats with peppers and aubergine as starters. For the main course I had a delicious Sogliola alla Griglia, black sole, and Marcus the Bocconcini de Pescatrice, monkfish, which looked equally good. We spoke little while appreciating the food. I savoured the perfect delicate tastes. Being quiet was not difficult, we were both at ease. Just to eat, be together, to listen to the soft hum of voices, the tinkling of delicate crystal glasses and the occasional cork popping was more than enough.

The delicious food and sumptuous surroundings were eclipsed by the conversation. Between courses we leaned in towards each other and spoke closely and intensely. I had thought that he was handsome, interesting and entertaining a couple of days ago. Now he tells me that for the first time in weeks he has had a couple of days off and it has revitalised him. He looks even more handsome and is even more interesting. He has wide, serious interests but his wicked sense of humour stopped the conversation from being heavy. He is obviously committed to his job. His crossness of the other day, aimed at whingers and slackers in the NHS, is obviously still there but in the background. If anything it makes him even more determined to change things for the better.

When he told me that his brother and parents had been killed in a road accident when he was young I looked closely at him. No, that is not the cause of his underlying sadness. He is at terms with that loss. He also said how much he loves the aunt who then raised him. The root of his deep sadness is elsewhere and recent. The only subject that we did not discuss, thank heaven, was previous relationships. I still cannot discuss that, I think he is in the same position. His forlorn air may lie there.

Neither of us could manage any dessert. Stephano asked if we wanted a coffee and a brandy. Marcus asked for a few minutes to consider it. As soon as Stephano left the table I could see what Marcus was going to ask and I knew my answer. It may only be the second date but I feel that I know him better than others I have been with for months. He leaned across, 'my present home is only a small, rented flat. I am still looking for somewhere to buy. The houses in that lovely terrace in North Street have all been snatched up.' I refused to rise to that. 'Even so it is a very comfortable little home.' Without hesitation and holding my gaze he continued, 'Would you like to come back with me for a nightcap?'

'Are your intentions honourable?'

'No.'

'Good, let's go.'

We walked to his flat, arm in arm, in silence. My mouth was dry and my heart thumping with anticipation.

We stepped through his front door; an inner door to the sitting room was open. The flat is small but it is also charming. He gallantly took my coat and hung it up. Then at the same time we both cracked and clung to each other kissing hard and deeply. We were devouring each other. I reached down and whilst standing on one leg, him holding and kissing me, I slipped off my boots. He pulled off my jacket and me his. There was no careful hanging for our expensive clothes. They were thrown to the ground, sod the creases. He led me into the sitting room and, still kissing me, unbuttoned and slipped off my blouse and lay me down on the sofa. He lay down half next to me, half on top then he leaned back a little and wide eyed looked at me and whispered, 'bellissimo.' He admired my flat stomach and gently ran his fingers down my tattoo. Then he kissed the head of the snake as it opened its mouth on the underside of my right breast.

Though the kiss he murmured, 'I have never kissed a snake before.' I could not reply, I was biting my lip to stop me from screaming with delight. He then ran his lips down its wide blue and green body as it curled down my side, under my belly button and then down further under my panties. Marcus whispered, 'where is the tail?'

'Mine or his?'

Now shaking with laughter he raised himself up and still smiling, kissing me on the lips as he ran his hands over its body, and at the same time over mine, he asked through a kiss, 'what does it signify?'

'Temptation. Power.'

'I think it may also represent Medusa and the power to destroy men.' As he said this he kissed my neck.

I softly bit his ear, 'that too.'

He slid down again, now exploring my left side. He

had not missed it. He ran his index finger across the scar below my ribs. With his experience in Afghanistan he must know what it is from. He did not ask how it had happened but with his fingers caressing it he asked, 'I can see that this is recent, does it still burn when touched.'

'No longer. It used to but now it is a strange, tickly feeling.' I had difficulty in getting the words out. Every time his lips and fingers touch me I have difficulty breathing.

He said, 'paraesthesia. That will go soon.' I very much hope not, I thought. When I touch it; there is only an odd feeling. When he does; a wave of delight flows down through me into my fanny. I can't wait anymore. I started to unbutton his shirt and ease it off his shoulders.

We heard it together and instantly froze. He looked into my eyes with panic, but more, much more, also apology. The front door opened and a shrill female voice called out, 'Marcus, surprise.'

Then quiet, she must have seen my boots and jacket. Then a sharp, hard, 'whose are these? What's going on?' He is still frozen, holding me. I was griping him but also thinking that the voice was not right, not genuine. The door burst open and in stormed a fairly pretty woman, my age but running to fat. She saw us clasped together and screamed. We were transfixed, unable to move.

'You bastard. You fucking bastard. I never want to see you again.' She tore at her ring finger and pulled off a large solitaire engagement ring and her wedding ring. She threw the gold at Marcus but I noticed that she held tightly to the diamond. Then she stormed out. The whole, odd feeling episode had lasted only seconds.

We disentangled ourselves and stood. Marcus picked up my blouse and held it for me to put back on. Then he put on his shirt saying, 'please do not leave yet. Please allow me to explain.' I nodded yes and sat on the sofa. He sat beside me and took my hand, holding it and asked, 'may I?' Again I nodded yes. I appear to have lost the power of speech. 'I am married but we are having a trial separation. Stephanie lives with her parents about forty miles away. We have left and sold our house in London. The removal people dropped some of her things here by mistake. I posted a spare key to her so that she could collect them whilst I was at work. I had forgotten about it. Other than then and tonight she has not been here. I have not seen her for some months and we have not communicated for almost as long, but, yes, I am technically married though for all intents and purposes it is over. I didn't know when to tell you. Please believe me. I am so, so sorry.'

I held his crushed face in my hands and kissed him softly. 'I do believe you Marcus. I have no doubt whatsoever.' I paused, thinking on whether or not to tell him. He started to speak. I put my finger to his lips and continued, 'I suspect there is more to this than meets the eye. You know her, I don't, but to me she sounded false, theatrical. I suspect she that knew I was here. I think she was aware that you had brought me back with you. I believe that her coming in and supposedly discovering us was all stage managed. I know she only said a few words but I am sure from the delivery that they were rehearsed. The throwing of the ring was also. A truly surprised woman would have either flounced out or thrown both. Sorting through them and keeping the expensive one is not a spur of the moment gesture.'

'How could she, as I said, she lives miles away?'

'Perhaps someone who knows her saw us in the restaurant. She could easily have driven here whilst we ate dinner.' I saw realisation come into his face. I walked to the hall and put on my boots, jacket and coat.

He looked at me crestfallen and asked, 'could we start

again?'

'I would love to Marcus. This evening has been wonderful. If you were to call me again I would be overjoyed. But do not call until you are divorced.' He looks completely distraught. I guess that I do as well. I closed the door behind me before I could change my mind.

I walked back through the now quiet city, beautiful in the streetlight. My breath streamed out white in front of me. My face was almost painful with the cold. My whole body felt numb but that had nothing to do with the temperature. In my mind I repeated over and over to myself like a mantra; rule 1, you must follow rule 1. It is too dangerous to break it, break it again that is. I don't know why mum calls it rule 1, it is the only one; no married men.

I walked down the Parade admiring the imposing gaunt grey stone of the castle floodlit to my right. I dared not look left to the warm entrance and guilt mirrors of the restaurant. I turned right, walked downhill and crossed the river on the old bridge then took a left alongside the river towards home. Pausing and looking over the limestone riverside wall back towards the bridge, the water gurgling through the arches seemed to be softly saying, "go back, don't be silly, go back." I dare not go back. I could not risk the same happening again. I would not survive it.

I pressed on through the narrow park. There was a low thin mist between the trees, across the footpath and spilling on to the surface of the water. I was still walking like an automaton. When I was alongside the foot bridge I turned right, uphill this time, walking towards my lovely house. I paused in front of the war memorial. It is at least eight feet high, I cannot even see my bedroom windows over the top. It must be thirty feet long. So many names, so many of them have the same surname. What did they feel? What did their women feel?

What do I feel now? This is, no, was, the first time I have warmed to a man for more than two years; the first time that I have kissed a man for more than two years; the first time that I thought that I was going to make love with a man for more than two years.

At the top, in front of my house, I turned to look across the river and saw on the other side, across the Market Square, the Culture Café is floodlit. Has it just been turned on or have I not noticed that before? I thought of sitting there with Marcus only two days ago, a lifetime ago. I felt completely untethered from myself.

I opened my front door and stepped in. Immediately I was hit by a sudden marooning emptiness in there. At last I started to cry. I had thought that I had forgotten how. Am I crying for me, for Marcus or for what happened in London?

I have no idea.

CHAPTER 8:
REBECCA, MOTHER

We stepped out of my front door, arm in arm, into a low but intense December sun. Cold and bright, it is a perfect day and only two days to go until Christmas. We paused at the railing to look across the river towards the small but idyllic city bustling in preparation for the holidays. Our arms locked, love flowed between us.

It is so good to have my baby sister here with me during my first Christmas in this house. I smiled at the thought, Julia, my "baby sister." Only two years younger than me, she will be twenty nine next year. Already deputy to the CEO of a major pharmaceutical company she will undoubtedly be CEO herself soon. Then, Mum and Dad, walking arm in arm, next to us, transfixed by the scene.

It is a little disappointing that Julia's fiancé, Chris, cannot be with us. The scientific expedition he is heading is, as was planned, deliberately stuck in the Arctic ice. They are missing each other but skype at least twice daily. Julia and I have never had secrets; it is as if we are part of the same person, so she has told me they enjoy skype sex every day. No details were spared, it sounds like a wonderful substitute. When I had added that it was good to hear at least one of us is getting laid she gave me a sad hug.

Mum and Dad walked through the park, down the slope past the War Memorial, and stopped again by the low wall next to the river. We went to stand next to them. Mum looked at us and said to me, 'this city is so beautiful. We were discussing it on the drive here last night. You are so lucky to have found this. Though, given what you have done it is only what you deserve.'

As the other three of us gazed across the river Julia turned to look back towards my house. As she did so I felt her tense, then freeze as she cried out, 'oh Jesus Christ, look out.' We all spun around and Mum also cried out in alarm.

I gave a little laugh and they looked at me with incredulity. There is a huge, vicious looking, black wolf-like dog purposefully loping through the park. He is headed straight towards us. 'It' OK, he's fine.' I called, 'Toby, come, good boy.' They all stiffened again as he broke into a run. He came right up to me. I bent down and scratched his ear and he gave me a slobbery lick on the cheek. Only when he then rolled on to his back for me to scratch his stomach did the three of them relax again.

Over the last few weeks I have regularly met Toby. When I have been running and I have met Luke and Samantha we usually stop to speak and they have always had Toby with them. On those occasions, as when I saw them a few weeks back, Luke is running, Samantha cycling and Toby loping along with an expression saying, "why can't we go further and faster?" I have developed a great rapport with them, with Luke and Toby that is. I chat with Luke whilst Toby leans against me so that I am forced to pet him. The Ice Maiden, as I now think of her, stands stony faced. My first impression when she walked in as Julian and I were starting to interview Luke was that she was frightened. When we questioned them she was initially offhand then seemed to warm a little. During the several times the three of us have spoken subsequently she has become more and more hostile. I am not sure why but I sense that she finds me threatening. Perhaps she is worried that I will start a relationship with

Luke and she that she will lose him. God knows I would like to and I feel he is interested as well. At our last meeting I asked if her leg is improving. I was trying to engage her but she clearly did not want to talk with me. She had reluctantly grunted, 'much better, thank you, I am due to start walking again soon.' Then, as always, she came up with some excuse as to why they had to rush back and she dragged off a resisting Luke.

I looked back along the path expecting to see Luke running and Samantha cycling towards us. To my surprise they are both walking though Samantha is holding Luke's arm, she clearly needs support. I thought back to when I first saw them; they do look like a couple. I stood up from scratching Toby as they came up to us. Mum, Dad and Julia are a little surprised to see them approach. They smiled, well Luke did at least, then he turned to stop and engage with us. As she held his arm Samantha had no choice but to stop as well. I said, 'hello.' Then I turned to my family, 'this is Luke and Samantha Cape.' Turning back, indicating them I said, 'Sebastian, Judith and Julia Fletcher, my family.'

Samantha barely nodded. Luke gave one of his warm, sexy smiles. He shook hands and nodded "hello" with Dad. Then he shook hands with Julia who appeared to have lost the power of speech and to be in danger of buckling at the knees. Finally he turned to Mum. He took her hand, initially shook it. Then whilst still holding her hand with his right he reached out and gripped her elbow with his left. He looked straight into her eyes and said, 'I am delighted to meet you, Judith.' Judith, not Mrs. Fletcher, and he did not mention Dad or Julia. 'Now I see where Rebecca gets her stunning good looks from.' He slowly let go of her hand, as if he was only doing so reluctantly.

I cannot believe what then happened. Mum simpered. My strident, bra-burning feminist, out-spoken Mum, is not only lost for words but she is simpering like a love-struck teenager. I realise that I should not be surprised, Mum and Julia are only acting in the same way as I had when I first met him. Afterwards Julian had teased me unmercifully for days. If I had been even half as struck as Mum and Julia then I would have deserved every word. Dad saved the day. Whilst Samantha glared and Julia and I looked at Mum in open-mouthed astonishment Dad asked Luke about Toby. Then they chatted for a few minutes, Dad and Luke that is. All the women, including me, seemed dumbstruck. When Dad asked Luke what his work is and Luke replied that he is a Professor of Earth Sciences Mum managed a strangled, 'oh, how interesting.'

I made the mistake of saying to Dad that I had been very impressed by the collection of geological specimens in Luke's study. Dad said that he did not know that I had visited the university. When Luke replied that they are all in his study at home, and that his house is adjacent to the police station, Mum and Julia looked at me wide-eyed. They obviously think that it is the geological equivalent of being shown his etchings. Even worse, during the whole exchange Luke had been looking at me fondly, almost eagerly. In fact, as he usually does. Finally Samantha who had been looking across the river with a glacial stare interrupted with a typical rude announcement that they had something else to deal with. They went off, again arm in arm, Luke saying that he hopes to see us all again over the holidays.

When they were out of earshot Mum said sharply, all simpering gone, 'I want to go for a coffee. That café over there looks good.' She pointed across the river towards the Cultural café, wrenched at Dad's arm, glared at me, then stormed off across the bridge. Mercurial Mum has transformed one type of smouldering into another. Julia and I followed. I tried to speak with Julia but she refused to look at me, she looks cross and anxious. I am clearly in trouble with both of them. I think I know why.

When we got to the café door Mum turned to Dad and said, 'why don't you go to the bookshop, as you wanted to.' That was the first that I had heard of him wanting to go anywhere. 'Come back in twenty minutes.' Oh bugger, we can always count on Dad to stand up for us daughters, he is being dismissed. Looking back at her I doubt that I will have Julia's support either.

Mum sat, not only at the same table but at the same seat as Marcus had. I was shepherded into the exact same one as I had occupied only a few weeks ago. It had been a very different atmosphere then. The waitress approached smiling. Mum immediately ordered for us all, without conferring, in a tone that sent the poor girl scuttling away. There was a stony silence. I tried to speak. Mum cut me off saying to wait until the coffee had arrived and that she then had something to say. Really Mum, I would never have guessed.

The moment that the now subdued waitress left our table, having brought the drinks, Mum raised her head. She fixed me with an angry stare that I have not seen since childhood. Then she started. 'Rebecca, I thought that you were sensible. I thought that you were a police officer, one trained in alleviating rather than creating difficulties. Clearly I am wrong, so very wrong. It is so upsetting. Not only that it is happening again but that you haven't learnt from the previous occasion.' I tried to interrupt but a flick of her wrist silenced me. I have no option other than to remain silent until she has finished. 'Rule one, rule number bloody one, can you not even keep one rule. It is not difficult. After all it is the only one. No married men, I repeat, no married men. We have discussed this with you. You have agreed, no married men. Have you forgotten what happened before? You were destroyed when John went back to his wife.' I bit my tongue;

that was unfair. John was separated when we started seeing each other, not exactly married, well, sort of not married. He went back to his sick child, not his wife. Admittedly though, she was there as well. In the current atmosphere I doubt that such nuances will be appreciated. Everything else that Mum is saying is completely true. Only now am I beginning to get over it. At least I think that I am. I was correct in what had I suspected Mum to be so angry at. Julian and I had also thought that they were a couple when we first saw them. In fairness to her I suspect that she is more worried for me than cross. I am desperate to correct the record, to stop her concern. I will have to wait.

The tirade continued for a few more minutes as our coffee went cold. The waitress kept glancing uneasily towards us, very different looks from those I received when I last sat in this chair. She is anticipating a scene, even more of a scene that is. We are already the chief entertainment in here. Eventually Mum settled into an exasperated and obviously worried silence. I put my hand out, held hers, and tried to start to speak. Before I could utter a single word Julia rounded on me. She effectively repeated exactly what Mum had been saying, but with tears in her eyes. Again I was not allowed to comment.

When they were both finally quiet, I asked, 'may I speak now?' They nodded. 'I have been trying to tell you that you have both got the wrong end of the stick. Thank you for your concern but there is no need of it.' They looked at me with identical, "don't take us for idiots, we were not born yesterday," looks. Julia went to speak but now it is my turn to cut her off. 'Firstly, he is not married.'

Mum nearly exploded, 'don't try to squirm out of it. Whether she is his wife or his partner everything I said still applies. More, now I think of it, you should beware of her. She was looking at you with daggers in her eyes. She may be an

Ice Maiden,' how interesting, Mum has used exactly the same expression as I employ when I think of Samantha, 'but she could easily make things very hot for you.' She stared at me, challenging me to deny any of that.

'Samantha is his sister, half-sister to be pedantic.'

Julia said with incredulity, 'they were arm in arm, what is going on?'

'Samantha was seriously injured a couple of years ago.' So was I, I thought. I know Mum and Julia think the same. It is just that my injuries were not structural. 'She has required multiple operations and the last one to her leg was only a few weeks ago. It is the first time that I have seen her walking, she usually cycles. I suspect that she needed his support.' They looked stupefied. Julia sat back. A fat tear of relief slipped down Mum's cheek. I wiped it away, squeezed her hand saying, 'I am fine. I am not in danger. I did try to tell you.'

Relieved smiles came to us all. Looking up I saw that the waitress' concerns had lessened as well. She is quite correct; a major scene was only narrowly averted. The other patrons look crestfallen. Julia now has a wild, delighted, conspiratorial expression and spoke, a little too loudly for comfort. I am pretty sure that the couple at the next table who were already earwigging heard. 'So you are fucking that gorgeous hunk. I hate you. You lucky sod.' Before I could stop her she reached across and hugged me.

When Julia finally let me go we saw that Mum's head was in her hands. She said in a mock wail, 'why did we bother sending you to private school. Watch your language Julia.' Then looking back up at me with a delighted expression, so different from only a minute ago, she continued, 'though her language was dubious the question is pertinent. Why did you not tell us that you are fucking a drop dead gorgeous hunk?' She so rarely uses the f word that Julia and I were stunned into silence. She was not finished, 'seeing the two of you together was explosive. He could not keep his eyes off you and clearly had difficulties with his hands as well. It was quite a turn on watching him look at you like that. If he wasn't screwing my daughter and if he had turned those Mediterranean eyes on me, in that fashion, I would have had to have him there and then.' If Julia and I were stunned before now we are paralysed. We talk together in such terms. I have overheard Mum make some fruity comments to her friends when she thought that I could not hear, but this. Not only in this language, not only in front of us, but to us. Then Mum thought further and asked, 'if she is his sister why is the Ice Maiden so antagonistic towards you. You are quite a catch yourself.' Julia muttered "thanks." 'Oh, don't be like that Julia. You are as well but we are talking about Rebecca at the moment.'

I had to act to stop their mounting speculation. 'You interrupted me before. I said, firstly. You have not heard the secondly.' They looked at me intently. I took a slow, deep breath. 'I am not having a relationship of any sort with him. We occasionally meet while we are out running in the park. We have never met on our own. I have only ever seen him when Samantha has also been there.'

Their jaws dropped and they looked at me with astonishment and then turned to each other in disbelief. When they had partly recovered they looked back at me and said in concert, 'why the hell not?'

The reality is that the Ice Maiden is blocking us but I thought that I should start from the beginning. 'It is to do with the manner in which we first met.' I hesitated. They gave impatient "go on " waves. 'I had to interview them as persons of interest in a case.'

Julia, wide eyed with delight, demanded, 'what sort of case?'

'An abduction; now it appears that it is most likely a

murder as the victim has not turned up after some time.'

Julia is now almost crying with excitement and whispered, 'gorgeous, a professor and a murderer. He is so sexy my panties are wet just thinking about him.'

Mum said, 'Julia, for heaven's sake.' Then she thought a little, smiled to herself and finally continued, 'you don't have to say it even if we are both feeling the same.' Julia and I looked at Mum flabbergasted. 'What are you looking at me like that for? Just because I am your Mother does not mean that I am not a woman.' There has never been any doubt, nor in fact any great secret, that Mum and Dad have a passionate relationship. Though they are both sixty neither look anywhere near that and they are both fit and slim. However Mum, though she obviously talks frankly with her friends, has always maintained that though sex is great to talk about such chat does not transcend generations. We all talk openly and freely of it but only to our peers.

I do not think that Luke is a murderer, even if Julian does, but I do agree with the rest. Even so I have to stop this rampant speculation. 'He is not a suspect; he was only a person of interest. I do not think he is a murderer and I am not even sure there has been a murder. You are both getting carried away. It is simply that we met in that fashion. It makes it difficult to take it further. Samantha is clearly resentful that I interviewed them.' I hung my head a little sheepishly. 'Anyway, he hasn't asked me.'

Julia threw her hands in the air as Mum snorted, 'you have a tongue in your head don't you. It isn't the nineteenth century you know.'

At that Dad came in, he took one look at us and said to Mum, 'it looks as if things are not as bad as we thought.' So, he wasn't dismissed. He deliberately left to enable Mum to grill me.

Mom replied, I noted a wild glint in her eye and wondered what was coming now, 'all is good.' She hesitated, I thought that I had misread her until she continued, 'I am tired after the drive yesterday. Let's leave these two to enjoy time together. We can go and have a lie down.' She grabbed his arm and practically dragged him out of the door. He looked nonplussed until just outside the door she whispered in his ear and they quickly strode off towards the bridge home, arm in arm, smiling all the way.

Julia said, 'tired? It's only a seventy mile drive.'

I replied, 'I doubt they will get much sleep.' We collapsed in each other's arms laughing with delight for our wonderful parents. I continued, 'I hope that she does not call him Luke half way through.'

She countered, 'with what he will be getting I am sure he would tolerate being called anything.' We collapsed together again.

As we recovered I looked up to find a smiling face that I recognised looking at me, the other waitress. She had obviously returned from somewhere else. Whilst unbuttoning her coat she said, 'I thought it was you. What a coincidence, I have just left your lovely boyfriend. I had to take my neighbour to the hospital and there he was. Sexy and a consultant doctor, aren't you the lucky one?' By now all of the other customers in the café, which is fairly full, were looking. She turned to the other waitress, 'Sally, you remember, the couple who were kissing so romantically when they left.'

Sally shouted back so all could hear, 'oh yes, three or four weeks ago. I knew you were familiar. I will never forget that kiss. It was beautiful.'

I felt myself colour, I could not face Julia but nor could I look at anyone else present. Eventually I tore my gaze from the table and met Julia's eyes. She was smiling lovingly and said, 'so you do have something to tell me after all.'

'Yes, but unfortunately it is not as good as it sounds. I was going to tell as soon as I could, but, well this is the first opportunity.' I told her all about Marcus.

When I had finished she held me for a while, we were both softly crying. I tried not to speculate as to what the others present were thinking now. At least we had given good entertainment. Julia softly said, 'I cannot believe that someone as lovely as you has met two sexy men yet has not got herself laid. Either you are doing something wrong or this beautiful city is full of idiots. Here we are, both hot, and neither of us is going to make love over Christmas.' She thought for a short while then said, 'at least Mum and Dad are keeping up the Fletcher average.' We both laughed and left with our arms around each-others' shoulders. We agreed that it was probably not a good idea to go back to my house for a while so went to look around the shops.

CHAPTER 9: LUKE, A CHANGE OF HEART

As we walked away from them, towards home, two different strands of thought played in my mind. Foremost is that the Fletchers really are a lovely family. I deliberately flattered the mother in order to curry favour with them all, but, of course, especially with Rebecca. I hope that I had not over-egged it. I had embarrassed myself with my gushing, enthusiastic comments. On the other hand it was at least true, like her daughter, in fact like both of her daughters; she is beautiful.

The second issue is not so good, that one is weighing on me. Samantha never misses an opportunity to attack Rebecca. I know that it is solely because Sam is worried about me getting close to her as Rebecca is investigating us; or at least Rebecca and Julien were scrutinising us. We have only had one official visit. By chance I did see Julian snooping around the van but they have not asked to inspect it.

Even so, at times, Sam's recent, uncharacteristic, irascibility is wearing. After this afternoon's chance meeting I am bracing myself for yet another tirade against Rebecca making any possibility of me having a relationship with her difficult. Today may be especially sharp after my comments to Rebecca's mother which now seem injudicious. Sam had practically dragged me away as soon as I had uttered them.

I smiled to myself as I thought, "stop kidding yourself Luke, all you are thinking about is Rebecca. The other issues only briefly flitted in and out," Samantha saw this and stopped walking. She turned to face me, leaned on the river wall and asked, 'what are you smiling at?' This is clearly a tease. Her bad mood regarding Rebecca has passed already. I shrugged, feigning innocence. 'Let me guess, is it just possible that you are thinking about the lovely Rebecca.'

I nearly fell over. Not only did Sam say, "the lovely Rebecca," it was also said in a pleasant, even affectionate, tone. This is the exact opposite of what I had been expecting and of her behaviour only moments before. Spotting my astonishment, more likely anticipating it, she squeezed my arm and said, 'I am sorry that I have been so disparaging about her. You know that it is only because I was so worried.'

Though I am still distracted and thrown by being wrong-footed I at least managed to pick up on, "was so worried," past tense. I had thought that she is still worried, apparently not or at least not so much.

'Rebecca is everything you need, intelligent and independent. Above all she is strong, both mentally and physically. The fact that she is so beautiful is only icing on the cake. The rest is what you truly want and need. I am sorry to have been so difficult of late but my thoughts regarding her are constantly flip-flopping. One moment I see how much you are drawn to her and how she could be the one to resolve your problem. The next moment the thought of her getting close and discovering what we are doing makes my stomach churn.'

No one else in the world would have been allowed to speak to me like that, telling me what I want and what I need. I would not suffer it even from our brother Jacob or any of our collection of four parents, no matter how lovely and well-meaning such remarks were intended to be. Our three different mothers are close to all of us but such a comment would still appear condescending from any of them, including my birth-mother. They would not give such advice no matter how strongly they felt it to be needed. The relationship that I have with Sam has always been different. Any conversation we have is like speaking aloud to ourselves. Between us anything goes.

Musing as she looked at the gentle river sweeping past, not even a swirl to break its smooth surface, Sam continued, still grinning, 'you oleaginous, sycophantic prat. Flattering the mother like that. You were lucky to get away with it. You certainly would not have were it not true. I thought the mother was going to take her knickers off there and then. In fact I thought all the women were, even the father purred.' She squeezed my arm lovingly. 'My lovely big brother, I would so love you to have a girlfriend again, even Rebecca.' She thought awhile then added, 'especially Rebecca. As I just said, she would be good for the difficulties that you have been having.'

An older couple went past hand in hand. He looked at us and then teased the woman, presumably his wife, saying loudly, clearly we were meant to hear, 'look at that, so in love. Remember, a long time ago, we were like that.' She told us to ignore him. They clearly are still in love. So many people think that Sam and I are a couple, no doubt because we are so close and do not look alike. The only thing that we do not do when out together is to hold hands, but we are tactile, like now with Sam taking my arm as we moved off towards the footbridge. Some have even suspected that we have a sexual relationship. If this is even hinted at Sam deals with them in such an excoriating fashion that they are quickly disabused. It was clear that Judith thought that Sam and I are married and that Rebecca is having an affair with me. That may well be what they are discussing right now. I wonder what Rebecca is saying about me?

All too quickly my mood darkened a little as I realised

what Sam had said before the older couple distracted me. She spoke of the "difficulties I have been having." Since the last attack on her by Robin, since seeing her nearly die, after all the hospital visits and the pain that she has suffered, I find it so difficult being a man. Could any of us do the same as Robin did in some circumstance or other? I fear finding the same urges to attack a woman in myself. For more than the last year I have hardly been able to even look at a woman in a sexual manner; that is until I saw Rebecca. I doubt that I will ever be able to hold a woman close again. I cannot envisage me lying on top of a woman, not even Rebecca; no matter how much I desire her. I miss holding them. I miss talking intimately. I miss making love. I miss it all so very, very much.

Being with Sam is satisfying and close, but so, so different. However much I love her it is still a totally dissimilar type of relationship, a different form of intimacy. I simply cannot face having a lover. I cannot face confronting my fears. I have never hit a woman. I have never even thought about it; but I feel that I may still embody the violence present in so many of us. Perhaps it lurks in me. I could not bear for it to break out.

'Luke, we haven't spoken of your thoughts and fears for some time. I think we should. We have done so much to try to alleviate the wrongs done by others. It is time to work on your pain.' I tried to interrupt, she put a finger to my mouth, 'my pain, mental and physical, is considerably less. I am putting it all behind me. I want you to try to as well.' Again she stopped me interrupting, 'Luke you would never hurt a woman, physically I mean. True, you have broken many hearts but that was not solely your fault. I know that you have never hit a woman. There is no doubt whatsoever that you never will. I know you have fears. I wish you would see a therapist as we have discussed so often but I stand by your decision not to. Luke, now the time is different. Even more, Rebecca is different. Surely you can see that, not only would you never hit her, but if you even thought about it I would be visiting you in hospital, not vice versa.'

At last we laughed at this. Shaking my head I replied, 'no. You would be identifying what was left of me in the morgue.' Then I changed tack, 'why this volt face, I was not anticipating it; why now.'

Now on the foot bridge we halted again and leaned on the rail as Sam took a deep breath. 'Three reasons, firstly, as I have just said, Rebecca. There is no doubt that she is formidable. Most men would find her daunting but she is exactly what you need, thankfully bloody sexy with it. You both are so attracted to each other; the sexual tension between you is electric. Her mother and sister, what were their names; Judith and Julia, they were also attracted to you but their obvious thoughts were eclipsed by Rebecca's. I know that I have been so antagonistic towards her, you know why, that is part of my second point. This afternoon, seeing you together, seeing you talking so easily with her family; I had a complete change of heart. Now I very much regret pulling you away.'

Metaphorically I rocked back on my heels. Previously I had thought that I could always read Sam but, as with another recent statement by her, I had not picked up on this. Then I realised that for the last few minutes; it has only been a few minutes, it feels like a wonderful long afternoon; for the last few minutes I have only thought of and only seen Rebecca. Sam smirked and tugged my sleeve, 'wakey, wakey, I am here.' She knows exactly what I am thinking on. Then she continued, 'I have no doubt what they are all talking about now. Rebecca's family obviously thought that we are married and that you are having an affair with her. I know at first, before my "Road to Damascus" moment, that I was glaring at her. They think you are having an affair and that I am about to kill one or both of you.'

So, I am not the only one thinking that. I wonder, are Rebecca's family similarly encouraging her to see me if they now they know the truth?

We turned to start walking home. Sam grimaced a little and held tight to my arm. After a few steps her leg obviously eased, she initially walked more confidently. Then she winced and we stopped again and leaned back on the rail. Ignoring the pain Sam returned to her comments. 'Secondly, as you know I was very worried, not worried, frightened, by her investigation. Well it has been weeks now and we haven't heard any more. There is nothing whatsoever to link us to...,' she dropped her voice and looked cautiously around, 'to link us to the James' investigation. We have undertaken several more corrections and all have passed without incident. I have checked the hospital records and none have turned up in A and E. What we are doing remains below the radar and even if it is detected there is no evidence. I think what we have done, what we are doing, is undetectable; even by one so accomplished as Rebecca. So far that is.' I noted her final qualification but let it slide.

With her current work, in pharmacy rather than as a medical practitioner, Sam is required to visit all units in the hospital in order to monitor drug stocks. She has managed to secure a specific responsibility for A and E. In order to gain and continue this she has had to make a point of currying favour with, even flirting with, the older consultant, Dr Wynn-Davis. She does not like this, calling him a repellent, misogynistic, fat toad; but it works. I am concerned that Wynn-Davis is retiring soon. Sam describes the other consultant, Marcus Rice, as a sexy hot-shot. He may be more used to young women flirting with him and so be more resistant. If he is alert then he may also be suspicious of Sam spending so much time in A and E. Worse, the incoming new A and E consultant is a woman. Unless she is gay she will also be immune to Sam's charms.

For the present moment though, our system works well with Sam being around A and E to spot the abused women being treated. This and her voluntary work in the refuge enables us to detect the abusers. Even so I have worries. 'Sam, it is fantastic that you can observe in A and E but as you know I am worried by you looking through the hospital records. You are leaving a digital trail.'

Looking at me with an indulgent smile, she said, 'stop worrying big brother. We have been over this many times. I always have two files open when I look at the computer in the department. One is for my official work logged on as me. With the other, for our unofficial snooping, I log on as one of the junior doctors. They are hopeless with their passwords and often leave them written down on scraps of paper. They do not remember from hour to hour whose records they have been looking at and they have no reason to check their own logging on anyway. As they are so busy it is hard for them but it makes everything safe and secure for me. People have no interest in me looking at the computer, supposedly ordering drugs. I can easily check medical records for the abused women and their details. If anyone does come by as I am undertaking this I simply switch from the doctors log-in to my official one. We have been through this, stop worrying.'

During this exchange we had remained paused on the footbridge. I leaned on the railing and looked across the river to the Market Square. The Culture Café caught my eye. I was briefly distracted remembering having coffee there with a girlfriend before Sam was attacked. It is such a romantic spot. It always seemed to be an auspicious place to cement a relationship. I gust of cold wind brought me back to the present.

Sam is correct. We have discussed this interminably.

To be more accurate I have raised it time and again. She is more than computer literate, she is an expert. If anyone can hide such an investigation she can. My concerns had flared when I had heard in the interview that Julian has experience in forensic computing. As Sam had said after they left, there is no indication for him to look at the hospital computer and even if he did so he would only see junior doctors logging on and off. Sam is also careful to log on as them only when they are on duty. Also she has checked that if the doctor logs on at the same time the antiquated hospital computer does not detect this. So, with them being so over-worked and moving on every few months, there is no detectable trail.

Sam indicated that the pain in her leg had eased and we restarted our journey home. We walked in a companionable silence at first, then I remembered what she had started to say. I turned to ask her, 'what is the third. You said there are three reasons for your change of heart. You have only given me two.'

Sam suddenly looked distressed and, most unusually for her, uncertain. She whispered to me, 'not here. Let's talk at home.'

I was briefly perplexed by her not wanting to talk now but quickly my thoughts returned to Rebecca. It has not only been because of Sam's disapproval that I have not approached Rebecca. Whilst I respect Sam and I always try to fit in with her opinions I remain my own man. Not often, but it does happen, we agree to disagree and go our own way. With Rebecca the chief problem has been a lack of an opportunity to approach her. Whilst I regularly see her in the park panting out an invitation whilst running after her would be difficult. It would have to be blurted out. Anyway, I can barely keep up with her, she is so strong and fast. I can hardly call her at the station. Though she gave me her card I presume that is a work mobile number. I would not to want to splutter out an invitation whilst thinking that she was on speaker with half of the station listening. I will keep my eyes open whilst training and undertake most of it around the war memorial where I often see her. An opportunity may present itself on the odd occasion that Sam is not with me. Surely even Rebecca has to rest from time to time. At least I am getting fit trying to engineer a supposedly chance encounter. Since I first saw her in the park I have begun training there as often as possible.

By the time we arrived home and then settled in what I call my "sitting room;" though it is in my part of the house Sam mostly joins me there so it is in reality "our sitting room; " I had forgotten about the third reason. When I finally cleared my head of Rebecca I spotted Sam's troubled expression and I remembered our promised chat. 'OK, Sam, what is the third, and obviously troubling, reason.'

She looked away, took a sip of coffee and scratched Toby's head. This is so unlike my lovely sister who is usually so direct. I cannot remember the last time I saw her prevaricate. What is worrying her? There is nothing troubling between us, especially since her re-think on Rebecca. We have no problems. Tomorrow we go to a family Christmas celebration at our joint parental home, the first one in which we will all be together for years. Dad, our half-brother Jacob and our three various mothers will all be there.

We are all close; we get on very well and always have a great time together. After a few drinks Sam, Jacob and I always return to speculating on the sleeping arrangements on the second floor. We do not venture there; we never did as children, confining ourselves to our rooms on the first floor and family rooms on the ground floor. It is however a superb subject for sibling conjectures. This year it is an especially wonderful Christmas as for the first time in three years Jacob will be there. Working in California, being so senior in the company and the Americans taking such a short break at Christmas it is often difficult for him to join us. Even though the four parents will no doubt take advantage of the glorious opportunity, for them that is, of us all being together. They will no doubt conspire and then berate us all for still being single. By the age I am now dad already had had two wives and two children and the five of us were all happily together in the same house. Christmas will be a chance for them to point this out. In spite of that we will still have a great time.

Whilst I thought this, time passed in silence. Eventually Sam spoke. 'The third reason is that what I am about to suggest will reduce future risk anyway.' She saw me look up with interest and anticipation; she would have expected this knowing that though committed I always want to minimise the fear of detection, especially for her. Seeing my expression she looked abashed but defiant. 'Luke, I think we should stop. Or, at least we should greatly curtail what we are doing and deal with only the worst offenders.'

The grandfather clock ponderously ticked; usually I find it relaxing, now it seems portentous. The mechanism whirred preparing to strike. I was paralysed, staring at her, for what felt like minutes. As the clock chimed, the "bongs" being softened by a damper on the bell, she held my gaze, challenging me. She knows how I will react and she is preparing to stand her ground. I cannot face her any longer. I stood and went to the window looking out across the green. With the winter sun and children playing around the statue it all looks the same, yet, in here, all feels so very different.

At last I can speak, I need to ensure that I have heard her correctly. 'Are you suggesting that we should stop the abductions, that we should stop doing our utmost to prevent these animals beating their wives and partners?'

She gave a defiant nod.

'Are you suggesting that we should turn our back on

ROBERT WILLIAMS

women who are suffering the same as what Robin did to you; that we should leave them to be let down by the criminal justice system as they have been for generations; as you were?' Instantly I regretted that cheap jibe. Whatever she is now saying Sam feels for them as strongly as I do, more so.

Sam nodded again but now downcast and hurt.

I immediately regretted the manner in which I had responded and I went and sat next to her and put my arm around her shoulder. I gave her a gentle squeeze. 'Sorry Sam, that was uncalled for. I know how you feel. I am just so flabbergasted.' I gave her another squeeze and she returned something between a smile and a grimace. 'Tell me more, why are you thinking this?'

'It has been building for some time. In fact it dates back to when we, that is you, had to kill and dispose of Brian James.' I went to speak. 'No, please don't interrupt. All my thoughts overlap so allow me to finish before you respond.' Reluctantly I nodded "OK."

'I know why what we did to James was necessary. I was co-author of Rule 2 with you, remember. Even so it felt that we had gone too far, disproportionate, when it actually became necessary. However much it seemed reasonable in preparation I felt it was wrong, disproportionate, when it was undertaken. I know that many abused women are killed but I am not sure that confers the right to do so on us, especially as we are both judge and jury.' She held her hand up to ask me not to speak. It was a gentle request, not an insistence.

'Another, and major, concern is that we are accelerating and breaking Rule 2. We agreed on one each month so that is would be less likely that a pattern would be detected. Whilst it would be good in one sense for our activities to become known, it may create true prevention, it would be so dangerous for us. Apart from risk to us it may curtail future work. In the first year we only dealt with five, admittedly I was in hospital or incapacitated for much of that time. This year we have undertaken eighteen, fifty percent more than agreed. Worse, two thirds have been in the last four months. We are accelerating. I know I am always there, I know it is me who unearths the cases, but I am sorry to say dear brother it is you who is driving this. You are always pushing to do more. I am sorry to say Luke that I fear that you are becoming obsessed by what we are doing. I know more than anyone how important it is but we cannot take on responsibility for all abused women. We must be more circumspect, for our sanity as well as our freedom.'

Whilst Sam had been speaking I had morphed from astonishment, through anger, to a mixture of concern and resignation. Perhaps a little shame mixed in as well. Sam does not know how easy it was for me to kill Brian James. It would be, or should that be, will be, easier still next time. Further, though I do not actively enjoy the treatment I give the despicable abusers at the farm, nor do I abhor it. It should be difficult for me to treat another human being in such a fashion, whatever the reason, however much they deserve it; but it is not. At times I find myself looking forward to it. It feels to be the correct thing to be doing and it is satisfying. I would be mortified if Sam spoke of this, however she has almost certainly intuited my feelings. Maybe we can leave that unsaid. I did not speak as I can see that she has not finished.

'Luke, I suggest that we return to our original plan and deal with only one a month. Let us tackle only the worst cases. We can then research them more thoroughly so we don't end up in the same position as we were with Brian James. You know how much I feel for the women being abused. On the other hand I am putting what Robin did behind me, especially as I am so much more mobile and as I said by the river most of the pain, the physical pain that is, has gone. Let's both continue what we have to do but also give ourselves time to have fun.'

I can see she is finished. She can see that I do not agree. I really have no choice but to go along with what she is saying but it is good that I do so anyway. We do not have to, and could not any way, agree to disagree on this occasion.

The discussion is concluded satisfactorily for both of us even though I have not actually said anything of import. A cheeky little smile came to her now softer expression. I asked, 'OK, what's so funny?'

'I was thinking about us having more fun. I bet that I can guess what fun you have in mind with Rebecca. I also suspect that she is one woman who can teach even my Lothario brother a thing or two.' She jabbed my ribs now openly laughing and mocking, 'you are blushing. You are an old softie.'

I can feel that she is absolutely correct. I am blushing.

CHAPTER 10:
REBECCA, TAKEN
BY SURPRISE

I sprinted hard for the last half mile of my training run. My path home, from the new bridge passing through the park alongside the river, was clear and I let rip. I came to a halt on the part of the path immediately below my house. I turned to face the river and leaned forward putting my hands on top of the cold wall as I gasped for air. A mist rising up off the water caused the reflected lights of Market Square on the opposite bank to look ghostly; it mingled with the white of my breath. It feels good to be outside. I always have a better workout in the fresh air even if it is near freezing and dark. For the first five weeks of the year it has been icy and I have had to undertake all of my training in the gym. Today has been milder; the pavements are cold and wet but they are not slippery.

This evening, as soon as I had finished in the station, I rushed home, changed and came out for a run. Leaving my front door I had simply crossed the road and descended the steep path down the sharply sloping park to the walkway alongside the river. Most of the paths through the park are dark but the wide, flat area adjacent to the river has street lighting. For the circuit I always take, starting from this point directly below the war memorial and my house, I initially turn downstream following the river. I cross the old bridge and then run upstream through the gardens on the opposite side until I meet the new bridge and finally turn back to here. It is a fraction shy of a mile. I have just completed five circuits in a good time. It has been a good end to a good day. My nemesis, Meadows, has been away for a couple of days and Julian and I made a gratifying arrest this morning. It was only a minor case but, even so, it was still satisfying to clear it. Even better I gave Julian the credit of the arrest. He gets the kudos and I get to avoid the paperwork.

I stopped for a moment longer to get my breath whilst looking across the river. Though only six pm, as it is February, it is completely dark. Today had brought one of those wet, winter afternoons where night falls at four o'clock. It has stopped raining but heavy clouds block any moonlight. Beyond the adjacent street light illuminating the path the river is a stately, inky black as it slides by. The matching lights in the gardens opposite that I have just run through are reflected and shimmer on the surface. They are a little clearer now as the steamy haze has swirled away with a faint puff of a wintery wind. Behind me the impenetrable shadows between the trees of the park slope steeply up for sixty yards until meeting the railings on the opposite side of the road from my house; from here, during the daytime, they are just visible above the top edge of the memorial. Yet again I feel so privileged to live in this gentle city, to be able to run in such a beautiful and secure area right outside my front door.

On the way out for my runs I take the diagonal path down through the park towards this riverside walkway and then I turn left towards the old bridge to start my circuit. At the finish of the final lap I always stop to catch my breath here. When recovered I backtrack upstream for a hundred yards and I then take the mirror image diagonal path which, at the top, meets the one that I leave on almost opposite to where I live. The reason for this alternative route home is that half way along this second, upstream route is the massive war memorial wall. In front of the memorial is a crescent shaped paved area the same length as the wall, roughly thirty yards, and it is is fifteen yards wide in the middle tapering to a footpath at each end. Opposite the wall, directly above me and overlooking the river, are railings to prevent people falling over the twenty foot drop on to the rock garden below it, in front of where I am now standing. The flat area in front of the memorial wall is ideal for my warm down and stretches. It is dark and in the evenings very quiet. I have the room and privacy to complete my workout without being ogled by passing men. In fairness to them many of the stretches, out of context, are very provocative. I have a great understanding of women who prefer ladies only gyms. I prefer the outdoors.

A shout behind me made me turn to look up. I thought, "bugger," a couple of yobs, they look to be teenagers, are prating around on the railings where I was about to go to for my warm down. They sound coarse and appear to be wearing shabby motley, presumably they consider it cool. They spotted me watching them and yelled, 'lo darlin', fancy comin up fu a gud time.' For some reason they found this hysterically funny. I ignored them and turned to look back across the river. After a few minutes I saw that my strategy had worked and they were walking away uphill. I gave them a little longer to clear the area. I did not want any cheap comments to spoil this beautiful day. I then slowly walked up to the memorial allowing time to ensure they are well away.

On approaching the workout area I looked carefully around. Though it is dark a crescent of moon has peeped from behind a cloud and is now giving just sufficient light to give the wet paving stones a silvery glow. I can see that it is empty. I pulled off my beany hat, shook out my hair, and turned towards the wall in order to lean against it for initial calf stretches.

My head snapped round as a threatening cackle came from my right. Two of them have not left. They had been hiding around the corner of the wall. They must have spotted me walking up to here and lain in wait. One is tall, heavily built, and seems slow and stupid. He appears to be one of life's mistakes, a wholly wretched character. The other one spoke, he is small and wiry but looks mean. His demeanour shows that he has a taste for mindless violence. They are not teenagers. I had not seen them clearly. They are in their thirties.

'Well, look at that. She's blond. I do like a blond bit.' As he said this I pulled my hat back on. There is clearly potentially a problem and I do not want them to be able to grab my hair to restrain me. He sniggered, 'that's not nice. Never mind, I will soon find out if you are a real blond.' So, my initial presumptions are confirmed. I do have a problem.

Thinking to myself that I really can't be bothered with this on such a lovely evening I turned to jog back down the path out of harm's way. I will call it in when I get home and have a couple of uniforms pick them up. I could tell them that I am a police officer. I could threaten to arrest them though as yet they had not actually committed a crime. Or, as I chose, I could simply take the longer way home.

As I turned a third one appeared from behind the other end of the wall, he must have been skulking in the dark as I came up. He is also small and mean looking. I am hemmed in. There is an eight foot wall behind me, railings and a long fall on to rocks in front, and there are yobos clearly intent on attacking me at either exit. I am thirty yards from my home, thirty yards from a well-lit reasonably busy path, three hundred yards from the High Street; yet I am as isolated here as if I am on Mars.

I moved backwards and I put my shoulders flat against the wall so that I can watch them all together. On my left the small one moved along the railing until he was in front of me, the big one stayed close to the wall. Then they all slowly moved towards me. This is a moment with meaning, a moment that changes the moments to come. They approached in a desultory fashion, one now in front of me, one from either side.

The small, nasty one who had spoken before now stands directly ahead of me, a couple of meters away. He spoke again with an adenoidal whine, 'Benny just wants a little kiss luv.' As he said this he mimed unzipping and zipping his flies. I have no intention of kissing him anywhere, certainly not there. I pretended to cower. I pressed the palms of my hands and the ball of my right foot against the wall.

He spoke again, the others have not uttered a sound. He is obviously the ringleader, 'no need to be frightened girl, m'be a little kiss.' They all sniggered, 'or what would youse say to a little fuck?'

I very nearly replied, 'hello, little fuck.' I bit my tongue. Better not to goad them. It is to my advantage that they think I am frightened. Any smart-arse reply may alert them. Under the guise of trying to squirm away I pressed harder into the wall. I felt the carvings of all of the names of the fallen imprint on my back. They have failed to spot that I am positioning and bracing myself, preparing a pre-emptive strike.

Benny then made another serious mistake. It could have literally been fatal for him but I chose to be gentle. No, not gentle, more like being less vicious. He had become emboldened by my apparent fearful quivering. He swaggered, he made a sickly grin from side to side to each of his fellow would be rapists. He took another step forward, this time more confidently. As his front foot touched the ground, in the instant he placed all of his weight on it ready to take the step to grab me, I struck.

Lunging and twisting simultaneously, pivoting on my left foot, I brought my hips into line and using the blade of my right foot and heel I delivered a roundhouse kick to the side of his knee. I spun back and rechambered against the wall before any of them had any conscious notion that I had moved.

In a split second of eerie silence I watched as Benny's pasty, pugnacious face contorted in pain. He started screaming and falling at the same moment. Damnit, he staggered and fell back. I had deliberately hit his forward right knee with a sideways blow hoping that he would fall in front of the big man to my left and help to block him. I am exposed on both flanks. If they charge together now my defence will be more difficult. Oh well, no battle plan survives first contact with the enemy. I will have to improvise.

They did not charge. That is a second amateurish mistake compounding Benny's cockiness. Initially they looked in astonishment at Benny who is now writhing and screaming on the ground. His knee is bent a hideous ninety degrees to the side. Though I am not a doctor I am fairly certain that knees should not bend sideways. Good, at least one will not cause me any problem. The others lost the initiative as they tried in vain to assimilate what has happened. They had expected that by now my face would be pulled into Benny's groin.

The big one to my left fumbled in his pocket and pulled out a long kitchen knife. He looks as if he is more likely to cut himself than me. Even so it is a knife, a big one. He pointed it towards me, his arm out straight. Good, that will easily be taken from him.

The smaller one to my right is clearly the slick, experienced one. A knife appeared effortlessly in his left hand. A smaller knife but it is in a more expert hand. He twisted and lowered himself; he is clearly anticipating a kick and preparing to counter. From the ground Benny shouted, 'cut the bitch, cut her good.'

The big one lumbered forward but the little one held back. The little one is the problem. I am obviously expected to be daunted by the big one and the other will strike as I am grappling with him. I have to immobilise the little one first. That he is left handed and on my right will help. If I make a false run to my right, as if I am trying to run past him, he will think that he will be able to swing the knife straight towards me for a stab to my side. When he strikes I will pivot, take the sleeve of his knife hand and pull it forward to pass in front of me. He will be unbalanced and his body will be unprotected in front of me. At the same time I will hit him hard, very hard, in the temple, with my other elbow. He will, unlike Benny, hopefully fall in the direction he will be moving and be on the ground in front of the large assailant. Possibly he will have dropped the knife. Anyway he should be either unconscious or so groggy that he will not be an immediate threat.

Even if the big one reacts quickly he will still have to get over the little one to reach me. I should have time to deliver another roundhouse kick, this time to the groin. If I am lucky he may simply run but I doubt that he has that much insight.

I paused. I will lunge right as the one to my left takes his next step. He started to move.

Before I could react a massive black shape silently flashed in front of me. If it had appeared a fraction of a second later I would have collided with it. In the gloom I could not initially work out what it is. Then I saw a huge jaw open and clamp across the outstretched arm of the one to my left. It is a colossal dog. The man screamed and the dog's momentum carried him over backwards with the knife thrown clear, clattering to the ground.

I mentally kicked myself for being distracted and quickly focussed back on the little one. He had not taken the opportunity to strike. He seemed confused, uncertain as to what has happened, as indeed so am I. At the same instant as I took this in a large man wearing black shoulder charged the little one and sent him spinning over. My would be attacker is obviously experienced in street fighting and the one to beware of. In spite of being taken by surprise and knocked flying he had held on to the knife. Instantaneously he regained balance and immediately started to get to all fours to retaliate. The man in black, who now had his back to me, lunged forward with a kick. I thought, I shouted in my mind, "don't do that, you will get stabbed in the leg." I kept my mouth closed not wanting to distract him. Anyway it is too late to have any effect; he is committed to the kick. The big man's foot drove hard into the other's stomach. Though unable to breath he still fought back and again tried to get to his feet wildly swinging with the knife. The man kicked hard again and caught him square in the balls. This time the knife flew out of his hand and he writhed on the ground.

Finally; I am able to process who it is who has arrived.

It is Luke, with Toby.

I quickly looked back at the large one to my left. Toby has released his arm but is lying with his frightening jaw half open, showing his white fangs, next to the chap's face. He unwisely started to reach for his knife. Toby gave a rumbling low growl that seemed to shake the ground. The lout lay still again. So much for Sam and Luke saying that Toby is a "big softie." I think that he will be reappraised.

I heard a scrape behind me and whirled around winding to strike. At the last moment I saw that it is Samantha pushing her bicycle with one hand and in the other is a 'phone held to her ear. I managed to hold back the kick but it was close. Samantha screamed and then shouted, 'no, no. I'm here to help.' She relaxed again when I had both feet on the ground and then looked at me in astonishment. 'Rebecca?' In the semi-dark, with my beanie hat on and wearing my new tracksuit, which being a present from Julia is not in my usual colour, Samantha had not recognised me. She spoke back into the 'phone, 'It's OK, I'm fine.' Then a pause as she listened and then she replied, 'I understand, on their way. Thanks, I think we are secure now.' She hung up and spoke to me, 'I called the police. I did not know that it was you.'

I said to Samantha that was great news, we need back up to deal with this. I turned back to Luke and the men on the ground. Luke is too close. I hissed at him, 'step away quickly. They may have more weapons. Kick the knives over here as you do so.'

The knives hit the base of the wall with a clatter and Luke stepped towards Samantha out of harm's way. As he did so I heard people vault the railing above and heavy footsteps, half tumbling, half running down the slope towards us. "Oh shit, what now?" There are at least two people charging down the slope. If they are Bennie's friends and similarly armed we are in serious trouble.

Then the best possible sound carried down. I caught the swish-click of police batons being extended. I heard the footsteps separate and they came around each end of the wall. As they did so I pulled off my hat so that the officers will instantly recognise me. For a copper, blond curls are often a disadvantage; people, not only men, assume that the wearer is weak and stupid. For instant identification in the half dark they are, however, an advantage. I don't want to be Tasered or batoned by mistake. PC Patrick Johnson came from my left towards the big man who is still stretched out next to Toby. WPC Sally Myers came from the opposite direction behind Luke and Samantha. Their batons are held ready as they appraised the scene. They looked at the men on the ground; Benny had started screaming again and attracted their attention first. I called out, 'Patrick, Sally.'

Taken aback to hear their names they looked at me properly for the first time and together gave an astonished 'Ma'am.'

They quickly recovered from their surprise and surveyed the scene. Seeing no immediate threat, Patrick looked at the dog lead that he saw Luke is now holding out and asked, 'is this your dog sir.' Luke nodded "yes." He seems so discombobulated by the whole situation that he cannot properly speak. 'Would you please put him on the lead?' The Big Softie is still giving the appearance of being viscous and he is the chief current focus of concern. Luke called over Toby and clipped him on. The man on the ground then started to move. Patrick pressed him in the middle of his back with the baton, whispering with menace, 'and you stay absolutely still.'

Whilst this was unfolding I had heard a siren approaching, blue lights flashed on the tops of the trees. Tyres screeched to a halt. It sounds as if they have stopped directly outside my front door. Two more pairs of boots crashed down the slope. Again there was the double swish-click and again they separated and came around the memorial from opposing sides. It is Sergeant Mike Fellows and PC Derek Cartwright. They also quickly appraised the scene, spotting me, again with surprise in their eyes, they said 'Ma'am.' I pointed to the knives behind me and then to the men on the ground. Derek went to stand over the one still holding his balls. Patrick stayed over the other. Benny is clearly no longer a threat.

Mike rushed up to Samantha who is standing

open mouthed in astonishment. Before Mike could speak Samantha held up her 'phone and asked, 'how on earth did you get here so quickly? I have only just called 999.'

Mike replied, 'we were in the area looking for these three. They had tried to molest two young girls but thankfully the girls managed to run away. But you, are you alright? Did they harm you? I'll radio for an ambulance.'

Samantha initially looked confused and then she realised what Mike had presupposed. 'No, I mean yes, I am fine. They did not attack me. They attacked Rebecca. That is, I mean, they were attacking Detective Inspector Fletcher when we arrived.' As Samantha said this I heard a groan of despair from Bennie, different from his cries of pain. I suspected that he had not picked up on my colleagues calling me ma'am. He probably thought they had said madam. Now he knows that he was attacking a police officer and though I was not on duty any chance of squirming out of his just deserts or any clemency has receded. Sam continued, 'my brother and I came along as it was happening. I called 999 from over there.' She pointed a short way back along the path.

Mike clearly did not accept this and presumably thought that she is in shock. He pressed again, 'before you called, did they hurt you in anyway?'

Samantha replied, this time very carefully and clearly. She can see that Mike is confused by the situation. 'Officer, thank you, I am absolutely fine. I was not involved. It was Rebecca who was being attacked.'

Mike looked at me and appeared flabbergasted. I nodded a "yes." He looked at the men on the ground, then at Luke and Toby, then at all of his colleagues. The four of them stood stock still, rooted to the spot, mouths gaping.

I interjected, 'Mike these three attacked me. They were

threatening rape. As they closed on me I kicked this little shit in the knee.' I pointed at Benny who has thankfully stopped screaming and is now simply whimpering. It is pretty obvious which one has been struck in the knee anyway. Christ, it is at a dreadful angle. 'Then the other two came at me with these knives.' I pointed with my foot. 'Before I could react, Toby, the dog, and Luke took out the other two.' I added, 'we all met here by chance. Luke, Samantha and I know each other from....' What do I say, it is not the time to say that I interviewed them as "persons of interest" or that Julian still considers them suspects? '.....from before.'

Mike, still standing in the centre of this scene, slowly turned around looking at us all. His face trembled. Then his features contorted into a rictus. Finally, he can control himself no longer. He exploded with laughter. He had to walk to the railing and hold on, shaking. He can hardly breathe as he is laughing so hard. Patrick, Sally and Derek also cannot hold back and started rocking with mirth as well. I know what they find so funny and I smiled along with them.

Luke and Samantha looked on in wonderment. This is clearly not the police response that they had expected. Even Toby looks intrigued. Benny yelled from the ground, 'what are you all laughing at? It's not funny. That bitch has broken my leg.'

With one intimidating stride Mike was looming over him. He had "accidentally" kicked Benny's leg on the way. After Benny's screams had died down, Mike snarled at Benny whilst pointing at Luke and Toby. 'You should thank this man and his dog. They have saved the lives of all three of you.' The heads of all three on the ground, along with Luke's and Samantha's snapped up looking at him, questioning.

After a deliberate, theatrical pause Mike continued, 'listen carefully. This is Detective Inspector Fletcher.' Now the expressions of the other two on the ground shifted to read "oh shit" and Bennie's consternation deepened. Mike continued, 'please allow me to tell you more about this first class police officer, the second in command of our station, the woman I am proud to call "Boss". DI Fletcher is also a third degree black belt in Taekwondo. Not only that, prior to coming to this quiet city with its dutiful residents,' he gave Benny a prod with the baton, 'and prior to her service in tough areas in the Met, she spent a year on secondment in Israel with the Israeli police studying Krav Maga.' Benny looked blank. Luke and Samantha appeared uncertain; they clearly do not know what Krav Maga is either. 'I can see, SIR, that in your no doubt wide and intensive education that you have not encountered Krav Maga. Let me say that it makes Karate and Taekwondo look like a Sunday School outing. You should thank this man,' Mike looked across and smiled, this time gently, 'and his savage dog.' Toby is already lying on his back with his massive paws in the air. Derek is bending down scratching his stomach.

Benny howled again, 'my leg my leg. Whoever she is she broke my leg. I have been assaulted. I need help, call an ambulance.' Assaulted? Mike looks as if he is going to stamp on the little runt's leg. Samantha stepped forward, 'excuse me officer. I am a doctor in the hospital.' I smiled at this, both true and not true. 'Let me assess his injuries.' She stepped forward whilst giving Mike a complicit smile. Mike stepped aside watching with relish as Samantha knelt down and grabbed Benny's leg and pulled. Whilst he screamed and writhed she held his ankle firmly and checked for a pulse. Standing up again she said, 'it's not broken and the circulation is good. He needs hospital care but it is not desperately urgent. Ask the ambulance to come but there is no need to hurry too much.' She glanced at the others and said, 'they are fine but to cover my brother and Toby in case of any frivolous complaint perhaps you should send them in as well. Get them formally examined.'

Yet again Benny screamed that his leg is broken and that he needs urgent assistance. Samantha looked at him with contempt and said, 'no, it is definitely not broken. That's a pity.'

Now grinning openly at the obviously cool and contained Samantha, Mike retorted, 'that's not very PC, if you don't mind me saying Doc.' His grin widened from ear to ear.

With a knowing, contemptuous stare at Benny, Samantha responded, 'actually it is. For a young man such as him a broken leg would heal in a matter of weeks. He has badly torn ligaments. He will need multiple operations and be in pain for years.' She stepped over Benny walking towards Luke. As she did so her foot "accidentally" caught Benny's leg, she has obviously copied Mike's technique. Whilst Benny screamed yet again Samantha muttered under her breath, 'believe me. I know.'

Mike instructed Sally to radio for an ambulance. The other PCs gingerly handcuffed and searched the men on the ground. As I had anticipated they found a knife in Benny's pocket. Then with glee they pulled from the pockets of all of them large bags of white powder. It must be cocaine. Holding them up Mike said, 'well, look at this. Given the quantity here they must be dealing. These three will not be littering our streets for some years.' On the ground three heads slumped back, finished.

Realising what has been overlooked in the excitement I said, 'Mike, they have not yet been formally arrested.' He nodded and looked to me as the senior officer. I shook my head, inappropriate as I am involved. Mike gave me a surreptitious shake of his head, not him either. I know he is over-burdened with admin. I looked at Patrick and Derek who firstly looked at each other and then back at me, not with pleasure, but with extreme consternation. Then I realised, not only are they great friends they are also great competitors. In the station there is an informal "collar competition," whoever gets to be the first to make one hundred arrests receives an unspecified prize. It no doubt involves a drinking session but it is the kudos that counts. They are neck and neck at ninety-eight. No matter how I divide up the arrests one will win in a somewhat unsporting fashion. Thinking further I remember Sally being teased as a "collar virgin." She is a new recruit and has yet to make an arrest. I turned to her and said, 'WPC Myers, would you please arrest these men.' All four of my wonderful fellow officers were delighted and the men cheered as Sally went through the arrest spiel. Luke and Samantha were grinning as this spectacle unfolded. I suspect that they realise this is not a usual police action.

Samantha stepped forward and interrupted apologetically, 'I have to go, I am on duty soon.'

Sally said, 'I am sorry doctor. I have to ask you to come to the station to make a statement.'

Stepping in I reassured Sally, 'I know and can vouch for both Luke and Samantha. I am sure that it would be in order if they called in tomorrow to make a statement.' Samantha agreed and thanked me. She said good bye and prepared to cycle off down the path. As she turned her bike and mounted Sally called out, 'no doc, wrong way. You must have been distracted by these events. The hospital is this way.' She pointed downstream.

Shaking her head Samantha pointed upstream, 'thanks but I also undertake voluntary work at the women's refuge. I am on duty there tonight.' She said good bye again to the four officers. Then, coming up to me she surprised me. She gave a warm loving smile. The Ice Maiden is smiling at me. Then my surprise turned to being astonishment, she gave me a tight hug saying, 'you are wonderful, an inspiration.' As if this was not enough I was then astounded as she planted a warm kiss on my cheek.

Thankfully she missed my stupefied reaction as she turned to Luke saying, 'see you around eight in the morning.' She thought no one could see and she gave Luke a quick, sly wink. Anyone observing may have thought that it was sexual, that she was promising something for the morning. I have no doubt that it is not. When I have seen them together they have been like Julia and myself; loving tactile siblings but nothing more. Luke looked taken aback by the wink, then realisation dawned and he returned a knowing smile. Something has passed between them. I have no idea what. I have the same with Julia, sibling communication. We can exchange ideas without actually talking. They are as close as I am with my lovely sister.

With that she cycled off leaving me even more taken by surprise by her behaviour than I was by the initial attack leading to all of this. I am completely wrong-footed by her altered behaviour towards me. Surely it cannot be solely because I kicked a crook in the leg. I also felt surprised by having heard of her duty in the refuge. That is silly of me, though I did not know she undertook such work it is predictable from what she has suffered. Predictable that is for a warm, considerate person; not for an ice-maiden.

Luke, Toby and I moved a little to the side and leaned on the railing looking down over the river. It still slid calmly by. People walked hand in hand along the softly lit path not thirty yards below and in front of us. They had no idea what has unfolded so close to them. I turned and gently said, 'thank you Luke. Thank you for coming to my aid. You were very brave and decisive.' I managed to avoid adding, reckless.

'You didn't need me. You could have finished them on your own, but thanks any way.'

'No Luke, you are wrong. Firstly there were three of them armed with knives. Yes, it is likely that I would have come out on top but that was by no means certain. You did not know that it was me and you did not know about my training. You came to the aid of a defenceless woman being attacked by three armed men. You could not have seen that the one on the ground was already incapacitated. Most people would not have done that. I have no doubt that Mike will recommend you for a police commendation medal and that it will be awarded. It is truly deserved.' He looks astonished. 'Luke, most men do not come to women's aid like that. I have seen the results so many times. From what you said when we first met I know that you were devastated not to have been able to help Samantha when she was attacked. That was not your fault, you were not there. That is the problem with domestic abuse behind closed doors. Your courage and actions of tonight must resolve the misgivings that I saw you still retain.'

I looked up at him, his long hair flowing, his dark eyes almost black and unreadable. I fought the impulse to kiss him. I had to look away to break his gaze before I did something stupid. As I did so I noticed Sally looking at him with admiration, and more, desire mixed in. She caught my eye and gave me a knowing, soft smile. She mistakenly thinks we are an item. I would so much like that to be so. I have little doubt that he is a womaniser. He is easy and warm with women. Being so handsome helps, certainly he could have most of the women I see looking at him when he is running in the park. I realised, that includes me. Womaniser or not I desperately want to experience him, even if only for a short time. It is now so long since John left, since I last held and kissed a man. I want him even if only briefly before he moves on. I thought to myself, "stop being sentimental Rebecca, you need a good screw as well."

Toby broke the spell, he nuzzled against my leg. I rubbed his head and said, 'Toby you are my big, bold saviour. Luke only took on the little one.' I neglected to add, "the dangerous one." 'Big, brave Toby felled the big one.' Looking back up at Luke I asked, 'I thought that you said he is only a big softie?'

'I thought that he was. I have never before seen him do anything such as he did tonight.' Luke paused thoughtfully then added, 'actually you do need to thank him. It is because of him that we found you.' I quizzically raised my eyebrows. 'Whenever you are around Toby seeks you out. He obviously thinks you are lovely.' There was a pregnant pause which seemed to suggest that Toby was not the only one. 'Sam and I were intending to walk alongside the river. We would not have seen you. When we arrived at the turn off leading up to here Toby set off along it as if on a mission. Intrigued we followed. As we came over the crest I saw a woman, you, being attacked before he did as he is lower than me. I realised that Toby had detected your scent. I started running. Initially he thought it was a game and ran alongside but as soon as he saw you he flashed past me and launched himself at the one furthest from him but nearer to you. It was him who gave me the idea to charge the other and he also gave me the opportunity by distracting him. I would probably have a knife in my stomach now if not for Toby.' I thought "that is quite possibly true. I gave Toby a big hug.

We looked up as we saw more flashing blue lights in the trees. Neither of us can see over the memorial wall from here, that is only possible from below by the river, I presume it is the ambulance arriving. After the distraction Luke faced me and turning those eyes on me said, 'if I am your saviour then I judge you owe me a favour in return.'

Intrigued and suspicious of what I am letting myself in for I reluctantly replied, 'I suppose so, go on.'

'In return I want you to do me the honour of allowing me to buy you dinner.'

My head spun. Recovering I countered with, 'should I

not be the one buying you dinner?'

'Absolutely not.'

I feigned reluctance, 'OK, if you insist. When?'

'Now.'

My jaw dropped. I can't take any more surprises tonight.

He saw me looking taken aback and said, 'I was going to work on a lecture tonight. Not only will I not be able to concentrate, but after this evening's events I feel a great need to get to know you. Clearly you are a woman of many talents. I want to hear about them. Whatever you had planned I guess that even with your sang-froid you will not be able to concentrate either. So I presume that you are free tonight as well.'

Thinking that I suppose I can make a bit of an effort and drag myself away from a book and the current Netflix series I said, 'yes. I would very much like to join you for dinner tonight.'

He beamed. 'Do you know Porcini in William Street?' Shit, do I know it? Yes Luke, I have walked past. I have looked in at the white linen and cut glass on the tables. Yes I have stood between the gas lanterns outside and read the menu noting that as there are no prices on it I probably cannot afford the Michelin starred food.

'I have seen it but I have not been in. It looks lovely.' Crap, it looks stupendous.

'Hold on.' He took out his smart-phone, Googled the restaurant, called them and arranged a table for eight 'o' clock. All this took but seconds. 'Good, all done. Shall I collect you at seven thirty, where do you live?' I pointed up the slope. 'You were attacked almost outside your house?' He looks astonished. I nodded yes.

'Thanks for the offer but as you may guess I want to shower and change.' I would want to look my best for Luke but I doubt that I will be allowed in other than in expensive designer clothes. 'Time will be tight. I can easily stroll over to there.' I pointed across the river; it is less than five hundred yards to the restaurant. 'I think that I will be safe for such a journey.'

He smiled seeing that he is beaten. Whispering, 'see you at eight, come on Toby,' he walked in the direction of his house. I floated past my colleagues towards my home and the shower. I already knew exactly what I am going to wear. Sally gave me a sly wink as I went by. Too many sly winks tonight and somehow they all seem to involve me. I feel out of control. Thank god, it is about time.

CHAPTER 11:
REBECCA, ROLE PLAY

I have been out to dinner only twice since being in this elegant city. Each time it has been with a devastatingly handsome, charming, intelligent man, taking me to a chic gastronomic paradise. Either I am doing something very right, I am here; or, very wrong, it is only twice. One thing I am definitely failing at, I have yet to be laid. I grimaced at my internal attempt at coarse humour. I am not good at hiding the truth from myself. I have been lonely for nearly two years.

My heart is pounding as I step between the elegant gas sconces, their flames warm against the cold of the night. With agonising anticipation I grasp the slim brass handle of the discrete black door. For the first time in months, probably years, I feel nervous. The unexpected dinner and the elegant restaurant remind me of the debacle with Marcus. It is not just because I am out of practice in the dating game and that the last occasion ended so badly. Also, I want Luke so much.

Stepping through I found myself in a lobby, there are potted miniature palms to either side, dimly but artfully lit. Double doors are in front of me completing a spacious ante room. It is cleverly designed. Above the palms and in the top half of the doors there are small glass panels set into the mahogany frame. It enables whoever is entering and the diners already present to inspect each other without being intrusive. There seems to be no more than eight, intimate, round tables. They are looking even more elegant from here than I previously thought when I have peeked through the window in the past. In addition to the white linen, crystal glasses and a single white rose, there is a solitary candle in the centre of each. The wood panelling on the walls has a gilt mirror set into it behind each table. Again so discrete, whoever is sitting facing the wall is able to surreptitiously look around the restaurant. It is so clever; you can come here to be seen and to look without being seen to be looking or to appear to be on show. There is another dining room through an arch in front of these doors, two medium sized rooms rather than a barn. This place may have a Michelin Star and foodies may be attracted by that. It is also unbelievably romantic.

The maître de has spotted me and is already barrelling towards the inner door. Obviously here one is not allowed to open doors oneself. I spotted Luke to my left. He is deep in animated conversation with an older woman on the next table. He has not seen me. It is the first time I have seen him other than in casual dress and not all in black. He is not good looking; he is knee-tremblingly striking. His glowing black hair is falling to the shoulders of his charcoal linen suit. His light olive skin is offset by a crisp, white, open neck shirt. Perfect.

My heart gave another flutter. This time there was a frisson of concern in addition to the other, unexpected, roiling emotions. I hope that Luke being dressed so similarly to how Marcus had been is not portentous. I brushed away the stupid suspicion.

The maître de opened the inner door with a flourish. Detecting the movement Luke looked up, spotted me and stood with a wide smile. The woman he had been speaking to turned with a welcoming smile. As soon as she saw me she froze, it immediately became a scowl. She turned to look at

Luke, I can no longer see her face but it is almost certainly with a glare. Then she quickly spun back to speak in hushed tones to the older man opposite her. He then looked at me and frowned. Luke is oblivious, he is looking at me. I am looking at him. I don't give a damn what is rattling the old bat's cage, electricity is surging between us.

I jumped as the maître de asked for my hat and coat. I had completely forgotten that he is next to me. I took off what Julia calls my "Anna Karenina" hat and shook out my hair. I glanced to the mirror to check it. Curls can be handy when wearing a hat. I had only gently put it on when I left, no "hat hair" has developed. It still looks good. Though doing that brief shake may have looked so casual surely most women in the room will realise that I have spent half an hour with a brush before leaving.

I started to untie the belt of my long, black, heavy woollen coat and undo the buttons. It is buttoned to the neck. What I have on underneath may be hot but it is not warm, it is cold outside. I had not wanted to arrive looking blue, hence the hat, coat and knee high leather boots. I slipped off my coat and the maître de passed it to a flunky waiting with outstretched arms.

Luke stepped around the table. In my vertiginous heels I am nearly as tall as him. He took my elbows and looked at me intently. He kissed me lightly on the cheek and whispered in my ear, 'you look absolutely stunning.' I realised that it is the first time that he has seen me wearing something other than a tracksuit. My dress is simple, a khaki, puff sleeve, midi dress with a crew collar, button front and tie belt. I have a solitary, plain, gold bangle on one wrist and a discrete, short, gold chain around my neck. Mum always taught both of her daughters, "KISS and get kissed." KISS; "Keep It Simple, Stupid," her advice has always paid off. Thanks Mum, her words had flowed through to me.

Before I could respond to Luke's compliment, not in the same words but I wanted to say something similar to him, he gave me a little push and abruptly said, 'for god's sake sit down, now, quickly.' I can see he is grinning. With a suggestion of a smile I did as suggested, ruefully raising my eyebrow at the same time. He received both messages loud and clear, "instruct me at your peril," and "what the hell is going on." In truth I am not at all perturbed by being told to sit. I can see that it is a game. 'Sorry to be blunt. If you look in the mirror behind me you will see the need for urgency.' I glanced up. At the table opposite him, behind me, there is a middle aged couple. He is portly, she is drab. There is however a quiet row taking place. She is the only one speaking. He is looking down shamefaced. I can hear her whisper in a savage tone but unfortunately I cannot hear what is being said.

I asked Luke, 'what on earth is going on?'

He replied, 'when you took off your coat he stared at your gorgeous bum. He kept on staring. He missed the evil eye from her. Now he is paying the price.'

I half choked suppressing a laugh. At this the old bat at the next table, the one who had given me a dirty look on my way in, tutted and frowned. I cannot see why she has taken against me. Then I realised what I have let pass. I looked sharply up at Luke with a mock glare and snapped, 'what do you mean, "gorgeous bum." Firstly you are being very rude so early on a first date, making such a personal and impertinent comment. Secondly, as I am sitting down, how can you tell?'

He threw his head back and softly laughed, 'surely you do not expect me to believe that is what you think. You know full well that I admire your perfect derriere, indeed all of you barely hidden by the close fitting track suits that I have seen you in. When we are running in the park I find that I do not have to overstretch my imagination. Why do you think

I allow you to overtake me? It is so I can appreciate you at leisure.'

'What, what, you think that you allow me to overtake. There is no way you could even keep up with me let alone pass. You are full of ....' Thankfully the waiter appeared and interrupted us as I realised that what I had been on the verge of saying should, perhaps, not be said in here. I cannot think of any other way to finish the sentence so I left it half way through, hanging. He set a fizzing glass of something rose coloured, with blackcurrants floating on top, in front of each of us. I hope it is what I think it is.

Luke said, 'I hope that you do not mind but I took the liberty of ordering a Kir Royale for each of us as an aperitif.' Don't mind, it is only my favourite drink.

'I do rather enjoy Kir Royale. It may even go a little way to redeem your awful comments.' I am grinning too much for this to have any serious intent.

He smiled, this time softly. He reached forward and touched his glass to mine saying, 'sorry, it was only my daft way of saying that you look absolutely beautiful. Thank you for joining me here.' He touched glasses again and said, 'to us.'

Before I could interpret the meaning of this the old woman next to us briskly stood up. They are leaving. As she swept past she gave Luke a look of strong disapproval and then a contemptuous one to me. At the door she turned for a final censorious glare. Unfortunately I caught sight of this in the mirror as I was taking a sip of the champagne. In trying to suppress a snigger I snorted, not the most elegant action. Thankfully I saw that Luke has as well. Whilst we wiped our chins and noses with our napkins I asked, 'what has happened with her. When I came in you were talking in a very friendly, animated fashion. She took one look at me and everything changed.'

'A few weeks ago Sam and I were in the park and they spoke to us. We have seen them there before, a few times. Previously we have simply been polite, we have said something bland, such as "nice day," in passing. That last time they stopped and chatted. It was clear that they thought that Sam and I are a couple. This often happens, as it did with Julian when we first met. When she saw you walk in she probably thought that I am being a naughty boy. She obviously likes Sam and doesn't approve of me being with a floozy, or a high end escort.'

He fixed me with an innocent "who me" look. I reached for the dinner knife in my place setting and he changed his look to mock horror. Then he laughed again, softly held my hand with the knife in it, leaned across and whispered, 'I can see than I am very much going to enjoy this evening. My companion is not only a beautiful, elegant professional; she is also easy to wind up.'

Again we laughed together; already we seem to be doing a lot of that. He can tell that not only am I flattered and pleased but also that I enjoy being teased. In my family, especially with Julia, that is a necessary skill. I said in a stage whisper, hoping that the people at the next table, on the opposite side from where the oldies had vacated, would hear, 'I hope to have a good evening as well but if you continue in that vein you do realise that I will kill you. You have seen first-hand that I am more than capable of that.'

They had heard. I think they had also spotted me reach for the knife earlier. They looked disconcerted until they saw Luke smiling. He raised his glass to them and said, 'don't worry. It is unlikely as Rebecca has taken her medication tonight.' Then turning to me with an expression of mock fear he said, 'you have haven't you?'

They laughed, toasted us back, and asked if I could keep any blood to a minimum so that they can continue to enjoy their dinner. The waiter had heard the exchange and was joining in the merriment. During this chatter I spotted two old maids on the far side of the couple, dressed to kill, whispering together with faded narrow lips and wooden expressions. Judging from their darting glances we are entertaining them as well. I am beginning to realise that I am not only already enjoying the evening, it is going to be most unusual as well.

We ordered, enjoyed the food and softly conversed. The initial frivolity changed into a gentle discussion. Luke is superb company. I came in here only an hour ago not really knowing him. He is interesting, knowledgeable and self-effacing. He has asked about my life and my family. He has gently probed without being intrusive. He is also very open; when I have asked about him he has not only answered with ease he has expanded beyond what I asked, volunteering further information. After such a short time I feel as if I already know him well. I am warming to him more and more; I can see that he feels the same. Our initial teasing has morphed into an amiable closeness. More, I intuit that we are drawn together by a sense of an unresolved past that be both carry. I guess his is related to the attack on Samantha. He is so empathic he probably divines mine.

When we eating I had luxuriated in the elegance of this restaurant. The interior is slightly baroque. There is a maroon wallpaper with a delicate pattern. The pillars and other features are picked out in gold leaf. Paradoxically the fact that it is a little old and faded makes it look even more sumptuous. The waiters had the appearance of being at a ballroom dance. They wore black uniforms with starched white shirts. Their shiny patent leather shoes flashed as they stepped sideways and back, turning on the spot, simultaneously balancing huge silver trays laden with fragrant dishes.

The waiter cleared the remnants of our main course. My duck breast with roasted figs and crispy kale was to die for. Having started with beetroot cured salmon accompanied by an avocado puree I have already eaten double what I normally consume in an evening. I said to Luke that though the food is delicious as I have already over eaten I simply cannot eat any desert. I told him that I was happy for him to carry on and order. He replied that he could not manage a pudding either.

Luke became still and thoughtful, he appeared to be preparing to say something momentous. Finally, somewhat abashedly he asked, 'we could have a coffee and a digestif here or we could stroll back to my house and relax with a nightcap there. Which would you prefer?'

I felt a warm glow of anticipation. It is not my usual practice to return home with a man on the first date. That is in my wide experience of first or any other sort of date in the last two years. The opening night debacle with Marcus had not been the fault of either of us and it was, in reality, then our second date. Having thought about it afterwards I am sure that his wife had set him up. I should not allow that to influence me. On one hand I have only got to know Luke properly this evening. On the other hand I feel that I already know him better than other people that I have been with for weeks. Yet more echoes of the evening with Marcus came back to me.

I like Luke, I trust him. I feel sure that if I go to his home he will ask to make love with me. I am also sure that he will ask. He will not assume or insist. I am even more sure that I will say "yes."

We held each other's gaze, his is uncertain, hoping not pressurising. He must be wondering why I am taking so long to respond. He does not know of the immense weight of the last time which is slowing my decision.

Eventually I replied. Why had it taken me so long? I knew before I came into the restaurant exactly what I was hoping for, what I would say. 'Thank you for bringing me here Luke. It has been wonderful. Though it is so comfortable and peaceful in here.....,' I reached across the table and placed my hand on top of his. I looked softly into his eyes. I whispered; it came out hoarsely, 'it would be good after today's dramatic events to unwind in private. Let's go back to your house.'

He gently smiled, squeezed my hand and without saying a word slipped away to pay the bill and to collect our coats.

Within seconds of my few words, so few but carrying so much promise, we are stepping out into the still cold night. The narrow, cobbled street is empty. The occasional street light fixed to the sides of the boutiques and solicitors' offices are losing the battle against the swirling dark. The sounds of revellers in the High Street carried up but they are muted by the time they reach us. We turned away from them towards another narrow street, leading to an even smaller passageway that I know leads on, behind and parallel to the High Street, to our destination, Luke's house. As we stepped away from the gas lights outside the restaurant Luke stopped, turned towards me, standing so very close he gently put his gloved hands on my shoulders. 'Rebecca, may I kiss you?'

In response I leaned forward. Even in my heels I still have to stretch up a little. It is difficult to say who kissed who but we kissed. It is our first proper kiss; I so hope that it is not our last. Though we only left Porcini's a few moments ago already our noses and lips are cold as they touch. In our hats, gloves and heavy coats all I can feel is the bulk of him pressed against me. His hands are still on my shoulders holding me tight against him. Our cool lips met and I felt a warmth flow through me, it is not from my winter clothing. Our touching cold lips became a warm contact, then an intense hot kiss. I doubt that we would have let go for hours if were it not that we heard the restaurant door open. We remained to the side, unseen in the shadow, as a couple stepped out. Quietly, reluctantly, we broke the kiss and started to walk towards his house. I hope towards our next kiss. As we made our way across the uneven cobbles he held my arm. It is clear from the way he is gripping it that it is not a chivalrous support. He knows full well from how I am walking that the cobbles are not difficult for me, even in these heels. He is making it clear that he simply wants to hold my arm. I pulled him yet closer.

Neither of us spoke, our breath billowed in front as we made our way along the increasingly narrow and gloomy passageways. At times we were forced to duck beneath low hanging branches growing over the old stone walls of the cottages, their walled back gardens lining the passage. Abruptly we stepped out into the road, opposite the side of the church on the square where Luke lives. It is the same road that I walk up every morning as I make my way to the station; the very road that I will walk along in eleven hours' time when I make my way to the nine o'clock briefing.

We turned left and continued for the hundred or so meters to enter the square. I have been along this road so many times. I have walked the same passageway that we have just left several times previously. Never before have I seen the square as it is now; nor have I felt as I do at present as we emerge. It is enchanting. The sparse street lighting is augmented by lights over the front doors of the pastel painted cottages. The statue in the centre is bathed in white from its own floodlight that makes the beautiful girl appear even more virginal. Luke's house is in the far corner from us, a little larger, a little elevated; it seems to be inviting me to approach.

When I have had to go to the station at night I have seen the square so many times yet I have never before seen the square as it appears now. This is not solely due to the lighting. I have also transformed. It is my appreciation that is complimenting what I see. This time though it is freezing I feel as if my skin is on fire; that my insides are melting; that the square is paved with heated flags. My heart is thumping so hard, surely he can hear it. This is the second time in one evening that it has pounded.

We walked on across the green. The house seemed to be smiling at me, knowing why I am coming and welcoming me.

After the cold of the walk the heat in Luke's house hit us as we entered. He took my coat. Whilst he was hanging it up I slipped off my hat, gloves and boots. I asked, 'where is the loo?' He smiled and said that he had to go as well. We are both feeling the effects of half a bottle of wine and two glasses of sparkling water each, followed by a cold walk. He pointed me to one next to the stairs and as he ran upstairs he said that we should meet in the sitting room. Then, teasingly, over his shoulder, he added, you probably remember where that is, it is the one where you interrogated me.

Before leaving the loo I checked myself in the mirror and ran a brush through my hair. I seem to be glowing. I do not think that it is only due to the wine.

Luke was already in the sitting room as I entered. He had brought in a tray with two brandy glasses and an expensive looking bottle next to them. I crossed the room and stood close to him. Looking at me he said, 'I have a fine cognac here or if you prefer I also have an excellent malt.' He paused, looked intently at me and asked, no, more stated than asked, 'I don't think that you want a drink, do you.' I shook my head. In addition to the still thumping heart I now had a lump in my throat and I dared not speak, it would be a croak. For the second time this evening he put his hands on my shoulders. I desperately want it to lead to the same as it had before. Now looking even more serious, almost troubled, he asked, 'may I kiss you?'

We kissed softly. Then he gently pulled me toward him and we kissed deeply. He put his hand through my hair at the back of my head and held me as he continued to kiss me. He did not pull me towards him or restrain me in any fashion, he simply held me tenderly as we kissed. I wrapped my arms around him. I was the one who pulled. I held him tight against me. I am the one not wanting him to slip away. He seemed reluctant to hold me close, he still held me gently. I could have easily pulled away from him, had I wanted to. I did not. I stayed in his arms.

Finally we stopped kissing. We still held each other, we stood with our foreheads touching, breathing in each other's breath. He ran his hands slowly down my back. He stopped just above my bum. In my mind I shrieked "don't stop." He spoke again, softly again, 'as I said before, you have a lovely bum. I have admired it every time that you have run past me. I so very much want to touch it, may I slide my hands down.'

'I would like that a great deal.' He gently held my buttocks and we kissed again. As we stopped I said, 'you are being very chivalrous.'

'I don't want to appear presumptuous or pushy. I want to check that you agree with what I so desperately want to do.'

'Well, I have reason to know what that may be. To make it easier for you let me say that I agree to what you want, I consent.'

'But you don't know what I want.'

'I know that it is one of two things. Either you want to

make love to me or I need to arrest you.'

He pulled a little away from me and looked at me, amused and intrigued, 'arrest me? What for?'

'Possession.'

'Possession of what?'

He looks genuinely uncertain. I moved my hands to his collar and gave him a playful tug and a quick kiss on the lips. 'A firearm of course.' He now looks totally bemused. 'From your expression I gather that you have not heard the quip that Mae West is supposed to have made.' He shook his head. 'Is that a gun in your pocket or are you just pleased to see me?'

He laughed out loud, whilst apologising he twisted his hips so that his erection is no longer digging into my hip. I quickly moved my hands to his belt and pulled him back around so that he is pressing into me again. I raised my hips and rubbed my groin against his hardness. The pleasure coursed through me, I nearly cried out. He did, he gave a moan of delight. On hearing his soft groan I pressed myself against him again, this time as the thrill went through me I could not hold back and something like a sob of pleasure came from me. Whilst still holding myself against him I pulled his head down, I kissed him on the side of his neck and whispered into his ear, 'I consent.'

He put his hands back to my shoulders and pushed a little. We tried to keep kissing whilst separating a tiny amount and tugging at each other's buttons. It was impossible. Finally we parted a little more. He held my wrist and said, 'let's go somewhere more comfortable.' He guided me out of the room and up the stairs. We stepped into his bedroom. I had expected something similar to his sitting room. I am completely wrong, surprised and impressed. His sitting room is dark panelled and full of treasures, almost cluttered. This is white and minimalist. There is a king size brass bed with white linen, the walls are a soft off white, the curtains and carpets a pure white. It is a gorgeous place to break my year of enforced celibacy, and a gorgeous, considerate man to do it with.

Luke tossed his jacket to the side and then started expertly unbuttoning the front of my dress. When he had exactly the minimum required undone he lifted my dress over my head. I thought, "as I suspected, a womaniser. I don't care, I am going to enjoy this." I stood in front of him in my bra, panties and a single gold bangle, nothing else. That is nothing else other than a soft, expectant smile.

He held me at arms' length and slowly, deliberately looked me up and down. I cannot remember when, indeed if, a man last looked at me in this provocative, appreciative manner. He ran his index finger lightly down my snake tattoo stopping at the edge of my knickers. Through another kiss he murmured in my ear, 'let's play snakes and ladders soon. I am sure that it is down the snakes.' I felt my abdomen tense at his touch and his suggestion.

He pulled away and looked at me again as he ran his finger up the curving back to its mouth on my breast. 'I did not expect any tattoo and certainly not one such as this. It is very elegant and extremely erotic.' I cannot speak. Then he put his left hand on my shoulder and started running his right one down the other side. He continued looking at me, every inch of me. He paused a little when he saw the small round scar under the left side of my ribcage. He gently caressed it. He did not ask what had caused it. From its shape it must be obvious but he did not comment on something so unusual.

He quietly and simply stated again, 'you are very beautiful.'

We kissed again and as we did I unbuttoned his shirt

and took it off him. He unbuckled his belt and removed his trousers, boxers and socks in one fluid movement. I saw him fully naked for the first time. He is also beautiful. He is slim, not heavily muscled but he is in excellent shape with each muscle clearly defined. He has wide square shoulders, so it was not just the cut of his jacket, he really does look like that. There is a little dark hair on his chest running in a line down his abdomen. His erection, now freed of the confines of his trousers, is again pressing into my stomach.

He again quickly and again expertly slipped off my bra and panties. Again I thought, "womaniser." I don't care. I think it will be for more than tonight but, even so, if I can only have him for a short while I still want him. I responded by holding the sides of his head between my hands and pressing our lips together whilst rubbing myself against his cock. He had his hands on my bum, lifting me up to him, moving his cock between my thighs. I felt myself pouring. I want him in me so desperately.

We had slowed a little, still kissing and caressing. There is an urgency between us but we are also taking time to enjoy this first experience together. He leaned to the side and pulled back the duvet. He half lifted me as I stepped back to lie on the bed. He lay next to me but left the duvet pulled down so, as he propped himself on one elbow, he could continue looking me up and down. He obviously likes what he can see. I deliberately, and I hoped provocatively, mirrored him, scrutinising him. I also enjoyed what I saw.

After a few seconds of gentle, slow, kissing he moved on top of me. I parted my knees so that he can lie between my legs. We are pressed together but he has all of his weight. He is on top of me but not lying on me. I wriggled my back to position myself ready for him to enter me and I started to move my legs to wrap them around him as he did so. I put my arms around his neck and pulled his face next to mine as

I nuzzled his ear. I held my breath and nearly exploded with anticipation as the tip of him pressed against my lips. He slid his hand down to guide himself in.

Almost instantly his erection subsided. He groaned in anguish. He played with himself a little trying to make himself hard but to no avail. I put my hand down to help but he gently took my wrist whilst shaking his head saying that it would not work.

He rolled to the side and lay next to me with his face down so I cannot see his expression. His posture is of total defeat. After a short while, still not facing me he whispered, 'I am so sorry. Please be certain that it is nothing to do with you. You look so beautiful and desirable. More importantly I feel that we are easy together, I have enjoyed being with you. I want you so very much. It is all me. I am sorry, very sorry.' He sounded hurt, ashamed and defeated.

I raised myself on one elbow and put my arm across his shoulders. I kissed him on the back of his head and whispered in his ear. 'Luke, there is nothing to apologise for. It has hardly been an average day conducive of sexual performance. You have been involved in a knife fight. I guess that was a first for you.' I paused as he nodded "yes." 'Also we have had a few drinks and it is the first time which is stressful for both of us. I understand. It does not matter. I am sure it will happen soon.'

For what felt like an age he remained completely motionless. Then he turned on to his side facing me. His face is sad but determined. He has something big to say.

'Thank you for your understanding and kindness. Unfortunately you are wrong. It is far more than that.' He hesitated and looked at me. I have no idea what is coming but I can see that it is not easy for him to say. I am intrigued as to what he is going to say. I am flattered that he is clearly going to open up to me. 'I have not made love with a woman for more than two years.' Then with a quick smile he added, 'with any one that is, not with a man either. I am, by the way, completely straight. My last time was in fact September two years ago, two years and six months to be pedantic.' My first thought was, "holy shit, that is exactly the same as me." My thought second was, " so much for my detective skills, thinking that he is a womaniser. I corrected myself, he probably is but not active at present."

He cleared his throat and looked at me. I made what I hope is a kindly "go on, I am listening" expression. 'Anyway, the last time I made love to a woman was at exactly the same time as Samantha was being beaten with a cricket bat.' I felt my eyes widen, "bloody hell." 'I feel so guilty not being there to help her. I knew that things were bad for her but I did not know that Robin, her ex, sorry, she has already told you that. I did not know that he was capable of such violence.' I said nothing. I can see that he is not finished. 'It is not the guilt. I know that feeling guilty is not rational. I do still feel guilty but that is not the main problem.' He rolled on to his back and stared at the ceiling. For a while he could not continue. I felt my heart go out to this man. I gave him a squeeze and kissed his shoulder again. He turned to look at me with a weak, grateful smile that broke my heart.

After a long silence he slowly restarted, his voice redolent with uncertainty. 'I have suspected from then that I am unable to make love to a woman again, any woman, including one as desirable as you. I remember when we first met you telling me that your original qualification and work was in psychology, perhaps you will understand my distorted obsessions.'

I could not bear to hear any more yet I am hanging on every word. I am still on my back in the position that I had taken preparing for him to enter me. I slid my feet down and now coyly crossed my ankles. I am sure that with what he is telling me he would prefer me not to be in a position to make love.

'I am fearful that I may become violent. I have never hit a woman, I have never thought of or fantasised about hitting a woman. I could not be with any woman that I did not consider an equal; that I did not respect.

Yet I fear it.

What if I were to do the same? I feel that if I were to lie on top of a woman, if I were to attempt to penetrate her, then that may appear to be violence. I fear that I may not have obtained her full consent. I feared that because of these thoughts I would be unable to make love. Here we are. I was, unfortunately, quite correct.'

Again he stopped for a while.

'Sam is the only other person in the world who knows this. When she saw how attracted I am to you, after a while, after an initial hesitation that is.' He tailed off again. What hesitation I thought? I knew that she was antagonistic to me from the start, only relenting very recently. There is more to what he is now saying but that can wait for another day. That is assuming there is another day. 'After her initial hesitation which came about because of the way we first met,' I still think there is more he is holding back, 'she changed her mind. She felt that as you are clearly so confident, so mentally, and now we know physically, strong; that I would not have these fears. After what we saw this afternoon, as she was leaving she gave me a "told you so" look.' So that is what the wink was, 'I thought that with you I would not feel the same. That what I had anticipated would not happen.

Well, I was wrong.

I am sorry to have dragged you into my stupidity. I know that I could not attack you. I know that not only can I not because of who I am, but also, if I even thought about it you would probably kick me in the balls or worse. Even so, I am sure I don't have to tell you, the gremlin in the subconscious wins.' He slumped back, spent. He lay on his back with his eyes closed, his face contorted with despondency.

I closed my eyes in horror and disbelief at what he has told me, his pain. After only one meal together he has opened up to me and bared his soul. He must feel the same about me as I do about him. Then another realisation hit me. He said this happened September two years ago. What a month that was. Samantha was being beaten, Julian's Lucy died and John left me.

I snuggled alongside him and put my arm across and my head on his chest. I said, 'thank you for being so candid. Let me think about it for a while.' I moved my head off his chest and put it on the crisp, white sheet. I did not want him to feel my tears fall on to his skin.

As I lay there an idea flashed into my mind. It will not go away. It is idiotic, it is dangerous. I do not have the experience to pull it off. I told myself to stop being stupid. I could make myself look ridiculous but that will pale into insignificance alongside the harm that I could do to him. If it goes wrong I could reinforce his fears, fire up his gremlin. I don't have any truck with that pseudo-scientific crap anyway. On the other hand I have to do something and I can't think of anything else. He is such a wonderful man. This cannot go on. If I leave now without making love with him then he may well be finished for life.

I forced my expression into the last thing that I felt like being, the bad cop in an interview. Without saying anything I rolled over and knelt across his chest. He looked pleadingly up at me, he started to speak, I am sure to say something like "no don't. I can't." I snarled in his face, 'shut up. Not a word.' He looked back in astonishment and not a little concern.

With my right hand I roughly grabbed his left wrist and jerked it hard, straight up above his head, deliberately hurting him a little and making him grimace. I held it firmly there and then did the same with my left to his right. I changed my grip and I held both of his wrists with my left hand, pinning his arms to the bed. Then I ran my right hand through his long wavy hair. I suddenly yanked his hair back bringing his chin up; at the same time I pulled his head forward towards me. As he gasped I roughly covered his mouth with mine and kissed him hard, pushing my lips on to his, forcing my tongue into his mouth. I pressed down violently through the kiss. He tried to speak through this. To stop him talking I bit his lower lip. He winced. I can taste blood. I have bitten him much harder than I had intended to.

He tried to move his wrists, twisting his arms in an attempt to free them. Yet again he attempted to speak. Keeping my mouth hard on his I brought up my leg and kneed him in the ribs. Lifting my head back, breaking the brutal kiss, if in fact it can have even been called a kiss, I looked into his wide eyes. 'Don't speak and don't move.' His pupils dilated in astonishment, he looks totally perplexed by what is happening. That makes two of us but at least I know what is coming next. He wriggled his legs and hips, trying to slide from under me. I whacked him in the shin with my heel. 'I said don't move.'

Finally giving in his body softened as he lay back but he continued to stare at me, now with intrigue as well as continuing alarm. I eased my grip on his wrists and hair, only a little, I am still in total control. Then I kissed him again, this time softly. I stopped pulling his hair. I cupped the back of his head holding him against me. I felt myself soften and melt. He felt it as well and he wriggled his legs. Again I struck his shin with my heel saying through the kiss, this time softly, 'don't move unless I say to. I am going to tell you what I want. I am not going to ask you. You will do what I say or you will get kicked and kneed.' I lay across him, my breasts on his chest, my legs spread on either side of his stomach. He must be able to feel how wet I am against his abdomen.

Still holding his arms and hair I turned his head to one side then the other, now gently. As I did so I kissed and licked his ears, neck and throat. He groaned. I gave him a little warning jab in the chest with my elbow, only softly, but he got the message. He then again lay quiet as I smothered him. I am becoming consumed with desire, I am fighting with myself. I must keep quiet. He must not guess that I am beginning to lose control.

Sliding my left hand down to his elbow I simultaneously slide the other from his hair to his other elbow and brought up my knees. I am now on all fours pinning his elbows above his head with my hands and with my knees gripping his chest. I twisted to the left so that my right breast came to be directly in front of his face. 'Kiss my breast.' He did. Holding his body still he kissed my breast, then my nipple. Finally he took my nipple in his mouth and gently sucked. Now I bit my own lip, I had to stop myself screaming with pleasure. He must be feeling the vibrations coursing through me. I turned to the right and told him to do the same with my left breast.

Within seconds all I can think is that I can wait no longer. Reluctantly, as it took my nipple out of his mouth, I moved down. I took my hands from his elbows to his shoulders so that I can slide down but I kept up the upward pressure, his arms still fixed away from me. Now I stretched and then slid my groin down his abdomen. As I did my mouth came level with his. I cannot look in his eyes. I nuzzled his chin to the side and kissed his ear as my thighs slid across his stomach. We both tensed and held our breath. He must know but I am uncertain what I will find. Will I have made him erect?

If, as I desperately hope, he has regained his erection then I expect it to be lying on and across his lower abdomen. As I continued to slide downwards and could not feel anything I initially became disappointed, then concerned, then as I slipped lower and lower I started to panic. If with this role playing I have not made him hard then I will look a fool. Worse, much worse, I will have compounded his erectile problem.

Then, suddenly, with a delicious shock that thrilled me. I found it, not with my thigh but with my pussy. He does not simply have an erection, he is rock hard. It is not lying up on his abdomen. I have not felt it before because it is pointing straight out. I gasped and he groaned as my downward slide came to a delicious stop with me resting against him, feeling him solid between the top of my thighs.

Still holding his shoulders, even though he is now rigidly still, I raised my hips and lifted myself over him. Then I pressed down on the other side so that my lips pushed against the underside of his cock, forcing it up and back against his abdomen, where I had initially expected to find it. With my lips still thrusting down and squeezing him, his erection pushing back up against me, I slid up and down the underneath of his shaft, wetting him whilst he is still outside me. He moaned again but with me still pressing his shoulders he did not, could not, move at all. I am the only one in motion, sliding against him. I bit my lip to stifle a scream of delight. However I still revealed what I am feeling by arching my back and him then being able to see my face, contorted with ecstasy, and my nipples, hard and still moist from his lips. We then looked into each other's eyes with naked desire.

I slid up to the tip of his cock. I raised my hips more

so that I am directly over him. I pushed down with my hips and took him in me, looking down, watching him slide in. He groaned again, louder. I let out something between a cry and a shriek.

Play acting is over.

I released his shoulders, placed my hands on the pillow, pushed myself up further so that I am now kneeling astride him and looked back into his eyes. They are open, boring into me, passionate and excited. He brought his hands down from above his head and put them behind mine pulling me into an intense kiss. At the same time started returning my thrusts. He let my head go, slightly pushed me away so that he can look into my eyes again. He did not speak, his expression said it all. His hands slid down my back slowly. Even with the thrusting of our hips I still felt his warm, strong hands on me, sliding over my shoulders, down my side and on to my bum. Then with us rhythmically, gently, moving together he held my buttocks. As we pushed together he pressed on my bum so that our contact was increased. As we moved apart he released and stroked me.

Very quickly the sensations intensified. I am overwhelmed, I cannot hold back any longer. I moaned, softly then nearly a shout, as my fanny started contracting of its own accord. An orgasm pulsated through me. As I gripped him inside me his back arched up, his hands gripped my bum harder and he loudly groaned as he shuddered inside me.

Afterwards neither of us moved for an age. He is on his back, his hands resting on my bum. I am sprawled across him, my full weight pressing down, my hands behind his head, my head lying on his chest, my thighs limp on his hips. After a while I said, 'I must be squashing you.'

'You are not exactly heavy. Even if you were I would not want you to move for a long, long while.' He moved his hands up and put his arms around my back. I wanted to lift up my head and kiss him but I seemed incapable of any movement. After a long pause he said, 'that was a Ferrari.'

I know I am being teased and I took the bait, 'OK, surprise me, what does that mean?'

'Very fast, very powerful and very beautiful; the reason that you have not heard it before is that I have just made it up. It seemed a good idea until I said it.' We shook a little in each other's arms laughing silently. I thought, " no Luke, that is not your best quip but I do like the sentiment." He paused further and then said softly, with a hint of regret, 'after a two year hiatus it is difficult to remember but I cannot think of having made love so intensely before.'

'Can I ask you something that sounds odd, I will explain?' He nodded. 'When exactly did you last make love, I know you said September just over two years ago, what date?'

He turned to look at me intrigued. 'That's easy. Firstly it was the day Sam was attacked. I am not going to forget that. Also it was September the eleventh, the 9/11 anniversary. I can hardly forget that either.'

'So, I beat you by two days. For me it was September the ninth, I win. I have been celibate for longer than you. Or should that be I lose?' His look of intrigue turned to astonishment. I felt that as he has been so openly with me that I should reciprocate. 'I was in love with a married man. I knew that he was married.He had separated before our relationship started, in fact before I met him. We fell in love, we moved in together. A week later his oldest child, then three, became ill. He went home and never came back. I was heartbroken and I thought that I would never recover.' The words came out without me being sure what they meant. They imply that I have now recovered. If I have then it was tonight. What has happened has healed us both, possibly, hopefully.

He looked thoughtful and finally said, 'so there is something good about me after all. I am not married.' I shook with silent laughter. I finally managed to persuade my limbs to move. I raised myself, kissed him and rolled to lie next to him. He continued, 'so this afternoon I find out that you are a Samurai Warrior. This evening I find out that you are a Dominatrix. Now I find out that you fell in love with a fool, let's face it he must be to leave you. What more is there to come?'

I playfully kicked him, 'I am not a Dominatrix.'

'You could have fooled me. Look at my poor lip.' We turned to each other lying side by side looking deep into the other's eyes. His lip is actually quite swollen. 'I am teasing, as you full well know. Now tell me what has just happened, what you did. Something I have thought about and feared for two years came true and you turned it around and cured it in ten minutes. When I say cured I hope to check that with you soon. I have to say possibly very soon. It may be the endorphins talking, but I do feel different. I feel that a dead weight has gone. I guess that you applied something from your previous work in psychology.'

I squeezed him and I put my head on his chest so that I can feel him without staring as we speak, 'that's good to hear. Please don't tell anyone in psychology what I did, I am no longer registered but I would still be banned for life.' I felt a silent laugh. 'Do you know of the history of psychotherapy?' He gave a shake of his head. 'It was started by Freud and then Jung, psychoanalysis was developed and this developed into psychodynamic therapy. Though these were the starting points from which the modern, proven and effective therapies were developed they have little scientific merit and are in reality a faith. Often they are only self-absorbed navel gazing.'

He interrupted, 'by the client or therapist?'

'Both. There are however a few ideas still in use. Have you heard of catharsis?' He gave another shake of his head. 'This is, in rough, non-scientific terms, the idea of healing by crisis. The idea is that by bringing an issue to the fore and persuading the client to confront it then it is healed. In the short term they have a crisis but in the long term they are helped. It is still used in a diluted form in phobias and post-traumatic stress. Obviously what I did was different but there is some overlap. By role playing a Dominatrix I wanted to demonstrate that you could have sex without dominating or harming the woman. By forcing you into being the submissive partner you were not able to believe, even subconsciously, that you were abusing me.'

He thought for a while, I almost felt him smile, 'so you were only role playing. I am disappointed. I was hoping that you would bring a whip next time.' I jabbed him with my foot again but he can feel me laughing. He turned me sideways so that he can look into my face and an intense, serious expression had replaced the playfulness. 'More seriously, thank you. I was not joking. You have relieved me of two years of fear.' He paused and then continued more ruefully, 'I very much want there to be a next time. Will that be possible?' I hugged and kissed him. He continued, 'I take that as a yes. Seeing as you are being so agreeable will you stay the night?'

I raised my head more so that I can look straight at him, 'I thought that you would never ask. Yes, I would love to.'

'In that case we need to sort out a practical point. I don't have a car; living in the city centre I have no need. The van for my moth collecting is, as you know, at the university. I doubt that you want to be taken home on a February morning on the back of my motorbike. Anyway that figure hugging dress would undoubtedly ride up, you would be forced to arrest yourself for indecent exposure.' A motor bike, something else new, I didn't know that he had one. 'Shall I order a taxi? There is an excellent company that I use regularly.'

'That would be a good idea.' I undertook a quick calculation in my head, taxi time, shower, walk to the station, 'please book it for 8.' He slipped out of bed and picked up his jacket taking the 'phone out of his pocket. He switched it on. 'I am impressed to see that you had your 'phone switched off during dinner.' I had suspected so; there had been no irritating distractions.

'I own the 'phone, unlike with most people it does not own me. I had expected so but I was pleased to find that yours did not ping either. I guess that yours is similarly off.' I nodded, yes. He opened an app, after a couple of taps he said, 'done, they always come to the side door off my parking area. Your colleagues coming early for work will not see your walk of shame to the cab in last night's clothes.' I burst out laughing. I should have been cross with him but it was exactly what I had been thinking. He slipped back into bed.

We lay there in a comfortable silence wrapped around each other. My throat is sore from all the talking at dinner. My lips are sore from all the kissing since. In short I feel great. The curtains are a little open and a white, ethereal light from the street lamp outside is bathing the room. With my head still I looked around, enjoying and admiring all. I feel as if I have known him for months. We have covered so much tonight. I found myself slipping into a satisfied sleep.

I awoke but lay for a luxurious while with my eyes closed, feeling him breath quietly next to me. I realised that it is the breathing of someone awake. I opened my eyes and found him facing me, his head on one hand on the pillow. He is looking softly at me. 'I thought that you were awake. It is still early, six thirty, but as we are both awake would you like a coffee?'

'I would love one.' He got up, put on a dressing gown and went downstairs. I went to the loo and I heard him talking to someone, Samantha must be here.

When he came back I was sitting up in bed with the duvet demurely pulled up covering my breasts. I felt deliciously naked underneath and I am wanting to test whether or not last night had entirely resolved his issue. I have little doubt that it has.

As I sipped a sublime coffee I asked, 'I heard you talking, is Samantha here?'

'No, she won't be back until after eight, you will miss her. I was talking to Toby. Sorry I forgot; you have not seen the rear of the house. Sam's annex is L shaped with one end abutting this house and where they meet we have an interconnecting door. So the two homes form three sides of an enclosed courtyard, the fourth side is the wall that faces the road to the rear door of your station. You can't see in from the road and the area is secure and private. Toby is mostly in with us but if we are both at work, or out such as last night, he is happy and secure in there. He has a kennel and his toys.' He spotted my raised eyebrows, 'yes that great big, vicious looking, lump has toys. He came in for a chat whilst I made the coffee. He has detected that you are here. I had to fight to stop him coming upstairs or he would now be lying across you on the bed, refusing to move. Actually, that is precisely what I would like to do.' As he said that he slipped off his dressing gown and he slid in alongside me. 'I didn't want Toby here. I want you to myself for a while.'

As he put his arms around me I asked, 'Oh really, why is that?'

We made love, slowly, gently and this time conventionally, in the missionary position. No role play was needed this morning. There was no hiccup needing attention. He moved on top of me almost weightless, I wrapped myself around him. It was utterly wonderful.

Afterwards we lay together in a post coital glow. The advantage of waking up early is that there is no hurry. Eventually, his voice heavy with regret, Luke looked at the clock and said, 'we need to get up soon. Your carriage will be here.' He kissed me again and in a hesitant voice he asked, 'may I see you again?'

'I would very much like that.'

'This weekend I am on moth patrol Friday night and all of Saturday. I need to process them quickly after collection the previous night, so I can't make it then. Would you like to join me for lunch on Sunday?'

'I was expecting to be wined and dined on Saturday but if you prefer the company of a few insects then I can wait until Sunday.' He looks a little concerned. 'What I really mean to say is; that would be wonderful. I will look forward to it.'

Reluctantly we dressed and went downstairs. Toby came in and was delighted to see me. As I was rubbing his head we were both startled as the side door opened. Samantha came in and walked straight up to me, she gave me a kiss on the cheek, 'Sorry to disturb you but I wanted to say that your taxi is outside. No hurry, he is having a coffee. I guessed that you would be here and Andy confirmed it.' I obviously looked perplexed. She shook her head smiling and continued, 'there are only two reasons why Luke would not 'phone me before he goes to bed. I doubted that he was dead so that left one. I took a taxi home as it is icy and I did not want to cycle. Andy is the taxi driver and we know him well. He said that he is taking Luke to North Street at eight. I did not disabuse him and say that Luke has no reason to go there, well not this morning anyway. I would love to see his face when you get in. By the way, that is a gorgeous dress.'

I felt myself reeling with the rapid run of events and the volte face in her attitude towards me. Samantha turned to leave through another door which I presume leads to her part of the house. As she went she called out, 'I will leave you in peace to.......er.........say your goodbyes. Rebecca, do up another button, we don't want Andy to crash.' I clasped my hand to my chest blushing and she continued, 'I am admiring the bruise on my brother's lip. I see that you had to defend yourself. Don't worry I will have extracted all the details from him before you get home. I will chastise him accordingly.' With a knowing smile and a flourish she left as abruptly as she had entered.

Luke is looking sheepish. 'Luke, you can't tell her, you must not. I would never be able to face her again.'

He put his arms around me and apologetically said, 'no hope, she will interrogate me until I bleed.' Then he stopped, thought for a while, then continued, 'I will make a deal. I will not tell Sam if you do not tell Julia.' He saw immediately from my expression that is not an option. 'I thought so. You share everything with her, I share all with Sam. I am sure that, for both of us, telling our sisters will not only make things complete but that it will not go any further.' He is so right.

Poor Andy nearly fainted when I got into the taxi and Luke leaned in and kissed me good bye. He obviously did not expect to see that on a frosty, but beautifully blue, February morning an unexpected woman in inappropriate clothes leaving Luke's house. He would not have seen it for two years.

It certainly is a wonderful morning. Andy wanted to chat, 'av you 'erd the news.' I shook my head. 'There was some incident last night right outside where we are going. Some woman copper was attacked by three thugs with knives. Not only did she beat them off she hospitalised them.' Not quite correct but close enough. I expressed suitable wonderment.

'What a woman eh, we need more like her. Mind you, luv, the f... sorry, the bloody trolls are at it already. They 're sayin' she assaulted them and should be locked up. A woman, cornered by three pricks....sorry.... with knives. She needsa bloody medal, it is them who need lockin up." Thankfully we arrived and I started to open my purse to pay. Andy said, 'put that away luv. The prof pays us monthly, he tips generously too. All is covered.'

As I got out he asked, 'are you late love? I can include a run to work if you need.'

'Thanks Andy but I am fine. I work at the Police Station and I like to walk across the river each morning.' He looked at me surprised then a big question came to his face. I decided to put him out of his misery, 'yes, I am a woman copper. It was me that you heard about on the radio,' I paused, 'and Andy, thanks for your support. The service needs more like you.' I closed the door and gave him a little wave. He sat there stupefied as I walked to my door. Before entering I turned and saw him on his radio, no doubt already reporting in his latest passenger. Whether to say simply that a woman had left the "prof's' for the first time in two years; or to report further that the "woman copper" from last night had been in his cab and appears to be bonking the prof, I do not know.

CHAPTER 12:
LUKE: WAITING
FOR SUNDAY

We stood next to the rear door of the taxi, near to each other. I was pleased to find that it was not just me, neither of us wished to part. I do not want her to leave. Pulling her close I kissed her again, 'thank you Rebecca. Thank you so very much. Last night and this morning have been wonderful. I don't just mean………,' I hesitated, what to say? Obviously not "the sex," but is "making love" too heavy? 'I don't just mean making love, I mean everything, being with you. Of course sorting out my, er…, issue was a bonus. I doubt that any other woman could have or would have done that.'

She squeezed me and said, 'it has been a marvellous time for me as well. I have loved every moment.' Now it was her turn to hesitate, then with a cheeky little smile that was so enticing I felt like carrying her back into the house, she continued, 'I would not wish to repeat the role play itself but it did lead to a very,' she glanced to check the taxi door is closed, 'exciting conclusion. The issue, as you call it, is no longer an issue. I am sure of that, especially after what happened an hour ago.'

I couldn't help myself, 'when we meet on Sunday, can we recheck that it is fully resolved?'

With her mouth she replied, 'are you are being very forward professor? I am not entirely sure what you mean but if you are implying that we participate in salacious activity then I need to remind you that Sunday is a day of prayer and contemplation.'

With her eyes she clearly conveyed, "oh yes please."

Reluctantly we had a last hug and kiss. I opened the taxi door and she slid in. As she moved through the door her coat pulled tight against her side and even from this angle I can see it outline her perfect figure. At that very moment the weak February sun reached above the roofs of the houses on the opposite side of the square and her blond curls shone in its rays. Andy had been engrossed in his coffee and reading "The Sun." Still looking forward he said, 'mornin' prof.' Then he turned and instead of me he saw Rebecca's shapely backside and thigh slipping in, her hair glowing, her wide enticing smile now turning towards him. Poor Andy, I thought that he was going to faint. He had been expecting me, not a sexy woman. Then I remembered that he had dropped off Samantha only fifteen minutes ago. I know he finds her very attractive. I often spot him looking at her, with appreciation, not lewdly. Not so much "poor Andy" as "lucky Andy," it is still only eight am on a frosty Thursday morning in February and he has already had two enticing customers.

Whilst Rebecca turned to find the seat belt I made the introduction. 'Good morning Andy. It is not me today. Please take Rebecca to North Street, half way along behind the war memorial.' He seems to have lost the power of speech, most unusual for him. I closed the door and as the taxi drove off, like teenagers, we blew kisses at each other.

I moved to the front of the drive and watched the taxi making its way slowly around the green. In the dark of the taxi interior I can just make out a face in the rear window. I think that she is looking back at me. It turned the corner and passed out of sight. I still cannot move. Rooted to the spot, unaware of the cold, I thought, "what a night. What an extraordinary metamorphosis that has taken place in my life in only one night."

Eventually I forced myself to turn back to the house and I thought of the next three days before I can see her again. Sam and I have what we now euphemistically call a collection tomorrow night. My treatment of him will take until late on Saturday. I had strongly considered cancelling it as Rebecca is free on Friday and Saturday. Not seeing her for three nights, I must be crazy. Tomorrow night's collection is however a particularly vicious abuser, we need to put him straight before he does more damage. I will have to wait. Thankfully as we have already agreed to meet that should lessen my anguish. Sunday lunch with Rebecca, magic, I will book the gastropub by the river. Returning to thinking about her I stepped back into the house.

Firstly Toby roughly pushed past me and looked out of the door. He is besotted with Rebecca as well and is obviously looking for her. "Besotted as well," I had thought, that implies that I am also besotted. At least my thoughts demonstrate that I am being honest with myself. I had locked Toby outside. Sam must have come onto my part of the house and let him in. Oh lord, let the interrogation begin. As I called the disappointed Toby back in and turned to face into my kitchen I saw Sam, hands on hips, confronting me. She has an ear to ear smile.

She started with a look of mock disapproval, wagging her finger at me, 'you look like the cat who has got the cream. I take it that you have had a good night.' She hesitated and then continued more gently, 'and that what I told my silly brother was correct. Your fears were unfounded.' I started to speak; she interrupted, 'not so fast. I am going to treat that lip first.'

She pushed me down into a chair and lifted up a bag of frozen peas, I had not spotted them in her hand. She pressed them to my lip, held for a while and released, then repeated the cycle saying that she needs to get the swelling down but does not want to give me a freezer burn. 'I don't know what you did to deserve a punch in the mouth but obviously you made up. Both of you had the "well screwed" look when I came in.' She finally took away the peas, 'now that is much better already. It is time to tell me everything.' I started to protest. She interrupted again, she is in control this morning, as always, 'Luke, you know full well that you want to tell me and even if you did not I would wring it out of you. Speak.' She sat in the chair opposite to me and folded her arms. She will not let me move until I have confessed.

'Rebecca did not punch me in the lip. She bit me.' Sam's eyes widened like saucers. Over the next ten minutes she sat speechless as I told her all.

When I finished Sam, who is still sitting, remained motionless and silent for a couple of minutes. Finally, quietly, she said with an appreciative shake of her head, 'what a woman. No wonder you look so besotted.' "Besotted," so we both think that I am, I can see that we are both delighted by it. Toby put his chin on my leg. He still looks besotted as well, so does Sam. She repeated with admiration, 'what a woman. I like to consider myself as a fairly strong and controlling person.....' I thought, she likes to consider herself strong. The woman who was in a coma for two weeks and has rehabilitated herself within two years to return to full time work and cycling. Sam is not strong, she is formidable. I forced myself back to listening to her. '....... but I doubt that I would have thought of doing that and I am certain that I could not have carried it out. I am so happy for my big brother. Now you can stop being daft and accept that women are lucky to be with you. You have nothing to fear.' She gave me a hug, held me tight for a while then continued, 'I guess that tomorrow is now off and that you will see Rebecca instead.'

'No.' I almost shouted it and Sam looks stunned. 'I have arranged to see her for lunch on Sunday. I want our collection to continue tomorrow as planned.' Sam looked at me sharply. She obviously considers that this is the wrong decision. 'We must carry on with our treatments Sam.' "Collections," "our work" and "treatments" followed by "drop off;" we use these not as euphemisms but we consider them accurate descriptions of our intent. Legally they may be abductions and torture, morally they are not.

Sam's mood changed sharply. Such emotional lability has been part of the new Sam since her injury. It is the one thing that I never speak to her of. I am not sure that she even realises how much the head trauma has changed her in this way. Mercifully it is the only longstanding damage. My previously always placid sister can now become querulous in an eye blink. Thankfully she can control it during her medical work, it is only in the family when she relaxes that it is exposed. We all understand her, it does not matter. With me it is an additional spur to undertake our work. I cannot help Sam but I can prevent it happening to others. If the criminal justice system effectively dealt with the abusers then "our work" would not only be unnecessary, it would also be unjust. In the present circumstances we must continue, even if it entails delaying seeing Rebecca again.

The more I do the longer and harder I treat them. Sam is convinced that I am entering a cycle of violence. It is not that. When I undertake the training of them I remember Sam's injuries. I see that I need to use maximum force to achieve the maximum preventative effect. I have seen that if they are forgiven, as they so often unbelievably are by the PC, unrealistic, pseudo-liberals as they pontificate from the unruffled security of their armchairs, then they will not see what they have done is wrong. They will not regret without instruction, they will not control themselves and desist. When I have finished with them they see the consequences and make better choices.

Sam let rip. The mood has turned in an instant. 'For god's sake Luke, I have said before, you are getting obsessed. It is getting out of hand. We discussed only a couple of weeks ago that we should only undertake one a month to prevent a pattern being detected. Not only are you insisting on doing more you are now dating the detective charged with finding us.'

'The police only know about Brian James and Robin. They have not connected the two. Further.................'

Sam shouted over me. 'Stop making fatuous excuses. You know that what I am saying is true. It is dangerous.'

'Now you are making excuses. You are the one who uses your work in the hospital and at the refuge to assess the victims and their abusers.' As I said the words I regretted them. They are true but Sam is in no mood for the truth. Also, whilst correct, they are definitely a spin.

Sam rounded on me. I thought that she was going to hit me. 'Don't you dare talk to me like that. You know that I only seek them out because if I did not you would charge off and take risks looking for them.' Even with the random vacillations of her mood since the injury it is unlike her to be so censorious. This was also a partisan spin but it is not the best time to point that out. Her reproof was harsh and it stung but, I have to admit, it was justified. We are equally involved. Though I do most of the treatment she is vital for detection and collection.

As suddenly as before Sam's mood switched back. She leaned forward and threw her arms around me. She put her head on my chest and gave a loud, solitary sob. Then she continued, now tearfully' 'I am so sorry Luke. I do not want to spoil your wonderful night. I am frightened for you, for us. You have to admit that you are increasing the number of treatments. Please let's just back off a little. Continue but reduce the number. Is that a deal?

'Of course, we must continue but that is a reasonable compromise.' I cannot remember when, if ever, I have wilfully deceived Sam before but that was a lie. Though the intention was good, to end this amicably, it was still a deception. I have no intention to scale down what we are doing. I will ease back for a short while and then increase again. I must do all to prevent the disgusting attacks. I failed Sam but I can make some amends by helping other women.

Sam looked up at me with a teary, weak smile. Then she brightened and said cheerily, 'I have an idea. It is a little weird but if you are in agreement please pass it by Rebecca.' I looked down at her suspiciously, what is coming now? Seeing my expression she playfully punched me in the chest and said, 'why not invite Rebecca here for Sunday lunch. I will cook and we can have a family meal. It sounds a bit odd, meeting the family on the second date, but I like her. I think that she and I will get on well.' She gave a theatrical shrug and continued, 'I have to go to the refuge at three this Sunday so I will leave you early. I am sure you can find something to do after I have gone, perhaps play you can play Monopoly.'

It was my turn to give her a playful jab. I thought for a moment, yes it is weird but I would like it and I am pretty sure that Rebecca will also. 'Okay, it would be ...different. I will ask her.'

Sam went to catch up on some rest. She told me that she had slept for some of the night but one woman talked until late and another woke early, both in a crisis. The second one is the wife of the man we are treating tomorrow. I managed to avoid pointing out the irony of Sam wanting to back off but I am sure that she sees it as well.

The rest of Thursday went quickly. I had seminars and lectures to give and research to keep up with. I worked hard to clear the decks in readiness for an early finish on Friday and being occupied all day Saturday. During the afternoon I called Rebecca three times to ask about Sunday's arrangements. She did not pick up. No doubt her work is more irregular than mine and on some days she gets sucked into crises. Unfortunately it also crossed my mind that she may be having second thoughts. I think not but last night was hardly conventional. I tried not to dwell on that. Reluctantly I sent a text to ask if she wanted to have Sunday lunch with both Sam and me. I would have preferred to ask something delicate directly. She did not reply. My concerns mounted.

During Friday morning and early afternoon, though I was busy, my mind kept returning to Rebecca. I have still not had a reply from her. I am now getting very worried. It seems that she must be having second thoughts.

Finally, late afternoon, whilst I was driving the van from Hogwarts to pick up Sam for our collection, a text came from Rebecca. [v v v sorry v dif 2 days would love to see u both Sun cant phn now wil xplain sun cant wt].

My heart soared.

The collection went like a dream, Sam and I have developed it into a choreographed art form. He was Tasered, bundled into the van and injected with ketamine within fifteen seconds. As I was applying the straps to his unconscious body, fixing him to the wheeled stretcher, Sam was already driving towards the Farm.

All of our collections now follow the same pattern. I lie in wait and Taser as they pass, at the same time Sam drives up with the van's side door towards me and already open. In the winter we have the advantage of the cover of darkness and we can take them in a quiet area anytime during the evening. The one disadvantage is that we have to abandon if they are wearing heavy clothing, the Taser may not penetrate to the skin and so may not work. Thankfully many of these low lives seem to think that it is manly to parade around in tee shirts, often in shorts, even during the cold weather. Such ridiculous garb, though inappropriate for the winter, is ideal for the Taser. I do have a stun gun back up but that would require contact, it would probably entail the application of rule two as we had to enact with Brian James. I would be happy with that. If left to me I would probably kill all of them, but not only is Sam unhappy, that may draw attention to our work.

We arrived at the Farm, university speak for an industrial area previously used for research, now forgotten about except by me. As always Sam drove in, left me there with the van and then she took her car to work. Plausible deniability, it makes me secure in the thought that most of the risk is on me. Once she has left I lock the huge gates which, along with the perimeter fence, have razor wire at the top securing the compound. Then I lock the outer door of the warehouse. Finally I bolt the inner doors enclosing the abuser and me into the walled off forge. Even if someone came around the outside of the building they would not see or hear anything of my treatment. The security cameras would show me of their presence and I could either lie low or deal with them.

In preparation for handling him and the potential risk of being seen I replaced the mask that I wear during the collection. Sam and I wear them at pick up but then remove them as soon as the abuser is secured in the box in the van so that any one we pass will not be suspicious. The masks are excellent and deceive most people giving the usual passing glance but they would not pass close scrutiny by someone observant.

I wheeled him in and secured the stretcher to the end of the pivoted metal arm, him at one end and the counterbalance at the other. I adjusted his position so that his head is still supported by the end of the stretcher, strapped to it so that he cannot injure himself whilst thrashing around. His head is overhanging the end of the arm, supported and held by an extension, so as to be in the optimum position. I took off his straps one at a time and replaced them with padding underneath so that whilst he is trying to escape he will not have any skin injury from the stretcher during the treatment. When he is returned in twenty-four hours' time the only blemish will be the small burn, nothing to indicate what he has mentally suffered. Then I re-secured the blindfold. Only then did I take off my mask. I retied the gag, loose enough for him to grunt in response to me, tight enough to prevent any screams distracting me. Being heard by others is not a concern; no one else will be able to hear anything from this internal room. Finally I stuffed the incontinence pads down the front and back of his trousers. So many of them are incontinent when I treat them; especially during the branding. They injure the women unfortunate enough to have become embroiled with them but cannot take any pain themselves. Then I sat back and waited for the ketamine to wear off completely.

It is cold, we are going to be here for tonight and tomorrow, I don't want to be shivering all the time and I do not want him to get hypothermia. That is not for any concern as to his comfort, feeling cold will be the last of his worries over the next twenty-four hours, it is simply that if he is unconscious then it will hardly be effective treatment. I lit a fire in my forge. I have been concerned that if any of them do go to the police then they will be able to tell them that, firstly they were transported in what they would be able to glean from the rattling is a van, then they were held near an open fire. Scant evidence, I do not think that is anything to worry about. It is insufficient to track me down and even if they came here it is circumstantial at best.

I warmed my hands as the charcoal glowed. I so enjoy my metal sculpting, especially the large works. I have seen Rebecca admiring the one in my front garden. I can't wait to tell her that it is my work and to show her the others. Though I have never won any prizes I am as proud of the sculptures as I am of my academic work. Enjoying the heat I thought back over the last few days. Wednesday night was extraordinary. She is extraordinary. I had anticipated a good night, I had feared my failure. At no time had I imagined anything even remotely similar to what had actually happened.

I thought of her stunning body. Sliding my tongue down the snake tattoo from her breast to between her legs drove me wild. Then the other surprise on her abdomen came to mind. I can only think of one cause for the scar below her ribs on the left, I must ask her if it is what I suspect. If so then she has also been a victim of crime though probably not abuse. Further she has seen many battered women; she spoke sympathetically about Sally James. Would she join this work? Dare I speak to her of it? That is for the distant future, for now I find myself smiling in anticipation of Sunday.

I forced myself to return to concentrating on the task in hand. When I constructed the counterbalanced arm to swing the large pieces from the forge, to be plunged into the water tank for the cooling phase, I did not anticipate the other use that only a few years later I would put it to. The work that I made it for, the life size warrior now in Dad's garden, is not only six feet tall it is also sixty kilograms. I only had to add a little extra counterbalancing to repurpose the pivoted arm.

He has been stirring for a while and is now wrestling against his bindings and trying to speak through the gag. It is time to start.

For the first couple of hours I remain completely silent,

the unknown, the threatening quiet increases the terror for them. I leaned on the opposite end of the arm from him and he rose into the air. It was the first time that he had any indication of being on something mobile. Feeing the movement and not knowing what is happening he pulled against the straps as I swung the arm so that he pivoted over the water tank. He would be fighting even harder if he had any idea what he is now positioned over and what is about to happen.

I lifted up my end deliberately slowly. Firstly this returned him to the horizontal. He has no idea that his shaven scalp is now only an inch clear of the surface. Then he started to tilt head down as I raised my end of the arm further. He started to wriggle, trying to loosen his bonds, as his head slowly dropped. As the back of his head touched the cold water he tried to scream through the gag. I paused with the back of his head just breaking the surface. Then I lowered him further until his ears and eyebrows are submerged. Only his nose and mouth are now clear and even they have splashes entering as ripples crisscross the tank. He is now frantic with terror. He is making futile attempts to break his bonds and to scream for help. I waited until I saw him take a few large gasps then I plunged his head under the surface. His whole head is now submerged, his collar is touching the surface, the rest of him is held clear and dry.

I lifted him out again after only fifteen seconds. I do not submerge them for too long for the first few immersions as I do not want them to inhale water and drown. I held him with his mouth and nose again only fractionally clear, the top of his head still in the water, for several minutes. Every so often I gave my end of the lever arm a little shake to make him think that he was again being plunged in. He shook with terror each time. Then I slowly submerged his mouth again, this time for longer.

I repeated this for the next two hours, varying the time and speed. Twice I lifted him above the horizontal and held him there for fifteen minutes or so. I watched until he relaxed a little, thinking his ordeal is over. Then I let him fall suddenly, his head plunging below the surface. I repeated the waterboarding again and again extending the submersion each time. It feels good to see him blue and gasping when I lift him out. In the coffee room at the university, only last week, as I dunked my biscuit in my coffee one of my colleagues caught me smiling to myself. She asked me what I was grinning at. From her demeanour she clearly thought that it was some lewd memory. If only she had known that it was this.

It is time to talk.

I lifted him to the horizontal and pivoted him to the edge of the tank so that I can speak directly into his ear. I took one of my voice modulators and silently went to stand next to him, my mouth to the side of his head but covered by the modulator so that he cannot hear me breathing. Everything is completely silent other than his whimpering. I let several minutes pass then, through the modulator, I screamed his name directly into his ear, 'TERRENCE.' He jerked with fear. I quietly moved to the other side and took out a different modulator; I have four and I aim to convince them that there are several of us here by using different ones at different times through the night. I spoke quietly this time. 'Terrence, we have brought you here for re-education. You have some vicious habits. You have been beating your wife. You have severely injured her. We aim to show you that this is not how to behave. We are going to show you what it is like to suffer pain and fear. Terrence, you will feel them both tonight.' I then swung him out again for another round of waterboarding.

I repeated this cycle through the Friday night,

Saturday morning and into Saturday afternoon. The message changed several times and each message was repeated many times. He was told that he must not beat his wife nor cause her any distress nor give her reason to be fearful. He was often told that his wife had no idea that this was being undertaken, she has no part in it and that he must never discuss it with her or anyone else. The aim is to inculcate this message into his sick mind so that whenever he raises his hand to her again he will desist.

In addition, on multiple occasions, he was informed that a permanent mark will be made on his penis near to his stomach and that doing this will be hideously painful. I always add that it will be on the top side so that he will see it every time he goes to pee. He was threatened that if he ever injures his wife again or tells anyone what has happened tonight then he will be brought back and his penis severed through the mark. I suggested in future that he thinks carefully about that every time he sees the mark. That is an empty threat. We have no way of monitoring him and it would be too risky to try to abduct the same person twice. He is not to know that.

With each piece of advice he was returned to the waterboarding and told to grunt and nod that he had understood. I also said, again a threat that is empty but he cannot assess this, that if he is not sufficiently convincing in his agreement then "we" will plunge him in until he drowns. In the middle of the night I took a break of three hours and dozed. Partly this is to keep me strong. Partly I do not want him to pass out.

Late Saturday afternoon, as it is beginning to go dark, I prepared for the finale. I have a leather marking tool which is intended to be heated and to burn an R on leather work. I heated this in the forge, in the summer I use a blowtorch. I pulled down the front of his trousers and pants making sure that the incontinence pad is under his penis. They usually wet themselves either before or during the final part. I clamped his foreskin with a spring clip, for the circumcised I put it directly on the shaft. It does not matter that this is painful; it is part of the treatment and nothing when compared to what is to come. He wriggled and gave a muffled scream but he is still held firm and gagged. I attached a short bungee cord to the end of the spring clip and hooked its other end to the toe of his shoe, pulling his penis out straight.

I took the branding iron out of the fire and held it next to his cheek so that he can feel the heat. 'This is going to brand an R on your cock. It is R for remember. Every time you see it you will remember our advice. You will remember that if you fail, if you speak to anyone about tonight, if you ever again hit or threaten or frighten a woman, we will cut off your cock.' Urine dribbled on to the pad. I pressed the branding iron to the top of his penis, close to his stomach, and held it there until the skin sizzled. The acrid smell of burnt flesh and singed pubs filled the air. He shook violently then fainted.

Leaving him attached to the wheeled stretcher I disconnected it from the ducking arm and wheeled him towards the door. I checked that the fire in the forge had burnt out. As I waited next to the door I thought about the others. This one is number nineteen. We started with Robin when he was released from prison. It will be the second anniversary of that next month as he had incredibly only served a few months. He was both more difficult and easier. It was more difficult as Sam was still so restricted by her injuries caused by him. She was barely able to drive. It was easier in that we did not have to restrain him or return and release him. He had to be killed. I would not countenance any risk of him attacking Sam again and she could not live with any such fear. After Tasering him I simply bundled him into the van and then I had given a massive overdose of ketamine.

That immobilised him immediately. He then quickly died, his breathing being stopped by the drug.

Disposing of his body had also been easy. A previous post-grad researcher of mine, Clive, had been studying eco conscious disposal of dead humans and animals. The politely named Natural Organic Reduction, aka human composting, is legalised in some States in the USA. There it is undertaken in specially constructed steel vessels. Clive wanted to take it one stage further and examine the results of simply burying the body with a high temperature composting mix, a concoction including wood chips, alfalfa and straw. The concern was that the temperatures reached in burial would not be as high as in the aerated vessels and may not be sufficient for complete composting and sterilisation. For obvious reasons he did not use humans but dead, full grown pigs which were sick and not suitable for consumption, were an excellent substitute. There was the additional advantage that disposal of such pigs is difficult and expensive for the farmer. Clive had a ready supply of porkers and was also looking at widening the whole process to dispose of slaughtered cattle, and sheep as well as pigs.

It had worked like a dream. In the above ground ventilated composting bins a human being totally decomposes, including bones, within sixty days. With the buried pigs at the lower temperature, but still a much greater heat than a garden compost heap, it took a few months. Clive expanded it further still by adding human sewerage to the compost mix. He thought, in my opinion quite rightly, that this could all be combined and developed into, not only eco-friendly disposal of humans, animals and sewerage, but also nutrient rich fertiliser production.

Before he could undertake more than a few of these, all extremely successful, he died from a ruptured brain aneurism. I tried to find others to continue the work but some were squeamish and others were rightly concerned that such off beat research may damage their career. Poor Clive, it is simply unjust that excellent researchers such as him die but scum, such as this creep here tonight, live. Had Clive survived I am sure that he would now be the head of a successful and worthwhile environmental enterprise. However hard his loss it has left me with many pre-dug holes in the ground and sheds full of the composting material, now old but still viable.

I had simply stripped Robin and put his corpse into one of the holes with Clive's composting recipe mix under and above him. I labelled it "Pig 80kg," dated it to when Clive was here and put turf over. After a year I dug it out and found to my delight and astonishment that he had simply disappeared, even his leg bones and teeth. There was only a rich, fresh smelling earth. I scattered the dark soil where Clive had been undertaking his research on human sewerage and I planted a tree there. In the unlikely event of any DNA being recoverable it will be mixed in with all the others present in the effluent. Brian James is now in the hole that Robin had occupied. He is possibly already "cooked" but I will leave it undisturbed for the full year.

Bang on time Sam's text came, she is outside. I gave the despicable Terrance a shot of ketamine then opened the doors and Sam drove in. Our drop off is a reverse of the collection with the exception that we leave them within an easy walk of their home. This is not for their comfort; we do not want them staggering through the city in the shell-shocked state they find themselves in.

If they can get home and recover before seeing the world then it will help us to remain undetected. Of course the wives or partners must see them. We have heard considerable encouraging feedback from the ones attending the refuge when Sam has been on duty. She is careful not to talk to them but has overheard them reporting to the other victims that "so and so" came back in a state after a day's mysterious absence and since then he has miraculously been non-threatening and not violent. Some have even been contrite.

I wheeled him into the van and I secured him in the hidden compartment. Previously Sam had found a good drop off point; she is an expert at detecting them. It is surprising how many dark corners with bushes are to be found in housing areas. Before the final dose of ketamine I tell them where they will be dropped and that they must make their way straight home without talking to anyone. I advise them that we will be watching; this is not true but again they are not to know that. They are told that they will be dropped with their eyes and mouth securely bound with gaffer tape but their wrists only loosely bound. They are to wait for a count of fifty, that I will be watching, and only then they can wriggle their hands free, uncover their eyes and mouth, and walk home. They stumble more than walk. Mostly they are so broken by the waterboarding that they can barely stand, let alone give any resistance. For the occasional one where I fear they may try to fight back I keep a stun gun handy.

Sam drew up to the drop off point after a drive by to check that all is clear. I wheeled him out of the recess and started freeing him from the stretcher. I had previously replaced the tight bindings on his wrists and secured them behind him. I replaced them with some loose binding. Holding the stun gun pressed to his neck I started the potentially dangerous manoeuvre. With my other hand I quickly released cleats of the bindings on his body. As I did this Sam had a last check up and down the street and slid open the van door. I rolled him out and as he hit the ground I leapt down, flipped him on to his back, so that he could not use his hands still bound behind. Then I dragged him behind a bush. This time there was the perfect finale of him being pulled through some dog shit. I had not seen or planned this but I thought it apposite and I will look out for more in the future. Immediately I ran for the passenger door of the van. Sam had already closed the side door and she had moved into the driver's seat. As I was closing my door she drove off and we pulled off our masks. We stopped in a quiet part of a near deserted carpark, stepped into the rear, removed our overalls and put them, along with the masks, into a duffle bag. Then I drove from there. I dropped off Sam at home, she took the duffle bag, she casually throws it into a storage cupboard that we have. If any one were to find it we would simply say that it was disused work and party gear. It is not hidden so why would it be suspicious?

I took the van back to Hogwarts and then walked home. After such days, though tired as I only have had a little light sleep, I always feel energised and excited. I feel that I am doing some good, keeping some of these abusers in check, compensating for not helping Sam. Tonight I am more than usually happy. I have tomorrow to look forward to, seeing Rebecca.

It has been an excellent start to what should prove to be a satisfying and enjoyable weekend.

CHAPTER 13
REBECCA, THE
ARREST

I hurried from the taxi to my front door. I let myself in and then I went straight upstairs, stripped off and dashed towards my shower. I ran the water until it became warm and I started to step in. Then I froze. I don't want to shower. I don't want to wash the delicious scent of him off me. Having no choice, I can hardly go to work smelling of last night, I reluctantly showered.

After quickly re-dressing, this time in my more customary track suit, I left my lovely little home with the low sun streaming through its back window, to walk to work. I will pass by Luke's house that I left only half an hour ago. Eight-thirty, that gives me plenty of time to arrive a little early for the meeting. I will not have enough time to ring Luke's doorbell for another kiss, unfortunately. I thought, "so much for me playing it cool being and hard to get.' Sex, no, making love, on the first date and now I would call on him again if I had the time.

I crossed the footbridge walking on air, smiling and saying hello to everyone I pass. Most smile back, some look at me as if I am mad. I walked up the cobbled passage and I was on the verge of crossing the High Street when I noticed the Boots Pharmacy a few doors down. Warning bells clanged in my head. I made a quick calculation. I thought, "bugger," and headed in.

I was the only customer but the dried up specimen behind the counter took her time coming to me. Having no time for pleasantries, not that they would help here, I asked, 'please let me have a morning after pill?'

She looked back in horror, tut-tutted, turned on her heel and disappeared into a back room. She was gone for an age. I looked at my watch. Now I will be a little late. No matter, Brutus and the Troop always keep us all waiting. It is part of their childish power-play. Eventually the pharmacist re-appeared. As she took the money she glowered at me and said, 'you should be more responsible. This is ridiculous at your age.'

Under normal circumstances I would have probably taken her by the throat and shaken her. Today, nothing will rile me. I will smile at everything sent to annoy me. I will rise above it all, even Brutus. I tried but failed to resist stabbing her and turning the knife. 'Oh but you should see him, he is so handsome. I couldn't hold back.' I ostentatiously looked at my watch, 'it was only an hour ago. The last time that is.' Well, I had not actually lied.

Her pinched, disapproving face now looks as if she has bitten into a very sharp lemon. I realised that she is probably only ten years or so older than me. From her demeanour I had originally thought that she was ancient. I thought, "lose three stones, scrape that thick plastic slap off your face, stand up straight and smile; you would actually be quite pretty. You could walk out in ten minutes as a new woman, except the weight but the smile would make up for that." I managed to keep my thoughts to myself but from her changed expression I suspect that she may have seen them in my face.

Having jogged past Luke's, that was hard; having taken the pill as I went by, that was easy; I arrived outside the briefing room only three minutes after nine. It is ominously quiet. Usually, until Brutus walks in, everyone is joshing about the night before. I cautiously stepped through the door.

Everyone was sitting rigidly to attention. Julian spotted me and frantically waved at me to get out but it was too late. Brutus was not only already there and wearing an uncharacteristic, sickly, pleased with himself, smile; he has also seen me.

He bellowed across the room. 'Good of you to finally join us DI Fletcher. We have just been speaking about you. I have appraised our colleagues of your disgraceful behaviour in the park last night and how you have brought the station, in fact the whole service, into disrepute.'

Holy shit, what is he talking about? What is going on? 'You can take that false look of shock off your face. It is ridiculous. The whole team have been told about your attack on those innocent young men. You were clearly in a frenzy, perhaps it is the time of the month or some other girly thing.'

'What on earth are you talking about? They attacked me.'

'I am not going to lower myself and argue with you about the undisputable facts. Two witnesses came forward and have given statements that you ran down to the war memorial and attacked the three saying that they had dropped litter. This concurs with what the victims themselves said.'

I stared back, stupefied into silence.

'Given your martial arts skills you effectively attacked them as if with an offensive weapon. You are under arrest. You will be charged with grievous bodily harm.' He turned to two of his sycophants, 'DI Phillips, handcuff her and take her to the holding cell. DI Whitlocke, keep a good distance and cover him with your Taser. Don't hesitate to use it if there is any indication whatsoever that she may resist. She has shown herself incapable of controlling the use of Taekwondo. ' They walked towards me grinning. I saw that Whitelocke is indeed holding out a Taser.

Julian leapt to his feet and started bellowing at Meadows. 'This is ridiculous. This is a set up. We know you are a crook. Those supposed witnesses are low lifes that owe you a favour.'

Pandemonium broke out. Julian's friends tried to restrain him; he looks as if he is going to attack the Troop. Meadows and Julian were both screaming at each other at the same time. Colleagues are straining to control Julian and shouting at him to back down.

In the midst of this, as Phillips and Whitlocke approached me, Sergeant Peter Bender; our kindly, rock solid, respected Desk Sergeant; unobtrusively got to his feet and stood between Whitlocke and me, blocking the Taser. He almost inaudibly snarled, 'put that down and get out of the way.' Whitlocke went pale but did not move. 'Put it down and fuck off before I break your fucking arm.' Again quietly said but with menace, only Phillips, Whitelocke and I were able to hear this threat. It carried even more weight as it is said in the station that Peter never ever swears whatever the provocation. Now ignoring Whitlocke, whose hand with the Taser seems to have lost the ability to stay up and the weapon slid down, Peter turned to Phillips and said, 'give me those you little creep.' He snatched the cuffs. 'Now we will take Rebecca to the holding cell together.' At this the fracas died down and all in the room stared at me. The Troop leered with smug delight, the rest looked on with horror.

Peter turned to stand alongside me. Out of their line of sight he gave me a wide grin and a wink. I fail to see anything to joke about. He gently turned me around. Making a show of taking my hands behind my back he tapped the cuffs together on my wrists. They made the chinking noise of them being secured but I found that my wrists are still free. He has knocked them together to make the sound of them closing but he has not locked them. Holding my wrists between us so that no one can see the subterfuge he steered me towards the door saying loudly, 'come quietly DI Fletcher. You are restrained, martial arts will not help.' Very softly in my ear he said, 'for a very, very brief visit to the cell.' Turning to the detectives, he shouted, 'come on Phillips, you can help. Whitlocke, you can go back to browning your tongue.'

As we left the room Julian shouted again that this was a set up and that Meadows is a crook. His friends struggled to quieten him down. I heard Meadows scream back, 'you are suspended Courtney. Get out of this station. I will have your job for this.'

Silent and mystified I allowed Peter to guide me to the top of the stairs. When the sprung door had closed behind the three of us Peter whirled around, took the unprepared Phillips's wrist and neatly handcuffed him to the radiator. Phillips yelled out, 'what do you think you are doing. Let me free, I am your superior officer. You will lose your job for this.' The Troop seem to be threatening the employment of half of the station this morning. Phillips obviously thinks it will help him to ape Brutus.

Peter smiled and softly said, 'I am quaking in my boots.' Phillips' confidence drained away. Peter gently shepherded me down the stairs, more of a request than an arrest. As we passed out of sight around a bend in them we heard the doors to the briefing room open and all of our colleagues, other than the Troop who leave through the side door, started to come out. Normally there is a babble of chatter, today they are silent. That is until they reached Phillips whereupon there was an eruption of laughter and catcalls. We heard him screaming at them to set him free. We stayed ahead, out of sight on the turning stairs, but it is clear that they are walking straight past him.

We arrived at the holding cell and Peter asked me to enter. He asked, he did not insist. 'I am going to lock you in Rebecca. This is for your own safety. If any of the Troop come down and start harassing you for the cell being unlocked then it would do you harm as you would undoubtedly injure them. I want to save you from yourself, not them. Also, please let me have your 'phone and any personal effects. I will keep them safe and private, no one can insist on seeing them if I have them squirreled away.' He took them and returned a couple of minutes later with a large envelope. He sealed my effects in the envelope, asked me to sign across the seal and then covered it with Sellotape. He then hid it deep in his uniform jacket. Throughout this he was grinning, smiling and at one time whistling. I cannot fathom why he finds this distasteful set up so positive.

Peter looked at me and registered my confusion. 'Rebecca, I am sorry to be mysterious. I am desperate to tell you what is going to unfold but it is not my place. Please bear with me. You will be out of here in a few hours. Please refuse to talk to anyone without my introduction. Shortly you will understand and no doubt you will be delighted as to what has occurred. Julian will be happy with the events as well. Back soon.' With that he locked me in the cell and skipped along the corridor.

Perhaps it is the endorphins left over from last night. Perhaps it is the joy of having been with Luke. Whatever, I do not understand not only what has happened but even more stupefying, my reaction. This is not me. I found myself sitting back on the cell bench passively waiting for whatever is going on to unfold. The usual me would be pounding on the cell door, acting, demanding.

After a short while Peter came back in with a

coffee and an almond croissant from the delightful Italian deli nearby. 'Not long now Rebecca, quicker than I had anticipated.'

Roughly another couple of hours or so passed. I guess that I have been in the cell for a total of three hours. Peter came back in. Now he is accompanied by another man who I do not recognise.

The stranger is wearing a thousand pound suit and equally expensive shoes. His wavy grey hair is expertly coiffured. As Peter stepped to the side the stranger held out a manicured hand, shook mine, and said in a mellifluous, public school voice, 'Ms Fletcher, delighted to meet you. I am Max Carruthers, your solicitor.' My what? Whoever you are I cannot afford you. 'May I call you Rebecca, please call me Max.' He swept me out of the cell with Peter beaming on.

I passively went along as he silently took my arm and gently shepherded me out of the deserted station. What has happened, have I had a personality transplant? I do not allow myself to be escorted no matter how gracious he is being. As we continued towards the front door Max spoke again, 'I suggest that we get to my car as soon as possible before the DS finds out what is happening and detains you on another ridiculous trumped up charge.' I thought, "Max, I cannot agree more. "

The moment we left the station door a vast black car swept up. A grey uniformed chauffer jumped out and opened the door for me. Moments later I was behind the tinted glass. Max slid in alongside me on the black plush leather. The limousine silently moved off. As we smoothly rolled along, Max held up what looked like a telephone and spoke to the chauffer in his partitioned off area. 'John, please pull over when it is expedient so that I may inform Rebecca as to what is happening.' Yes John, please do.

We pulled into a lay by in front of the new bridge. I

realised that we were heading towards my home yet I had not told "Max" or "John" where to go. In fact, I have not said a word. Max spoke softly. 'This must be very confusing for you and I am sorry to say that I can only partly explain. Things are happening on a need to know basis and some of the information is way above my pay grade.' What, above your pay grade? There is no hope for me to find out then. 'Firstly, I have been engaged by Julian Courtney's firm to represent you. There is no charge to you for this, indeed I will not be charging Julian either. Firstly his company is an excellent client of ours. Secondly, after what he has told me I am already a great admirer of you and I regard it my public duty to help. I need to ask formally, do you agree to me representing you, I come on Julian's recommendation?'

I managed to stammer a grateful "yes" whilst thinking, what the hell is Julian's firm? I thought that he is a copper.

Max continued. 'It is clear that the charge against you is false. I have taken the liberty of speaking to the Crown Prosecution Service on the telephone as John drove me here. My company's office is only two streets away from their head office in Petty France. I often meet with them and this morning I spoke to the DPP herself about you.'

This is becoming surreal. He works in central London. He must have left within half an hour of my arrest. He has spoken to the DPP about me. I swallowed as he went on. 'The DPP assures me that here is no possibility whatsoever of a case ever being brought against you. However I have been instructed to advise you that other sources request your help. I cannot divulge their identity as in fact I have not been told who they are. However, it is plain that they are very senior. They ask that you agree to the charges and suspension from duty remaining in place at present. For reasons that I am again not privy to, apparently this will be an advantage to the police service over the next few days or weeks. I am in the difficult position of recommending to you that you agree to this even though I do not know why it has been made and so I cannot inform you why. I can say only that it came from the highest level as a strong personal request. I am sure that if at any time you change your mind I would have the charges dropped within minutes. Do you agree to this subterfuge?'

Now, gripped with a burning curiosity, I readily agreed.

'Wonderful. I have been asked to inform you that Sergeant Bender will call on you at home at six pm this evening. He has taken the liberty of asking Julian to be there as well. I have been instructed to ask that you do not contact anyone about this issue in the interim.'

John then drove us to my door. I realised that though I had not said where I live this confirms they knew all along. As I stepped out of the limousine Max jumped out alongside me. As he shook my hand he said, 'it has been delightful meeting you Rebecca.' I have still not said more than a few words. 'I have no doubt whatsoever that this silly charge will go away and that you will soon be back in post. Unfortunately this means that we will probably not meet again; unless, that is, at one of Julian's firm's excellent soirees.' He shook my hand again, climbed back in and the car glided off as I stood dumbstruck thinking, "Julian's firm's soirees?"

After recovering I had an early light lunch. Unbelievably it is still not quite one o' clock. I seem to have had a month's worth of experiences in the last four hours. On second thoughts, counting last night that should be a lifetime's worth of escapades.

Then, with an unplanned five hours to kill and nothing else to do, I caught up on some housework and read a novel.

More accurately, I tapped my fingers on the table willing the clock hand around.

At a quarter to six Julian arrived. We filled each other in on what had happened. I told him my story. He said that he had been suspended and ejected from the station. Shortly afterwards he had received an enigmatic 'phone call from Peter and, like me, has been pacing in anticipation since. I was just about to grill him about "his firm" when the doorbell sounded again. I ran to answer it.

In came Peter, now in civilian clothes. Peter is cock a hoop, effusive, delighted, and completely unhelpful. He effectively put us on hold saying that it will be of great advantage to the service if we would we attend a clandestine meeting in the Oak Suite of the Park Hotel at two pm tomorrow. He did not advise on how this would be helpful. He did not explain why our suspension and my charge are such causes for celebration. He apologised and said that he is dying to tell us but that it is above his pay grade. I am hearing that a lot today. Who on earth do I have to meet to find someone of the appropriate seniority to tell me, now us, what the hell is going on? Peter handed over the envelope containing all of my personal effects, still sealed. He mysteriously also gave me a new 'phone and asked me not to use my usual one, not to answer it and preferably not even to switch it on. He strongly requested that we do not to speak of the day's events to anyone and that tomorrow we enter discretely and not in uniform.

Julian and I spent the evening in the company of a couple of bottles of wine making fruitless speculation. I thanked him for engaging Max, hoping that he would divulge something regarding "his firm." He brushed this off and changed the subject. I thought, "Julian you should know me better. I will have the thumbscrews out next time." We had arranged to meet early tomorrow. Julian knows the layout of the Park Hotel and told me that the Oak Suite is a small conference room directly off the main lobby. He said that if we get there early and we wait in the reception, behind some large plants, we will be able to monitor who arrives.

Whilst Julian was with me I was burning with curiosity. On several other occasions, I thought to ask him about Max mentioning Julian's company and what is it. Whenever I mentioned Max or tried to thank him for engaging Max on my behalf Julian changed the subject again. Tonight I will respect him not wanting to go there. As his senior officer, whilst thinking this I realise it is an excuse, as a nosy parker, I want to know everything.

After Julian had left I sat alone brooding on the day. It had started on such a high, descended into chaos and stupidity then ended in mystery. I am desperate to speak to Julia or Mum but I dare not, what on earth could I say? I would dearly love to call Luke but again, what to say? "Hi, it is the woman you screwed for the first time last night, remember me. Guess what, I have been arrested and suspended. Would you like to hook up for a celebratory bonk?" I stared at my silent, switched off, 'phone. Finally I went to bed and examined the ceiling for a long, long time. I realised that it is exactly twenty-four hours since I first made love with Luke. More has happened in that day than happens to many people in a year, most of it unexpected and surprising. No wonder my head is spinning.

....

....

We were skulking behind two enormous Yucca plants from half past one. At a quarter to two we jerked alert as we spotted the three purposeful people arrive. They strode across reception talking animatedly and swept into the Oak Suite. As the door banged behind them I wondered if I had been hallucinating. How is it that the three of them are together? Two of them, yes, that is understandable. The third, that is incomprehensible. He has no reason to be in this city.

Julian said, 'Jesus H Christ, did you see who I saw?' I nodded yes. He carried on in an incredulous voice, 'they are not in uniform but the one on the left was definitely our Chief Constable, Claudia Wentworth. The one in the middle was Detective Chief Inspector Martin Fox, the most senior detective in our division. I didn't know the guy on the right.'

He must have been surprised that I did not answer him. I wanted to but speech was temporarily impossible. He turned and looked at me and saw my jaw hanging slackly. He realised and asked me, 'you do, don't you?'

I nodded. Eventually I managed a croak, 'he is Commander Rupert Lightman, my ex-boss in the Met.'

As Julian looked on stupefied there came a cough behind us. We turned to see Peter Bender, also in plain clothes, who said blandly to us, as if there was nothing unusual about us spying on three very senior officers going to a meeting, 'good, everyone is early. Let's go in.' We followed him like sheep as he marched into the suite without knocking. They are all still standing. They beamed smiles at Julian and me, then they looked expectantly at Peter who said to the Chief Constable, 'sorry Claudia, you need to pay up. They were behind the Yuccas.' Claudia? Not Ma'am?

The Chief Constable took out a purse and handed a twenty pound note each to both the Commander and Chief Inspector. She smiled at us and shook our hands. 'Sorry, we had a bet. I said you would be looking from the bar and the others said from the yuccas. Anyway, it is all first names here, mainly because we want to ask you to undertake something off the record. Also, to fill you in as to our relationships, Peter is my brother and all four of us were at Police College together. So, that means we are more friends than colleagues.

We often debate as to who has the best outcome, us going for high office or Peter choosing to stay as a proper policeman.' So that is why the obviously talented Peter is still a desk sergeant. She chirpily enquired, 'who do you think made the correct decision?' As if the opinion of two relatively junior officers on the career decisions of three of the most senior could possibly be of interest to them.

I panicked. How to answer such a loaded question?

Julian said loudly, clearly and without hesitation, 'Peter.' They all nodded agreement. I was astonished at both his audacity and his answer. I thought that he was bound for the top. He is implying that he wants to stay in uniform.

The Chief Constable; Claudia, whatever, I am struggling to think of her as Claudia; continued. 'Let us cut straight to the chase. Before we tell you what is going on and what we are asking of you, we owe you an apology. You have been stationed here under false pretences from the very start of your appointments. Everything about your work has been engineered behind your backs. We apologise for that. When you discover why, then we trust you will understand the necessity for this. Rebecca, you must be wondering why you were not promoted after your peerless work in the Met. Julian, we cannot tell you what she did other than it was extremely impressive and dangerous.'

Julian interrupted, brave man. People do not usually survive interrupting the Chief Constable, I mean Claudia, I mean.....I don't know what I mean to say. She smiled. She bloody smiled and inclined her head to listen to him. I am beginning to consider the possibility that I have developed a psychosis. Julian simply said, matter of fact, as if it is a mere bagatelle, 'I know what happened Ma'am.......er... Claudia.'

They all tensed. An instant later Rupert exploded at me, 'for god's sake Rebecca, that is under wraps. It is not just you at risk, it is the whole team.'

Julian interrupted again. Please Julian, be careful. I willed him to shut up. As with the Chief Constable he is not one to suffer being interrupted. I wanted to warn Julian that the Commander is not called "the Bear" because of his forename. Again quietly, as if it is of no consequence, Julian said, 'Rebecca did not tell me. I found out myself with a little online digging.'

They looked astonished. Rupert is the worst affected, his face is a mask of incredulity. He cannot speak. Apparently on his behalf, Claudia asked, 'Julian, we know of your expertise. Are we to believe that you hacked the Met?' The shock of this being said aloud seemed to affect Rupert like a slap to the face, he rocked back on his feet. 'Please be frank, I am not concerned by whatever fun you may have had but by the security implications.' Claudia then faced Rupert and they exchanged looks of despair, they are reaching for straws.

'Ma'am,' deliberately and playfully not Claudia, 'surely you would not think one of your officers would commit a crime? If this impossible event occurred I am sure that I would be able to report that the Met is secure behind defences more solid than those of banks and insurance companies. Only by chance would it be penetrable should such a would-be hacker have both inside knowledge and, in a most serendipitous addition, stumble on something by an almost unrepeatable episode of chance. Nothing is beyond improvement and the computer world is moving daily. To cover this I could suggest some minor tweaks to the IT department of the Met, were it that I had actually looked myself. In the meantime, in the opinion of my company, who in the spirit of assisting the service have undertaken some exploratory tests without charge, I can assure you that the Met computer system is as near to impregnable as is possible.'

They looked stunned. At least I had prior knowledge

of this, my first heads up for more than twenty-four hours. Two "oh shits" slipped out, one a female voice. He has effectively told them that, yes, he has hacked the Met, but no, there is no need for major concern. Then they looked at each other and laughed in disbelief and relief. During this release of tension I saw a furtive glance pass between Claudia and the Bear. If it were different circumstances, if it were not them then I would interpret it as sexual. I must have misread them.

Claudia continued as if nothing had occurred, ignoring the fact the Julian has not directly said how he found out, 'actually, as you are both currently suspended what we are going to ask of you is in fact a crime, but please don't tell anyone.'

She motioned to the table and we all sat. That is a relief as my legs are beginning to wobble with all the revelations coming from the top brass. I realised that the meeting has not even started yet. Claudia continued in a gentle, unruffled voice as I fought to calm myself. 'Anyway, as I was saying. Rebecca you must be wondering why you have not been promoted and why you were encouraged to move to this delightful, but relatively small, city and station. Julian, though you now intimate that you wish to stay in uniform you must be surprised as to why your detective training has been delayed.' I thought, yes Ma'am, Claudia, whatever. Though I have not discussed these points with Julian I have definitely been thinking on both of them. She breezily carried on, 'I have to confess that the four of us have conspired to bring you here and for you to work together.'

I looked at her and then towards Peter. My face must have betrayed my thoughts that this is impossible. Peter spoke, 'it was simple to manipulate Brutus to place the two of you together. When you each arrived I spotted that he saw you, individually that is, as a challenge to his Troop. I could tell that he wanted you both out of his way. I said to him, supposedly just an aside in passing, that I thought you were both troublemakers. I intimated that it is a pity that you were not working together because if you were to do so I predicted a major debacle. That would be a perfect excuse to get rid of you both at the same time. I gilded the lily by saying that I had heard that you were both reckless. He swallowed the bait and here we are. I must admit we have arrived more quickly and more dramatically than I had anticipated. I was trying to think of a situation that I could contrive to bring this about when the three charmers in the park did it for me.'

Julian and I looked at each other with amazement then, together, we roared with laughter. They all joined in. There is considerable relief in their chortling. I guess that they were concerned that we may be outraged by the subterfuge wrought on us. When we had calmed I looked at Peter and naively said, 'well, it is good to get all the surprises over before the meeting starts.'

A wide grin split Peter's face as he replied, 'not so fast. The best is yet to come.'

Claudia continued as if talking about the cake display at a village fete, 'we wanted you to develop a working relationship together and for Peter to check that it was effective before springing a challenge on you. He assures us that your teamwork is of the highest order both in terms of your relationship and your results. Being suspended, thus not only out of the station but at a loose end, puts you in an ideal position to consider a difficult investigation that we wish you to ponder. We will describe it to you now and ask you to think on it overnight. Please let us know tomorrow if you will it take on. I have yet again to apologise to you, we cannot give you any longer to think on it. What we will ask is time limited. I should forewarn you that it is not only demanding it is potentially dangerous. It could also backfire.'

She hesitated, looked at the others, then continued, 'on all of us that is.'

Julian and I spoke immediately, interrupting her, talking over each other, 'I accept. Delighted to be of service Ma'am.'

Claudia sighed, took out her purse again, turned to Martin and Rupert and handed them another twenty each saying, 'I will never ever again be conned into a bet with you two buggers.' They grabbed the money with alacrity and all three turned to us with big thankful smiles, Peter beaming to the side. 'Over to you Martin.'

Martin, or until five minutes ago DCI Fox or Sir, looks troubled. He slowly and softly spoke in an apologetic tone. 'I regret to inform you that we suspect that your chief of station, DS Meadows, along with a group of other senior officers who we understand have been given the moniker, The Troop, are corrupt and are abusing their position by being involved with organised crime.' He paused.

Rupert broke the silence that lay heavily between us. 'I note that you are not jumping to your feet saying, "oh no, not our boss, he is a thoroughly decent chap." Your expressions are telling me that you were already suspicious. Even yours Rebecca; that is saying something as when you worked for me I could never read you. It drove me nuts.' At last smiles came back to us all.

Martin continued, 'as you are already aware we have concerns regarding the operation of a gang in this area. Thankfully we have little gang crime here and we fit the caricature of a small, provincial cathedral city. However, some organised elements are here as they are everywhere else. They seem to be increasing their activity and to date the supposed attempts to close them down have got nowhere. I say supposed as the only action so far has resulted in the arrest of the small time competitors, not the main gang, who we guess are being supported by Meadows and his Troop. The main activities are likely to entail sex trafficking, prostitution and drug dealing centred on a pub-hotel in East Street.'

I am beginning to see where this is going. I like it. Before I could process this further I became aware that Julian had stiffened, the others spotted it as well. Martin gestured for Julian to speak. 'I live in the apartments adjacent to the railway station at the end of East Street. During my evening runs I go down East Street and then turn left alongside the Langley Hotel. They have a small car park at the rear. I have often seen Meadows' car parked there along with others owned by the Troop.'

Grinning, Martin shook his head. With a wide smile Claudia said, 'am I right in thinking that in the first five minutes we have formed the basis of a team and had our first breakthrough.' Everyone nodded. Still smiling she continued, 'at this rate I will postpone going to the loo in case I miss the first arrests.' Now everyone laughed but with a serious edge, it is a breakthrough.

Rupert took over. 'As you have no doubt guessed we are asking you to form a team to investigate this. Obviously this must be with the utmost secrecy. To this end we have asked five officers, who Rebecca has previously worked with in the Met, to come here and to assist you in the initial investigation. We consider that the majority of the station are clean, first rate officers, Peter assures us of that, but as yet we are uncertain how far the tentacles of corruption spread. In view of this we wish to contain the investigation between us here and the incoming team until we have established who is culpable. Obviously, if and when we come to arrests, you will need considerable local involvement and support. Peter can organise that at the last moment. He already has provisional teams drawn up.' He paused and looked straight into my eyes and said deliberately calmly, 'Rebecca it is Tony Cartwright, Alison Hughes, John Davenport, Simon Jones and Charlie James.'

He looks serene, he must know what this means to me. I could not stay seated for a moment longer. I leapt to my feet. They all leaned back as I rushed around the table and hugged Rupert. Turning to the others he said, 'told you she would be pleased.' Then to Julian he said, 'they are the team from when what you don't know what happened took place.'

Dead pan, Julian replied, 'oh, really.' He knows full well, he could probably write their biographies.

Martin restarted as I returned to my seat after my uncharacteristic emotional spectacle. 'The team will arrive late in the evening two weeks on Sunday. We tried hard but it proved impossible to extricate them from some serious work in the Met any faster than that. You can have your first meeting the following day, that is the Monday morning. We have booked this room.'

I asked, 'I was already astonished as to how the three of you came together here at less than a day's notice. This is now unbelievable. How on earth have you reformed the team at two weeks' notice?'

Claudia answered, 'it has not been easy. Two of us have disappointed a government minister today. When she heard the reason, not only was she happy to postpone our meeting, other doors suddenly opened. This investigation is being undertaken at the highest possible level. If, or I am sure that I can say when, it is successful, you will be feted from on high.'

Julian spoke, I had seen him brooding through this exchange, 'If I may, I would like to make a suggestion.' Claudia said "of course" and Julian continued, 'if prostitution is possibly involved it may be better to avoid meeting at the hotel. I have never heard of prostitutes being based here but you can be sure they attend. My flat is less than half a mile from where Meadows goes drinking and presumably where we will at least start. We could meet there. Also there is parking in the basement with a lift from there to my level without going through reception. The garage entrance is discrete, behind the railway station. All could drive in, park in visitors slots that I can pre-book, and make their way to my flat without being seen. I have plenty of room and spare keys. We can establish a temporary control centre there.'

They were impressed and delighted. It was arranged that the team all meet at Julian's flat on the Monday morning. I simply cannot believe that I will be seeing them all again in just over two weeks. When I asked which flat we should go to Julian simply replied, "top floor." He has been very reticent about where he lives and I have not gleaned any details. Respecting his privacy I have not asked. On the other hand I am intrigued, especially now. Perhaps I will find out about both his home and his now obvious continued involvement in a computer security company.

After a few moments of us each looking at the others, wondering what more to say or ask, Claudia said, 'we seem to have come to a natural and highly satisfactory conclusion.' She theatrically looked at her watch, 'three pm. We have finished in an hour what I had set aside the whole afternoon for. Marvellous, I think fellow officers, friends, this bodes very well indeed. I know full well that I need not say this but please indulge me. Do not enter the station. If any of the Troop call to interview you then tell them to contact Max Carruthers who knows to prevaricate.' To Julian she teased, 'I wish I could afford a solicitor who knows the DPP.' Then back to us both, 'please, please be careful. We do not want a repeat of what happened to you Rebecca. This gang could be very nasty.' Then she did something that seemed even more out of character than it was for me hugging the Commander. She stood, came around the table and enveloped Julian and me in a joint bear hug whilst the others patted our backs.

We all shook hands and left the room. Julian and I walked towards the city whilst the others headed for the car park. We were uncharacteristically silent. When we reached the end of East Street he pointed at the top of a smart looking tower and said, 'that's me, there. See you in two weeks.' There is a big twinkle in his eyes. He knows that I am burning with curiosity and he is going to make me wait.

When I got home I opened the envelope Peter had returned to me and switched on my 'phone for the first time in now more than twenty-four hours. I panicked when I saw that I had missed three calls from Luke. Then I saw his text and my heart flipped. As he said himself it is unusual in effectively meeting the family on only the second date. I do not know how I will face her as he will have told her what I did. Even so I think that it is a delightful idea and I immediately and readily accepted. The moment after pressing send I thought that perhaps I was too effusive, hardly cool. Then I thought, sod it, that is what I feel. I can't wait.

I exercised hard for the evening and then fruitlessly tried to read. I went to bed knowing that it is hopeless to expect to sleep. For the second time in two nights I looked at the ceiling but tonight is so, so different. I am so energised. I am seeing Luke on Sunday and I am starting a major investigation in a two weeks' time. More, I am heading it. I realised that one word sums up the last three evenings and two days. Starting with my behaviour with Luke, through my arrest to my new role, in the middle finding out a little more regarding Julian; there is only one word, astonishment. The events that happened to me, my arrest, meeting Carruthers, the clandestine operation; these are all surprises, they have come from outside. What truly amazes me is my behaviour; role playing a dominatrix, hugging a Commander and a Chief

Constable. All of these are completely out of character for me. Then I realised, I have not even considered being attacked at knife point and hospitalising a culprit. Those must be all in an average day's work for a woman like me, not worth bothering about. To my further astonishment I then found myself slipping into what is obviously going to be a deep, satisfying sleep; hopefully with dreams of anticipation of Sunday.

CHAPTER 14: LUKE: SUNDAY LUNCH

Sam came in to my study where, for the last hour, I have been supposedly trying to read. In reality I have been pacing up and down, constantly looking out of the window, jittery with anticipation. With deliberate, teasing, calm she said, 'lunch is all ready, we can relax now and await our visitor.' Then, while looking intently at me with a knowing smirk, she added, 'she is of course your guest, you are the host, I am only the gooseberry. As for relaxing, it appears that only I am capable of that until she arrives.' With a sigh of exasperation, I am now being baited, Sam pleaded, 'is there any chance of a drink? That is if you can tear yourself away from the window.' I reluctantly stepped across to the other side of the room surreptitiously looking at the clock as I turned. Sam observed, 'it is one minute to one, thirty seconds later than the last time you checked the time. I can see, big brother, that you are being cool about her visit.' Bugger; does she miss anything?

Sam glanced out of the window then put her hand to her forehead in a theatrical gesture of relief, and continued, 'here she comes. As I expected, bang on time. You can stop fretting now.' I froze, my hand half way to the bottle, my heart suddenly thumping . I looked across to Sam who is now staring hard across the square. She said, now softly, more to herself than to me, 'bloody hell. Look at her. She is on fire.'

I raced to join her next to the window and stared out

at the beautiful woman striding across the square, coming to see me. As she passed the centre the knowing smile held by the statue of the young, virginal woman seems to be appraising Rebecca, giving approval. Rebecca does indeed look stunning. She is wearing a long, loose, check blazer; a cream cashmere polo jumper; loose jeans that have to be designer, and loafers. It is not the clothes. It is not the clothes nor her athletic figure and poise. It is her. Sam is correct, she is radiating excitement. She does seem to be on fire. Moving away from the window and turning to walk out of the room, Sam said, no longer teasing, now with love for me in her eyes, 'I will busy myself in the kitchen whilst you .... as you .... well, say hello.' She squeezed my arm as she passed me and disappeared.

I forced myself to wait for the doorbell to ring and I then sauntered to open it casually as if I had not been watching Rebecca approach. She came in and gave me a hesitant peck on the cheek as we struggled to speak. Finally we both managed a strangled "hello." I took her jacket and we went into my study. I closed the door behind me and then I turned to look at her.

We both cracked at the same instant. Throwing our arms around each other we kissed hard and hugged. Finally our lips parted. Still holding me close she spoke softly into my ear, 'I had planned to play it cool, at least at first.'

Laughing I said, 'snap. That ridiculous idea vanished as soon as I spotted you walking across the square.' She raised an eyebrow in appreciation. 'Not that I was looking out for you of course.' She kissed me again, now softly. I caught her perfume, she is only wearing a little making it subtle and alluring. It smells exotic; there is incense with smoky, woody notes.

There came a knock at the door and Sam yelled out, 'can I come in? Are you still decent?'

We reluctantly pulled away from each other, Rebecca laughing helplessly at Sam's brazen comment, me pulling an exasperated grimace as if to say, "my difficult sister." I called out, 'you can come in if you promise to stop being rude.' Sam strode in saying "no way" to me as she swept past to Rebecca. She gave Rebecca a hug and a kiss on the cheek as they said hello. Without any polite conversation, any introduction, anything further that would vaguely pass as normal intercourse, Sam ploughed on. I spotted a mischievous grin on her face and I thought, "oh shit, what is she going to say now." Rebecca has seen it as well; in fact it is difficult to miss. She looked at Sam quizzically. I moved forward to interrupt but before I could Sam stepped back and ostentatiously peered past Rebecca, looking behind her, then behind the sofa and over at Toby's chair. Eventually, with an exaggerated grimace of exasperation, hands on hips, she said to Rebecca, 'ok, where have you put it. I want to see.'

Knowing that she is being set up Rebecca wisely said nothing but simply smiled, one of her eyebrows raised yet further. Sam folded her arms with a defiant expression and stared back with mock, grim determination. Rebecca eventually gave in and asked cautiously, knowing that she is about to be teased, 'you win. What have I put where?'

'The bag that contains all your bondage gear and whips of course; I would like to see them.'

Rebecca let out a wail and sank backwards on to the sofa covering her face with her hands. I shouted 'for god's sake Sam,' but I cannot keep the laughter out of my voice. The door burst open and Toby bounded in, obviously concerned by the piercing cry from Rebecca. He ran up to her and put his chin on her leg as if to say, "don't worry, I am here to protect you again." Behind her hands I can see that Rebecca is shaking with mirth. Sam looks very pleased with herself. I gave up and asked, 'would you like a drink?'

Her face still covered by her hands Rebecca said, 'a very big one.'

As I poured the drinks Sam went to sit next to Rebecca and took her hands. She leaned forward and whispered something into Rebecca's ear. I struggled to hear but only caught Sam saying, 'you were absolutely wonderful.' They smiled at each other and had an awkward hug. No doubt they were talking about Wednesday night. Louder, and more light heartedly, Sam asked, 'what is your perfume? It is delicious and very seductive.' Yes Sam, I thought, it is, or at least it is seducing me.

'Pomegranate Noir by Jo Malone.' As Sam nodded I thought, "what a good name, the thoughts it is evoking in me are certainly noir."

Finally I handed them the drinks and Sam said with an ostentatious flourish, 'why thank you Luke. Kir Royale, you know how much I like that. Thank you for spoiling me.'

Before I could object to this Rebecca chipped in, 'actually I don't like it at all. For you though Samantha, I will suffer it.' They chinked glasses and Rebecca winked at Sam. I mentally gave up. I have no chance with these two who are obviously bonding and colluding. Then I spotted the twinkle in Rebecca's eyes. Her intense look at me said, "you remembered, thank you."

I am in the company of two strong women who are clearly intending to enjoy teasing both each other and, probably mostly, me. Wednesday night's dinner was dramatic enough. Here without the normalising influence of a restaurant it is terrifying to anticipate the possibilities. I am delighted at this. I sipped my drink. I looked at the tall cut glass with its light pink petillant contents; I have forgotten to buy some blackcurrants to put in as they had in the restaurant. What the hell, it does not matter. Where on earth did they get them from at this time of year anyway? Actually

I do not care for Kir Royale but today it tastes delicious.

I looked at them both with appreciation as well as apprehension. I sat back contentedly and watched them as they chatted affectionately. I am so glad that Sam is warming to Rebecca. Obviously Rebecca likes Sam as well. The two elegant, beautiful women talking on my sofa seem to fit in so well in this room. The low February sun is bringing out the warmth of my wooden panelling as well as the ancient patterns in my polished rock slices. The crackling and smell of the wood fire is complimenting Rebecca's perfume and, along with the occasional waft of roasting beef, are combining to a soporific contentment. I took another sip and looked at Toby, his massive head still on Rebecca's leg as she absently strokes his neck, his soulful brown eyes looking up at them both with adoration. As I sit opposite to them all I am content to quietly watch. Probably I am wearing the same expression as Toby.

Sam sat up a little briskly, surprising us, then said, now seriously, 'Rebecca, in truth, I owe you an apology. I am sorry for being so offhand with you when we have met over the last few months. I should be honest, I was not offhand, more downright rude. Obviously it related to how we first met. You did nothing wrong, indeed what you did was both professional and essential, but I found being interrogated very difficult. Heaven knows what it would feel like if I was guilty. I am sorry.'

Rebecca said firmly, with a mock frown that implies it is now her turn to tease, 'it is a good job that I was only gently enquiring then. If I had been interrogating you I would have brought my whips along.' After we finished laughing at this she continued, now gently, 'there is no need to apologise, I realise how you must have felt. It is only too frequent. Many people refuse to even look at us after we have chatted to them at home. If we take them into the station it is worse. Again, there is nothing to apologise for. I am glad of the opportunity to meet you properly. I am very much enjoying your company.' She jerked her head towards me, 'it's a pity he has to be here though.' Together, smiling, they gave each other a conspiratorial hug. I realise that I am in a minority and I am going to be on the receiving end of much of today's banter. As they sat opposite me I started to feel rather vulnerable. Then as she looked warmly towards me, over the top of Sam's head, I belatedly spotted the affection in Rebecca's words and expression. My chest gave another flutter.

Returning to being serious Sam continued, 'are we still suspects, that is if he is still missing.' I froze, this is dangerous Sam. On the other hand I want to know the answer as well for two reasons. Do we need to be careful or even stop? How do I deal with a relationship with Rebecca? It is only date number two but clearly a relationship is developing and after Wednesday we are already close. Sam and I scour the news and net for reports of any of the men we have treated. To our delight, with the exception of a couple of reports recording the disappearance of Robin and Brian James, there has been nothing whatsoever.

Rebecca said, possibly a little too quickly, 'I never considered you suspects in Brian James' disappearance, and yes, he is still missing.'

Sam also picked up on Rebecca's too quick and too careful answer and she continued, 'well, at least that is good to know. However I am intrigued that you specified "I" and "James." This implies there is more to tell. What do others think and what about Robin?' Whilst saying this she sat back on the sofa in order to be able to look directly at Rebecca. I felt myself become very still as I sat facing them on the opposite one. I am now beginning to feel nervous. Sam had not divulged her intention to pursue this line.

Rebecca clearly hoped that the moment had passed but Sam

fixed her with another determined look. Rebecca shook her head and said, 'ok, ok, I give in, again.' She stressed the "again" and turning to me asked, 'is she always like this?' I gave a, "this is nothing shrug."

Rebecca continued now speaking to us both, 'I only ever regarded you as possible witnesses or perhaps persons of interest, never actual suspects. Because of the coincidences with your ex-husband's disappearance Julian was initially suspicious, less so now.' That minor comment made my stomach churn. So he is still considering us. 'On the James' file you are not recorded as suspects, I could not be here if you were. In fact there are no suspects, simply a big fat dead end.' She is clearly not happy with that and reluctantly carried on, 'in fact my only dead end case since I have been here.' How pleased I am to hear that. I am sorry for her but overjoyed for Sam and myself. Rebecca pressed on, 'with regard to your ex-husband I did review the file. Actually, Julian did and he reported to me. Obviously, given the circumstances, you were initially suspected but your alibis were rock solid and you were very quickly exonerated. That file is technically still open but as with James there is nothing useful whatsoever in it.'

Sam replied, 'thanks for your candour Rebecca. I find it difficult that you have not heard anything about Robin. You probably remember me saying that as his mother has not heard from him I consider it most likely that he is dead. I would prefer to see the body. I doubt that I will sleep easy until I am certain he will not return.'

I see that Sam is laying down a smokescreen. Even so the very mention of the man I murdered, however justifiably, in front of the accomplished detective looking back at his case still fills me with foreboding. My head is beginning to whirl. The champagne is mingling with the risky sweeps of the conversation.

Toby saved the day. He had kept his chin on Rebecca's leg throughout the talk. She had been continuing to absent-mindedly rub the thick ruff on the back of his neck as we were talking. She stopped and he gave a little yelp of dismay and nuzzled her to restart. Rebecca moved her hand and some of Toby's hair had caught on it and came away. She held her hand up looking in wonder at one long, thick hair hanging from her finger nail. She said, 'sorry Toby, I seem to be scalping you.' She turned her hand, still admiring the strand, jet black at one end, and continued, 'look at this you lucky boy. Your hairs are so thick and you cleverly shade them so they darken towards one end. How do you do that you clever boy? Toby, so many women would kill for hair like this.' She then looked pointedly at me and my long, black hair and continued, 'some men would kill as well.' My heart stopped as I heard her words. Then I realised that she is musing and had not accurately constructed the sentence. She had meant, "some men would kill for hair like this." She is teasing as mine is so similar. At least, I hope that is what she meant.

Sam also looked startled, she quickly said, 'Vera would strongly disagree with you.' Rebecca looked quizzical and Sam realised that she does not know who Vera is. Sam continued, 'Vera is our cleaner. We, that is Luke and I, are clean and tidy but she has to come in three times a week, largely because of Toby. She has young children so she is here during school hours and we do not often see her. Every time we meet she moans about the amount of hair that Toby sheds and how difficult it is to hoover up. In reality she loves him to bits. When we are away Toby goes to stay with her.' Then Sam's stomach rumbled and she finished, 'let's eat. I am hungry.' Walking towards the door she turned and pulled our old family monopoly board out of its drawer. With her impish grin back in place she turned to Rebecca saying, 'I am not sure if Luke has told you but I have to go to the refuge at three.' She ostentatiously put the board down on a side table and continued, 'I will leave this here in case you are stuck for something to do this afternoon.' With this she flounced out.

Looking at Rebecca I shook my head to communicate apologies for my mischievous sibling being so trying. She took my arm and whispered, 'I don't like monopoly. Will you tempt me with something else?' Like teenagers we held back and had a surreptitious, expectant kiss until Sam yelled from the dining room asking what is keeping us.

We had a superb lunch. We rarely eat meat but Sam had decided to cook a traditional roast beef. She is an excellent cook. We frequent a specialist butcher when we do eat meat and the result was delicious. Whilst enjoying our food we had a general, wide ranging chat. It was perfect for getting to know each other. When we have Sunday lunch Sam insists that it is semi-formal. We sat at the dining table with a white damask table cloth and our best cutlery, china and glasses. We also had candles in silver candelabra. Even when it is only the two of us these effects add to the atmosphere. With Rebecca here being old fashioned accentuated the warmth flowing across the table.

As the kitchen area is only separated by a counter Sam could continue chatting whilst serving the food. She had insisted on doing everything today. The only difficulty is that, as always, Toby had sprawled across the centre of the room and Sam has to step dangerously over him as she moves in and out. Sam and Rebecca hit it off, they complement each other being so different yet still gelling together. There was only one glitch that surprised me and that I do not fully understand. To my great surprise Sam spoke about thinking of dating again. She has told me but she must be feeling very in tune with Rebecca to have raised it with her. Rebecca spotted something in Sam's demeanour and asked if there was anyone specific in mind.

Sam hesitated and blushed; then she surprised me further by saying that there is. This is the first I have heard of this. It is so unlike her not to speak candidly to me of all her thoughts as soon as they arise. I sat back and listened intently.

Sam said that she was very attracted to one of the doctors in A and E. Rebecca asked who. Sam and I both know that Rebecca's work takes her there regularly and it is likely that she has met them all. Sam said, the new consultant, Marcus Rice. Rebecca looked stunned and abruptly tensed. After a while she stammered that, yes, she has seen him and, yes, he is very attractive. Sam immediately quizzed her on why she was so taken aback. Sam is obviously concerned that Rebecca knows something about Marcus Rice that will be relevant to her. Rebecca replied that she thought that he is married. Sam said, with a relieved laugh, that he is but the rumour is that he is separated and getting divorced. Then Sam continued saying that as Rebecca knows him she will mention to him that she has met Rebecca, it will be a good ruse to start a chat.

Rebecca then looked even more startled and jumped back, nearly knocking over her wine, quickly and loudly saying, 'no, no, don't do that.' When Sam asked why Rebecca looked almost distraught and finally said, again stammering uncertainly, so unlike her, that she had had a disagreement with Marcus Rice and it may not help to mention her name. She seems very unsure of herself. I feel that there may be more to this and Sam also looks suspicious. However, the moment passed and we continued on to lighter subjects.

At the end of the meal Sam fixed Rebecca with one of her unwavering looks and, whilst making an elegant conjuring gesture, demanded, 'time for you to tell us.' I have no idea what she is talking about. Rebecca, however, does not appear surprised. 'You are on fire today Rebecca. You seem to be getting on well with the man of the house, Toby that is, but I suspect it is more than that. You were attacked at knife point only three days ago but I guess that is all in a routine day's work for you. So what is it, what's going on?' My bloody sister, sometimes I think that telepathy must exist and that she can do it. The moment these words came out I saw how prescient they are.

Rebecca sat back, looked at us earnestly, then she unveiled the reason. She calmly told us about her arrest and suspension. We were both spellbound. At the end I thought that I am not surprised that she is excited. Sam thought otherwise and pressed on, 'now you can tell us the rest. What you have said is undoubtedly dramatic but it would worry and dismay you. You are neither. You are stimulated.' As Sam spoke I can see the incisive truth in what she was saying.

Rebecca now looks hesitant again. 'I do not wish to be rude. I cannot tell you. That is not my decision but I have been tasked with leading a team to pursue an undercover operation. In such work we all have to maintain absolute secrecy. The married members cannot even tell their spouses. As the team leader it is possible that I may have to censure a member who has spoken to another. That would be hypocritical if I had done the same. I am sorry but I cannot say any more. It is not that I do not trust you. In fact even saying what I have is breaking the rules. Obviously I do not think you would tell anyone, I would not have said anything if I thought that, but please, please do not even hint at it to any one at all. Even the fact that there is an operation is secret.'

Sam said, again frightening me, 'don't worry, we are very good at keeping secrets.' Oh shit, why did she have to say that? 'You can be absolutely certain that neither of us will breathe a word in any circumstances. Will we Luke?' I could not speak. I sat there staring. 'Luke, wakey wakey, we will not say anything will we?'

After a while, ignoring Sam's question I asked, 'Rebecca, are you in danger?' They looked at me realising that I had not answered Sam as I was frightened.

'Not too much.'

Now I am even more worried. I pressed on, 'that scar, is it what I think it is?' I put my fingers just below my ribcage on the left indicating which scar I meant. That was actually a redundant gesture as I have first-hand knowledge that it is her only one, one of a pair that is. Sam is clearly puzzled by what appears to be a non-sequitur.

Rebecca's eyes brightened. I thought that she was relieved to find out what is worrying me. I misjudged her. She has spotted an opportunity to tease me and to change the subject. 'That depends on what you think it is.'

She is going to make me say what I think and possibly make me look foolish. Now both Sam and Rebecca are giving me "go on" looks. They waited. I tried to get out of the spot they have put me in by not replying. Eventually they won. Prodding the area again I stuttered, 'I am no expert but I can only think of one thing causing a scar like that.'

Sam stood. With an exasperated air she pulled up her blouse and said, 'he should know Rebecca. I have one as well. It is a splenectomy if it is there.' She showed her scar resulting from the injuries sustained when Robin attacked her. We shook our heads and Sam looked mystified.

Rebecca stood and lifted her jumper showing the one centimetre round scar and then she turned to show the slightly larger one in line behind it, totally unlike Sam's single, thin, linear mark. Sam blanched and whispered, 'that's a bullet wound.' Rebecca nodded.

Dry mouthed I managed to ask, 'what happened?'

'I was on an undercover operation when I worked in

the Met.................... Stop looking so panicked. It is unlikely this one will turn out to be as dangerous.' Unlikely, bloody unlikely, I don't like the sound of that. 'At the end of the mission I was on the team that went in to make the arrests. We knew that the gang we were rounding up were always armed so we were also carrying firearms and wearing bullet proof vests. They were all in a cellar bar. As I was running down the stairs towards them, one of them, the gang boss, came out shooting. My left arm was holding the stair rail for balance and trailing above and behind me so pulling up my vest and his bullet passed under it. Thankfully it was what they call in the films a flesh wound. It passed through and a scan showed that my spleen was bruised but not ruptured. Major surgery was not required, the wound was only tidied up.'

Transfixed Sam gently enquired, 'what happened to the shooter. I presume it was a man?'

'Yes it was a man. He is dead.' Neither of us spoke but our eyes asked "what happened?" Now reluctantly, Rebecca continued, 'I shot him in his head.' She paused and looked at us uncertainly, not sure what our reaction may be. Still silent we both gave understanding and supportive nods. Seeing our favourable, non-condemning response Rebecca continued more certainly, 'we knew that he often wore a bullet proof vest as there were frequent shootings between the gangs. It was the entrance to the club and innocent bystanders surrounded us. One had already been injured by his wild firing. I had to stop him and I only had one option. As he shot at me I shot him. I deliberately shot him between the eyes. I killed him.'

The room went deathly quiet. Toby picked up on the change in atmosphere, he did not understand and his tail uncertainly thwacked against the floor as he lay sprawled, now by Rebecca's feet. I gulped. Rebecca is looking at the table. I can see that she is not upset by the shooting but still concerned as to how we may feel about it. I can feel Sam's eyes burning into me, questioning and challenging me, asking, "how does this relate to our activities?" I reached across and briefly held Rebecca's hand. Then I diffidently ventured, still uncertain how to proceed. I eventually managed a response. 'I am pleased to hear that there are people in our police service who are brave enough to deal with criminals in a manner such as that when it is necessary.' I paused, should I say the rest of what I am thinking? It seems presumptuous as I hardly know her. 'I know this is a daft thing to say as I have not known you for long and I am not involved in anything similar,' I felt rather than saw Sam's worried expression, 'but I am proud to be sitting next to you.'

Sam relaxed then also squeezed Rebecca's hand and added, 'me too.'

Rebecca looked up at us both and smiled with relief that we are supportive. I guess so many would be critical and quick to condemn. I pressed on, 'if I were in the position where it was necessary to kill a criminal to protect others, then I doubt that I would hesitate. In the incident you described I would consider it moral. Arrest and a jury trial is obviously preferred but in those, and I can envisage other circumstances, summary justice for the protection of others is necessary.' Sam squirmed. She gave me a sharp "shut up" look but, much to her chagrin, I pressed on. 'For me that is hypothetical.' I felt two faced saying this but I need to hear Rebecca's opinion and how it reflects on what we are doing and I can hardly tell her the truth, not yet anyway. 'How do you feel? What did you think of the possibility before it happened and now that it has is you outlook the same?' I feel as if I am dancing the two-step but I have to know her opinion.

It was Rebecca's turn to squeeze my hand. 'Thank

you for saying that. So many people's knee jerk reaction is to condemn the police. They fail to appreciate the context. I am fine with it. I feel the same way that you do. As in all such cases there was an investigation but I was cleared of any wrongdoing. In fact, sorry but again this has to be kept secret, I was given a police medal. As the investigation remains secret and some of the gang are still at large, then few know that and fewer still know the circumstances. I also had compulsory counselling but that was unnecessary and after a couple of sessions it became a friendly chat for the rest of the stipulated course. The only concern I have, not for then as it did not happen, but for a possible future similar situation, is that I might have missed. He was surrounded by innocent club goers. For their protection I had to act but that in itself put them in danger, albeit less hazard than his wild shooting. I fired before his bullet hit me but I was still half falling downstairs. I could have killed an innocent person. He would certainly have killed more, probably including me. If the circumstances are repeated I will not, cannot, hesitate to do the same again. Anyway that is an unlikely hypothetical. Most police officers never shoot anyone. Even then I rarely carried firearms and I never do now. I try to keep to arresting rather than shooting.' This last part was said with a smile and the atmosphere lifted a little.

'Actually, Rebecca, I want to press you further on your thoughts as, whilst hypothetical, I have, in the past, certainly considered murder. I need to tell you as it may reflect on your opinion of me. I want to be open and honest.' Rebecca looked startled but Sam froze in fear at what I was going to say. 'When Robin was released from prison after such a ludicrously short time I felt that Sam was again under considerable threat and that the criminal justice system had failed her. The fact is that it indeed had and still does fail society in domestic abuse in not protecting the victims.' Seeing her disagreement, before she could speak, I said, 'I know, I know. The rights of the possible offenders need to be put in the balance and I would not want it any other way. It is extremely complicated and, though critical of the system, I find it near impossible to envisage one that combines respecting alleged offenders' rights as well as fully protecting victims.'

Rebecca relaxed and nodded agreement. Sam still looks as if she is sitting on hot coals. 'Remember, at that time, I had thought for weeks that Sam was going to die. This was followed by having to stand back and watch as she suffered multiple, painful, procedures and months of gruelling rehab. When we were told that he was being released I thought that the only way to protect her was to murder him. To be frank I did start planning. Then, thankfully, he disappeared. However my worries are not over, what if he comes back? What should I do then?'

I saw Sam relax a little. She can see that I am hiding in full sight. That is partly true. In addition I am keen to discover Rebecca's philosophy on this, out of genuine interest in her views. Also I am asking in the desperate hope that she could join our work in the future, maybe, who knows?

'I am not demeaning your understandable, in fact laudable, thoughts but if you were to undertake anything at all, from threatening him to injuring him, then you would be acting as a vigilante. I cannot support such actions, either philosophically or as a police officer. In any civilised society there must be the rule of law, a presumption of innocence and a right to a fair trial. When punishment is necessary we must be careful that it is only administered by bodies with the appropriate checks and balances. Most philosophers consider that judgment, retribution or punishment by individuals is not legitimate. This power is transferred to the State to ensure it is undertaken both proportionately and justly.'

Rebecca paused as she considered further, then reluctantly continued, 'also, I think it is correct that on the whole we do not undertake capital punishment. I realise that sounds hypocritical as I have told you I deliberately shot someone dead but that was in exceptional circumstances for the immediate protection of others.'

'Surely there are possibilities where we could all be in such circumstances and be forced to act. Further what about people whom the State have failed when there is no doubt who the perpetrator is, I would include Sam in this group? If we have a contract with the State and hand it the power but it fails to act, then it is the State who has reneged on the contract, not the person seeking justice.'

Rebecca looked at me again, seeming a little uncertain, 'I cannot condone vigilantes. Think of the times they get it wrong. Remember during the child abuse hysteria a few years ago when an innocent man was attacked and PEDO daubed on his wall. Not only could they not spell paedo but they did not know the difference between a paedophile and what he in fact was, a paediatrician.' She hesitated yet again and then diffidently continued, 'I am saying vigilante, you are saying people seeking justice. Technically both are correct yet I would guess we agree that there is a vast difference, morally and emotionally. It is an extremely difficult area. You probably guess from the manner of my reply that it is something that I have studied and wrestled with. I agree that the justice system is often inadequate but I cannot see a better alternative.' Finally she smiled and shook her head, 'give me three yobs armed with knives. I would choose that challenge any day over this one.'

I squeezed her hand again but still I pressed on. 'I hope that you do not censure me for considering murder and for pushing you for your opinion. I was not being critical or seeking your support for my thoughts. I genuinely wanted to hear what you think. Thankfully, unless he returns of course, it is hypothetical.' Throughout this exchange Sam had looked serious and was also listening attentively to what Rebecca said. On my last comment she flashed a hard look at me and shook her head. Rebecca, however, is engaged with the discussion.

When I had said "censure" Rebecca had given a "certainly not" shake of her head which emboldened me to continue. 'I would never condone the knee jerk reaction of people who have not considered the philosophy or investigated the offences properly. However there must be circumstances, again I think my thoughts about Robin are included in these, where the evidence is in no doubt and the police cannot act because of the criminal justice system.' I hesitated, is my next question too far? 'What if it was Julia who had previously been gravely injured and was in imminent danger of being attacked again by the same man. What if she were at high risk of being seriously injured again, possibly killed. What would you do?'

Rebecca's eyes blazed. She said without prevarication or doubt, 'I would kill him. In such limited and specific circumstances, such as I did in the different circumstances on the steps of that club or in the hypothetical situation you describe, I would not hesitate. I would kill him.' I was taken aback by the vehemence in her voice. She obviously feels as we do that pontificating on vigilante behaviour when sitting in a philosopher's study is a million miles from some real world necessities. Rebecca most likely sees many heart breaking cases that underlies her obvious frustration.

Sam pushed back and said with a somewhat forced, jovial smile, 'well now that we have finished a gentle after Sunday lunch chat I will get coffee. Then perhaps we can move on to something lighter and non-contentious such as sex, politics or religion.' We gave a relieved laugh. Then with a wicked grin, as she went to make the coffee, Sam continued whilst looking pointedly between us and not directly at either Rebecca or me, 'if you don't mind can we not mention sex.' We all laughed again, the heavy moment has passed but I feel that I have made progress in developing my thoughts and exploring Rebecca's.

Over coffee I slipped into a contented silence. I lounged back in my chair admiring these two enchanting women as they amiably chatted together. They are so different in both appearance and temperament. They are both so lovely in both appearance and temperament. My relationship with each is also very dissimilar but I am so very close with Sam and I feel that I am already getting so close to Rebecca. Then I mused on a similarity we all have. Rebecca is obviously excited and satisfied by an undercover operation in which, whilst administering justice, occasionally people are killed. So are Sam and I. The only difference is that Rebecca's work is officially sanctioned yet criticised by many. Our abductions and my treatments are officially condemned yet would be supported by many. Toby let out a huge sigh as if to say, "stop thinking such heavy, challenging thoughts. Just enjoy the moment." So often Toby is spot on with his opinion and can communicate it clearly without speech. I returned to simply enjoying the afternoon.

After coffee Rebecca slipped off to the loo. As soon as the door closed behind her Sam fixed me with another one of her hard stares and started. 'Be very careful Luke. You are in dangerous waters.'

'I am being careful and I do not agree. Anyway, you are the one who started by laying down a smokescreen about us being suspects.'

'You misinterpret me. From my point of view an open discussion, not appearing to avoid discussing a topic is the best way of keeping our secret. I meant your relationship with her. If it is as intense as it obviously already is on only the second date, then, my lovely soppy brother, I think you are falling in love. Both of you that is. You do not want a relationship to start on a basis of deception. Leave the lies to me.'

I was stunned by what she had said. It was so incisive and at the same time so challenging. Before I could reply the door opened as Rebecca came back in. It is a heavy wooden door so I had not heard her approach. Hopefully this also means that she had not heard our conversation. Rebecca looked between the two of us. Sam looks serene and I probably look as if I have been caught with my hand in the cookie jar. Sam said, 'no need to speculate, I will tell you.' More double-speak that I cannot follow. 'Yes, we were talking about you.' Rebecca laughed at Sam's frankness and asked if it was good. Sam made the "so-so" gesture with her hand. Again we are all laughing. I have had more laughing since I have been with Rebecca than in the last two years, more kissing as well. We made our way back to sit in the front room.

After a little more, thankfully non dangerous or demanding, chat, Sam said that she had to leave. She is going to the walk to the refuge as her leg is improving so much, possibly it is just her excuse to leave early and to allow us to be alone. She is so lovely and thoughtful. Sam collected her coat and bag from her part of the house. The she returned and kissed us both goodbye. As she left the room she turned and said with yet another infuriating grin, 'please wait until I have at least got through the gate.' She flounced out before we could reply. We turned and watched her walk down the path.

As the gate closed we moved to face each other again. The mirth of Sam's throwaway line has already gone. Rebecca and I exchanged hungry looks. We threw ourselves together.

We held each other tight and kissed hard. My lip is still so sore and it hurt like hell but so what, I kissed her harder. Then, still mouth to mouth, devouring each other, we were swaying through the door and up the stairs whilst tearing off the other's clothes.

CHAPTER 15:
REBECCA: THE
REUNION

I strode up East Street towards the railway station and Julian's somewhat mysterious flat. I cannot complain that I have not been invited there before, that he keeps his home completely separate from his work. I do exactly the same. Emotions surged through me. Eight forty five on a grey March morning, even this beautiful city looks tired and drab today and there is a spattering of icy raindrops in the gusty air. Yet, internally, I am again on fire.

I have a nosy interest in seeing Julian's nest. More even than that, I am looking forward to the reunion with the team I worked with in the Met. They were my life for nearly two years ending in a dramatic finale. Two of us were shot, there major arrests, enquiries and all of it being in camera. Now we are back together. I have to pinch myself to check that I am not dreaming. It is unbelievable that after my arrest and the incredible result, only two and a half weeks later, I am not only seeing the incredible team again but I am now leading them in a major internal investigation.

In spite of all this professional excitement for once in my life I am having difficulty in focussing on the job; much of today's feeling of exhilaration is coming from a different place. My nickname in the Met team was Laser though it is not deserved today. I always liked that but I have to admit, though only to myself, that I am also proud of my new one, Tibs. I will have to pull myself together before I see them or I will lose both and be called something like Scatty. My problem is that Luke keeps intruding in my thoughts, taking my mind off the job. Only has been two weeks, already we are so close. After our lovely Sunday lunch, the kindly teasing of Samantha and the passion in bed during the afternoon, we then talked and talked until the evening. Lying naked in each other's arms for hours we talked about ourselves and each of us asked about the other. I immediately felt then that I already knew him so well.

The two weeks following my arrest have been an emotional roller-coaster at work and at play. As far as the station is aware I am suspended from work. The team were not able to meet until today so I have been at a loose end. On one hand I have been on tenterhooks waiting for the investigation to start. Julian has started digging on line. I have tried to do some snooping but it has been difficult as I must not be seen. On the other hand I have been free to spend time with Luke. He is in a lull in his academic work and other than a few lectures he has also been free. We have spent several, wonderful days and nights together. That is now likely to change as I guess that I will be fully occupied until this task is completed.

I had arranged to enter in full view through the lobby to the apartments where Julian lives. It would be expected for us to liaise as we are suspended together and it would look more suspicious if I was skulking around the rear entrance. He has texted the door codes to the underground car park and the lift to the team. They will drive in and go straight from the car park to his floor so their arrival will be unseen.

The entrance door now facing me is discrete, though there are large windows either side I cannot see in as they are of etched glass, no frilly net curtains here. I pressed the bell and waited to be buzzed in. Instead the door was opened for me by a uniformed man and he ushered me into what looks like the reception to a five star hotel. As I sank into the carpet with the chandeliers twinkling far above me I admired the floral arrangements. Behind them was a massive, impressionist style painting of a hazy, brown ship being tossed on a wild, dark blue sea. After a long trek we arrive at the receptionist's futuristic, curved, glass and chrome desk and he consulted a list on his screen.

After checking my name and confirming that I am indeed expected he escorted me to the lift and he even called it for me. As the door opened I noted from the overhead display that the other lift arrived at the car park at the same time as the doors in front of me silently parted. Perhaps it is the team arriving? The uniformed man even pressed the button for the ninth floor for me and bade me good bye as he adroitly stepped out. Am I imagining it or did he give a little bow? Open-mouthed I looked around at the wooden panelling and brass fittings. There are even fresh flowers on a pedestal. I had guessed that Julian's flat would be smart. I have surmised that during his previous work he was well paid. This opulence is more than I had anticipated and this is only the lobby and the lift.

The lift doors opened and I stepped out. Before I could assimilate my surroundings the adjacent lift doors opened and out came the team. Tom, Alison, Simon, Charlie and John all stepped out. We have not seen each other for nearly a year and so there was a couple of minutes of hugging and back slapping. Finally we stood back and took in the surroundings. We were all silenced by the wide open hall with plush wall paper and brass wall lights. A spiral staircase with glass sides and a brass banister swept down and the chandelier above twinkled. Taken aback I looked at them and saw their inquiring faces. I shrugged and said, 'I haven't been here before but I guess it is this door.' There is no number, no name plate, but as it is the only one my detective skills were not stretched.

The door opened as we approached and Julian stepped out saying that he had heard a hullaballoo and guessed that it was the Met. That was an excellent start. There were further teasing exchanges and all were introduced. Julian bade us in.

We were all quietened again as we assimilated his huge entrance hall whilst he put our coats into the silently sliding, floor to ceiling, fitted cupboards. Then he opened the inner door and led us in. We halted in a stupefied bunch a little inside the door. Simon was muttering and pushing as the leaders had blocked the doorway. Julian waved his arm and said, 'good view from up here isn't it.' We were all looking at the room. We had not yet reached as far as the view.

It is vast. The floor of this one room is the same area as my house. The height of the central atrium and the two full length windows on the two walls in front of us are the same height as my house. We all walked silently to the window and turned around. On the two walls which do not have windows there is a gallery. One side of the gallery has a panelled, book lined library; the other has banks of computers. Alison, who was our computer guru during the Met operation, took them in and uttered, 'holy shit, there is more computing power there than in Microsoft.' Her fingers twitched. She is having to restrain herself.

Julian retorted, 'that is an exaggeration but I admit my array is powerful.' I saw Alison continue to fight to restrain herself from scurrying up the curved open stairs and cuddling the hard drives. It will be interesting to discover who has the greater computer skill of the two. I can see that they are already locking horns. I turned back to look out of the panoramic windows. At first I was distracted by a train passing in complete silence nine floors below. The windows are triple glazed. Then I looked South and West and I spotted the top of the church in the square where Luke lives. I am not going to be effective at leading this team if I keep looking that way.

Tom said, 'my brother has told me that he thinks there is someone on the take in the station. Now we know who it is.' Grinning he looked at Julian who shrugged. I raised my eyebrows at Tom silently asking, "who is his brother?" 'My little brother is PC Dereck Cartwright.' I know him but I did not know that he is Tom's sibling. He is one of those who attended the attack on me. Little brother, he is at least six foot two.

Julian is clearly going to leave them all guessing so I interjected, 'to put you all out of your misery and to prevent any more scurrilous speculation,' I pretended to glare at Tom who mocked a penitent head hang, 'I will inform you that before joining the service Julian worked in computer security. We can all presume,' I theatrically waved my hand around, 'that he was well rewarded.' Alison and Julian again stared at each other, each giving the other a smiling, combative, "I will beat you" look. I quietly thought to myself that I may not have used the correct tense. I suspect that Julian is still more than a little involved with whoever he worked for.

Julian ushered us over to the kitchen area which is so discrete that I had not even seen it. As he made coffee he suggested that we all set up at the vast dining table as it will be the best place to be able to work separately. We will have sufficient space to concentrate yet still be together. In keeping with modern policing we all put our laptops on the highly polished mahogany after Julian had assured us that the varnish is indestructible. He gave us his wifi password and we all connected. Alison's brow immediately furrowed and her fingers flashed. Whilst we chatted amiably, the old team and Julian getting acquainted, she tapped furiously.

After a few minutes and many expletives she suddenly slumped back and cried out, 'holy Mary mother of god will you look at this.' She turned her screen to us and there was a photograph of Julian sitting at the head of a long table in a plush board room with JCCS in large gold lettering behind him.

We looked from that to Julian who spoke only to Alison, 'I am very impressed that you found that at all, let alone so quickly.' The look on his face clearly shows that he is in fact both extremely impressed and challenged. Round one to Alison but I can tell from his expression that Julian is sharpening his claws.

Julian sat like a statue with an inscrutable soft smile and made no further comment. After a pregnant pause Alison capitulated and read the text below his photograph, 'strictly confidential memo to IT Directors of JCCS Banking and Insurance Clients. I wish to inform you of changes following on from our flotation on the Stock Exchange. Firstly the flotation has been very successful and enables further development of our services. Secondly, whilst our accounts are now in the public domain all of our clients' accounts and their security systems are completely separate and remain subject to client confidentiality as they contain sensitive information. Client accounts are totally secure and secret. Finally, in order to pursue other activities in the field of security, I am stepping down from much of the day to day business of the company. I wish to assure you that our security assessments will be undertaken by the same team that you have been dealing with before. I retain a controlling interest in the company and I will be in regular, at least weekly, contact with the Consultant in charge of your portfolio. Yours, Julian Courtney, Founder and Director of Julian Courtney Computer Services.'

Julian looked serenely out of the window. The team

looked at me and they can see from my expression that I had had no idea that Julian is still engaged in such a company. Alison stated, it was not a question, 'so, you are a hacker. A top level poacher turned gamekeeper but still a hacker.' A broad smile crossed her face and she looked at him almost reverently and continued softly, 'I can't wait to work with you.'

I told the team how Julian knew about our previous assignment together. Now they are all looking at him with reverence.

We fell back into a discussion that after the revelations was initially stilted. It quickly slipped back into a friendly banter. A respectful comradery had re-emerged between the original six of us and Julian was immediately accepted in by the others. He was teased further with Tom picking up on the phrase in the memo, "other activities in the field of security." He opined that he had not heard being a wooden top referred to in that manner before. After a few minutes more chatting John light-heartedly questioned me saying, 'tell us Rebecca, have you found a squeeze in this fine city?'

Before I could even think what to say Julian chimed, 'she is seeing Luke Cape, a Professor of Earth Sciences at the University.' I rocked back, stared at Julian. I tried to glare but it came across as astonishment that he knew. Picking up on this they all hooted and the emboldened Julian continued, 'well at least I think it was her who I saw leaving his house a couple of weeks ago, on a Wednesday morning at eight am wearing last night's clothes. She had obviously been taken to somewhere very posh and she had returned the favour in the time honoured fashion. He lives behind the station and, when going in, I spotted someone looking very much like Rebecca leaving his house. It may not have been her though, possibly a doppelganger. I have to admit that though the face was identical this woman was wearing a very sexy dress, not an Armani tracksuit.' As they all roared, behind my blushes, I thought, "so much for avoiding the walk of shame."

Out of the corner of my eye I had seen Alison pounding the keyboard and seconds later she cried out, 'holy shit, Rebecca, you are screwing him.' She yet again turned her screen towards us all continuing, 'you lucky sod. He is gorgeous.'

Looking at the screen John said, 'bloody hell. I would screw him as well and I am straight.'

I had not seen it before. It is a superb photograph of Luke obviously taken on a geological field trip and used in the University literature. He was standing on the edge of a cliff in brilliant sunshine with a view of a turquoise sea. There is a Mediterranean looking village behind and an excavation to the side. His hair was streaming back in the wind and his loose white linen shirt billowed open. In one hand he held a shining, black rock sample and in the other a geological hammer. No wonder the University had used it. He looked inviting, masculine, intelligent, and as Alison had said, drop dead gorgeous. I thought to myself, yes Alison, I am screwing him, and I am delighted to be doing so.

Simon asked how we had met and again before I could even begin to answer Julian interrupted again, 'he is a suspect in a disappearance, probably a murder.' They all sat back as I rounded on Julian and, too quickly and too sharply for them to believe, I told both Julian and them that he is most certainly not a suspect.

Julian and I argued. It was our first ever cross words. The useful no he isn't, yes he is, adult exchange with much of it being in the vernacular. The others, after recovering from their surprise at this flare up, asked Julian why he thought that Luke is a suspect. After Julian told them of all the circumstances, including the disappearance of Samantha's husband, none of them could look me in the eye. Alison's face wore a curious expression and, at a shrewd guess, I think that all of the men consider that Luke's involvement is at least possible.

Eventually Tom cleared the air by saying, 'whoever did it I would like to catch them. Not to arrest them. I would give them a bloody medal.' They all heartily agreed, including Julian and this led to a partial rapprochement between us. We moved on with, to my surprise, a form of tenderness within what is now, already, indubitably a team.

On second thoughts it is not so much of a surprise, previous joint experiences have been unveiled. All of us except Julian have previously discussed a similar conundrum. At one time during our operation in the Met we had discovered incontrovertible evidence of horrible violence being undertaken against innocents by a couple of vicious thugs. We could not arrest them as this would have blown the whole operation. We discussed, off the record, summary justice before they could hurt more people. We all wanted to and at one or other time during the debate we all, including me, agreed that it was necessary. Eventually we concluded that we should follow the rule of law. They were arrested and given life imprisonment in the end but in the meantime they had maimed two other people who had done nothing wrong other than go into the wrong pub. We all have to live with that and we all carry the guilt. I am uncertain what I would do if a similar situation arises. I want to be lawful but I cannot get the images of those innocents being brought in by wheelchair out of my mind.

I thought of seeing Sam's scar and limp and hearing her story. Julian obviously thinks that Luke has responded to what he has seen Sam go through. In my heart I know that it is not Luke, he is too kind and gentle. It would be implausible. In my head I know to avoid thinking on it.

At last, turning to my responsibility as team leader, I rapped the table and insisted that we start planning. John smiled saying, 'good to see that Laser is back in focus.' Julian raised an eyebrow and John continued, 'Laser was Rebecca's nickname. It seemed to embody her approach. Does she have one here?'

I started to threaten Julian but again he spoke over me, 'Tibs.' Now all the others raised inquisitive eyebrows. I kicked Julian but he still carried on, 'Tough. Intelligent. Beautiful. Sexy.'

All the men laughed out loud but Alison looked ruefully towards me and quietly muttered, 'I could live with that.' Then she looked wistfully away. My heart, all of our hearts, went out to her. She is a lovely person, a superb copper and a computer wizard. However, to call her plain would be a compliment.

Finally we are underway. Though, as it is still only nine thirty and we have already gelled as a team, I consider that it is an excellent start. I told the team of the background of Meadow's behaviour and the Troop around him. I also suggested that we started looking at the Langley Hotel. Given Julian's observation that Meadows often parked there and that it is suspected as being a centre for drugs and prostitution it is as good a start as any other.

Then, after innocently asking if he could speak, Julian dropped his bombshell. 'Over the last couple of weeks I have been, ...er.............., shall we say ....looking at.......... various police officers' financial accounts and travel arrangements. Not only me, I had the help of many of the people you saw in the JCCS photograph. They were delighted to help, regarding it as a public service as well as an interesting aside. Also, of course, they are used to operating in total secrecy. To say that they uncovered some interesting facts is an understatement.' I noted that Julian was attributing the success to his team but I am sure he was front and centre. 'Our erstwhile colleagues are cash strapped police officers. Their wives, they are all married, and some of their children are quite wealthy. The source of this money was found to be, most unusually, from cash deposits. What is more this said filthy lucre is now hidden away in obscure accounts and trusts.' We all sat back, initially dumbfounded. Then Tom started to applaud and we all joined in.

Julian took a mock bow and continued, 'too soon dear colleagues, too soon. There is yet more. I have two other major discoveries to impart. Firstly the owners of the Langley Hotel are a certain James Coyle, known as Jim, and his sons James, known as Jimmie, and William, known as Will. The father and his father before him were suspected of being involved in organised crime in Northern Ireland. It appears that things became too hot for them there and they relocated here where they have kept a very low profile. Several family members, including some of the women, have spent time at what was then Her Majesty's Pleasure but only for lesser offences. They have avoided conviction for what are clearly their serious activities. It is obvious that they operate as a criminal gang.

Secondly, the Coyles, Meadows and members of the Troop travel several times a year to Mallorca, often together or at least on the same 'plane. There they hire cars using a single account linked to two adjacent houses in Soller in the west of the island. The Coyles own one and as you can guess, it was paid for by monies originating from cash, the folding variety which given the amounts necessary must have, over several months, filled several suitcases. The adjacent one is owned by Meadow's son who is only eighteen.' Julian showed us the villas on google earth. They are huge and opulent. 'As you can see it is not a bad second home for an eighteen year old who, surprise, surprise, paid using monies originally deposited as cash. In all of these transactions the spondoolies had been laundered through a couple of accounts to look legit. The Spanish authorities were diligent but, in spite of this, still skilfully hoodwinked.'

The team exchanged disbelieving blinks and sat back smiling. Tom said, 'surely we have enough to arrest them and search their properties already.' We all agreed but I pushed for prudence, to have it sewn up before we moved. Reluctantly they admitted that was a better option and we brainstormed ideas on how to progress.

Within minutes a plan was born. Julian and I could not be seen to be investigating and so we had to keep out of sight. Julian and Alison were to spend the week in his gallery, on the prodigious computer array, digging further and documenting more incriminating evidence. As soon as this had been agreed Alison kept looking up to the bank of screens, she seems to be salivating, she cannot wait to get her hands on Julian's computers.

Simon and John, as the two bachelors, are to go to the Langley and see if they could procure the services of two prostitutes. They have done this before when undercover in London and they assure me that full intercourse does not occur. In order to keep cover, they have to receive some attempted masturbation but this does not result in the usual happy ending. They tell me that it is not difficult to remain flaccid. All they have to do is think about the girls' drug habits, who else has been with them that day and what they might catch. Apparently many men, when they visit ladies of the night, do not perform and simply want to talk. That is ideal as gentle, careful questioning by Simon and John, without penetrative sex, then does not raise suspicion. They joke that they can undertake the investigation without anything being raised.

Tom will tear Alison away from the computers for one evening and go to the bar where they will pretend to be a couple and try to purchase drugs. This was arranged for Wednesday evening as we also immediately booked tickets online for Tom and me to go to Mallorca for a couple of days, leaving tomorrow and returning Wednesday afternoon We are going to see if we can unearth anything that will definitely tie Meadows to the villa there.

We were thinking of extending our brief and of trying to take down the Coyles as well as Meadows and his Troop. In view of this I called the Chief Constable to obtain her approval for both the plan and the contained increased remit. I had the direct number that she had given me, to be used only for this investigation, on speed dial. I called putting it on speaker so all could hear. She answered on the second ring. The team broke into silent laughter, yet again shaking their heads in disbelief. A Chief Constable contacted after only two rings, this clearly has the brass involved.

'Rebecca, this call is earlier than I anticipated. Is everything OK.'

'Yes Ma'am.'

She interrupted. 'Start again and address me correctly please.'

It was not a request. 'Yes Claudia.' The others nearly fell off their chairs and two had to run to the other side of the room stifling their guffaws. I outlined our proposals.

After I concluded there was a long pause. I was about to ask if she was still on the line when she said, 'well, Laser, that is meteoric even by your standards.' How the hell does she know my moniker? 'Sorry, I forgot, that should be Tibs now.' I am still on speakerphone and the others are by now uncontrollably shaking. Without pause she added, 'I sanction that sound plan and you can all consider the warrant granted. There are some people watching this with interest from a very lofty position. The legal niceties will be no problem.' She hung up. We looked at each other open – mouthed. We clearly are all thinking the same. We judge the Chief Constable to be in a "lofty position." Who on earth can she be alluding to?

As one we silently moved to the window and looked contemplatively across the city. I am, no doubt the others also are, musing on the enormity and the speed of what is happening. Our previous enquiry had taken months in preparation and had not included investigating colleagues. This is suddenly no longer amusing. We stood in a troubled silence. We all felt the dissonance of wanting to go in hard to take down corrupt officers who are bringing disrepute on the service. On the other hand it is difficult to criticise or condemn our fellows as usually we have to close ranks to overcome the frequent abuse we suffer.

Julian finally broke the silence saying, 'well, eleven o'clock. That is not too bad for two hours work. I will put on some more coffee. I feel like adding something stronger to it but perhaps that should wait.' We all soberly nodded.

....

....

Twelve o'clock on a cool, damp Friday morning, for the final day of this already momentous this week we again sat together around Julian's fine table for coffee. I examined the faces of my colleagues, my friends. All of us are feeling a conflicting surge of emotions, excitement mixed with apprehension. Both are spiced with the disappointment that we are having move on one of our own and the disbelief that we have arrived at this point in only a few days. We have discussed and we all, except Julian who was not even in the service then, agree that taking down the criminal gang in London was satisfying. Repeating this here will be similarly so for the now seven of us. Arresting a group of nasty, bent coppers will be a combination of gratifying and distasteful.

I looked at the team with incredulity and admiration, especially Alison and Julian on whose cyber prowess our success is built on. Four days and two hours of this the fifth; it took eighteen months last time.

They looked back at me expectantly and I croaked, 'I think we should move tonight, do you agree?' Six clear, loud yesses returned. In eleven hours' time the operation will explode into action. I called Claudia. Last night we had delivered a boxful of evidence to her. Mostly computer printouts, some reports of physical investigation and some photographs that Tom and I had taken in Mallorca. The high burden of justification of such an action falls on her. Even so, it is the road to perdition for us all if we get it wrong. All seven of us continue to have difficulty in accepting that I am expected to call her Claudia but there are no smiles this morning. Today is deathly serious. This time I did not even have to say her name, on the second ring she answered with, 'my congratulations to the whole team. Please proceed tonight as you suggested. Best of luck.' She hung up. Now we did, finally, all smile together.

This week has been so busy that I have not been able to see Luke. He wanted us to meet and it was so difficult to refuse. He understands that I am involved in something major and that it is not my choice to turn him down. Again I cannot believe how close we are already and the mutual understanding we have. He is involved in one of his moth collections tonight and so would not be able to see me anyway on this particular evening. I am uncertain where he is working. I hope that when the city lights up at eleven he will not be disturbed.

I then called Sergeant Benson, Peter, Claudia's brother; I am struggling as to how I should address those around me. They do not have the same problem. I am now openly Tibs to them all. To me it still sounds like a bloody cat no matter how envious the other women are of it. Peter is going to have a busy eleven hours. We are divided into several teams. The seven of us here will split into two groups with separate roles in the raid. Peter is going to contact eight of the most trusted PCs in the station to join us at six pm when they will be briefed. Four of them will join each of our groups. Boy, are they in for a shock. At present they are probably on patrol looking forward to a quiet night with the family. That will make two teams, one of seven and one of eight, which will hit the front and rear of the Langley simultaneously. Each will be in an unmarked van with an additional separate driver. Peter knows of two, both women, with consummate driving skills. One is Barbara Sturgis and I took him aside and asked for her to be placed in the group that I am heading. That is seventeen officers in total. In itself that is a major operation but there is yet more.

Peter is also assembling five other teams to hit the homes of Meadows and the Troop to arrest whoever is there and start the search for further evidence. He has already taken into limited confidence five team leaders. They have been briefed that there is to be a large operation this evening but not of its details. They have decided which four others they will each ask to join their team and they will contact them at nine pm to attend in secret a briefing commencing at ten pm. So for tonight's massive operation the only people who know the details are the three who set this up, Claudia, The Bear and Martin; Peter and the seven of us. The eight officers who will join us, the two drivers and the five team leaders know something is happening but they do not know what. The twenty others still think it is a normal Friday and will know nothing until the team leaders contact them at nine this evening. I hope that there is no major incident tonight. The station will look like it has been abandoned.

The week had progressed as if it had been choreographed. Tom and Alison brought forward their trip to the hotel. On Monday night they went in as a couple looking for some excitement and wanting drugs. Within half an hour they left with a packet of cocaine which is now in an evidence bag. They had been directed by the barman to the reception for the supposed hotel rooms which doubled as a drug supply counter. All manner of drugs had been freely available. The supposed receptionist, in reality a dealer, had a couple of bouncers watching carefully from a side room but everything else was open. Clearly the dealer and bouncers thought that they were secure, presumable due to protection and cover up from the corrupt Troop.

Early on Tuesday morning Tom and I boarded a flight to Mallorca, hired a car in the airport and drove to Soller. I had never been to Mallorca before and I found the large airport and the motorway outside Palma busy and soulless. As we drove westward it became rapidly more rural and attractive. Tall mountains reared up in front of us, I had not realised that Mallorca has mountains. We passed through a very long tunnel and emerged on the other side into a different world. The road descended towards the west coast down a lush valley with a river tumbling down alongside. Soller proved to be a beautiful old town and appeared to be a wealthy area. The coast and port were nearby and accessible by a quaint railway. We checked into a gorgeous town centre hotel. Minutes later with the use of google maps and Julian's researches we were outside the villas. They were stunning. Massive white buildings with shouldered terracotta roofs were surrounded by palm trees. Unfortunately the security was also impressive. There were tall walls and through the substantial gate we could see the villas were closed up with bars on the windows and doors.

We debated what to do. We knew that the families were all in the UK. We had hoped there would be retainers present and that we could blag our way in. We were not there officially, there had been no time to organise it and we feared a security breach anyway, so we could not openly force our entry. We decided to beak in. We were on our own. If caught we would be treated as common criminals, which in Spanish eyes we would have been. Most likely we would be arrested and probably jailed, at least for a time, in a holding cell. We had to try. We decided to make our first attempt on the one we thought belonged to Meadows.

The outside wall had been no problem. We had easily slipped over and then we had moved cautiously between the palms to the house. We could not see any CCTV and we assumed that there would not be an alarm as if the villas are the results of crime the last thing the owners would wish is anything that would alert the police for any reason. However the doors and both ground and first floor windows were heavily barred and when we were close we could see them to be impregnable. Then I had spotted a skylight that seemed to be open a chink. We argued about who was to try to enter and who would stand guard. Neither of us would back down so we tossed a coin. Tom won, or lost, depending on how you view it.

We had pulled ourselves up to a balcony. I had then given him a leg up. He had grabbed the overhanging low gutter and had easily swung himself up on to the gently sloping roof. The trees had hidden his approach to the skylight. He had previously palmed a knife from the table when we were shown the dining room in the hotel. He had slid this under the window latch and opened it with ease. Tom had then lowered himself in and softly closed the window behind him.

Then there had followed an agonising twenty minutes as I waited. I dared not call him and for all I knew he had been caught in a trap. Every rustle in the trees made me think that silent alarms had alerted gang members who were approaching. I had been far more frightening waiting there than if I had been inside. Finally I heard him walk down the roof and he jumped back down beside me. There was no time for pleasantries. We ran to the wall, vaulted over and then casually walked down the empty street, hand in hand, acting like two tourists so in love that they were oblivious to the surrounding villas. It had taken a long time, most of the walk back, to calm down from risking both the police and the criminal gang. As we walked we had pretended to exchange sweet nothings. In reality Tom assured me we had enough to incriminate Meadows and that there was no point in pushing our luck and trying to enter the Coyles' villa. We had proof they owned it anyway.

After leaving the area of the villas we had dropped the pretence. Our conversation during the return to our hotel was not of two enjoying their holiday and confessing their mutual adoration. He had whispered, bingo, we can go home now. At the hotel we looked through the photos he had taken on his camera. He had found, in the sitting room, photographs of Meadows with his family, side by side with the Coyles, all holidaying together both in the villas and in Soller. In an office he had found utility bills and legal documents all showing that Brutus's is the name used for all official correspondence even though Meadows Junior is the owner. We e-mailed them back to the others who were overjoyed.

By then, back home, it was still only six in the evening on the Tuesday. We had only assembled the team thirty two hours before. We had dinner in the beautiful square in Soller which is dominated by a vast cathedral to one side. Tom had remarked that I was looking wistful. I admitted to thinking about Luke and told him that I had been reminded of Luke as he also lived on the side of a beautiful square with a huge church. Tom chided me to stop being ridiculous, it had been apparent to him that, other than when we were outside the villa, I had been thinking of Luke all day. As always he was correct. We had returned to the UK the next morning.

During the Wednesday afternoon Peter had called round to liaise with us during his day off. He had entered through the garage and even though I had warned him what to expect in Julian's flat he had taken several minutes to assimilate it. Peter had then discussed with Alison the recruiting cascade that he had devised in which his initial five team leaders would be informed and they would then contact the officers that they trusted and had chosen for their teams. Only then would people begin know something of what was happening. Only when all were assembled an hour before the operation would the plans be disseminated. Alison had built on this by setting up a What's App Group and a group text alert. Peter had supplied the mobile 'phone numbers of the whole station, those belonging to the Troop were recorded but kept off the list. Alison had written an emergency text message alerting all the station other than the Troop to the What's App Group. When they signed on all of them, in addition to the teams, would be given the outline that a major operation was about to happen and then they will be requested to join the briefing if possible, even if not on duty.

We realised that possibly half of the station would attend and so we needed a venue to meet and brief. Again stalwart Peter came to the rescue. He is on the Board of the local cricket club and as it is offseason it is not in use. I did not know it but apparently it is in a quiet road on the edge of town, there is ample parking and a large function room that has computer projection facilities. Alison also prepared a briefing presentation that could be projected in the cricket club and then specific tasks are to be sent to the 'phones of the teams and any other volunteers as they drive to the roles allocated to them. Julian had already downloaded maps and plans of the Troops houses and plans of the hotel. Now, as there is a possibility of increasing the number of teams, we added the Coyles' houses. The father and brothers are known to be in the hotel each night so we did not anticipate any armed resistance there and we wanted to secure any evidence in their homes.

So, the strategy is set. Only the seven of us going in and Peter in the control area will know the full details until an hour before action. The five team leaders have an inkling that something is afoot but they do not know what. No one else will know anything at all until they are asked to attend the briefing. At the cricket club Peter and the team leaders will finalise the teams. Peter's tech savvy sixteen year old son, Gary, is thrilled to be involved. He will be at there with his Dad and he will send the maps and plans prepared by Alison to the teams of officers' 'phones. Peter will organise the others who respond to the text into additional ad hoc teams and decide where to send them. His son will then forward the details of their specific hit to their 'phones and they can study the layout of the property whilst following google maps to the appropriate house. It will be a precipitous event with many chances of it failing but we dare not risk a leak. We have no option.

On the Wednesday night Simon and John had gone to the bar posing as two half-drunk lads on the town wanting a good time. Within the hour they were at the same reception and minutes after that upstairs in the rooms. Both found the girls they had been offered to be eastern European, drugged and fearfully submissive. In John's case he was sure that she was underage. The lack of sex seemed to come as a relief rather than to arouse suspicion. There was little conversation as not only were the girls reticent they spoke little English. However it was ascertained that they lived in the hotel in some form of dormitory at the rear. On the way out both of them had difficulty in leaving the girls to their fate and not assaulting the sneering bouncers.

Then, Thursday morning, another superb opportunity had come our way. This was partially serendipity but mostly due to the perseverance and brilliance of our computer wizards. They found that Whitlelocke was booked on a flight from Stanstead to Henri Coanda Airport in Romania the following day, that is this morning. Backtracking through his credit card accounts and airline manifests they discovered that he went there every three to six months, staying only a couple of nights. On each occasion, when he returned, his credit card showed that he had not only booked his return flight but three to five women with Romanian names were also booked with one way tickets. We surmised that he was in charge of collecting girls to work as prostitutes. They were probably lured with the promise of secure occupation in the UK only to find what was really expected on arrival. No doubt they were then either encouraged or forced to take drugs and their passports were held until they were deemed to have paid for their trip, probably that never happened. Whitelocke may be corrupt but he is also young, good looking and debonair. We surmised that he was sent to complete the charming of the girls who had already been groomed locally. This was all supposition but we all agreed that it was also near certain.

After hearing of Whitelocke's trip I had had an idea. I told the team that Whitelocke was one of the ones sent to arrest me and that he backed down with only a stare and a soft verbal threat from Peter. I proposed that he could probably be persuaded into turning on the others in exchange for a promise of leniency. They jumped at my suggestion and it was immediately incorporated into the plan. We agreed that we should arrest him at the airport, his latest check in was six in the morning. As he would be expected to be in transit and working in Bucharest then we hoped he would not be missed, at least during the day, on Friday, or, as it now is, today. We would have all day to interrogate him but that meant we were committed to our swoop on the hotel and houses on this evening. If we left it any longer with him being out of contact and the possibility of this being noted by the Troop then suspicions may be aroused and evidence may go missing.

Simon and John had travelled to Stanstead on Thursday night. They liaised with airport police and together with them they had arrested Whitelocke at five thirty am this morning. On searching him they found he had concealed in a chest wallet 80,000 Leu which is roughly equivalent to £14,000. He had no excuse prepared to be carrying this amount. When challenged he panicked, broke down within half an hour and he had admitted that he was the errand boy procuring girls. He was placed in custody at the airport so there was no risk of him being seen in custody back here. Unbelievably Simon and John are due here, at the table in Julian's flat, by three this afternoon.

This incredible week has led to us now sitting here with a plan and the Chief Constable's go ahead. It is breath taking. We went over the details again and again. It seems so rushed. There remain so many uncertainties and guesses. We have not undertaken long term exhaustive surveillance. It feels as if we should investigate more, look harder, find what we have missed. On the other hand with Julian and Alison's hacking we have all the layouts of the buildings and sufficient evidence to warrant an arrest and search. As it was obtained illegally, both the computer hacking and the break in in Mallorca, our evidence will not be presentable in court but along with years of circumstantial observations by Peter which were reported officially to Claudia, not just sibling chat, they justify our action. Hopefully during the swoop we will obtain definitive, usable evidence.

The cascade thought up by Peter and developed by Alison will allow us to have at least seven teams briefed and ready to go within the hour. If the What's App group works well we may have more.

Then I raised the elephant in the room but I could see that everyone was thinking the same. The Coyles are an organised crime gang. We have had no sightings of weapons and no reports of guns being actually used in our city for years but we have to be prepared to face them as we know that they sometimes carry weapons. None of us want to carry firearms again but I and the Met team are all licensed to do so. I have not done so in my present post but my previous registration is still up to date. We decided that we had to carry them. Tom and Alison left to collect them from headquarters. We amended the alert text to include that as many officers as possible should bring bullet proof vests along with all of their usual equipment. Some will not have any available as they are likely to be leaving social events. We had to pinch ourselves to remind us that this will be an ordinary Friday night and most citizens, including our colleagues, will be enjoying a social night. They are unlikely to be going for a pint or a romantic dinner carrying their vests and batons. Peter will take into account what equipment they have when attending and those without vests, batons and sprays will be kept away from the Coyles. Of the seven of us six will be carrying firearms, Julian cannot. We will split into the two teams, each with three carrying firearms. I am leading one. We will lead the raid on the Coyles.

So, we start the cascade at ten tonight and move in at eleven. All we can do now is to wait. Ten hours of pacing and coffee. I am tingling with a combination of nerves, anticipation and excitement all mixed in with a fear of failure. Ten hours to brood on the unknowns and uncertainties. Once the briefing at the cricket club starts they will evaporate as I fire up the teams. I hope.

CHAPTER 16: LUKE: GUNSHOTS

I bundled him into the van and secured him in the hidden compartment as Sam simultaneously started to drive off. I moved into the front compartment and buckled into the passenger seat before we had even reached the edge of the car park. Our technique is now the same every time and it is as polished as a Strictly routine.

The site of this collection had been a little different. It is on the edge of a large car park which is adjacent to both a shopping area and the railway station so it is mostly busy. However this repellent character does not leave his work at the adjacent ten pin bowling alley until nearly eleven pm and our previous surveillance showed the area is then quiet.

During the week, when I had been assessing the suitability of using this place, I had noted and I had been concerned by the tall block of flats overlooking the railway station and this car park. Their entrance is very discrete so I had not noticed it before. They look expensive. The top one is a two storey penthouse and has panoramic windows overlooking much of the area. My concern was that the collection area is overlooked. However, I judged that in the dark corner, where we planned to wait in ambush, that we would not be visible from any of the flats as I bundled him into the van.

Yesterday evening, while looking up during my last surveillance, I could make out a group of people in the penthouse window who appeared to be holding a meeting. It was difficult to see but one resembled Rebecca. It could not have been her though as she has gone off somewhere abroad on her clandestine investigation. I am not sure where she has gone to nor when she is back. It is all very hush-hush. The openness of the car park forced us into using the one secluded corner but this did bring an advantage that, in addition to avoiding been seen from the flats, Sam did not have to drive up. She had simply sat waiting in the van.

This evening, whilst I had waited for him to leave his workplace I had noted that the lights in the penthouse were off. It appears empty tonight so we will not be seen from there. As it is Friday the obviously well-of owners are probably at an expensive dinner. Finally tonight's target had emerged. I had followed him from the approach to the bowling alley whilst looking around, checking that there were no passers-by. When he was alongside the van doors I had Tasered him and here we are, less than a minute later, driving away.

We drove down the ramp and pulled up to the car park exit and then we waited as some traffic passed in front of us. We have the outward appearance of two innocent people going home after we had enjoyed bowling or having returned by a train. I glanced at my watch, 11.20, we are a little later than usual but there is still plenty of time for the treatment. There is a busy intersection to our right, we had to be patient until there was a gap and then we will pull out, turn left and drive along the main road to the bypass. We aimed to cross that at the roundabout then drive straight on for a few rural miles until arrival at the Farm. We sat calmly, all is routine.

Then I caught my breath and I felt Sam tense as we heard sirens coming from our left. We looked further down the road and saw a police car with lights flashing and siren screaming as it hurtled towards us. Then another, and yet another, then a fourth; between them we can see unmarked cars but they all appear to be travelling in a howling convoy. With the overwhelming noise and dazzle of multiple blues and twos they hurtled towards us. All other traffic is urgently pulling over as they expertly weave in and out. We are trapped. A car has pulled behind us. It would be suicidal for us to pull out; anyway we can hardly outrun them.

Sam looks terrified. I felt the same at first then I realised what should have been immediately obvious if we were not concerned by the presence of a drugged and bound man behind us. I said to her, 'they can't be coming for us. Even if we were seen there was simply not enough time for them to get here.' We both tried to relax a little but it was impossible to do so with him out cold behind us and the blinding cacophony now only yards away. Then I added, 'it is very odd. They are all coming from out of town, not from the police station.' These observations were completely unhelpful. For both of us it is the same, they are factually spot on and emotionally completely unbelievable.

The noise reached a crescendo and the blue flashes lit up the whole area. They were hard on us and then all around us. The sirens and the lights are overwhelming.

We both exhaled with relief as they flashed past in front of us. At the intersection, as cars and pedestrians scattered, they split into four pairs. Each pair had one police car and one unmarked car. One pair hurtled straight on, one swerved right towards the Park Hotel and the other two skidded left down East Street towards the centre of the city. The tyres of all of the cars were squealing and the rear of the cars sliding as they made their turns.

Seconds later, all is again eerily quiet. The traffic did not move at first. All eyes are turned in disbelief in the directions they had disappeared in.

Eventually we can move forward. We turned into the

main road relaxing again.

Then, to my horror, I can see in the distance ahead more flashing lights and yet more police cars weaving in and out, again coming towards us. We cannot risk being stopped or caught in any hold up. Urgently I barked at Sam, 'quick, take that road over there.' I pointed to our right and a little forward to a barely visible opening a few yards past a grim church. She looks astonished and reluctant. I shouted, 'go, go now, before it is too late. I will explain.' She quickly indicated and made the turn into the street. We had only progressed about twenty yards down it when, to our further relief, all the flashing lights and noise passed behind us, continuing along the main road.

More calmly I continued, 'sorry to bark at you like that. I know this road from the genuine moth collection. It is very narrow but there is little traffic and we will easily get through. It goes down the hill between these terrace houses. Initially it runs parallel to East Street then it turns away towards the river. At the bottom it joins the larger side road that turns off East Street alongside the Langley pub. This is the other end of the road that opens opposite the car park and picnic area overlooking the weir.' Sam nodded, now understanding. Some summer evenings we go to sit there. 'We can take a left there then follow it for a mile or so until it joins the main road that we have just turned off. If all is quite then we can resume our original route. If there is still police activity we can cross the main road into the housing estate and wind our way through coming out on the bypass near to the bridge club. That is where we made a collection a few weeks ago.' Again she nodded, now fully orientated and calm again.

As I said this and we slowly and unobtrusively made our way down we both relaxed further. Sam does not know this road but she knows the other routes I suggested and with another little nod she indicated being in agreement with the plan. Then she brightened and said jokily, 'actually that excitement back there was very reassuring.' I looked at her askance. 'Don't you see? With all of the county's police roaring off in the other direction there will be none left to stop us on our way.' We laughed together at this. Though a joke it is also true. Even when an old ducks held us up for what felt like an age, manoeuvring her car on to her driveway, we felt at ease and sat quietly together. We exchanged friendly waves and smiles with her as we moved gently on. We are now back to a routine collection and treatment. Having completed so many the stress is much less and the operation is getting easier each time. That is until being surrounded by police tonight. Thank god that is over.

We neared the end of the road and looking ahead I can see the junction where the side road between the Langley pub and the main road we have just left crosses in front of us. At the junction, the road we are approaching makes a tight bend, the concave face towards us. At the bend, on our side, the houses fall back and there is a communal grass area allowing a good view in both directions. Opposite there is an attractive parking area. It has a white picket fence all around it enclosing both the parking area and a picnic site on a bluff sitting a few feet above the river. The weir downstream of the city is in front and the castle and park are situated on the opposite side of the river. It is one of my favourite spots to sit during a tranquil summer's evening, though the other weir a couple of miles upstream of the city, is even more delightful.

For the first time however, though I have been around here on many previous occasions, I spotted a tiny road, in reality little more than an alley, joining the junction from my right. Ignoring that, I looked back at the river. After the frights on the main road the memories of warm evenings here thankfully returned. Sam has obviously also recalled them and we both breathed more easily.

When we were only twenty yards from the junction I heard a screeching of tyres coming from the right, the direction of the Langley pub. I immediately went straight back into panic mode thinking that it is unbelievably yet more police. A large, smart, black saloon careered around the bend barely making the turn with its tyres howling in protest. Before I could process what is happening a white van, one of the types with windows and ten or more seats in the rear, hurtled out of the alley. It is clearly trying to get in front of the car which I now see is a Lexus. The van was initially alongside but with superior acceleration the Lexus started to pull away. I gasped, Sam screamed and braked hard. There is clearly going to be an accident. The van then deliberately turned sharply and rammed the rear of the car. It was no accident.

We watched in horror as the scene seems to unfold in slow motion. The car is now completely out of control. The driver is twisting at the steering wheel but to no avail. It spun and then slid sideways through the gate to the car park but as it entered side on it destroyed the both gateposts as it smashed through. That caused the car to spin more and it then slithered backwards across the car park. The air bags deployed and I can no longer see the occupants. The car mounted the slight rise, hit a picnic table, catapulting it into the river, and then carried on backwards through the picket fence. I thought that it must surely plunge into the water but as the rear wheels went over the edge the underside caught on the embankment and it jerked to a halt.

That was the last I saw of the car as the van now blocked my view. That driver is in complete control. I can see now that it is a police woman. She steered at considerable speed through the now widened entrance. I thought that she would ram the car again and send it over the bank. Instead she expertly undertook a hand brake turn. The van turned through one-eighty degrees with the driver, who still seems completely relaxed, now side on to us. It slid sideways a few feet and then shuddered to a stop.

Immediately all the van doors flew open. From the rear a woman officer in what looks like a bullet proof vest and a riot helmet sprang out. There is a pistol at her hip and a baton in her hand. Sam and I gasped in unison. We could not see her face but from her build, from her gymnastic leap demonstrating a powerful grace, but mostly from the blond curls escaping from under the helmet, it is certainly Rebecca. She disappeared from view as she ran around the van racing towards the car. At the same time we could see through the windows that the passenger door of the van, on the opposite side from us, burst open and someone jumped out. The sliding door on our side jerked open a second later. Several police jumped out, one being another woman. Inside we can see more wrestling with the rear door on the opposite side but it has jammed. They gave up and followed their colleagues exiting on our side. All of them are in the same combat style gear as Rebecca and several are carrying guns. They split into two groups and went around opposite ends of the van.

Seconds later we heard a sharp bang, more like a crack. Then another followed almost immediately afterwards. I have only heard a pistol fired on the TV or in the cinema but I have no doubt that they had been gunshots.

I thought, "Rebecca."

I unclipped my seat belt and started to open the door. As I did so we saw the policewoman driver step out looking extremely distressed. She tried to hurry around to the other side but is clearly in pain, perhaps she has been injured in the ramming.

Sam lunged across, pulled the door closed and hissed, 'don't be daft.'

'But Rebecca may be shot again.'

'It is far more likely that Rebecca has shot someone else. Even if she has been she is surrounded by police who undoubtedly have much more first aid training than you.' She paused as I assimilated this. More softly and kindly she continued, 'think of our cargo. Now buckle up and try to look innocent.' Reluctantly I did so. I sat stock still, mentally paralysed, thinking only of what could have happened to Rebecca. Sam saw this and took charge. 'I cannot turn around and I dare not go right as that will take us back into the city and god knows what we will meet there tonight. I will have to turn left even though that will take us directly in front of the police. Thankfully they all seemed preoccupied at present on the other side.'

Sam waited for a while. All remains quiet, uncannily quiet after the explosive action of a minute ago. She then drove sedately towards the junction. Before we arrived she had to brake hard again as two unmarked cars flew around the corner from our right and slithered to a halt in front of the car park entrance. From each car out jumped four more police in a motely of clothes. Each is wearing a police vest. One also has a police jacket on. Otherwise three are wearing dinner jackets and another has on a polo neck sweater and chinos. None of them are in normal police gear. Thankfully they also disappeared around the van.

Again Sam cautiously moved forward. I craned my neck looking back. We cleared the van and on seeing the scene horror and delight filled me. Rebecca was uninjured, standing and looking down. Relief flowed through me. Then I spotted that she was looking down at a male police officer who is on the ground, obviously seriously injured. While I looked the policewoman driver reached the scene and threw herself on to the man on the ground, obviously distraught. I whispered to Sam, 'Rebecca's fine, let's go.' As the words escaped my mouth, with mounting fear, I saw two of the original police who had jumped out of the side door look up, spot us, and come running towards us. Both are armed.

Before I could warn Sam they appeared alongside us banging on the van side and making "put down the window" gestures. They split and one came to each side window. One barked at Sam, 'name and what is your business here.'

Before she could reply the other who was looking intently at me shouted across the cab, ignoring us, to his colleague, 'Tom, it is the professor.' The one called Tom eased back a little, looked closely at me, then he said more gently to Sam, 'and you are, madam?'

'Samantha Cape.' Their eyebrows shot up as if this was a revelation. 'His sister, Luke is here for university research and I am assisting.' They looked extraordinarily relived. I cannot work out how they know my name or why they are relieved that Sam is my sister and not my wife as so many assume. It hardly matters to them.

Without warning the one on my side ripped open the sliding side door and stuck his head in the rear of our van. I went stiff trying not to react or show my fright at that. Sam responded the same way. Thankfully both of the police are intent on inspecting the van and did not spot our distress. He shouted "all clear" and I breathed again as he slammed the door shut. The one referred to as Tom quietly said to Sam, 'sorry to disturb you. On your way now.' I went to speak and to check that Rebecca is completely uninjured. He saw me start and roared, 'GO.' Sam quietly drove off.

Now thoroughly rattled, we drove on in silence along the street. Shortly we came to the main road that we had initially turned on to after leaving the carpark. That had been about ten minutes ago. It felt like ten years. I am beginning to get jittery. Given our cargo I am having difficulty coping with being surrounded by and being stopped by police.

There is clearly a major operation under way and by them concentrating on this, paradoxically, it probably makes us more secure. Even so it is shredding my nerves and I can see that, despite her strength and sang-froid, Sam is barely keeping it together.

Sam came to a halt and looked at me uncertainly. The fastest way to the farm is to turn right and to follow the main road out of the city. I thought about this, then I said to her, 'I can't take any more excitement tonight. It all seems quiet now but I thought that before. Let's cross over into the housing estate and work our way through the back streets.' Looking relieved she drove across and into the estate. I can see that she is still frightened. So am I. For god's sake I am an academic, not an undercover agent.

Sam knows the route through the estate from our previous collections, though none have been quite like tonight's drama. After a hundred yards she turned right on to a yet smaller street that leads down to the bridge club where we can turn onto the bypass. We had only travelled a few yards along it when, yet again, we heard wailing sirens, this time coming from behind us. Sam looked in the mirror and I turned around to look out of the rear window, Together we said, 'oh shit.' Another pair of cars is travelling at speed, coming up behind us. Is that the seventh pair? That is not counting the ones that flashed behind us when we initially turned off the main road. Again the first is a police car and the second is unmarked. For the third time this evening panic surged through me as they slid around the corner and hurtled towards us. As they came close they started braking hard, slithered alongside and skidded to a halt directly in front of our van blocking the road. They are targeting us. How do they know?

Four police in full riot gear leapt out of the first car. I started to breathe again when they ran away from us towards the house to our left. The two in the lead are carrying a battering ram. They ran to the door and without stopping, in one fluid action, they knocked down the door. It did not open. It was flattened backwards on to the hall floor. They dropped the ram and all four disappeared inside.

Then I looked towards the other car. Four people had jumped out. I presume they are police but they certainly do not look like them. Two are wearing dinner jackets. I recalled that three policemen at the river had also been wearing them. The only woman was dressed for a romantic night. She has a skimpy blouse that is flying open as she ran showing that she is not wearing a bra. Her short, tight skirt is riding up. The only things that would have looked unusual on a date were the incongruous police boots that she is wearing. The last man is in football gear including the football boots. They ran to the side gate. The first two in their dinner jackets did not even try the handle. The gate splintered open as their shoulders hit it together. All four of them disappeared into the garden.

At exactly the same time as they passed from view a front bedroom window opened and a wild looking man in pyjamas jumped down onto the grass and started to run towards us. Sam hit the button to lock the doors but he passed in front of the bonnet bouncing off it in his haste. He has been spotted.

The scantily dressed woman and the foot baller exploded back out of the gate and sprinted, again worryingly towards us, but it is clear they are after the pyjama man. The footballer's studs caught in a grating and he went flying. The woman ran like the wind and caught pyjama man on the opposite neighbour's lawn. She performed a flying tackle and he hit the ground hard as her blouse flew completely open and her skirt pulled up to her midriff tearing over her hips. She had effectively taken him down whilst wearing only a thong. Sam said, 'Christ, they should sign her for the Lions.' I thought, "no Sam. That was an illegal tackle. She had brought up her knees and caught him square in the balls as he hit the ground. He is writhing in agony.

Then the footballer caught up and hauled him to his feet and lifted one arm hard up behind his back. The woman tried and failed to make herself decent again. She has mud down one side, a torn blouse and a ripped skirt. Her breasts and thong are clearly displayed. Then one of the dinner jackets arrived. Smiling his respect at her he slipped off his jacket and put it over her shoulders. Gallantly he looked her in the eyes, not down at her breasts. He is tall, she is average height. His jacket came to her mid-thigh. Now she is decently if oddly dressed. The mud and grass stains are still evident on the side of her face. He then saw us. It was the first time that we have even been noticed. All had been so intent on the entry and chase. A cold fear went through me but he simply waved at us that we should turn around and leave. They then lost interest in us as the man was roughly bundled into the back of the police car still moaning in pain and holding his balls. As we drove off Sam said, 'did you recognise him?'

'No. Who?'

'The man in pyjamas; he is a policeman.' She is correct. I now remember seeing him pass our house going in to the station. He has always been in plain clothes but often in a police car so I have always presumed that he is a detective.

In an agitated silence we drove towards the Farm. To my great relief we did not see another police car. After half a mile or so Sam started to snigger then gave a frightened half-laugh, saying, 'do you remember when we were children and Dad used to watch all those repeats of 1970's TV shows?' I looked sharply at her. This is more than a non-sequitur, it is a knight's move. I feared that she is becoming hysterical. I feel on the edge myself. 'Tonight has reminded me of them. The first police action was like one of those American cop series. The second was straight out of Monty Python.' She is spot on. We both started to laugh out loud together.

Then I sighed, 'oh, what a night.' At the same time we looked back at each other and burst into another round of laughter as we remembered singing the Frankie Valley song with our grandmother. It had been one of her favourite songs from her youth.

We could not resist. We sang together,

'*Oh what a night,*

Late December back in 63.'

We laughed so much that we could not continue. Though laughing we are both close to hysteria. Then Sam finally gasped, 'I am pretty sure that he was referring to an all-together different form of excitement.'

I shook my head and sang,

'*I felt a rush like a rolling ball of thunder*

Spinning my hear round and takin' my body under.'

'I certainly felt like that earlier.'

Sam nodded saying, now again looking simultaneously serious and frightened, 'so did I. So did I.'

I looked back at the hidden compartment. He is likely still drugged though tonight we have been delayed and he may be coming to. Even if he is awake he will not be able to assess our voices through the panelling. If he hears us singing he will think that he has been abducted by lunatics and hopefully he will be even more terrified. Little will he know that our singing is not celebration, it is near hysteria. We are as frightened as he probably is.

We arrived at the Farm. Sam dropped me off and I unloaded the chap who is now writhing around but securely bound, gagged and blindfolded. As planned Sam then drove to the refuge. She is not on duty tonight but is deliberately going in supposedly as a social visit, she will still have to sign in and out giving some alibi for her and a little for me.

I set to work on the shit that we had collected. I found my mood darkening and I took it out on him. Whirling through my head were the images of seeing Sam in the hospital, beaten, unconscious. Ringing in my ears were the words of the consultant bracing us for the possibility of Sam being left with serious brain damage. Thankfully he was wrong but it must have been close. He described her recovery as "miraculous." Joining all that, tonight, I have the sounds of the gunshots, the sight of the badly injured officer on the floor and his colleague weeping over him. Also I recalled the story of Rebecca's shooting and the feeling of running my fingers over her scar. How close it had been for her as well as Sam.

I became furious as the night wore on, the tiredness, the images, the stress of the evening, they all fermented within me. I worked on him more and more. I cannot protect all beaten women. I cannot directly help the police. However, I can make sure that these bastards never, ever, again attack an innocent woman. Three times he was unconscious when I levered him out of the water. I don't give a damn if he dies. I slapped him harder and harder until he came to. When I branded his cock I held it there until it burnt through the skin into the flesh. He passed out for the fourth time.

CHAPTER 17:
REBECCA: THE RAID

Tom smirked at me as he spotted me looking at my watch, again. Though it seems as if it is half an hour since I last looked it is only the second hand that has moved half way around the dial. 2255 hours, we go in in five minutes. He shook his head. He knows that I am not nervous. It is simply that I am raring to charge in and to take them down.

He is correct, I am not nervous but I am anxious. I am not anxious that I will be shot again, like the last time we all went in together. I am anxious for the mission. This must not fail. Too much is hanging on the outcome. If we fail the good guys will lose their jobs and the bad guys will go free. I am also curious. I do not really know what we will find tonight. My curiosity is at war with my anxiety.

To distract myself I regarded my superb colleagues here with me in the van. I forced myself to think of our situation, to think of them. We are all sitting quietly together in an unmarked, common or garden white van. It is completely unremarkable and unnoticeable. We are parked in a small side street, off East Street, which is on the opposite side of the road from the Langley pub. Julian is in the passenger seat. We have positioned the front of the van to enable him to look diagonally down this road and across East Street itself. He can discretely watch the front of the Langley. The rest of us are screened from view to anyone in the pub by the wall of the building on the corner of the two roads. If they did bother to look this way they would see only one man, waiting, of no consequence.

All is quiet. The bouncers have thankfully positioned themselves inside the door. Being under the pub floodlights they would not be able to see us over here anyway even if we were all in view. Belt and braces, I am in charge and I have tried my best to make sure that there will not be any hiccups tonight. Even better than planned; in addition to the bouncers not being able to see us them being inside means they will not even have a seconds warning of our imminent dramatic entry. They will not know what hit them.

I hope.

Alongside Julian is Barbara. Following her recent surgery she is not supposed to be here but she turned up, grabbed the keys and insisted on driving at least. We had to threaten her to stop her putting on a vest and taking an invasive role. She looks fantastic following the op. After the despicable teasing by Brutus the station became aware that Barbara had always been extremely distressed by her massive boobs. She could not afford the surgery for a breast reduction. A callous NHS consultant had weighed them in his hands and then he rudely pronounced they were not heavy enough to qualify for NHS surgery. Apart from his pompous, uncaring bedside manner I had been left wondering how massive a woman has to be to be considered for help. A whip round had been organised by the kindly Peter. He must be the best desk sergeant in the country. Within twenty-four hours so much had been collected that, not only could she book surgery with another decent consultant, but also she could afford respite care for her Mum. Peter tipped me off that in addition to the whole station, other than the Troop that is, being so generous there had been a single massive cash donation. Literally it had been left in a brown paper envelope. I am sure that it was from

Julian but I did not ask. I simply regarded him even more highly.

Barbara does not know of the large contribution. It had been type-written on the envelope that it was requested to be kept as a secret donation. Only Peter and I know. So that is not the reason she has been getting so close to him. She cares; so does he. They spend a lot of time chatting together. Others have noticed and joked with me but they have also been sensitive enough to not tease either of them. Julian's bereavement has become known. Recently I noticed that he has stopped wearing his wedding ring. I gently asked him about this and he told me that Lucy, when she was dying, had made him promise that after a while, she stipulated a maximum of two years and preferably less, that he should look for someone else. It is now a little over two years.

Some of my Met colleagues are here with me in the van, the others are in the second van behind us. Along with me they are all carrying firearms. We discovered from an earlier casual walk-by that all of the Coyles are here and, judging from their bulging jackets, some are carrying guns. In view of this we amended the plan so that all armed officers will be in the hotel together. I desperately hope that this will intimidate them and stop any shooting and that there will not be a repeat of last year's public shoot out.

The others with us are the first arrivals from Peter's cascade system which is working superbly. The call went out at 2130. At the last minute we decided to make it a little earlier to give people time to assemble. The risk of a late leak was considered small. One of the Troop had been in the station on duty. He had been quietly arrested and put in the cells without a 'phone before 2200. His house will still be raided at 2300 for evidence. He has deliberately been put in the same cell as I had occupied. He will be there somewhat longer than I was.

By 2215 the five other team leaders had each assembled their entire posse. They had described themselves as "posses." There is indeed a wild-west tension in the air. By 2217 the others here in the van had arrived and been allocated to be with us. They are bursting with pride and enthusiasm. Then it became a stampede. By 2225 all the police cars including the unmarked ones had been filled. Other officers arriving have been demanding to volunteer using their personal vehicles. Behind us, in addition to the van, we already have four unmarked cars with five determined men and women in each.

I looked forward through the windscreen and watched the Friday night revellers parade up and down the street. It all looks too normal. It is disorientating and making me feel dizzy. The women are in tight, short skirts showing off their fat legs. One pretty young woman is in a long black coat which has striking gold trim; she is the only one out tonight dressed for the temperature. Even so her face looks so cold; that may be just the Goth make up.

The men are dressed for Ibiza in August, not the UK in early March. The women are wiggling, the men are strutting. All are looking for a mate. It appears that they will at least mate. All are oblivious to the presence of what is similar to unexploded ordnance in the dark street, only yards from them. Out there are shouts, horns and a general hub-bub. In here is a stalking quiet.

My 'phone is on silent but I felt it vibrate, looking at the screen I see it is Peter. I put it on speaker with the volume low. All in the van craned their necks to listen. 'Rebecca, I want to give a quick update before you go in. Virtually the whole station has turned out. They have all been allocated targets. Gary has sent the briefing to their 'phones and they are either on their way or going to their cars as I speak.'

'Great news Peter, please give my thanks to your

wonderful son. To undertake such a responsible task as the briefing at his age is a credit to you both.'

Peter replied, I can hear the pride in his voice, 'I will do that after I have taken him outside and poured a bucket of ice water over his head.'

'Go on; tell us. What on earth are you trying to say?'

'Some of the WPCs have turned up in the clothes they were going on the town in. Shall I say Peter has had his eyes full as well as having to deal with his computer tasks?' He heard us all snigger.

I interrupted, 'I am glad to hear that at least one of the weaker sex can multitask. He must be a new age man.' Soft groans came around me.

Peter continued, 'that is not all. You should see some of the lads. Two left the pitch and are in their football gear. Five are in dinner jackets; they were at a Lodge dinner.'

I chipped in, 'what do you mean, Lodge? Surely we do not have any of the silly handshake brigade in our fine station.'

'A few but we keep them in their box. Anyway, bless 'em, they do have some redeeming features. They refused Meadows admission to their soirees.

We have only had one person 'phone in with a weak excuse as to why she is not coming. Jenny, she is in labour. She said that she will come along later but may have to bring the baby.' The van shook with silent laughter as he rang off.

I looked at my watch, 2259. All the others are watching me. All over the city doors are about to splinter open, the occupants of those houses and most other citizens are unaware, unprepared. It feels surreal. I pointed to the pub.

We stepped out slowly and quietly. Barbara's door

opened, 'no Barbara, stay. It is not only your surgery; we may need the van urgently.' Reluctantly, seeing the wisdom in this, she pulled it closed without a sound. On seeing us exit all the others in the cars behind stepped out. The team in the van are joining with us. The others have been designated teams A,B,C and D. Tonight there is simply too much going on to think up inspiring names.

Having parked on the left we stealthily crossed to the other side of the street so that we cannot be seen from the door of the Langley. This street is empty and the hordes on East Street are not looking this way. There are more than thirty of us, I feel that I have an army behind me. I lifted my hand and they silently paused. I peered around the corner. The door has a couple of customers having a smoke just outside of it. There is no bouncer in sight. When there was a gap in the light traffic I dropped my hand and we ran.

Silently and swiftly we crossed the road. The people out for Friday on the town looked on with jaws dropping. One girl screamed. As I crossed the pavement in front of the pub I saw that the gold trimmed Goth had walked back down. Momentarily our eyes locked. Her face remained expressionless but she slightly inclined her head as if starting a dance. I can see that she knows what goes on in here and that she is wishing us well in stopping it.

I led half of the squad in through the front doors. The others, with Tom leading, sprinted down the side street alongside the Langley to the rear door. As arranged two of the volunteer PCs came alongside me, one on each shoulder. I went through the centre of the double doors and they peeled off and each shoulder charged and dropped a bouncer. The astonished thugs were handcuffed before they even knew what was happening. The back-ups allocated for the two who took down the bouncers were not needed and they moved forward alongside me.

We poured down the corridor scattering and ignoring customers. By now the air was full of screams. We burst into the bar before anyone had even properly stood up. Everyone in there froze with their bums just above the seats. Four PCs peeled off left, vaulted the bar and wrestled the two barmen to the ground before they were able to get hold of whatever weapon it was they were reaching for. Alison, who had pushed up next to me, shouted, 'Coyles, ahead, next to the pole.' I looked forward and there were the two brothers half sitting, half trying to stand, at a table directly in front of a floor to ceiling pole. A naked girl slid down it and turned to run. Alison and I, along with two more PCs were on them. They are both half drunk, slow to react and they looked warily at our raised batons. Though they are vicious animals they realised that any resistance would result in a beating. We had them handcuffed together around the dance pole before they could think further and challenge us. They were roughly frisked and handguns taken from their jackets. All doubt is now removed. The Coyles are armed and there is one more to go.

The bouncers, bar staff and Coyle brothers are now secure and out of the fray. The drinkers are scattering, we ignored them. They have probably not done anything wrong. Some may have purchased drugs but that is not our mission tonight. We grouped in the middle and looked. There is no sign of Meadows or Coyle senior. I whisked around as a scuffle behind me broke out. The officers who had handcuffed the bouncers and bar staff had been approaching from behind to join us. They had spotted three of the Troop trying to sneak out from an alcove where they had hidden. They tackled them and quickly overcome them with the help of a couple more who ran back. They had to call for more handcuffs, 2305 and already we are beginning to run out of them.

So that is two Coyles, three Troop here, one in the station cells and Whitlocke arrested at the airport. That leaves one Troop, Meadows and Coyle senior along with a few more bouncers at the prostitution reception come drug dealing area upstairs.

I split the team. I, along with Simon, led the majority up the stairs to overcome the bouncers there and to check the rooms. Alison and a few others started to sweep towards the rear to join Tom's team, who are clearly entering through the back entrance, in a pincer movement. We can hear crashing and screaming as Julian, Tom and John along with eleven other PCs worked their way towards us. They are blocking the rear stairs. We are going up the front ones. Meadows and Coyle must be trapped somewhere.

We burst into the first floor reception. There are three huge bouncers. All are trying to bundle drugs into bags, presumably hoping to either get away with them or to dispose of them. They have baseball bats to hand and they made the stupid mistake of reaching for them. All three were immediately Tasered. There was initially difficulty handcuffing them as they had fallen in a huddle. Like the Coyle brothers, now embracing the dance pole, we handcuffed them together, arm to arm, in a circle. Then with a fourth pair of cuffs we secured the ring of them to the handle of the safe. Now they are restrained we started to move along the corridor.

Each door was kicked open in turn. Behind each there we found a screaming, terrified girl. All look emaciated and hardly more than children. Behind every girl, reaching for their trousers, was a fat middle aged man. We did not have the time or manpower to arrest them all. We had prearranged that we pulled their trousers either out of their hands or off them and confiscated them. They can go home trouser less and face the inquisition and consequences there. I have no beef with prostitution or with men attending women who choose that profession. I have a huge problem with johns using girls who are obviously trafficked and abused as these terrified, scattering waifs undoubtedly are. Feigned ignorance or innocence does not absolve them of responsibility. Unfortunately, for tonight, we do not have either the time or the personnel to detain them.

One man ran from a room and was tripped up by one of the officers in plain clothes. I am sure it was an accidental trip, as if. As he sprawled on the floor with blood spewing from his ruined nose, I looked past him and saw the girl he had been with come to the door. She stood there cowering, her barely pubescent body is naked and unmoving in front of all the men charging around. She is clearly used to being on display. Her breasts are just budding on her scrawny chest. She is definitely a minor. Two of the WPCs put sheets around the girls and shepherded them into their dormitory. As they realised they were being rescued rather than arrested they started to cry with relief.

As we continued through the hotel battering down doors screams continued to come from the girls still in the rooms. They are remain unsure as to what is happening. The men were sinfully quiet. I looked through the remnants of one door and spotted a huge fat man in his boxers. He looked like a baby circus elephant on its rear legs. The child-like girl was shaking with fear. The thought of him forcing her to give him a blow job filled me with repugnance. I locked eyes with him and the odious creep started to shout at me and complain.

That was a step too far. He has made a terrible mistake. I raised my baton high and strode into the room. I was assaulted by the stench of semen, sweat and misery. I lunged at him as the officer inside, the one who had burst open the locked door taking the lock and hinges off in a single charge, yelled at me, 'no Ma'am.'

I had no intention of harming him and allowing

him to offset his crimes with a complaint against me. He reared back in fear looking up at my baton. Whilst he was distracted, or should that be intimidated, with my other hand I grabbed his boxers and tore them off him ripping them into shreds. He whimpered as I then pointed my baton down at his groin. I said softly, almost inaudibly, 'don't worry sir. No one will see your cock as you walk home. It is covered with an apron of lard.'

The PC, now smirking, bundled him out of the door. I pulled a stained sheet off the bed and wrapped it around the trembling girl. I led her out to join the others and she also cried with relief as she realised that she is now safe.

With grim, determined officers on either side of me, I continued through the hotel with its looming shadows and corridors trailing off in different directions. We checked room after room, finding only a few more johns and girls.

Tom and Alison came running up the rear stairs. They had completed the sweep down below. There is still no sign of Meadows or Coyle. Julian had spotted a door half way up the stairs and diverted, pushing his way through. Seconds later he stuck his head out and bellowed, 'this way. There is another set of stairs that is not on the plans.' We barrelled down following him as he went back through the door. It led to a spiral staircase and at the bottom I can see a small doorway discretely placed in a corner. I thought, "shit, they have put in an emergency exit, presumable for exactly this sort of situation."

The stairs have been hacked into the floor of what was probably an old store room and there is a small original window adjacent to the top of them. I glanced through it and spotted Meadows and Coyle. They are struggling to cross the car park to the rear of the pub. Their difficulty is caused by them carrying a large heavy looking trunk between them. Before I could think on what it could possibly contain they dropped it. The corner hit the tarmac hard and it split open. Out of it poured bundles and bundles of money. Thousands of pounds were caught by the gentle breeze and carpeted the car park. Meadows knelt down and tried to scoop some up. I am astonished at his avaricious stupidity. How can he be thinking of money in the situation he is now in? Coyle did not hesitate, he ran to a large black Lexus further along. Meadows spotted him and followed.

I shouted, 'they are on the car park, go, go, go.' They all tried to move fast down the stairs but as they are narrow and spiral even sliding down the rail took time and only one can go at a time. Some ran back to the rear main stairwell. I pointed to one of the PCs, I did not have time to use his name, I shouted again, 'call Barbara, block the car park.' He immediately understood and pressed his speed dial. We had put all the teams' numbers in each of our 'phones for such emergency use.

One group of us streamed onto the carpark in a single file forced on us by the narrow stairs and doorway. We ran towards the car. The other group who had used the main stairs exploded from the rear double door in a pack, only yards behind us. Coyle has now jumped into the passenger side and Meadows into the driver's seat. He started the engine and drove off with the tyres screeching. The first PCs had missed the car by inches but they are unarmed. They could not stop it anyway. The only hope had been to stop Meadows getting in to drive. The car slid sideways out of the carpark and turned right to follow the side road out of town. At the same instant as they cleared the entrance the van driven by Barbara skidded to a halt across it, inches behind them. If only I had spotted them seconds before and we had been able to alert Barbara a fraction earlier they would have been trapped.

I yelled across the car park, 'front van team, in the van with me. We will chase them. A and B cars, back to your cars and follow us. Rear van, C and D cars secure the building and the detainees.'

Barbara started reversing towards us. Julian got to the van first and pulled open the side door and passenger door. The rest of us threw ourselves in the side door. Julian closed it behind and he leapt into the passenger seat as Barbara gunned the engine and set off in pursuit with tyres squealing. Julian had to grab for the seat and pull himself in as the van accelerated. We all had fallen in a heap in the rear. We struggled to unwind ourselves and buckle up as the van swayed and skidded down the road. Julian is still struggling with his door but on a left bend he managed to close it and clip in his seatbelt. I have ended up on the rear seat but I can still see clearly between the heads of my fellow officers. The fully laden van is no match for the Lexus. I can still see its taillights but it is getting away. As it went around a bend it finally disappeared from view and there was a chorus of 'oh shit' from several others.

Barbara is completely focussed. Even through the horror of travelling at such speed along a narrow bendy road we can all see that she is eerily calm. Without warning she spun the steering wheel and we careered left into a narrow entrance barely wider than the van. Again she floored the pedal. Tom yelled, 'what the fuck are you doing?'

Without moving her head Barbara calmly replied, 'short cut.'

It is. We all realised this together. This alley is straight. The road the Lexus is on is bendy and I know from running that a little further ahead it takes a considerable loop. I do not know where this one opens out but obviously our driver does. The van raced along, the sides barely a foot or more from the tall brick wall. The squealing of the tyres and agonised whining of the over-revving engine were amplified and reflected back from the bricks. In sharp contrast there is a pregnant quiet inside. I, and I am sure all of the others, are thinking, 'are we going to make it.' I grinned at my own double meaning. Are we going to make it and get ahead of them, or, are we going to survive this bloody alley? We flashed past a lamppost that narrowed the street yet more. We barely made it through to the tune of several groans, near screams.

Julian turned to face us and said, 'don't worry. Barbara was taught to drive by her father who was a stock car racer.' Hardly reassuring I thought. I am pretty sure they crash all of the time.

Simon had been chatting with Barbara earlier and had clearly noticed her surname. He asked, 'was your father Alan Sturgis?' I thought "for god's sake don't distract her.' Then I noted the "was." Barbara nodded. Simon turned to us and said sotto voce, 'do you want me to tell you that he was killed in a race accident.' There was a chorus of no's.

Alison cried out in some alarm, 'Barbara, have you seen the next lamppost?' She again simply nodded and kept her foot hard down. I looked ahead and spotted that in their infinite wisdom the council had placed the next streetlight opposite to where the corner of a building jutted out, narrowing the alley yet further. There is no way that we can get through. We all instinctively pushed together into the centre of the van and held our elbows in; as if that will make any difference at this speed.

Barbara held her nerve and we went between the lamp post and building at what must be seventy miles an hour. There was instantly a cacophony of tearing metal and breaking glass.

We are through.

We rocketed out of the far side. Both wing mirrors

have been torn off but the body of the van, and our bodies, are all through.

Ahead I can now see the end of this narrow alley, thank god. It joins the road from the Langley at an angle in an area where there are some gardens with a car park on the other side overlooking the river. I remember it now. On our left as we exit there will be a narrow road, at least I considered it narrow until I was driven along this alley. That little road goes up the hill and opens on to the main road opposite the car park close to the railway station. Everybody looked and saw together, or rather didn't see. No Lexus in sight, we must be ahead of them. Barbara yelled, 'I will block the road around the next bend. It narrows there and they will not be able to get past us.'

We came out of the alley like a cork from a bottle. At exactly the same time Meadows and Coyle roared from between the houses, along the road coming from our right. I thought that we were going to collide but Meadows is barely in control and his car has slid on to the wrong side of the road and Barbara controlled us on the left side. For an instant the vehicles were neck and neck. Then the superior power of the Lexus kicked in and they drew ahead. More "oh shits" were shouted. At the instant they were pulling away Barbara spun the steering wheel left. More screams came out. Then she whipped it hard right and the front of the van rammed the tail end of the Lexus.

The car is completely out of control. It spun anticlockwise 180 degrees and went sideways through the gateway to the carpark taking out both of the gateposts on its way. The Lexus then slid back around 90 degrees in the opposite direction and skidded backwards towards the river. It catapulted a picnic table into the water and continued backwards through the fence. I thought that it was going to plunge into the water. The rear wheels went over the bank and it jammed there. The boot is hanging over the edge of the river bank. The bonnet is on the picnic area but the car is secure.

Barbara calmly remained in total control. She had continued our turn, which was initially into the Lexus' rear, until we were heading at a considerable pace through the now widened gate. I thought that we were again going to ram the Lexus and that it, and possible us, would finish up in the river.

Barbara spun the wheel right and touched the handbrake. The van slewed. Then she spun the wheel left and controlled it. The skid had taken us through another 90 degrees so we are now sideways on to the Lexus with the passenger side facing it. Before the van had stopped shaking Julian was out of the passenger door and I was out of the rear. The driver's side sliding door crashed open and some others jumped out. I heard 'fucking jammed' as other officers tried to open the passenger side sliding door. I was aware that behind me they gave up and exited through the far side.

That means Julian and I are running towards the Lexus a little in front of everyone else. Julian is on the passenger side towards Coyle, I am racing towards Meadows. Behind Julian are Alison and Simon. I can hear boots pounding behind me but I am unsure who has exited first.

In the car the air bags have deflated. Meadows and Coyle are struggling out of the car. Each has the door half open and an arm and leg are coming out.

As I closed on Meadows I glanced across to Coyle. "Oh god, no." Coyle's left arm is out of the car and being raised. He is holding a pistol. I screamed 'GUN.' Julian did not have time to react. Coyle fired. Julian went down hard. The gun turned towards Simon. He is too close and yet also too far. There is nothing he can do.

Alison is a little ahead on the other side of Julian. She brought down her baton with full force across Coyle's wrist. I heard a bone snap and Coyle screamed. The gun discharged. The bullet went harmlessly into the river as Coyle's hand had been knocked backwards by the baton as well as being broken. The pistol flew out of his hand and away into the bushes. A fraction of a second later the full sixteen stones of muscle that we call Simon collided with the passenger door. Coyle's arm and leg that are half out were shattered as the door crushed them onto the frame. Simon's elbow then hit him in the temple. Coyle slumped down inert.

I looked back at Meadows. He is now more than half out on the driver's side. He is reaching into his jacket. Oh shit, he is armed as well.

I am close enough.

I spun into a roundhouse kick and caught him square in the balls. As he doubled forward Tom, who must have been one of those directly behind me, grabbed his hair and arm and threw him across the bonnet. As Meadows writhed, vomited and fought for his breath, Tom wrenched his arms behind him. A PC, who had also been close behind me, roughly cuffed him and threw him down to the ground. Meadows doubled up, vomiting, howling with pain from my kick. His face is contorted in a rictus as he rolled in his own spew.

Meadows was roughly turned over as he writhed on the grass. His hand movement had been seen by the others and they were looking for a gun. They found a packet of white powder, presumably cocaine. I guess that he was hoping to throw it into the river. Did he really think that ridding himself of a few drugs would mitigate the deep shit he is in?

I twisted around and raced over to Julian. Barbara had struggled out of the van and is painfully hobbling towards us. She does not look injured. It is hopefully only her stiches restricting her. I arrived first. Julian is on his back with his eyes closed and does not appear to be breathing. There is blood gushing from under his helmet, so much blood. It is spurting out, soaking the grass of the picnic spot, covering his jacket. There is an astonishing amount of blood. Also a flap of scalp is hanging down and behind it I can see something white. I think it is brain tissue.

As when I was shot the bullet passed under my vest, from the low angle Coyle shot and Julian being so tall, the bullet has passed under the edge of his helmet. We had decided not to wear the full motorcycle type riot helmet as they would have restricted our movement and vision as we went through the pub. We opted for the smaller ones like a bicycle helmet. How I regret that now. It had been a team decision but I am the leader. It is my responsibility. It is my fault that Julian now has a terrible brain injury.

Barbara arrived and threw herself down. She screamed, 'Julian, oh no, Julian.' He gave a short gasp and his eyelids fluttered. As his eyes closed again she softly sobbed, 'don't die Julian. I love you. Please don't die.' He lay motionless and she lay across his chest sobbing. I can see that he is breathing but it is very shallow. His injury looks frightful.

Two cars slithered to a halt at the car park entrance. I looked up. It is A and B cars arriving and ten officers are racing out. All was quiet for a minute and then I heard a violent metallic banging. I looked back and saw that Tom and John had stopped a white van. I cannot see into the van as there is a reflection from a street light. The engine has stopped. The driver's window is beginning to come down. Tom and John are relaxed and their weapons are holstered. It looks innocent. I turned back to Julian. From behind I heard Tom shout 'go' and the van moved off.

All is now eerily quiet. The soft sound of the weir is really no sound. The reeds of last summer are whispering in the breeze. Barbara's sobs are bodily shakes. There is no crying to be heard. There is a smell of wet vegetation. The tang of Julian's blood and the reek of Meadows's beery vomit cut though the earthy undergrowth scents. Meadows and Coyle are wriggling. Julian lies deathly still.

CHAPTER 18: LUKE: DISTRAUGHT

Initially we seamlessly slipped into a beautiful routine. For two weeks Rebecca and I met several times each week. She had told us that she was involved in some undercover operation but for two weeks she appeared not to be at work. I wanted to ask her what was going on but I forced myself not to. I did not want her to think that I was compromising the necessary secrecy. We had gone to the cinema or we had walked with Toby under the streetlights, arm in arm. Once weekly we went out to dinner. Once or twice a week she stayed with me. On other occasions, to my dismay, she went home after we have finished making love. She seems to want to keep a distance between us. I half agree with her, our relationship is progressing more quickly than usual but I would be happy for it to do so. I am surprised, even a little hurt, that I had not been invited into her house. On the two Saturdays we broke the usual dating tradition and we did not meet. Rebecca was at a Taekwondo competition. I had a collection and correction on the Friday nights and leading into the Saturday.

Sunday morning is always a training session for Rebecca. After that, on two blissful occasions, she came to my house for a traditional Sunday lunch each weekend which we deliberately made into a more formal date even though Sam is here at the beginning. Rebecca was so relaxed then even though she had spent the previous three hours kicking and punching big, athletic men. Sam cooked superb roasts. After we had all eaten together Sam went goes off to the refuge. Toby lay back with his eyes closing as he digested our leftovers. Rebecca and I went to bed. We made love and then we lay in each other's arms, sometimes talking, sometimes just holding each other. It was routine, predictable and utterly wonderful.

That all started three weeks ago and lasted for a blissful two weeks. Then there was a week that I did not see her. She was totally committed at work and she even hinted, in one of our few phone calls, that she was out of the country for a few days. I had been hoping that today, the third Sunday, we would return to the new and delightful normality.

Not today.

Yesterday had been dreadful. On Friday night we were reduced to near hysteria by the police activity and being stopped ourselves whilst we had a drugged and bound man in the van. Then, over Friday night and during Saturday day, whilst still suffering the remnants of our fear, as I did the correction Sam sent me texts updating me on the news of the massive raid and that a police officer had been shot. We had assumed so but it was still upsetting to hear it confirmed even though we knew that it was not Rebecca.

Now Sam and I know not only that Rebecca had been involved in a huge operation, which included tackling a violent gang and corrupt police officers, but that she had led it. The local and national news all reported that the operation had been led by DI Fletcher. None had discovered that DI Fletcher's first name is Rebecca yet all have spoken highly of "him." I have spent two days swollen with pride that such a woman has held me in her arms. As what she has achieved has sunk in I have become even more astonished at her talents. Stupidly, as the action is now over, I am fearful that she may have been injured. I fear for the officer who has been shot. His name has not been disclosed nor the extent of his injuries but as he has been shot in the head they must be frightful.

I have only managed to exchange a few texts with Rebecca since Friday. We normally call each other several times during Friday and Saturday but this had not been possible. Though it had been the weekend after all the arrests and continuing searches, with all of the work required, she had only briefly managed to tell me that everyone at the station had attended for duty and all had been ferociously busy. Finally we had spoken for a couple of minutes on the 'phone last night. She had still been fraught but was able to say that she can come around today for Sunday lunch; in fact the Chief Constable has ordered her to take today off.

Since seeing her leap from that van on Friday night I have been on tenterhooks. After the gunshots, if I had not seen her standing as we were ordered to drive away then I would have been utterly distraught. Sam obviously thinks that I am anyway, she is most likely correct.

This time I made no pretence of being cool. I paced my study waiting for her to arrive, staring out of the window as I walk up and down past it. Toby has detected my perturbation, nothing gets past him. He is curled in his chair supposedly relaxing, his head on his paws, but he is fully alert. His eyes are swivelling, fixed on me, as I anxiously walk and wait. On the 'phone Rebecca had sounded so tired and distressed. I know why. I saw her there at the time her colleague was shot. She will know him. She will care for him. I caught myself, why am I presuming "him." Am I making the same misogynistic mistake as the reporters who assumed the lead police officer was a man? Whichever, I fear for him or her; being shot in the head at close range can only be catastrophic.

I made no effort to hide that I had been looking out. I opened the front door as she came up the path. She looks exhausted. I wrapped my arms around her and she hung on to me with her head on my chest. This is not the usual Rebecca. She seems vulnerable. We went into my study and she sat, more collapsed, on to the sofa. I sat next to her, my arm across her shoulders. So far neither of us has said a word. Toby took one look and leapt down from his chair and strode across the room. He sat at her feet, put his chin on Rebecca's thigh and looked up at her, his nut brown eyes full of concern.

Sam came in from the kitchen. With one fleeting glance she became aware of Rebecca's distress and sat next to her on the sofa on the opposite side from me, mirroring me, also putting her arm across Rebecca's shoulders.

Sam has immediately intuited the chief cause of Rebecca's distress and simply stated, she did not ask, 'it is your colleague, the one who was shot. That is what is upsetting you.' She paused then softly continued, 'we know that a police officer was shot but there have not been any details on the news. It must be someone that you know.'

Rebecca's head snapped up and she looked from Sam to me with grief and pain in her eyes. She started to shake and put her hands over her face and was then wracked with silent sobs. All we could do was to hold her tight. After a while she tried to speak but her words initially came out garbled.

Sam gently asked, 'is this the first time that you have spoken about it other than in an operational sense?' Rebecca managed only a slight nod between sobs. Sam said, 'take your time.' We both squeezed her tightly.

Rebecca calmed. She looked briefly at us through red-rimmed eyes and then had to look down again. After a while she stopped shaking, she took a deep breath and she croaked, 'it was........... Julian.............' She tried to carry on but could not.

Sam and I exchanged looks of horror. It was bad enough knowing that a police officer had been shot. Wrongly, it feels even worse that it was one we know, like and respect.

Rebecca shook and shook then tried again, 'but.....but............' More heaves, then she made a huge effort and took her hands from her face and firmly put one on her thigh and the other on Toby's head. That seemed to contain her. Gathering herself she spoke slowly and deliberately, obviously finding it difficult to continue, 'Julian was shot in the head but he is fine. Well, not fine, but alright, there is no serious damage.' She stifled a sob, wrung her hands and then continued. 'When he was on the ground I saw a frightful wound, blood everywhere and what I thought was brain tissue underneath.' I cringed with horror. 'When I went to see him in the hospital I found out that it was only a scalp wound. Apparently they bleed like crazy,' Sam and I looked at each other with relief, not only at Julian not being seriously injured but also at Rebecca now coming out of her distress. She continued, now a little more calm, 'I am so sorry to be so hysterical. It was so busy over the last couple of days that I have not had the opportunity to think about it. Walking here was the first chance that I have had to process it all. Sorry.'

Sam took Rebecca's face in her hands softly turned it towards her. Then she kissed Rebecca on the forehead. I should have done that instead of sitting here like a rabbit in headlights. Sam said, 'I am amazed to find out yet more about you.' She paused theatrically. 'It has in fact come as quiet a surprise.' Rebecca and I looked at her with concern but this melted when we saw Sam's cheeky smile. 'Yes, Rebecca, it is quite a shock to discover that you are human after all. It is indeed a shock to find that you, like the rest of us, can sometimes be overwhelmed.'

We all laughed and hugged as Rebecca wiped her tears

away. At last I thought of something useful that I can do. I poured us all a drink.

Much calmer now, Rebecca took a sip of the stiff gin, a Kir would not suffice today, and then she continued. She told us further details of how Julian was shot and that when she had run over to him she found him unconscious. The bullet had gone under the edge of his helmet. She described how she had seen a torrent of blood and under the edge of his wound something white that she had thought was brain tissue. Rebecca had assumed that Julian had been seriously brain injured. She had blamed herself and though distracted by the continuing operation and all of the arrests she had agonised for hours. They all had.

Then fantastic news had come from Barbara who had accompanied Julian to the hospital. The copious blood was due to a long scalp wound. The white tissue had been bone. The skull had not been penetrated; there is no serious brain injury. Julian had been knocked unconscious and has long suture line on his temple but is not gravely injured. In fact he is sitting up in bed, complaining about having to stay in for observation and wanting to come back to help with all of the work. Rebecca, who is currently the most senior in the station following the arrests, has had to telephone him and order him to stay in hospital, or at least to stay away from the station which is the limit of her control.

We all sat back with a sigh of relief. Sam and I now know that no officer, especially not Julian, has been seriously injured. It is also clearly the first time that Rebecca has described the incident to anyone. That plus her walk over has helped her process it. She looks so tired, that must make assimilating and coming to terms with all of this more difficult for her.

Sam sat back a little, giving Rebecca and I more space together, but still kept a hand on Rebecca's shoulder and looked at her with concern. I put my hand down to her side and, through her blouse, I felt where I know her scar to be. I whispered, 'it is the same as happened to you.' They both looked at me in surprise. I continued, 'the bullet passed under your protection and thankfully only caused superficial damage but came within millimetres of creating a serious injury.' They looked at me, initially surprised, then they realised what I said was true. This seemed to relax them both and we all sat back more on the sofa. We fell quiet for a while. Toby relaxed, went back to his chair and in seconds was snoring.

I innocently restarted, 'we were so worried when we saw you leap out of the van and seconds later we heard what we presumed were gunshots.'

Looking across the room, not seeing Rebecca's response, Sam added, 'I had to pull him back to stop him jumping out of the van and running to you. He wanted to help but I guess a couple of the very effective looking policemen there would have killed him before he even got close.'

Sam and I both jolted as we realised at the same time that Rebecca is now sitting bolt upright looking aghast. 'You were there?'

Taken aback I stuttered a reply, 'yes, we were driving to the car park to undertake a moth survey.' I felt myself colour a little at the lie and Sam looked at me sharply. Hopefully Rebecca will think the embarrassment is part of the general confusion. 'We saw the van you were in roar out of the alley then ram the car. We saw the skidding and then watched you jump out.' She sat stock still, open-mouthed. 'Rebecca, we thought you knew. Two of your colleagues stopped us and interrogated us. One recognised me and told the other who I think was called Tom that I was "the professor." He emphasised that knowingly and Tom immediately understood. We had no idea what was going on or how they knew me.'

'Tom saw you?'

'Yes. I had assumed he had told you. After the heads up the other also recognised me. Then Tom quizzed Sam and only relaxed when he found that we are brother and sister. He had looked from Sam to you. I guessed he knew that I was seeing you and initially thought that I was being unfaithful. It was clear that he was looking out for you.'

'I saw them stop a white van. I could not see who was in it. I was more concerned about Julian who was at my feet.' Then she smiled, her lovely warm smile, the first time today. 'So you were going to run over and protect me.' I sheepishly nodded. 'I was surrounded by fired up officers who do not know you. In addition to me five others were armed. It is a toss-up as to whether, as you ran between them towards me, you would have been severely injured in a tackle or if they had finally run out of patience and would have simply shot you.'

Sam snorted, 'exactly. I had to hold him down. He may be intelligent but he is not sensible.' Then it was her turn to look wistful. She held Rebecca's hand and whispered, 'we thought that it may have been you who was shot. We could not see you standing until they ordered us to drive away.' They had a little hug and Sam repeated, 'we thought that Tom would have told you.'

'I have hardly seen him since then. We have been working flat out processing everything.'

Then I asked what has been intriguing me, 'how did they know who I am?' Rebecca laughed out loud. The afternoon is getting easier by the minute. She then told us about the Met team, Alison's researches, and the comments made about me.

Sam snorted again and said, 'oh do shut up Rebecca. He is big headed enough as it is.' She is also smiling and Rebecca gave me a squeeze. I very much hope that I will have the opportunity to meet this team. During our too short 'phone calls they were the main subject Rebecca wanted to talk about and she has spoken about them in such a warm tone. Not only do they sound like extraordinary people they are also obviously close to Rebecca. I only briefly met her family and that was in difficult circumstances as they then thought that Sam was my wife. I would like to meet these other people. Rebecca has clearly been through a lot with them and she has love and respect for them all.

I fell quiet as relief flowed through me. Rebecca has made a coup. In addition, Julian is not badly injured. Finally Sam broke the temporary silence. 'We have heard on the news that a certain DI Fletcher has been very successful in a major operation taking down an organised crime gang. There has been some mention of corrupt police officers involved as well. He, we have noted the "he" with considerable amusement, is being feted. When are you going to let them down and tell them that this stunning operation was undertaken by a mere woman?' She paused and then continued with one of her teasing looks, this time it is directed at Rebecca. 'At least we have found out today you are human and therefore a woman. Until this afternoon I suspected that you were like Superman and from the planet Krypton.' Sam had demonstrated that she is not an expert on the superheroes mythology but we both understood her intended meaning.

Rebecca laughed again, whether at the Krypton mistake or the press mix up I am not certain. 'I am certainly not a superhero. I don't think they get as tired as I feel. However, it is not only my gender they have backwards. The Chief Constable, who, shock horror, is yet another "mere woman," will have great fun at their expense in a press briefing tomorrow. She has already told me what she is going to say. I will not spoil her thunder; it will be at 10 after we have a station meeting. Look out for it live on the radio and TV. I have no doubt that it will go viral.'

She continued but now more reluctantly, 'unfortunately that is not all that they have wrong. The initial investigation that I was tasked with was to look into police corruption and I am sorry to say we found a great deal. When we stopped, for want of a better word, that car the passenger who shot Julian was the crime boss. The driver was our station head, DSI Meadows. It was him that the chief investigation was about. It was partly fortuitous and partly engineered by the Chief Constable and others that I had been suspended and then I was feed up to be given the opportunity to start the investigation. Unfortunately I was not allowed to shoot him but at least I was able to kick him in the balls. It was the same kick that you saw me deliver to that yob in the park.'

I winced, remembering the power in that kick. We all laughed but it was a sad laugh. I, and I am sure Sam as well, can see that it is hurtful to her to find a colleague to be corrupt. Then Rebecca continued, 'as I said the press have it backwards. There had previously been suspicions about goings on at the hotel but we had no idea of the extent of it until our investigation of Meadows started.'

Sam interjected, 'so, in three weeks you have not only cleared police corruption but unearthed and closed down a crime syndicate as well. I take it back, you aren't human. You are a superhero.' Rebecca shook her head grinning but Sam pressed on. 'Luke thinks you are a superhero but I suspect that is for other activities that many would consider criminal.'

Rebecca went scarlet and covered her face but this time in a jokey manner. Then she said, 'it was certainly not only me. The team I was previously in were seconded from the Met. We actually worked from Julian's flat. I had not seen it before but he has a massive penthouse flat with two storey windows overlooking the railway station. It was superbly situated with fantastic facilities. It was a great improvement on the dingy cellar that we are usually allocated.'

My blood ran cold. Sam does not know that I had thought I had seen Rebecca and then realised, or now I should think wrongly concluded, that I was mistaken. It actually had been her looking out. When I was assessing it she had been overlooking the precise spot where I had later undertaken the last abduction. What if she had spotted me? Sam and Rebecca chatted on for a while. I then realised that they were looking at me. It must be obvious that I am miles away, two miles away at the station car park to be precise. Sam said, 'Luke, you look taken aback. What is on your mind?'

What to say? Thankfully a deflection came to me. 'Rebecca, you were previously second in command. Are you now the station boss?'

She ruefully shook her head. 'Technically, at present, I am. As I said there is a big meeting tomorrow before the press conference. The whole station will be there, with only a few officers drafted in from outside to answer the 'phones. In order to accommodate everyone it will be in the Ballroom of the Park Hotel. I am sure that the Chief Constable will bring in a temporary DSI while the permanent one is sought. Whoever is the stand in will be announced then.'

Sam looked cross and said sharply, 'they can't do that. It must be you after such a stunning operation and being next in line anyway.'

Rebecca smiled and shook her head. 'No, I have not been in post long enough. Anyway, as the Chief Constable is a woman I doubt the station could handle another weak link in the chain.' This was clearly meant as a joke but Sam harrumphed.

Sam looked at the clock and said, 'sorry but I must go.' To Rebecca she added, 'I have another shift at the refuge this afternoon. Whatever the reason I should go, I suspect that I may look green and hairy if I stay.' With her naughty face back on she added, 'no doubt you have catching up to do.' Before I could think of a suitable caustic reply she added, 'my darling brother has been far too busy worrying about you to do anything remotely useful. He certainly did not have the band width left available to think about you being fed. I have cooked a venison, port and pickled walnut casserole. Do leave some for me when I get in later.'

Sam stood and started to leave. At the door she paused and turned back saying, 'no doubt I will see you in the morning.'

To my horror Rebecca quickly and strongly said, 'no, no. I have to go home. I must catch up on some sleep. There is a big meeting tomorrow and I must be alert.'

As Sam left Rebecca turned to me and, giving me a gentle kiss on the lips, continued, 'a lie down this afternoon may help though. Afterwards please make sure I get up and go.' I tried to interrupt but she put her hand to my cheek and silenced me with a kiss. 'Please don't ask me to stay. I could not resist. I must get some sleep tonight and, knowing you, I would not get any here.' Grinning at her comment about knowing me, I thought, "knowing you as well Rebecca, you are quite correct." Now considerably relieved I took her hand and lead her in to eat.

We chatted comfortably over lunch, or as she reminded me, more correctly over Sunday dinner. We deliberately avoided the subject of the raid. I had simply told her how stunningly effective she had been; then we passed on to other interests. I am sure that she needs a break from her operation so I deliberately raised some other matters that I have been intending to discuss with her.

For the first time I told her that I am attending a conference in California in July and that I have been asked to give one of the keynote lectures at the World Congress of Earth Scientists. I tried to present this as blandly as possible but she can see that I am so excited by this; that I am both proud and humbled at the same time. She replied that she was honoured to be entertained by a world star. I laughed at this but she said seriously that in Earth Scientist circles surely I must be. She is correct. I had not thought of it that way. Then I reached the million dollar question that I had been postponing as I do not want to be disappointed. I explained that Sam is coming with me and that we are staying with our brother Jacob who lives near to the university where the Congress is being held. Will she come with us?

Rebecca sat back obviously both surprised and very pleased. I can see that she so much wants to come and my heart soared. Then I came back down with a bump as I saw her face fall.

Rebecca sadly said that she was honoured to be invited and would love to come; but. I hate bloody buts. She explained that July is the most likely time for the new permanent DSI to be appointed and also there will need to be several more new DIs recruited to replace those arrested. As second in command she will need to stay here to help with all of the inductions. On one hand I am disappointed but, on the other, I am delighted to see that she genuinely and strongly wanted to come. She is clearly as disappointed as me. Though it is a negative outcome even asking her has intensified our relationship. She squeezed my hand in a warm apology. Then she thought for a moment and continued, saying that she will think about it; there is the possibility that if she is only away for a few days then the Desk Sergeant may help. There is a glimmer of hope. My heart soared.

Then it was her turn to probe me. She asked about my motor bike. I have mentioned it in passing but I have not given any details. Rebecca wanted to know what sort it is and when will I take her out on it. I assured her that the first warm, dry day we are together I will take her for a jaunt. I asked her to guess what it is like. She had picked up on me saying jaunt. She surmised that it is either a vintage bike or a scooter, one of those with a double front wheel. I left her guessing saying that she will find out soon enough. Boy, is she in for a surprise. I hope that she will still be keen to get on it after she has discovered its true nature.

Then it was my turn again. I said that I have a free day on Wednesday and I asked if she will she join me for a day out? I suggested that I take her to see the Farm and after, if we continue a few miles further out of the city there is a lovely country pub where we could have lunch. She asked if this would be on the back of the motorbike or in the research van. She teased that she is not sure she can trust my riding on one or my roving hands in the other. I said neither, I will hire a car.

When she had had time to think about it again her face fell. As I had anticipated there is too much work at the station this week. She will have to be there especially as she may be acting DSI for a while longer until the interim one is parachuted in. She promised to let me know if she can make it but she is not hopeful.

We returned to my study and sat quietly together for coffee. Then it became clear that we are thinking the same. Without saying anything we took each others' hand and went upstairs. I slowly undressed her as she leant against me passive and compliant, wanting me to do it all. I slipped off my clothes and we slid between the sheets. Our lovemaking this afternoon is so different and sublime. She is uncharacteristically lying still on her back as I slowly enter her. Her hands are softly holding my shoulders and at times her eyes are closed. It is a delightful, gentle togetherness. It seems to be what she wants and needs. It is certainly what I am delighting in.

At one stage whilst her eyes were closed and I was raised above her I looked down and thought yet again what a beautiful, admirable woman she is. She seemed to sense that I am looking intently at her and her eyes flashed open and caught mine. As we continued to slowly move together she softly asked, 'what are you staring at?'

'A very beautiful and accomplished woman.'

She smiled, lifted up her thighs and wrapped her legs around me, crossing her ankles behind me and powerfully pulling me even deeper into her. As she did this she pulled my head down and whilst nibbling my ear whispered, 'are you being naughty professor? Are you trying to charm your way into my knickers?'

After we had made love she slipped into a contented sleep. I quietly got out of bed and I left her there for a while. I cleared up downstairs and then I sat with Toby quietly thinking about my luck in finding this remarkable woman. After only a couple of weeks I am already so close to her. We have gelled so well. It is a complete turnaround for me after the last two years of not being to be able to be with anyone. I feel complete again.

Reluctantly I went back upstairs to wake her to go. She is still softly sleeping. She looks like an angel with her golden hair on my pillow. I put my hand on her shoulder and gently squeezed. Her eyes softly opened and she looked into mine. Without speaking she pulled me down and kissed me. I so much want her to stay but I had to say, I had promised. 'I have called a taxi. Andy will be here in twenty minutes.'

'I don't want to go. I want to stay here with you. You must force me to leave.' That is the last thing I want to do and by saying she wants to stay she has made it even more difficult. Reluctantly I pulled the sheet back for her to get up. Seeing her naked made it even worse.

Andy arrived as always bang on time. I had arranged to travel back with her. Again I had to promise not to try to go into her house. I was going to walk back and so we took Toby. Rebecca had expressed surprise at Toby being allowed in the taxi. I explained that this was a benefit of being a regular customer who tips well. Even so Toby has to squeeze into the front foot well.

We sat in the rear and Rebecca immediately snuggled down next to me with her head on my shoulder and her eyes closed. She is still so tired but at least now relaxed. Andy immediately started his usual tirade. 'Lo Prof. Lo love. Er you're a copper aren't you love. You musta 'erd 'bout the op over the weekend. Bloody marvellous your lads.' I felt Rebecca start to shake with a supressed snigger. 'Its bin all ova t' nuse. Your chap DI Fletcher, he must be some bloke. He sorted it all out.' Rebecca is now almost uncontrollably shaking and sputtering with concealed laughter. I am fighting to keep a straight face. On and on he went for the entire journey, thankfully it was only a few minutes.

When we reached Rebecca's house, as we were getting out, Andy leapt out to open the door for Toby. He always does this as he likes to give Toby a pat. Handing Toby's lead to me he turned to Rebecca, he held out his hand and said, 'we 'avnt properly met. I'm Andy, Andy Price.'

Rebecca took his hand and said, 'good to meet you. I am Rebecca, DI Rebecca Fletcher.'

Andy's face lit up, 'Fletcher, you must be related to that chap who....who...who.' Poor Andy's face contorted in dismay and embarrassment as the penny dropped.

Rebecca beamed at him and said, 'yes Andy. I am him.' She continued to smile at him and kissed him on the cheek saying, 'I hope to see you again soon.' As she stepped to her door I looked back at speechless Andy who I thought was going to faint. He should have learnt his lesson when he had previously failed to realise that it was her who took on the thugs in the park. Even with basically good men such as Andy the assumption of female weakness seems ingrained. Looking at the chagrin in his face I suspect that he has finally appreciated this mistaken viewpoint.

As we got to her door she turned to me with a determined look and is obviously going to implore me not to ask to come in. I put a finger to her lips and interrupted, 'let me know if you can make Wednesday. I know and I understand that it is difficult. The whole week may be difficult for you. I would love to see you any time.' I kissed her good bye and reluctantly but contentedly turned to walk back with Toby.

That evening, when Sam came home, after sorting out a few domestic issues we sat together and I spoke to her about Rebecca. She largely only listened. She has previously teased me about falling head over heels for Rebecca but in reality is delighted for me with only the one obvious exception and worry. I had already asked Sam if she would be happy for me to invite Rebecca to California. She had been delighted at the idea and is disappointed to hear that, though keen, Rebecca will probably not be able to come. We would both very much like her to meet Jacob.

I talked more about California. I am getting very strong vibes from the department there. I said it is possible that they are building up to offering me a job and I asked Sam how she would feel about relocating. As always, she can read me like a book, she had guessed and she was already prepared. Sam said that she would be delighted to go.

There was no discussion about me going alone and us being parted. I have made it clear that for the foreseeable future, really until Sam has the security of a long-term partner, I would never consider that. As I had anticipated Sam will be delighted to go but she surprised me by throwing the obvious question back at me, 'what about Rebecca?' I don't know is the short answer. It is too soon in our relationship to ask her and I cannot think of going without her. I will cross that bridge if I ever come to it.

I said that there is a possibility that Rebecca and I will have a day out on Wednesday and if so I will show her the Farm. I said this flippantly but underneath I am very wary. I am pretty sure that I know what Sam's reaction will be. She did not lose her cool or get cross but she did become very worried. We went over old but unresolved ground with the tension mounting. Sam is worried about Rebecca being there. I feel things are better hidden in plain sight. Again she threw at me the fact that I am deceiving Rebecca and that is not a good start to a serious relationship. She dragged up and hurled at me the lie I had told earlier today about collecting moths when we saw the action at the weir.

We had become very heated but when she saw the effect this had on me she backed down and came and put her arm around me. I sputtered that she is correct and it is cutting me in two but I cannot see any other route at present. Sam nodded sad agreement. I told her I continuously think of telling Rebecca, I even hope that she will join out work, but that is a one way street. I must be sure of her response first. Sam agreed saying, "very sure indeed."

As we had come together again after a spat I thought it was a good opportunity to resolve another issue that we have previously fought over. I have had an idea that may settle our dispute. We so rarely argue that we do not have a tested mechanism to deal with such problems. I have desperately wanted to increase our number of treatments. After seeing the police officer on the ground last Friday this has now become unbearable, I feel like a pressure cooker about to explode. As she gets over her experience Sam wants to do less and to put it behind her. We both see and understand the others point of view but that does not stop it being unresolvable. I suggested that we tell Jacob what we are doing. As we are all so close I am certain that Jacob will not inform the police and, indeed, I think he will support us. Sam agreed and we decided to carry on at the present rate until we see Jacob in June and then take his council on whether to escalate or to back off. We both agreed to accept his opinion and that will be our policy on our return.

I went to bed both content and emotionally exhausted, what a weekend.

CHAPTER 19: REBECCA: THE STATION MEETING

I feel so good today.

After making love with Luke following lunch yesterday I slept until seven this morning. Firstly in his bed and then, after he chivalrously escorted me home, in my own. I even dozed through most of the taxi driver's ramblings.

I am refreshed. A good job has been done. I am off to find out what my new working arrangements will be. It is a good day.

Whilst musing to myself I strode up East Street. I can barely believe that it is only a little more than three weeks since I walked up here, at the same time of day, on my way to the mysterious meeting . A mere twenty-three days during which life has spun on its axis. This time I am to attend the meeting called by Claudia, the Chief Constable, when she will address the entire local service regarding the events of the weekend. We will also be told of the management arrangements for the station from now on.

That is at nine am. I have been asked to attend at eight-thirty to see Claudia in the Oak Suite of the Park Hotel, the same room as we last met. Then at nine we will move to the ballroom. The meeting is being held there in order to accommodate so many people. The briefing room at the station is simply not large enough. Furthermore it still seems contaminated by the Troop. I will ask for it to be painted to rid us of them.

We desperately need this guidance from the Chief. The station is rudderless at present. On the other hand there is still so much work to do and it is somewhat of an interruption. I am glad that the Chief has to attend a media briefing, in the same ballroom, at ten. Our station update will have to be short and I can then get back to work.

I had been surprised to be asked to attend in full uniform. I can only think of one reason for this. It seems impossibly fast but, given the speed the Chief moved at three weeks ago, it must be that she already has an interim station head coming and she wants me to meet whoever it is, most likely him, today. It feels odd to be in a skirt but I have to confess I enjoy wearing the uniform. It compliments my colouring and shape.

I feel good.

As I walked up the street one cheeky lad, no doubt he wanted to impress his mates, wolf-whistled me. I waved my handcuffs at him and they all amiably laughed and waved back. I always carry them when in uniform, even dress uniform. Not only are they complimentary, if they were needed it would look stupid to be without them.

I stepped into the lobby and I approached the Oak Suite door at eight twenty eight. Before I could enter I was intercepted by Peter who said, very formally, 'good morning Ma'am.'

I smiled and I decided to play his game, 'good morning Sergeant.' I moved to enter. He blocked my path and he turned to knock firmly on the door. I was taken aback and suspicious. Three weeks ago we had walked straight in.

We waited. He stared at the door. After an age I finally heard a brisk 'come in,' Claudia's voice. Peter, again with deliberate formality, opened the door and then he bade me go in. I froze. It is only not Claudia behind the desk. All three are again present, the Chief Constable, the Commander and the Chief Inspector. They are all also in full uniform and sitting to attention. Claudia waved me over. She pointed to a seat in front of the desk saying, 'good morning DI Fletcher. Take a seat.' Peter stood to attention to the side.

I immediately twigged. The off-the-books operation is over. Normal service is resumed.

'Good morning Ma'am, Sirs.' It actually feels easier.

Without preamble, skipping pleasantries, The Chief started. 'DI Fletcher; we wanted to see you before the station meeting to discuss an operational concern. Before we do so there is another complication that I need to clarify our joint opinion on before the later media briefing.' She looks so serious. This is not good. 'During the operation last Friday one of the suspects sustained two fractures to his left arm, one fracture to his leg, a skull fracture and concussion. Another suspect received a kick to the groin requiring him to be hospitalised with severe testicular and penile bruising. There is apparently the possibility of a penile thrombosis that will leave him impotent and at least one testicle will need to be removed.'

She looked sternly into my eyes.

Anger flared in me. Are we being disciplined? Should you not also refer to Julian being shot in the head? Can you not congratulate the station on a job well done? After a long, hard stare at me she continued, 'would you please comment on the injuries they received? Do you consider an investigation as to whether or not the action resulting in them being badly injured was appropriate and proportionate?'

Bloody hell, I am being disciplined. Is this why they wanted me in uniform?

I took a breath to compose myself. I think the Bear gave a brief smirk but he rapidly returned to his previous serious expression. I may at least have one ally. Whatever, I am not going to take this lying down.

Returning her stare I almost spat back at her. 'Ma'am, we were fired on. We previously had good reason to suspect that some of the gang would be armed. This was confirmed and during the operation we found that three of the suspects were indeed armed, the two sons as well, but only the father with the fractures had the opportunity to discharge his weapon. When Meadows reached into his jacket I reasonably thought that he was also reaching for a weapon. I found later that the other three officers who saw him put his hand in his pocket had thought the same. In addition to protecting myself I had an immediate duty to protect the team. A weapon had been discharged, an officer had been shot. Six of us were armed yet did not even draw our weapons. In view of all of these incontrovertible facts,' I nearly shouted the word "facts", how dare they sit there criticising, 'then, yes, I consider our response proportionate?'

I tried to stop there but I could not. 'I think the officer who caused the fractures to Coyle should be commended for tackling an armed man. He should be honoured for not shooting, not censured.' I tried to rein myself in but the implied fault-finding of my wonderful team had rattled me. 'I am sure that you are aware that it was me who kicked Meadows in the balls. I consider many officers in my position would have shot him. Indeed in order to protect the others this could be considered, not only justifiable, but necessary.' Too late, I realised that as I worked thorough my reply my voice had become increasingly louder and harder and that I am staring at her. Five minutes ago I innocently strolled in thinking, "what a good day." Now I am livid.

They all relaxed back and smiled. What the bloody hell is going on here.

The Chief nodded at the Bear who then spoke for the first time. 'DI Fletcher, I do not consider your response merely proportionate.' He emphasised and ironically rolled the word "proportionate." A proportionate response would have been to shoot the buggers. Your action was restrained.'

I sat back startled as they all stood. At a warning cough from Peter, I suppose I should now think, "Sergeant Benson," I belatedly jerked to my feet. Now all smiling warmly they came around the desk and shook my hand. The Chief said, 'well done DI Fletcher. That is well done for both what you did last week and for not hitting me a minute ago. That is the ridiculous type of questioning you will undoubtedly face from the media. We wanted to prepare and rehearse you.'

Horror flashed through me. I wanted to cry out, "what media. I am having nothing to do with them." 'Your response was perfect in the words used. I trust that with the practice we have just given you, and having worked through your understandable ire, when you speak to them it will be with an oleaginous, empathising sincerity oozing from every pore.' What does she mean, "when I speak to them?" The day was good, then bad, then good again; but with this "media" threat I fear for what may come next.

The Chief paused, then she said, 'please sit. I have something else to tell you.' As we all sat I thought, "what on earth is coming now." 'Everyone who attended on Friday is receiving a commendation. You will be given a Police Medal.'

My jaw dropped. Before I could think about a reply the Bear said, 'and this bloody time at least you will be able to tell people about it and show them what you have so well earned.' Again they all stood and shook my hand. My attempt to speak was waved down.

For the second time we sat, then the Chief continued, 'that brings us to the third and equally important point that the three of us wish to raise with you. I warn you that whatever answer you give you will gravely disappoint one of the senior officers here, either myself or Commander Lightman. One of the two possible answers will also distress DCI Fox and Sergeant Bender.' Sergeant Bender, so even he is to be addressed formally today; not as "my big bro." I braced myself for yet another surprise. 'You are to be promoted to DS with immediate effect.' I blinked disbelievingly. Before I could comment she continued. 'We wish to offer you a choice of new posts. Either you remain here as station head, or, you return to the Met where Commander Lightman will install you as the leader of a serious crimes team.'   Now I stopped blinking and stared disbelievingly. I had expected a surprise not a revelation. Seeing my disbelief she softly continued, 'no rush. The station meeting does not begin for...,' she glanced at the clock whose tick now seems like a detonation, 'forty-five minutes.' We have only been here for fifteen minutes, it feels like a lifetime. 'You have half an hour to give us your decision. Would you like to go outside for a coffee?'

I sat immobile. The Chief looked at me expectantly. After a minute I was finally able to speak. 'Thank you for the promotion Ma'am. Either position would be an honour.' Am I saying this, am I here? I can clearly see both my duty and my wishes which thankfully coincide. I glanced at the Bear who immediately intuited my reply. I saw disappointment reach his eyes as I continued. 'I can give you an immediate answer. The station here is currently rudderless. Partly due to this and partly due to me now being embedded here I would be honoured to take your kind offer of station head here.' Luke had also flashed into my mind but I kept that to myself. I saw the Chief, the DCI and Peter, that is Sergeant Benson, beam.

The Bear stood and with a grim resigned smile he said, 'let me be the first to congratulate you. I am disappointed but that is what I expected. You are quite correct, you are desperately needed here.'

The Chief and the DCI also stood and, along with Peter, they again shook my hand. Is that the third time in only fifteen minutes? I think that I spotted a tear in Peter's eye. I realised that I have already made my first decision as DS. I am Rebecca; he is Peter. The Chief spoke again, 'we have to have a formal advertisement and afterwards an appointment board so you are technically only acting head until then. The Minister has called me supporting your appointment. It is what she wants and this was said in a tone suggesting that mere mortals such as us should not disagree. Thankfully, we all strongly concur.' I thought, "holy shit, the Minister?" 'I am sure that with her influence, and as all of us here want the same result, that your official appointment will be a formality.' They all nodded.

With a characteristic Knight's move The Chief continued, 'would you please let me have your jacket?' Bemused I stood and slipped it off. The Chief handed it to Peter who stepped out of the room returning moments late without the jacket. The Chief gave me an enigmatic smile and I retained a bemused silence. I vowed to never again be surprised by this trio. What are they up to now?

Taking a breath and looking at me determinedly she then surprised and horrified me yet again. 'We will tell the station the good news at nine. Immediately after that your first task is to lead the media briefing at ten.' I tensed as I thought, "oh no, anything but that Ma'am." Spotting my expression she said, 'yes, that is what I imagined when facing my first news presentation. It is actually quite enjoyable when you get into it. You have already rehearsed the only awkward question.'

Finally realising that I have been set up from the moment I entered, I shook my head and smiled resignedly, yet again, at the three of them. 'I will set the ball rolling. DCI Fox will tease the reporters with a little misdirection and he will then introduce you. I suggest you speak for ten minutes. That is a surprisingly long time and you will need to instruct them that you will not take questions until the end of your summary. You will probably face a long grilling then, but for details not criticism, I hope.' I did not like the sound of, "I hope."

Still reeling I jumped as a knock came at the door. Peter opened it, took something and said 'thank you.' He came up to me and held open my jacket to help me to put it back on. I gasped, my DI badges have been removed and DS ones are sitting in their place. I turned to him wide-eyed as he helped me slip my arms in. It is the same jacket as ten minutes ago yet feels totally different. 'Take care Ma'am, they are only pinned on.' His voice is croaky and, yes, there is a tear in his eye.

'Thank you Peter.' I emphasised "Peter." 'Peter, did Julian tell you what I threatened if he continued to call me Ma'am?'

There were guffaws from behind me and Martin called out, 'we have all heard that, Ma'am.' More guffaws.

Pretending to be cross, but my smirk gave away my true feelings, I spoke again to Peter in a theatrical ordering tone. 'My first instruction in my new role is that I am to be called Rebecca. The second is that a WPC uniform in my size is to be placed in my new office. I will continue to go on patrol weekly.'

From behind me the Chief wailed, 'I would love that opportunity.' Then she continued, 'come. It is time for the station meeting.'

She led the way out of a side door in this small conference room. I had not seen it open before. We went through into a narrow corridor and at the far end I can make out the stage of the ballroom. I realised that the Oak Suite doubles as a changing room for the bands and for the actors when they stage concerts or plays here. The ballroom is clearly full and a loud hubbub is carrying along to us. As we approached the wings, still concealed by the curtains, there came an explosive roar and cheering. Peter surreptitiously peered between the curtains, then he turned to speak to us in a low voice. 'It is PC Courtney. He has just arrived. It looks as if he is wearing a white turban and he is having to lean on WPC Sturgis. Otherwise he looks fine.' I thought, "leaning on Barbara. Did he hear what she said as he slipped into unconsciousness?"

Peter paused as the noise died down again. Then he walked out alone. The Chief indicated that I should stay back. The others clearly know what is about to unfold. Again I am wrong footed by this conniving trio who are being aided and abetted by Peter. As he crossed the stage he held up his hand to quieten them. Initially it fell silent but then some wag started to sing 'dar da dah, dar da dah,' in a burlesque rhythm. Immediately many took up the theme.

Then another yelled, 'get 'em off.'

Claudia quietly asked of me, 'did you recognise that voice?'

'Yes Ma'am.'

'DS bloody Fletcher, you know precisely what I meant. Tell me who it was.'

'No Ma'am.'

In a mock cross tone accompanied by a twinkle she

hissed, 'that appears to be your first insubordination in your new role.'

Before I could agree the Bear growled, 'I am surprised it took her so long.'

Whilst we all hid in the wings, quietly shaking with supressed laughter, Peter held up both of his hands and the room finally quietened. At last he is able to speak. 'No doubt a few of you are already aware that our esteemed leader, DS Meadows, has had to stand down because of exceptional circumstances.' Jeers followed this and again Peter held up his hand for quiet. 'There are to be several announcements this morning but the first and major one is to inform you of the new reporting and management arrangements. A new DS has been provisionally appointed awaiting final confirmation by the board, I am assured that will be routine.' The jeers were replaced by incredulous gasps. With a wide grin back at his sister who remains concealed Peter continued, 'yes, it is astonishing. Apparently the powers that be are capable of action in less than a year and without quadruple documentation.'

This was met with cries of agreement. If only they knew who is standing feet from them. Claudia hissed, 'that brother of mine has always been a pain.' Even so she looks delighted.

Peter called the room to order again. 'I am delighted to say that it is my task to inform you who the new boss will be.' Now there is a deathly hush. He paused for a long moment, then, he finally and quietly said, 'actually, I won't tell you.' Moans echoed around the room. 'I will show you.' A murmur was followed by an expectant hush. He turned to me and waved me forward.

I froze. The Bear prodded me and my feet, which suddenly weigh fifty kilos each, slowly carried me out. As I emerged from the wings pandemonium broke out. There are cheers and screams. Then came a round of wild clapping and stamping as someone called out and drew attention to my new insignia. I looked around shamefacedly, I do not deserve this. Many, not only women, are in tears. I waved at them feeling like a Queen and another round of cheering erupted. It went on and on. As it continued I spotted that, not only are all the station here, the Met team are as well. I fought back my tears.

Then there was an abrupt halt. Silence engulfed the room. The whole station had turned back towards the wings with mouths open and looks of consternation. There came a violent scraping as all jumped to attention.

I turned and saw the Chief, the Commander and the DCI marching out in file. They are not walking, they are actually marching. They came to the centre of the stage and in military precision turned to face the audience. They also stood rigidly to attention facing the now worried looking crowd. The room seemed to hold its breath. Most people here would not have seen so much brass together since their graduation. Hell, other than my secret medal ceremony two years ago and my first trip here three weeks ago, nor have I.

Then I heard the Chief counting down from four, slowly, sotto voce. What on earth are they up to now? On one they ripped off their hats, threw them in to the air and started cheering and clapping. After a brief, shocked silence the room erupted again. The three turned back towards me and started shaking my hand and clapping me on the shoulder. All others in the room started stamping on the floor in unison. It is deafening.

After what felt like an age the Chief faced the room again and held up her hand for silence. There was no barracking as Peter had faced. The hush was immediate. She spoke loudly and with authority. However her voice is also laced with obvious emotion and affection. 'Some of you will recognise both me, Claudia Wentworth, the Chief Constable, and, DCI Martin Fox.' She indicated to him. 'Only a few visitors, the Met team you worked alongside last Friday, will recognise Commander Rupert Lightman.' She now indicated the Bear. 'He was DS,' she emphasised the "S" which raised an appreciative murmur from the crowd, 'Fletcher's Commander in the Met and he was responsible for seconding the excellent Met support to here. I think you already know Sergeant Benson, my brother that is.' More gasps accompanied this revelation.

She took a long pause as all in the room looked at the three. Then she continued, now for the first time in my hearing, with an emotional quiver, 'It is a great honour to have the opportunity to be your commanding officer. During the last several years it has brought to me nothing but pleasure. Watching you all work, often in the most demanding of circumstances, has been humbling. However, nothing, absolutely nothing, none of all the astonishing achievements that you have wrought during my tenure, prepared me for what happened last week. The skill, speed, dedication and professionalism that I was privileged to observe from you all last Friday and from the team laying the grounds for that action was breath-taking. We,' she indicated the Bear and DCI Fox, 'could only watch from an unmarked car outside the Langley.' Holy crap, I had no idea they were there. 'From the bottom of my heart I thank and applaud you all.' She paused and surreptitiously wiped away a tear as a soft applause followed. 'You are all being given a Police Commendation and DS Fletcher and PC Courtney are being cited for a Police Medal.' I already knew about mine but Julian's was an unexpected addition. I glowed with pride for him more than myself as clapping again filled the room.

The Chief continued, 'we all have further announcements to make this morning. I am delighted to inform you that, in recognition of your superlative work on

Friday and the fact that so many of you worked unscheduled over the weekend, that I wish you to take two days paid leave this week.' Cries of "thanks Ma'am," came from the floor. Then she added, 'I am ordering DS Fletcher to take leave on Wednesday and Thursday, as I had to order her to take leave yesterday. I have no doubt that if I do not do so she will be exhausting herself at the station..' Smiling at me she added, 'we all know that she will not leave her new post without an order. I say those two days and not tomorrow as she will be required to commence seeking replacements for the tragic loss of the Troop with some urgency. We will be drafting in temporary DIs in the interim. For this week, during the ordered absence of DS Fletcher, and whilst she is engaged in reorganising the station Sergeant Benson will control day to day arrangements.' As she spoke she emphasised each "order" to me, each "S" in DS and "tragic" regarding the troop. The muttering and suppressed laughter grew with each and now broke out into more cheering. All I can think is, "I can see Luke on Wednesday."

The Chief stepped back and the Bear moved forward and spoke. 'I want you all to know, especially my officers from the Met, that earlier today I tried to persuade DS Fletcher to return to lead a team in the Met. She declined. Apparently she prefers,' he looked meaningfully at Julian, 'the quiet life here in the sticks.' Laughter and applause rang out. 'Our loss is your gain.' He looked to Tom, Angela, Charlie, Simon and John, who all stood together to one side, and said, 'sorry team, I did try.'

They all started chanting, 'we want Laser, we want Laser.....'

Tom's brother, Derek, stood next to him. He playfully punched Tom in the shoulder and started chanting in return, 'we have Tibs, we have Tibs............' The whole of our station immediately joined in. The Chief grinned from ear to ear and allowed this insubordinate ribaldry and rivalry to continue for a while. She then shouted for order and, wisely, they all know her reputation, the room again fell silent.

The Bear now stepped back and DCI Fox moved forward. 'It falls to me to deliver the bad news.' Another hush and many looks of concern came. 'On Friday night commencing at eight pm there will be a celebratory party in The Mill.' More cheers came as I thought, "that is only two hundred yards from my front door." He held up his hand for quiet, 'worse, the Chief has arranged for the food and drinks to be paid for by the service.' Again he raised his hand to pre-empt more cheering. 'There are several more items of bad news. We,' he indicated himself, the Bear and the Chief, 'will not be there to prevent any excessive drinking or rowdiness.' Again he had to hold up his hand. 'A team is being brought in to cover the station so you may all attend. However, the very worst news is that you can all bring your significant others.' Now the clapping and cheering was irrepressible.

Someone yelled out, 'is Tibs bringing the Prof?'

There were wolf whistles and a woman, I am fairly certain that it was Angela, shouted, 'yes please. He is drop dead bloody gorgeous.'

Another called out, 'does he like being handcuffed?'

As the catcalls went round I thought of our first time. Not handcuffed but he was certainly restrained. I felt myself blush bright red. Thankfully with the stage lighting this was not visible from below. The Chief, who seems to never miss anything, conspiratorially whispered, 'so, that's a yes then.' Before I could make any useless denial she stepped forward and called them to order. 'Meeting over. We have to prepare for the media briefing. It is live on BBC News so they need time to prepare. As you leave, under pain of death, do not speak to the media. We have plans to set them up and get our own back for a change. Do not give any details of what you have been told here. You will be able to watch on the screens outside as they get a well-deserved come-uppance. ' Oh shit, and I had thought that the idea of this media briefing could not get any worse. I am going to be on TV and it will be controversial. 'There are coffees and pastries for you all in the bar. There will be nothing stronger from me until Friday.' Chatting amiably they filed out as my presentation distress soared.

As soon as the last officer left the room hordes of journalists poured in. My heart sank as I saw so many. They are all looking quizzical and they are asking every police officer as they left what on earth all of the rumpus had been about. Each and every one smiled back and shook their heads. Then the cameras and screens were wheeled in. I thought that my confidence had already hit rock bottom. I had been wrong. In walked Miles Porton, the aggressive, condescending News Anchor and debate show host. Anyone but him would be preferable if I have to face questions. I have to distract myself. I texted Luke. [fantastic news promotion and I can make Wed. Awful news I have to give the media brief and it will be on BBC News 24]

Almost immediately a text returned, [congrats we will all watch]

[no no no no I meant don't watch] Then I thought and sent another text. [who is we] I know that Sam is on duty.

[tough WE will. I am supposed to give a lecture at 10 they will prefer to see you only 100 of them u will hve 100s of 1000s on tv]

Oh shit.

I looked across the floor as I heard some shouting. Pompous Porton was screaming at a make-up woman who was turning away in tears. He is snarling and being aggressive. I had previously deduced that underlying his obsequious, superficial charm on TV he is clearly unpleasant. I caught the eye of the make-up woman and taking my handcuffs off my belt for the second time this morning I nodded at him and waved them in the air. He did not see but she immediately understood and came over to me, now smiling. 'Thanks. I was going to come to see you to ask if you wanted a touch up, now I am here I can see that it is not needed. You look beautiful and radiant. Good job, I have used it all up on that ugly prick.' We laughed together and as we did I looked back at him. I had not realised before, yes, he is ugly in spite of what must be an inch of slap.

Ten am came too soon. I found myself sitting at a long desk which had been moved to the centre of the stage. The Chief is in the middle. Martin Fox to her right, the Bear to her left and I sat on his left. The only good I can find in being here is that at least there is a modesty board on the desk. I presume that I will have to get used to skirts again. Only for formal functions though, I will continue to wear my track suits at the station.

At ten exactly the Chief moved to the lectern and the room hushed. Porton, with incredible hubris, tried to wave her to wait as he had not started his introduction to the camera. I can see on the large screen to the side of the room that the BBC is still transmitting the news from the studio.

The Chief ignored Porton and spoke. 'Good morning every one, thank you for attending this briefing. Before you are told of the operation last Friday there is another announcement. As you may already be aware, and this will confirmed in detail during this briefing, the operation was led by DI Fletcher.' The news has finished, the camera in front of us had a red light flash up on the top and the Chief's head and shoulders in close up detail appeared on the screen. She is being broadcast to the nation. Flashes were coming from every corner and cameras clicked. I inwardly groaned as I realised that in a few minutes time that will be me. 'Further, during the operation, the Detective Superintendent previously leading the station was removed from post.' There were a few guffaws from journalists who clearly already know more. Porton looked cross and perplexed; clearly he has not bothered to prepare fully. 'I am delighted to announce that, pending the official appointment by the board, DI Fletcher has been promoted to Detective Superintendent and placed in charge of the station.' As when it was announced to the station, there were gasps of astonishment and respect at this sweeping and rapid change. 'With no further ado we will move to the introduction of DS Fletcher, the newly appointed station leader head and the leader of last Friday's operation, who I know you are keen to meet.'

The Chief came to sit down. I am perplexed. I had been told that Martin Fox would speak next but she has just said that it will be me. Spotting my consternation, as she approached the desk the Chief nodded at me to stay put. Yet again they are up to something. We all heard clearly in the now quiet room that Porton is speaking to the camera, his false face is now on the screen. He pompously said, 'finally we are to see the elusive DI Fletcher. We know little of him other than he is a man of action and a rising star. He must be some chap to have led such a raid. At last here he is.' I felt the Chief shudder with suppressed laughter as Martin very slowly and deliberately walked to the lectern. Now I see it, they are setting up the journalists. Especially Porton, who has switched on his stereotypes and jumped to conclusions. Martin tried to speak but Porton shouted him down, 'DI Fletcher, now DS Fletcher, congratulations, how do you feel?' Again Martin tried to speak and again Porton interrupted. For a minute or so Martin is unable to get a word in edgeways.

Whilst this charade unfolded, my 'phone, which is on silent, vibrated. I am station head. Even though I am at a briefing I have to look, it may be an emergency. Holding it below the desk I opened the text. It is from Luke. [You look so hot.] Looking back at the screen I can see the camera has pulled back and now I am visible to the world. I cannot look at that so I continued with the text. [if you want to make love on wed scratch your left cheek once for each time] This relaxed me as I smiled at his comment which I suspect is also serious. I scratched my cheek five times and then innocently looked at Martin. At my first media briefing I am having text and TV sex. At least it has taken my mind off what is roaring down the tracks. My 'phone vibrated again but I dare not look.

As I looked back at Martin a tall, elegant Indian caught my eye. She is looking at me, not towards the podium. She has deliberately attracted my attention. She tapped her shoulder where my new badges are, once as she looked at me, once again as she then looked at Martin. At least she knows police insignia. She knows that Martin is not DS Fletcher. She has probably guessed that I am. She gave a warm conspiratorial wink. I returned a smile and a nod.

At last Porton shut up and Martin is able to speak. He made a theatrical pause and then portentously spoke. 'I am Detective Chief Inspector Martin Fox.' Chortles broke out around the room. Elbows were jabbed together and amused looks thrown in Porton's direction. For once he is silent; he looks as if he feels cross. He should feel stupid. The Indian reporter caught my eye again, her smile wider still. 'I am tasked with introducing DS Fletcher. I think, however, that it will be better if I simply hand over to DS Fletcher.' At this he briefly glanced towards the empty wings. Then he slowly walked back to the desk.

Porton had recovered and decided to go on the attack. 'The police are being deliberately mysterious about DS Fletcher. Finally it looks as if we are going to meet him.' He directed the camera to turn towards the wings saying, 'we will ensure that this station is the first to show you this man.' He has clearly swallowed Martin's misdirection.

As this unfolded Martin sat down. The Chief nodded that I should make my way to the lectern. As I did so I realised what I want to do. I do not want to tell the world what happened last Friday. I want to tell Luke. We had spoken on Sunday but I was then tired and emotional. Now I am going to calmly tell him what happened.

I walked to the lectern as if I was walking up his path, knowing that he is looking out of his window. I made sure that I am standing square and straight, I want to look elegant for him. I turned at the lectern and I faced the TV camera square on as photographers' flashes and clicks surrounded me. Except it is not a TV camera. It is Luke. I am looking through the lens at him. The background noise of the photographers is no more than Toby snoring. The room fell silent except for Porton who is still looking to the side wittering on about the delay in seeing this elusive chap. His camera man has seen me and is trying to get his attention but Porton is intent on being the first. He was the last. Finally he realised that the room has fallen silent and he looked back, startled to see me here. At last he also fell silent.

I again looked at Luke and finally I spoke, 'I am Detective Superintendent Rebecca Fletcher.' The room erupted with everyone cheering, except for Porton that is. I still looked into the camera, into Luke's kind, understanding eyes. When the brouhaha had settled I continued. 'I have a tortuous tale to impart and I ask that you do not interrupt. It will be quicker and easier for us all if you kindly allow me to tell you what happened without pause. I assure you that there is no time limit on questions at the end. I will remain here until you have all been satisfied.' They all sat down, surprised but clearly impressed and obviously they consider it to be a good approach. All except one, Porton, who remained moving around and speaking into his microphone, calling for the camera to be on him.

I can see only Luke sitting in his lecture hall with his one hundred students behind him. I have not yet seen it but I imagine the hall to be soft, warm and wood-panelled like his study. Most Unis are concrete and have cold looking lecture halls. With Hogwarts, though I have only seen the outside, I suspect that my guess as to the lecture hall appearance is possibly correct. The universities outer appearance is in fact like the description of the fictional Hogwarts and I surmise the inside is as well. I spoke to handsome Luke as he sat on his wooden bench. I spoke slowly, softly and calmly. I spoke to an intelligent caring adult.   Porton, in his constant distracting prattle, seems to be addressing truculent children.

Over ten minutes I gave the details of the investigation, the raid and what we had found. Admittedly I glossed over the fact that so many we arrested were our own. I did not flinch from it, I did tell them but I quickly passed onto and emphasised the breaking of the crime gang, especially the release of the sixteen girls, all of whom were trafficked, three of whom were under age. I gave details of Julian being shot and the injuries sustained by Coyle and Meadows. I neglected to say that Meadows had been my predecessor.

I came to the end. I had asked Julian and Sally to pop back in. They had slipped into the rear unnoticed. Several other coppers are scattered around so even if they had been spotted their presence would be unremarkable, well, except for Julian's bandages.

'I would like to conclude with two fine examples of modern policing that humble me and enthuse me to lead this station.' The room sat up. 'The first is PC Julian

Courtney.' I waved at Julian to stand and he walked a little unsteadily to the front. 'PC Courtney is the officer who I described being shot. As I have already related to you he unflinchingly tackled a man who was suspected to be armed. As you can see he is thankfully not seriously injured but he came within millimetres of losing his life. That you already know. What you don't know is that in the prior investigation.........' I paused to scowl at Porton who is still prattling on, distracting from my praise of Julian. I can accept him speaking over me. I cannot accept him detracting from Julian's well earned praise. Others in the room were now glaring at Porton also. I bit my tongue and carried on more loudly, drowning him out. '........PC Courtney used his incredible computer expertise and the operation was based on what he, and another colleague who is also a computing wizard, uncovered. Further, our investigation was undertaken in secret and he allowed us to be based in his flat and for us to use his home computing set-up' I neglected to add that his computers are more powerful than most banks.

People started to applaud Julian but were again interrupted by Porton. I fell silent and I stared hard at him until even he realised and shut up. Those around him had stopped scowling at him and are now grinning at me. They realise that I have had enough. 'Before I come to the second example please allow me a small digression. In today's police service we strive to find the truth and to present it to people. We regard the great British public with respect. At all times we treat them as worthy adults. We do not talk down to them and inflict our own pompous, opinionated distortions upon them.' During this I continued staring at Porton. The room erupted with cheering and laughter. I heard the Chief spluttering behind me. Because of his botox Porton could not frown. Because of his lip filler he cannot purse his lips. In spite of the thick make up I can see him turn crimson with rage which is accentuated by his bouffant, bleached hair. On the wall screen I can see this is being transmitted, the camera is on him. The camera man is wearing an, "at last" smile. Given that all around him are now jeering Porton finally backed down and shut up. I am now able to continue.

'The second example that I want to give you is WPC Sally Myers' I waved for Sally to stand and come forward next to Julian. 'WPC Myers has already seen action earlier this year when she was one of the officers who came to my aid when I was being attacked by three knife wielding thugs.' I glossed over that they were all already on the ground when the back-up arrived. Perhaps I should take up politics.

Someone shouted, 'was it you who hospitalised the leader or was it WPC Myers.' Someone is alert to the actions of our service.

'It was me.' More claps rang out. 'Anyway, let us return to Friday last. The call for officers to attend an urgent operation went out at nine forty five pm. At that time WPC Myers was in an expensive restaurant in the centre of town, elegantly dressed and being wined and dined by her beau. The restaurant had just fallen silent as her boyfriend had sunk to his knee to propose. A text came in with a special tone we use to make the recipient aware of its nature. She realised it was an urgent call from the station. She looked at the text and ran from the restaurant before answering. One hour and twenty minutes later, still in her finery, she was chasing a criminal, She rugby tackled him, then arrested him, single handedly. During this she tore her clothing and sustained a blow to her left eye and to the left side of her face.' The camera zoomed in on her showing that a bruise has bloomed and a greenish hue is spreading down her cheek though it does not distract from her beauty and obvious happiness. 'Another hour later, only after taking the suspect to the station, she returned to find her boyfriend.

The restaurant was then closed. He was not at his flat. She eventually tracked him down to his parent's home and asked if the offer still stood.'

I deliberately stopped speaking at that point. Excited cries rang out, 'what did he say? What happened?' Sally did not speak. She raised her left hand to her cheek so that it is next to her bruising with the back of her hand to the crowd. Her ring sparkled. The camera zoomed in and the screen was filled with her bruised radiant face and the ring twinkling to the side. The room erupted with cheering for the nth time today.

'Now, please ask your questions.' They came thick and fast but all were polite and respectful. It seems to be a very different atmosphere from the usual braying. I am enjoying it. Even when taking questions from others I still reply to Luke.

Most were incisive and penetrating points that it was a pleasure to deal with. I deliberately avoided looking at Porton but I had the impression he had finally shut up anyway. After a while a young reporter put his hand up and asked if he could raise a less serious point which is intriguing him. I replied, 'of course.' He asked how we had managed to undertake the investigation crammed into a bachelor flat. I thought of the facilities provided by Julian which surpassed even the most sumptuous Canary Warf office. I replied truthfully. Two sat at his computer station and the rest around the kitchen table. We made do. He, clearly impressed, copied my phrase and said, 'modern policing.' Yes, definitely politics for me if I get fed up with policing.

Then the elegant, thoughtful looking Indian woman who had twigged the initial ruse by Martin put her hand up. 'I would like to raise a very serious point.' I indicated that I am happy for her to continue. 'Two of the people arrested sustained serious injuries. One had not one but multiple fractures. There are often concerns about brutality and heavy-handed actions from the police. Would you say that your actions were proportionate? Will there be a compensation claim from the men you arrested?'

The room went quiet. This woman is obviously well known to them all and they respect her question. Also I can see that they are thinking the same and want an answer. Inwardly I quietly thanked the Chief for the stunt she had pulled only a couple of hours ago. I now looked away from the camera, that is away from Luke, and I addressed the reporter directly and politely. I am greatly helped by my confidence in the answer. I gave the same reply as I had given to the Chief but without the anger. I emphasised the shooting of Julian and that I was one of the officers inflicting one of the injuries during the arrests. That shocked them. I added that I had also been armed. They were even more shocked at that. When I said that though I had just witnessed Julian shot in front of us all and that none of the six of us who were armed had even taken out our weapons a murmur of appreciation went around. She thanked me warmly and is obviously more than satisfied that our response had been appropriate.

I decided to risk a question of my own. I looked back through the camera at Luke and I quietly asked, 'would anyone else wish to comment on the proportionality of the response given by the team that I was responsible for?' I am laying down my reputation. I heard a sharp intake of breath from the Chief and "wows" from around the room.

A hand went up at the rear and a tall, burly older man slowly stood. 'Ma'am, I do not consider your response proportionate at all.' He spoke in a heavy American drawl. The room became still. I may have pushed too far. He continued, 'before I came to journalism I was in the American infantry. I was leading a squad through a village in Basra during the Iraq war when there was a single unexpected shot from a sniper.' Now we are all hanging on every word. Where is this going? 'One of my men, one of those that I was responsible for, was shot in the head and fell to my feet. As your good man here had fallen near to you last week my equally good man fell at my feet all those years ago. The difference was that the rear of my man's head had been blown off. I took an RPG, that is a rocket propelled grenade launcher, off one of the other men. Then I instructed them to move on keeping their heads down but also showing the sniper they were moving. I hung back and watched. As expected I saw the sniper fire from an upstairs window. Thankfully he missed that time. I fired a grenade through the window. I did not miss. We found six bodies in the room along with a few other body parts.

When one of your men is lying at your feet, next to you, shot in the head, that is a proportionate response. You, Ma'am, if you do not mind me saying, were not proportionate. You were restrained.'

There is not a stir in the room. Finally I managed to ask, 'what happened to your man? Did he survive such a terrible injury?'

'He was dead Ma'am. He had two boys, now men. I do my best to continue to help but they are having difficulties being fatherless.'

I commiserated with him. That seemed to bring the meeting to an end. I thanked them all. Porton disappeared. All the others filed out and animated conversation broke out in the lobby.

The Chief came over to me with Martin at her side. 'DS Fletcher. I asked you to be oleaginous and empathetically sincere, implying falsely. You were not. That was sincere passion. You spoke as if you love the people you were addressing. It was a credit to the service and I feel honoured to have been behind you.' She grinned and then said firstly to herself, 'oh stop shilly-shallying Claudia.' Then to me, 'you were fucking brilliant.' They both warmly shook my hand. Quietly Claudia continued, 'you have made many friends today. They will be useful. Keep them well briefed especially the one who asked the difficult question. Not only did she mean well she is also very influential.' I am pleased and surprised, I did not recognise her. 'Watch your back when you are near the enemy you made.' There was no need to ask who that may be. Then, together, we walked to the lobby where an impromptu discussion continued.

After a few minutes general chit chat a reporter singled me out, the one who had asked the "proportionate" question. She shook my hand and proffered her card, I recognised her name. She is a well-known and much respected crime correspondent. 'I am sorry for my question. I thought it better aired here than by trolls on the net or by a group of pseudo-leftie, pseudo-intellectual, effete university professors.'

I spluttered with laughter and with tears in my eyes, as she looked at me astonished by my over-reaction. I said, 'my boyfriend is a university professor.' She clamped her hand over her mouth at her imagined gaff. I squeezed her elbow. 'No, don't worry. He is nothing like that and often moans about many of his colleagues who are. He would warmly agree with you.' We laughed together and seemed to form a bond. We chatted on for a while, not only about this case and crime, but life in general. After a while I thought it a good idea to take another risk with her. I gave her an additional briefing, from a "senior reliable source," no names. I described the actions of Meadows and the Troop and gave many more details on the Coyles. It will come out anyway and I prefer it to come from her and not someone with an agenda. She much appreciated my candour and we parted. I am sure that we will meet again.

Finally the crowd dispersed and I can get back to work. I realised that I had left my 'phone on the desk in the hall. I went back in and as I was picking it up a movement in the wings caught my eye. Turning towards it I was amazed to see the Chief and the Commander in a passionate embrace. They were almost eating each other, the same as Luke and I do. They are at least fifteen years older than me. I don't know why that matters or why I should be surprised. I hope that I am not succumbing to Porton-like stereotypes. They are so engrossed that they have not seen me. I made a hasty quiet exit. Well, well, I know he is a widower and she is divorced. They are both passionate, sincere people, so, power to their collective elbows. My only concern is that I had not spotted their relationship. I am supposed to be a bloody detective.

CHAPTER 20: LUKE: THE FARM

Parking is tight. Finally I manage to find a slot near to Rebecca's house but only on a double yellow line. Reversing in is difficult. I drive so infrequently these days that I am out of practice. Even when we make the collections Sam undertakes most of the driving. At last, I am in and I cannot see any wardens. I picked up the flowers and the newspaper and, yet again aping an overeager teenager, I ran to her door nervously grinning.

The door swung open before I could even knock and she pulled me in and embraced me. I had to hold out my arms to prevent what I am carrying being crushed. When she finished kissing me I said, 'you are as good as me at playing it cool.' She kissed me again. 'Careful, careful, these flowers are for a wonderful lady. I don't want you to damage them.'

With a big smile she asked, 'so who is that? You found out on our first date that I am no lady.'

'I have forgiven you for that abuse.' She snorted but her smile widened even further. 'They are for you.' I handed them to her. 'Happy anniversary.' She looked at me quizzically. 'Happy one month anniversary.'

Initially she smiled again; then it was replaced with a thoughtful look, 'is it really only four weeks. It feels like ages.'

'I am sorry to hear that I am boring you so much that time is dragging.'

She jabbed me hard in the ribs saying, 'don't play the poor victim with me Cape. You know exactly what I mean. So much has happened. That is why it feels like a long time.' Yes Rebecca, that is one of the reasons that it seems such a long time. The other is that I feel so close to you but I cannot say that yet. 'They are lovely. I will get a vase. I cannot think of when I was last bought flowers.'

A flash of sadness crossed her lovely face but thankfully it soon passed.

It is my first time in her house so as she walked back to the kitchen and utility room she showed me around. I told her exactly what I thought. It is delightful. The downstairs is mostly open plan, just a divider between the sitting and dining area to the kitchen. It is painted in pale greys, similar to my own hallway, and has a light wood. This combined with the rear kitchen window overlooking a little garden; the bay window to the front overlooking the park, river and town; tall ceilings and open plan stairs, they all together give a wonderful, light airy effect. She put the flowers down and stood next to me at the foot of the stairs. Looking pointedly up them she softly said, 'and the bedroom is up there.'

Grinning I said, 'I am on a double yellow.'

She pretended to flounce off but I held her hand as she said, 'so, I am not worth a ticket.'

I held her close to me and we kissed again. 'I want you so much, right now. However, even better, I would like to look forward to a spectacular afternoon.'

'What a brilliant idea.' She squeezed me and turned to get her coat.

Again as she tried to go I held her hand. 'From what you have said, or rather not said, I don't think that you have seen this. I am surprised that no one in the station has drawn it to your attention.'

As I held up yesterday's Guardian, without looking at it she replied, 'they have told me that I am in the local rag, The City Guardian. It is in my in-tray, deliberately at the bottom under a very large pile. They teased me that my photo is in it. I take a lousy photo, I cannot bear to look............' As she looked at the paper her voice tailed off. She was silent for a moment as she took in the front cover. 'Oh Shit.'

I held out the paper pulling it taught between my two hands. She can now see that it is not a local newspaper, it is the national Guardian. On the front, midway down on the right, there is a head and shoulders photo of Rebecca which was obviously taken at the media briefing two days ago. She is square on, caught in a winning smile directed at someone in the audience. Even in black and white news print she looks radiant. Her wide, square shoulders are accentuated by her uniform and epaulets. Above her is written in large type, "stunning." Below her in much smaller type, "police raid, see page 3." It is clearly meant to imply that it is not only the raid which is stunning. I am very surprised that they printed what will be interpreted as a sexist comment by some, particularly by some women not as stunning as Rebecca. Presumably the editor will say that they were only referring to the raid.

I turned to page three and she gasped and sat down holding it and reading it. Her mouth opened wider with each line. I have read it so much that I know it by heart. I am quiet as she peruses it. The whole page is covered with more photos of her and her team including Julian's bandaged head. There are graphic accounts of the raid and its success that is again, probably to appease the PC brigade, described as "stunning."

'Oh my god.'

'I guessed that you had not seen it. I bet that the whole of the station are whispering behind your back waiting for your reaction to being a "page three" girl. I was surprised that the Guardian finally managed to get at least one thing correct. You do look stunning.'

'Don't be daft. They meant the raid.'

'If you think that the double-entendre was not deliberate then you are then one being daft.' She went to playfully punch me again. I am sure that it was only playful because I am able to easily parry it and hold her arm. If she had meant it I am certain that the first I would have known about it would be when my head hit the floor. I pulled her close and whispered in her ear. 'When are you going to accept that you are not only a beautiful person but that you look beautiful as well.' After a brief pause for this to sink in I added, 'you are a stunning copper as well. I doubt any other could have pulled off last Friday.'

'You are biased by what I let you do to me.'

'I think you are the one who does things to me.' She held me close and blushed. Whether her embarrassment was at what I had reminded her that she had done, or at being called beautiful, or both, I do not know. It does not matter, they are all true. 'That was not a complaint by the way.' Now she is laughing as I held her. 'Anyway I thought that you were stunning when you came to interrogate me and that was before I found out how depraved you are.'

'I didn't interrogate you.' She accentuated 'interrogate." 'That was just a chat.'

'Christ, I would not like to be given the third degree by you. I would take the Spanish Inquisition any day.' I stepped aside from yet another punch, from all my teasing it is what I should expect, and I said, 'come on, before I get a ticket. Can you imagine the poor copper or meter maid when they realise the new commander is driving off in a car they have just ticketed?'

'I am not a Commander, they are much more senior and only in the Met.'

'I bet that is not what your new underlings say.' I ran for the door before she could swing again.

We drove slowly through the city in a gentle, quiet accord. I guess that she is thinking of what I had shown her in the paper. I am thinking of her. I managed to click into driving again and only ground the gears a couple of times. When I did so for the second time she took my hand off her thigh, where I have rested it between gear changes, and exhorted me to concentrate on driving. I deliberately took a circuitous route turning right at the Langley pub and going down the road Rebecca had raced along only five nights before. I pulled in opposite the car park in almost exactly the same spot as Sam and I had been in.

The car has gone but the wreckage of the fencing is still strewn around. She had fallen very quiet since turning into this road. I hope that I have not made a mistake in bringing her here. 'Sorry but I had to come here with you. I had to see it again with you sitting safely next to me. When I saw you leap from the van and then heard the shots I was so frightened for you. Now sitting here again I can only feel and see how magnificent and courageous you were. I wanted to say that to you. I wanted to look at you and say it directly to you, right here.'

She squeezed my arm. 'Thank you for that. Also thanks for bringing me here. It helps me to process what happened. I can't believe it even though I was involved.' She looked at the spot where Julian had fallen. 'I can't believe Julian was shot and I can't believe that he has not simply survived but has only minimal injuries. When I looked down at him I thought that the bullet had entered his brain.'

She faltered and wiped away a tear. I squeezed her hand and she looked at me with gratitude in her eyes. It had been a risk but thankfully bringing her here seems to have helped.

'I know exactly how you feel. I can't believe it either even though I saw it unfold with my own eyes, right here, directly in front of me. Shall we?' She nodded and I drove on. We passed the end of the road Sam had turned down on the night so that we could avoid any more police. That spectacularly backfired but we got away with it. I could not tell Rebecca that we had seen that arrest as well. I would have to explain why we had turned off the main road. I quietly drove on out of the city.

As we approached The Farm concentrating on driving became more and more difficult to do. Earlier today Sam had yet again tried to persuade me not to take Rebecca there, saying how dangerous it is. At the time I repeated my view that the best place to hide is in full sight. The closer we approach the less sure I am.

I started by showing Rebecca the outside. 'The buildings were originally a brick making factory but they have subsequently been used for many purposes over the years. When the university acquired them and I started using them for our research, now seven years ago, the outside was rubble and weeds. One of my post grads, Clive, took on the clearance. With some funding for diggers plus conscripted undergrads, he levelled and cleared the area. Then he started his research. All the grave sized holes you can see were dug out by the diggers at the very start. He commandeered the diggers in the evenings when the workers had gone home. He dug the holes in preparation for his experiments. The ones filled in with mounds of earth and fruit trees on top, twenty two of them in all, were where he started his research on Natural Organic Reduction. Unfortunately he only had time for a basic start.'

Rebecca chipped in, 'Natural Organic Reduction?'

'It is the mother of all euphemisms. The process is effectively human composting.'

'What, you have bodies in there?'

'Yes and no; yes to bodies but no to humans; they are all pigs.' Not entirely true, two are human. Rebecca relaxed a little hearing that as far as she knows they are pigs. I continued, 'human Natural Organic Reduction is legal in some countries but the composting is undertaken in tanks. Clive wanted to make it as green as possible and he was experimenting with undertaking it in a grave but using additional material to increase the temperature of the surrounding compost. He also put perforated pipes around to increase the oxygenation. The temperature reached is much higher than a garden compost heap but less than the tanks used elsewhere. He only had time to dig up and assess a small number of pigs before he died.'

'Oh, I did not know he had died. I wondered why you were implying he had left. I am sorry to hear that. What happened?'

'He had a brain haemorrhage. It was a terrible loss. He was a brilliant researcher. If he had lived I am sure that he would by now be heading a major company combining a green ethic with a good service to many people. Many farmers have to pay to dispose of dead animals; they made a donation to the research as well as providing the pigs for us and would have been happy to pay for the service. Many people want to be buried in an environmentally conscious way. It worked brilliantly. Using a combination of wood chips, alfalfa and straw around the animals they composted down in a few months, including the large bones. He used pigs as they are so close in size and shape to many humans. He went further.' I pointed to a very large mound, roughly ten meters across, to the side. 'That is where he composted the solid remnants from human sewerage. Again it composted well without the usual smell. It gave a rich medium much of which is spread all over this site. That is why the growth is so vigorous. After he died and the experiment had to be discontinued I planted trees over each filed grave as a memory to him. He would have wanted to be composted here but that was not legally possible. The trees are all that I could do for him.'

Rebecca looked sad but then, obviously wanting to cheer me up, I get morose when I talk of poor Clive, she picked up her feet looking at each shoe in turn. 'You mean to say that you are walking me across human poo. You romantic devil you.'

I laughed, I can see that she is not suffering the yuck factor that many people have when thinking of sewerage. If only they knew. 'Not poo, it is rich compost. Look.' I reached for a spade that is leaning against the sapling planted over where Brian James is quietly rotting. I bring over compost from the sewerage heap and regularly put it around all the trees. That hides the fact that some have been planted since Clive died and that it is not pigs underneath. Only two humans so far but there may be more.

I drove the spade in and turned over dark, rich, sweet smelling earth. 'Many people do not realise that over a million tons of the solids from sewerage treatment plants are spread on farms each year.' She looked horrified. 'Yes, it is true. When the sewerage treatment process is finished the clean water is put into rivers or the sea but that leaves the solids. Some goes to land fill but much is put on arable fields. It has been clearly shown to be safe but there can be some smell until it is ploughed in. Clive's process composts it more quickly and in addition it reaches higher temperatures so it is even safer and that also removes the smell. If only he had lived. I am sure he would have created a combined process for humans, animals and sewerage.'

I took her hand. 'Come, if you don't find walking through poo romantic let me show you my moths and my forge.'

She laughed again and hugged me, then she put her head on my shoulder as we walked along. God, it is good to be with her. 'Actually I am finding this fascinating and I was only winding you up. I don't object to well-rotted compost wherever it is from. Dad is a keen gardener and I used to love helping him turn over the compost heap and looking at all the wriggly things inside. We found an adder's nest once.' Then she stopped, she has obviously realised something. 'What do you mean; your forge?'

'Though our relationship seems so long to you, as I alluded to earlier that is probably because I am boring you.' I received a mock scowl for that. 'As we have only been together for few weeks I have not told you everything about myself yet. I am not simply a one track earth scientist.'

'Two tracks, earth science and sex.'

Now it is my turn to scoff at her. 'There are many things you do not know and have not seen. For example, I am upset that I have told you about my motorbike but you have not insisted on admiring it.'

She interrupted, 'actually, I would like a spin on it.'

'Done, I will take you out soon. Also you do not know that a hobby of mine is metal sculpture. I enjoy making large outdoor works. I should say, "I did enjoy." Since starting the moths study I have not had much time.'

She stopped suddenly and looked at me. 'Is that huge, beautiful piece in your garden one of yours?' I nodded. 'Luke it is fantastic, I have been meaning to comment on it. Not only is it beautiful but it is also intriguing. Can I make a guess at what it represents?' Again I nodded and I wondered what she will say. 'It is complex and I will probably make a fool of myself.' She hesitated and I indicated that I wanted her to go on. 'I think it is meant to represent tectonic plates colliding and giving rise to mountains. It is so delicate yet so dramatic.'

It was my turn to suddenly stop and look at her hard. Now I am even more impressed by her. She is a warrior, a lover, and now I find that she is an intuitive artist as well. 'Oh sorry, am I completely wrong?

'No, you are completely correct. Most people need hints before they see it.' We walked on. As I passed the outside sheds I opened the doors. 'I will show you Clive's raw ingredients.'

'You have bodies in there as well?'

'No, I meant, as you full well know, the other ingredients. I love the smell of them. Though they are now two years old as it is so dry in here they remain in good condition.' Yes, I thought, they are still in a good enough condition to do the job for me. 'This is alfalfa and as you can see these are straw and wood chips.'

She ran her hand through the alfalfa and smelt it. 'Gorgeous, I adore the smell of silage and this is similar.' Everything she says makes me feel more compatible with her. Our thoughts and opinions interlock.

So far so good but there is nothing about the outside to suggest that there are more bodies than the pigs being composted. The interior has more on show. The inside is where the danger lies.

We reached the heavy doors to the old warehouse and again I felt so unsure, so exposed. Taking a detective into here now seems ridiculous. I wish that I had listened to Sam. I unlocked the top of the range Chubb deadbolt and we went through to the cavernous warehouse. Most of the interior is open plan but two inner rooms are kept locked. I opened them and as I did so I realised that the lock on the forge is so much stronger than the lock on the moth laboratory. Is that a giveaway? Does that show that more goes on in the forge and that I want to keep it hidden? Again I cringed at this oversight; I should have made them identical.

Then I nearly panicked as Rebecca said, 'you have serious security here.' What do I say? Thankfully I did not have to think of a reply as she quickly continued, 'very wise. You need it with the site being so isolated.' I breathed again.

We went into the laboratory and I demonstrated some of the apparatus for identification, assessment of, and preservation of the moths. It is in reality only a pretend laboratory set up as a blind. This apparatus is an excuse in case I am spotted coming here at night. I could undertake some work here but all the moth work is done in the university and I would certainly never bring students here again.

Then we moved on to the part that I am now dreading, the forge. I still think of it as the forge though for two years the only thing I have tried to bend and beat here is disgusting male behaviour. Immediately she fastened onto the one item that I feared discussing above all. Laughing Rebecca asked, 'what is this? It looks like a ducking stool.' There is a huge tank full of water with a cantilevered arm several feet long next to it. It is clear that the arm can be lifted and swung out over the water. Again her observation is uncannily correct but this time I cannot tell her.

Thankfully I had a reply ready as I had intended to refer to it as that. 'Yes, it is.' I forced a smile and she looked at me as if I was trying to wind her up. If only she realised that I am telling the truth. That is, "was telling the truth," now I have to lie again. 'I use it for ducking my work when I am forging. As you can see from the one outside my house I like to make large pieces and it is impossible to lift them without apparatus even when they are cold. They are of course, in parts, literally red hot when being worked on.' I moved the arm which is currently pointing away from the forge to demonstrate. I swung the end across the water and it came to rest over the forge. 'I fix the piece I am sculpting to the end of this arm to heat the part in progress in the forge. I can then move it out, still on the arm, to the bench for the work. When I need to cool it I can then swing it further across and plunge it into water.' She nodded at this seeing exactly what I meant. Indeed, what I had actually done until the attack on Sam. Now, since its repurposing, I just move the end from the bench to the water. There is only a little fuel on the forge to keep us warm. That is only to keep me warm and them conscious. It is not for use as a smithy.

We walked around the forge and the laboratory as well as the old cavernous brick warehouse. Though its original use was industrial the construction and design is in a beautiful Victorian style. We strolled about, arm in arm entirely at ease, talking about moths, sculpture and the building. As well as it being delightful to be with her the insightful interest that she showed in all three enthralled me. I feel so good and so at ease with her. Additionally, thankfully, I had been correct and Sam uncharacteristically wrong. Rebecca is clearly enjoying being here and seeing an additional part of my life; even if one of the purposes of this place remains concealed. I will never have to be reticent about talking about the Farm. The additional use it is put to remains hidden in full sight. In case she ever decides to come out to see me when I am supposedly assessing the moths, in reality treating the shits, I had to tell a lie.

Another lie that is; I hate lying to her. I want to tell her all and ask her to join us but that will have to wait a little longer. Perhaps Sam and I can discuss that with Jacob when we are in California. This latest lie; only a little white lie, was me telling her that when I am undertaking the moth work I am locked in the laboratory. I said that not only will I not hear anyone come I would not be able to admit them as I have to control the humidity. That is at least true of when I am working on moths in the University lab, not the real reason for not being disturbed here. I feel bad lying to her but I cannot risk her finding out about our work until I am certain that she will join in with us. I think, I hope, that will happen someday. I have seen how she becomes taut when Sam's attacks and injuries are mentioned. She obviously cares for Sam as well. Am I jumping the gun, does she in fact care for me? I think so. I hope so.

We drove on to the pub. Though it is only six miles downstream from where Rebecca lives it is a different world here. In the city, as there is a weir where last Friday's action took place, the river is wide, deep and slow. It flows between the embankments upstream of the weir in the middle of the city itself. Here it emerges from between tall trees on either bank and then rushes white and noisily over shallows and boulders. The Fisherman's Arms sits on the bank at one side of a lush meadow. It is ancient, thatched and the walls are wattle and daub. At weekends it is predictably busy but today it is only half full and we found a superb table in a timbered alcove. We can see across the bar yet at the same time we have privacy. Near to us an open wood fire crackled and spat.

I looked at her, I pinched myself. It hurt, apparently I am not dreaming, I really am here with her. I said, 'I think there is only one way to eat in a traditional English pub; that is to have traditional English pub fare. I am having steak pie and a pint of Adnams.'

'Perfect, I will have the same.' As I went to the bar to order I realised that I had not been the slightest surprised at her choice. I had not actively thought of it before, but now I am, I realise that I had already subconsciously worked out that she would not be a small glass of sauvignon blanc and a prawn salad woman. With all of her exercise she probably requires more calories than me. In spite of enjoying pies and pints she is so lean.

The food was perfect, rich and satisfying. The company was even better. I tried to ask her more about herself. Though we feel so close already in reality I do not yet know her that well. "Yet;" am I again being presumptuous.

Initially it was difficult. Rebecca is not reticent. She just seems unused to talking about her own life. Eventually I had to pretend to refuse to take her back, saying I would leave her here unless she told me all of her secrets. She tried to parry by saying that she need the run anyway after that pie but eventually she relented.

We spoke about her mother, father and sister. When I had seen them, though it was so brief, I had immediately detected how close they all are. I asked, 'have you told them about me?'

'Of course.'

'What do they think?'

'Oh, you know, how lucky you are.'

I ignored that but I had to ask the overwhelming question, 'I hope that you have not told them everything.'

'What do you not want me to tell them?' This was delivered with a cheeky grin.

'You know damn well what.'

'Only Julia.'

'I am not religious but I pray that I will never meet her again.'

'She can't wait to see you again.'

After our jokey exchange we fell quiet for a short while as I plucked up courage to ask her.

Eventually she said, 'out with it. I can see you are building up to tell me something.'

I took a deep breath. 'As I said soon after we met, at the end of July Sam and I are going to California for ten days for the Annual International Symposium of Earth Science. There will be two thousand Earth Scientists in one city.' She gave a theatrical yawn and pretended to nod off. I playfully kicked her foot and after she had pretended to wake up I continued. 'You should be impressed. Yours truly is giving one of the key note lectures.'

She sat up sharply, 'I am impressed. I am very impressed. Is that on your moth research?'

'No that is a side interest. I am talking on my chief research on tectonic plate movements. It is not the science I wanted to talk to you about. Sam and I are staying with Jacob, our half-brother.' She nodded, she remembers me mentioning him and us staying with him before. I couldn't go on. I found myself tongue tied.

'Luke, what is it?'

I blurted, 'have you thought about it? Will you come with me?' All my confidence slipped away as the words came out and I saw her immediately look sharply at me. I stammered, 'sorry, sorry, one month is too soon for such a suggestion that is also so far ahead. I shouldn't have asked you and embarrassed you.' I immediately regretted asking her again. I should have been more aware of her wanting to take things more slowly and to still keep some distance.

She leaned across, put her arm around me and gave me a playful shake. 'You silly, silly man; I am not embarrassed. I am flattered.' Then it was her turn to fall quiet and look troubled.

Now it was my turn to press her, 'now you go on.'

'Luke, I don't think I can come. I would dearly love to. I am delighted that you have asked me. The problem is that it is only three months away. The station is under immense pressure. Not only will I be needed for the day to day running but that is probably the time we will be appointing and inducting new detectives.' She squeezed me again. 'As you said when you picked me up earlier, it is on the calendar only four weeks but in terms of life events it is more than that. It is certainly not too soon to ask. Let me think about it but for now I have to say no. I will work on it. I so much want to come.'

'I understand. I would love you to join us but I hadn't thought it through for your work.'

'That's my job.' She paused then continued, 'if I can make it there is a condition attached.'

'What, don't tell me you want sex while we are there.'

'OK, two conditions; in addition to that I want to come to your lecture.'

'It's a deal.'

We finished our meal and drove home. As we approached the city I asked, 'where can I park near to your house.'

'It's tight around there. Let's go back to yours; anyway I want to see Toby.'

We drove the rest of the way in quiet. A comfortable quiet as we had done so much talking in the pub. It was good sliding through the countryside with her head on my shoulder. As we passed the turn off to the Farm the sight of it caused my worries to bubble up again. Worries about her finding out what Sam and I do morphed into another concern. Rebecca made light of it today but she is very reticent about me even coming into her house, let alone staying there. What is the reason for her keeping me at arm's length? On one hand we seem so close already. On the other she is holding something back.

Surely she cannot suspect me? Is that the reason?

Even if she does not have her suspicions I feel so bad about lying to her. It has preyed on my mind since Sam drew my attention to the implications of doing so. Beforehand it had seemed sensible. Now it makes me feel duplicitous. For the present though it is the only option.

CHAPTER 21:
REBECCA: THE PARTY

It is one week to the day since our raid; that is only one week. I find it incredulous that not only is it all over but that the operation came both to such a good outcome and was concluded so quickly. The Chief Constable was generous in funding tonight's party and she was correct in forcing me to have a couple of days off. I now realise how much I needed that break. My day out with Luke on Wednesday was delightful. Yesterday was well spent sleeping and catching up on domestic duties.

Surprisingly today has not been too busy. We have had a quiet day. Perhaps the criminals have been frightened off by the media reports of last week. The Chief arranged for a skeleton staff from the adjacent forces to come in at lunchtime so we all had most of the afternoon off. None of us feel guilty or that we are skiving. We have all worked so hard over the last few weeks; especially my team undertaking the clandestine investigation. We deserve it.

I have just realised that it is only ten days since Tom and I were illegally scaling a wall in Solero. It feels like it was months ago.

I have been ready for a while and so I am enjoying looking out of my front window at the remaining glow following a glorious sunset over the city. Luke had called to say that he is running fifteen minutes late and that he will collect me at 8.15. That is unlike him, he is usually so punctual. It is of no concern; the party is likely to go on for hours. As it is to be held at the Mill Pub which is by the old bridge only a short walk from here we will only be a little late. I pass it on my runs, it looks charming but I have yet to go in.

I have one concern. No, it is not a concern it is a thrill of anticipation. Other than Julian, not counting Tom and Simon's very brief glance at the raid, none of my colleagues, no, none of my friends, have yet met Luke. I feel nervous but I guess that he feels worse having to meet over a hundred of them, including partners, in one go.

The doorbell rang at eight-fifteen on the dot. Adhering closely to arrangements that we have made is yet another thing we have in common. As he had warned me that he that would not be here until now I count this as being on time. I flung open the door and then had to catch my breath. Finally I managed a strangled, 'hi.' He always looks good but I have not seen him like this before. He normally wears mainly black, smart to casual. Tonight he has worn smart to very smart. He is wearing a wool twill suit in a classic navy, suede loafers, a narrow stripe blue and white shirt with button down collars, a club-type tie which is presumably either his school or university and, naturally, a polka dot handkerchief. I will have to watch him carefully tonight; the women will be all over him.

He smiled as I stood there looking him up and down, immobilised. Finally he capitulated and said, 'the usual custom is to invite me in but if you wish I will go away.' I grabbed his collar, pulled him through the door and kissed him. He continued, 'thank god, I thought you had forgotten how.' He looked me up and down appreciatively and then said, 'I didn't realise that you have legs. They are lovely; you should wear a dress and show them more often.'

'You have seen them before.'

'Hardly, they are either covered by a track suit or wrapped around my back.'

'If you give me any more of that cheek they will not be wrapped around you again.' He gave me an amused, "really," look. 'Anyway you saw my legs when I wore a dress for our first date.'

'Your dress that night was longer and you were sitting down most of the time. That is most of the time that you were actually wearing it.' He is correct, other than when I was sitting or wearing a coat my dress had only been worn for seconds. Then he looked me up and down again, this time more slowly and deliberately. Good; I can tell that he likes what he is seeing. 'Wow, I guess that dress did not come from Tesco.' I am wearing an off the shoulder Bardot split frill midi dress. The split up the left side, though part covered by the frill, is high enough to show my leg and still be decent, well nearly decent. I had bought it especially for tonight and I am now thanking my lucky stars that I bought the black one and not the dark blue. If I had been wearing the blue we would be matching.

I twirled around to show him all of it. He makes me feel so good that I can do this in front of him; normally such a manoeuvre would be way outside of my comfort zone. Then I pointedly looked him up and down. 'And you scrub up very well. Very smart, I approve.' I thought but I did not say, "not only smart Luke, you also look unbelievably sexy." With his shoulder length black hair, dark skin and Roman nose he looks like a southern European male model. No, it is not the looks and clothes, it is his poise.

'I thought that I should make an effort. I am after all, for tonight at least, the new boss's swain. More, it is our first time seen out together.' So, I am not the only one considering the importance of that.

'Are you going to behave?'

'Possibly.'

'Not good enough, you had better.'

'OK, if I must.'

'Are you nervous?'

'I am on parade in front of a hundred coppers who are all intent on looking after their wonderful boss. What do you think?'

'So am I. Come on, let's go.' I draped a pashmina over my bare shoulders and we walked out into a glorious evening.

He deliberately made a slight detour to pass in front of the war memorial. We paused in exactly the same spot where I had been attacked, astonishingly only four weeks and two days ago. He turned me towards him. He held me and softly said, 'I am not sure whether I want to beat those yobs to a pulp for attacking you or to thank them for bringing us together.'

We kissed again and I replied, 'leave the corporal punishment to Toby.' We embraced. After a while I said, 'come on, we will be late.' I took his hand and started to walk but he still dawdled.

As we approached the Mill we both remarked how attractive it looks. It is a fine old, three storey, stone building on the corner of the old bridge. It opens on to the path we are walking along and there is a stone wall opposite overlooking the river. In my trepidation I found that I was tugging his hand and trying to rush ahead. He gently resisted with a soft smile and head shake. I cannot believe that I am nervous but I so want to make a good impression on my first function as the boss. He said, 'easy, you look great and you will be marvellous. Anyway, look, it is very quiet. I bet that we are the first.' I had not realised. It is now twenty minutes after the start time and there is no sign of anyone going in.

We stepped into the ominously quiet bar. One of the staff, by his demeanour I suspect him to be the manager, came up to us. To my surprise he shook my hand first and said in a heavy Italian accent, 'DS Fletcher, good to meet you.' How does he know who I am? Perhaps he saw the media briefing on the TV. He then shook Luke's hand but did not meet his eye. In fact they are both avoiding looking at each other and they seem to be finding something amusing. 'Please follow me. The party is in the function room. You are the first to arrive.' I thought, "we are the first, what is going on, it is eight twenty?" 'I will come with you and put the lights on, the bar staff will follow.' He beckoned me to go ahead. As I walked down the corridor with the manager and Luke behind me I heard him mutter, presumably to Luke, 'bellissimo.' My mind flew back to Marcus and the Italian restaurant. He is another lovely man; if his wife had not come in would I be with him now? I pushed that aside to concentrate on this evening and especially Luke.

We came to a double door which I presume leads into the function room. The manager stepped to one side to open it and Luke came close behind and put his hand on my back. The manager flung open the door. The room is dark and after the bright corridor I cannot see in so I hesitated. As I did so Luke gently, but purposefully, pressed me forward.

Somewhat surprised I stepped in to the room. As I crossed the threshold all the room lights came on and a cacophony of cheers and clapping broke out. The whole station and their partners are already in the room, waiting. Luke has set me up. That is why the bugger was late and dawdling. I turned to berate him and saw his ear to ear grin with Julian at his side shaking his hand. The sods have set me up together. Before I could speak several powerful hands grabbed me and lifted me into the air with yet more cheering and shouting. I was carried around the room having to lean down and shake all of the proffered hands as the cheering continued.

Finally we had completed the circuit and I was returned to the floor next to Luke. Before I could speak he quickly said, pointing to Julian who is still next to him, 'don't hit me. It was his idea.'

I turned to Julian and saw that Barbara is standing arm in arm with him. That surprised me and Julian took advantage of my distraction. He passed to my left hand a glass of champagne saying, 'congratulations on your work and promotion boss.' He held out his right hand to shake mine. I grabbed it and startled him by pulling him towards me. Instead of hitting him I kissed him on the cheek, then Barbara as well.

Luke said with a pretend sulk, 'don't I get one as well. I did help.' I pulled him down and kissed him hard on the lips to another cheer from the crowd.

For more than two hours the party flowed. Luke and I moved around all the people. Everyone wanted to speak to us. As the drinks took effect the women stopped shaking Luke's hand and started kissing him instead. Then they held his gaze for a little longer than usual. Each time he smiled at them and then he stepped back to my side, slightly behind me to leave me in the limelight and with an arm gently around my waist. He is making it clear that we are together but he considers himself the guest at my function. The team from the Met had got to know all the locals well during the week and all present are in jovial groups.

At five to eleven some activity started to one side. I craned my head to see what is happening and to my surprise several of the men are carrying in a door. In fact it is more than a door, it is a door and its frame combined with some timber poking out sideways extending the frame so that it can be held. It was placed in the centre of the room and then held upright with powerful police hands supporting it but I noticed that they are standing to one side holding the timbers; they are not in line with the opening.

The room lights dimmed and someone shone a torch on to the clock on the wall. At ten seconds to eleven everyone in the room, that is everyone except Luke and myself who are standing bemused, started counting down, 10, 9 ,8, 7.

At one second to eleven Simon stepped forward and to my astonishment I see that he is carrying a sledgehammer. On eleven he swung it and smashed open the door. Then I realised, it is exactly one week to the minute from the commencement of our raid.

Someone lifted a plastic, child's, pretend police helmet and put it on Simon's head. Hands grabbed him from behind and then more behind them and Simon started a conga dance. A cheer went up and Luke and I looked at each other with our mouths open as the sixteen stones of muscle of Simon, which a week ago had crushed Coyle in the car door, danced the conga through the door frame. It is childish, ridiculous and utterly wonderful. The whole station joined in and they all danced the conga through the door. As I followed on, with Luke holding me behind, as we passed through the doorframe I thought, "a DS and a science professor doing the conga. I can't believe it. I have not danced a conga since I was thirteen and I was embarrassed then." The last of us passed through the door then we all fell about laughing at ourselves and the party resumed.

A little later Luke and I stepped outside for a breather and we found Julian and Barbara, arms around each other, standing at the wall overlooking the river. So, they are openly a couple now. We sidled up to join them. We chatted together for a while and then the conversation split with Luke talking to Barbara and me with Julian. I steered Julian away from the others and spoke to him softly so they cannot hear us. 'Are you and Barbara an item now?' I hardly had to ask but I wanted to gently open the subject.

He softly smiled and nodded yes. After thoughtful pause he then added, 'well, we are becoming an item. It is still early days.' I returned a smile of approval but I can see there is more he wants to say. 'When Lucy was dying she made me promise not to forget her but also to move on after a while and find someone else. She said a year and I sort of agreed but not quite. It is now over two and I see that she was correct. It is time.'

I squeezed his arm with my agreement. Then, even more cautiously I asked, 'did you hear what Barbara said when you were shot?'

He blushed a little. 'Yes but she does not yet know that. I have promised myself that I will tell her tonight that I had heard.' I have the distinct impression that is not all he will be telling her. I hugged him and we returned to speaking with the others.

After a little longer Tom, Simon and Alison came out from the party and joined us. A little in his cups Tom said, 'we want to meet the suspect before leaving.'

The others, including Luke, all tensed and I flared. 'Tom, don't be ridiculous. You cannot say.................' I tailed off as Luke relaxed and he then squeezed my arm.

'Easy Rebecca, I can speak for myself.' Though a little chastised at the deserved rebuke I glared at Tom. Luke spoke but now to Julian, 'am I still a suspect.'

I said sharply, 'no.'

Julian said softly, 'yes.'

'Julian, for such a good officer you are talking rubbish. How can you possibly say that ....' I tailed off as Luke squeezed my arm again. I looked sharply back at him. It is obvious that he had not been rebuking me; he was merely drawing something to my attention. I realised that I had been shouting. My over-reaction has clearly made the opposite impression that I had wanted to give. Tom, Simon and Alison are now looking even more closely at Luke and with a police look, not a party-goers gaze.

Julian and I glared at each other. All the rest now look awkward. All, that is, except Luke who remains calm and retains a smile. Luke said, with a matter of fact air, 'as the only non-police-officer here may I address this?' We all regarded him with interest, including me. We have hardly discussed this but he has obviously thought more on it. What on earth is he going to say?

He took our silence as an approval to continue. 'I don't think there is enough evidence to regard me as a suspect.' He grinned adding, 'not yet, anyway.' We all relaxed a little more as he is obviously easy with the discussion. 'However, I was in the vicinity of the abduction and I only have my sister as an alibi. Further, I am aware from the media and a previous interview that the person missing had been guilty of domestic violence. In addition to me being in the vicinity it was stated in the first interview that Samantha had been the victim of such abuse. She said so herself. I have already told Rebecca and Julian that I would kill to protect Samantha from further harm and I bitterly regret not stepping in before.'

Tom, Simon and Alison took a sharp breath. He had openly said that to Julian and me during the initial interview but they have not heard it before. To them he added, 'my sister was seriously injured in a domestic violence attack two years ago. Thankfully her husband disappeared on the day he was released from prison and so my criminal action has not been required. On that day we had a rock solid alibisj so we were not suspects then.'

I thought to myself, "actually Luke, you had a reasonable alibi but it was not rock solid."

'In view of all of this then I must at least consider myself as worthy of interviewing. As you know this has already been undertaken once.' Giving me a squeeze he said, 'and look at the mess that got me into.' They all laughed but I am still cross with Tom and Julian. Looking at Julian he said, 'if you want to speak to me again at any time I am happy to answer all of your questions.'

Now speaking to Julian alone Luke said, 'to you, I would add that Jock Anderson must be rolling in his grave.'

We all looked mystified by this apparent non-sequitur. All except Julian who looked embarrassed, perhaps even ashamed. To enlighten us Julian said, initially to the others, 'Luke and I went to the same university college.' Then to all of us he continued, 'Mr Anderson taught a course in critical thinking that was so acclaimed no one missed it whatever they were studying.'

Luke again picked up the thread. 'Considering me someone of interest is reasonable. Considering me a suspect is to commit the classical Prosecutor's Fallacy. Jock would knit together his bushy eyebrows at you.' I knew what that is and clearly so does Julian but the others look blank and so Luke explained. 'The Prosecutor's Fallacy is to assume that because the person may have committed a crime that they did do so even if there are only few or none others in a position to do so. For example, if a very rare blood type is found at a crime scene and a person who could have been there is found to have the same rare blood group then that still does not mean they committed the crime. You need to discover how many other people in the reasonable vicinity have the same blood group and they should all be suspects as well. I was in the vicinity but I daresay so were many others with vehicles and some of those others may also have relatives who have suffered domestic abuse or are sympathetic to the plight of such women for other reasons. They are equally deserving of a chat.'

A somewhat chastised Julian added, 'I like to think of it as the Doctor's fallacy. Medics are hopeless at assessing risk and have scant statistical understanding. They commit a similar fallacy all the time. They often think that simply because a test is positive then the diagnosis is certain. It is not, it is only somewhere between possible and likely. They need to consider the base rate of the disorder in the community, or the frequency in the group the patient belongs to, and also the false positive rate of the test. Only then can they assess the likelihood of the test being accurate and not simply a false positive. To fully assess the overall usefulness of the test they also need to consider the false negative, the ones missed by the test. A positive test is not a simply a truly positive test. It is the sum of positive and falsely positive tests. Doctors mostly do not consider the people wrongly thought to be positive and the ones missed in a test. They thoughtlessly give a knee jerk to the print out in their hand. Put another way, the Bayesian priors need to be accounted for.'

Julian had said this with a considerable vehemence and I can see that, in spite of him being criticised, it is not directed at Luke. Julian is looking into a memory, not at one of us. I guess that Lucy's death had a contributing miss-diagnosis.

Alison said, 'enough, my head hurts. It seems the conclusion is that all we should do with Luke is to have a friendly chat.' She sidled up and putting her arm around him said, 'I would be happy to perform that arduous task. That is unless you think the boss is doing a good enough job.'

We all laughed and the tension passed.

Tom, Simon and Alison drifted back in to the party. Julian said to Luke and me, 'we are just off.' Then to Barbara, 'I will go and retrieve our coats.'

As he left us I asked Barbara, 'are you going to his flat?' She gave a very happy nod. 'Have you been there before?' She shook her head. 'You know that we did our planning there so I have seen his flat. I should warn you..........'

She interrupted me with a laugh saying, 'no ma'am. Sorry, I mean no Rebecca. I have two brothers who are in bachelor pads. I am used to the mess men live in. I assure you I will not even notice.' I looked behind her. I had described Julian's apartment to Luke who is now trying to suppress laughter.

Julian came out and as he approached, before he was in hearing, I said, 'don't say I did not try to warn you.' I could not resist the tease. Luke sputtered but Barbara missed that as Julian put her coat over her shoulders.

As they walked off arm in arm I thought that I should leave. It is getting rowdy inside and I am sure the last thing the team want is the boss looking on, inhibiting them. Luke and I crossed the bridge and headed for his house.

CHAPTER 22
REBECCA: THE WEIR

I sat naked on the end of Luke's bed looking out of the window and across the beautiful square. Even at three am, even before the moon has come up, in the never quite dark of mid-July I can see well. As I watched, over a couple of minutes, the full moon crested the houses at the far side. Now I can see as well as during the day. A fox and a tabby cat are crossing diagonally in opposite directions. Initially their trajectories would have collided in the centre. Each diverted to avoid the other. With no reason to fight and aware of the damage each can mutually inflict they wisely avoided conflict by slightly modifying their actions to appease and to avoid the other. Oh that we humans could do the same.

I am unable to sleep. I am blaming the stifling heat. After the heavy unseasonable rains in the beginning of the month we now have record breaking temperatures. Except I know that is not the true reason for me being fully awake in the small hours.

I have to tell him.

The thought of telling him and what it may do to our relationship terrifies me. I have to tell him. I cannot tell him. It is no wonder that I cannot sleep.

To distract myself I tried to think of my work over the last four months since being made the station chief. It has been busy, very busy, but so satisfying and undoubtedly successful. We were swamped with applicants to replace the

Troop who are now all on remand. By chance, and not by my design as I have been accused of in the press, all but one are women. Along with me, I am a rarity as a female DS, plus a woman chief constable, we now have the highest proportion of female senior officers in the country. That does not matter to me. What matters is that they are all so effective. They were appointed simply because they were the best candidates. No accusation of positive discrimination can be justified and so cannot detract from their truly deserved appointment. Their initial success is already embarrassing to those who carped and the letter pages are pointing this out to them.

With Luke I have settled into a satisfying gentle routine. He is also so busy. He is preparing for his lecture at the congress in California, now only a week away. He also pulls an all-nighter every week or so with his moth study. In spite of our joint commitments we see each other at least three times a week when I come and stay here. Sunday lunch is a regular feature. Often Samantha joins us for that and I am bonding with her as well. She is a gentle, yet strong and resilient, woman. Luke complains that we gang up on him but I can tell that he is delighted that we get on well. So am I. She discretely always finds an excuse to leave us together during the Sunday afternoon. During the week we meet up for a couple of evenings and nights on an ad hoc basis. Whatever our work commitments we manage at least two nights together.

It is not working. This musing is not stopping my mind returning to the pressing worry. I only managed a few seconds thinking about work before my mind returned to the unavoidable necessity.

I have to tell him.

Luke slipped out of bed. I had thought from his breathing that he has also been awake for a while. He sat next to me in the moonlight and together we looked at the fox who is now sitting at the base of the statue. The moggie has disappeared. A tingle went down my spine as he nuzzled my ear saying, 'as it is obvious neither of us can sleep I have a suggestion.' He looked at me with a cheeky grin.

No prizes for guessing what his suggestion is. I decided to tease him. 'And what may that be?'

His grin widened and he stood, took my hand and pulled me to my feet. He kissed me and then I started to move back to bed. To my surprise he pulled me back saying, 'do you ever think of anything else?' What I had thought he was going to suggest was clearly wrong. Now I looked at him. I am disappointed but intrigued. As he started to put his clothes on he said, 'come on Rebecca, get dressed. You can't go out like that.'

Go out, it's the middle of the bloody night. Curiosity is starting to eat at me but I guess if I ask what he is planning I will not get a straight answer. His demeanour is that he wants to surprise me. I slipped on my panties, trousers and my blouse. I cannot face my socks and bra in this heat. I stepped into my sandals and followed him as he walked downstairs. We went out of his kitchen door into the courtyard. On one side of it is Luke's house, on two others is Samantha's L-shaped bungalow. On the fourth side there is a wall with a wide door leading to the little road between the square and the rear of my station.

I have not actually entered the courtyard before. It is Toby's domain. He is sprawled on the concrete floor with his back against two of the tall flowerpots. He lifted his head and thwacked his tail as we stepped into the yard. He did not sit up. Not only is the heat too much for him he seems to be able to divine that whatever is unfolding does not involve him. His vast head slumped back on to the cool stone but his eyes still followed us.

I gave in and asked Luke what is going on. He simply gave an enigmatic smile and walked across the yard. I should have expected that. He approached a wide door at the end of Samantha's house. When I had previously spotted the unusual opening, whilst looking out of Luke's kitchen window, I had thought that it must be a store room. He opened the door, it hinged outwards, and he bade me stand to the side holding it. Clearly whatever is happening requires the full width of the door. He motioned for me to stay to the side so that I cannot see into the room. Uncharacteristically I did as instructed. I will let him act this little drama but I did put my hand on my hip and indicate that he is pushing his luck. He ignored me and stepped in.

Seconds later he came back out holding two crash helmets which he handed to me with an increasingly wider smirk. They are dull black and their visors are half-silvered. They look aggressive.

So that is it. We are going on his motor-bike. What a stunning idea for a hot night. Previously he refused to discuss the bike with me when I had asked him what he had. He teased me when I tried to guess, saying that I had to wait and see. I still tried to guess. Firstly I suggested a vintage bike, say an old Bonneville. "Perhaps", was the only reply. Then I said one of those big scooters, the ones with the double front wheel. That was met with "maybe." Eventually I gave up and threw a cushion at him. Now I am finally going to find out but these helmets do not seem to fit either of my guesses.

There came a grunt of effort from the room. It must be big, or at least heavy.

As it emerged my jaw dropped. I have never before seen a motorbike such as this. The helmets look merely aggressive, the bike looks evil. It is massive and dull black. What is troubling me is that it also looks so different. I cannot fathom what is so odd about it and that is really bugging me. I only know that I have never before seen anything quite like it.

He saw my expression and, probably deliberately, misread it, 'magnificent isn't it.'

'Yes, it is truly amazing but something is different. It almost looks wrong yet I cannot see why.'

'Have a guess. What do you think it is?'

'It looks like a Harley but not like any other Harley that I have seen.'

'Well done, it is a Harley. Look again, what do you not see?'

He is obviously enjoying teasing me about this bloody bike yet again. It is infuriating. I know I can see what is different but I can't describe it. He asked, "what do I not see?"

Then it hit me. 'There is no exhaust pipe.' He nodded. 'And there is no petrol tank. It is an electric motorbike.' Now I am even more amazed. I thought electric motorbikes were all small, almost big bicycles. This one is a massive Harley.

'Spot on, it is a Harley-Davidson Livewire. Come, let's go for a spin.'

As he pushed the bike through the yard door into the road behind the station I suddenly felt a frisson of trepidation. I have not been on a motorbike since my teens and even then I was controlling it. I had envisaged a gentle putter around on some old vintage girl. Now I am facing with straddling a huge, mean machine. Luke propped the bike on the side stand whilst we put on our helmets. Apparently I have Samantha's but our heads are the same size and it fits perfectly. Knowing she rides it relaxed me a little. If anything she is more cautious than me and if she can sit on this then so can I. Luke stood on the footrest to help lift his leg over. As it is so tall and wide I found it easier to do the same.

'All set?'

I nodded yes then quickly said, 'slow and easy please.'

'Don't worry, I will keep you safe.'

Not actually what I had asked but I let it slide. Then I realised what he has forgotten and I laughed in his ear, 'we are not going anywhere until you start it.'

He turned and smiling shook his head. Then I realised what I had missed. He had not forgotten. He has switched it on. It is not necessary to start it revving. We gently moved off in total silence.

As we turned into the square Luke accelerated a little. It is surreal. There is only a faint hum from the engine. The only real noise is a soft swish from the tyres. We rode around the square and then alongside the church which looks even more gothic in the moonlight. Luke then turned the bike down the cobbled street, the one I walk up on my way to work. It will take us down to the High Street. I felt like a ghost moving silently between the buildings. The occasional late night drinkers staggering home are completely unaware of us as we float by. I saw poor Simon curled up in his doorway. The lads on night patrol often keep a sandwich or pie from the canteen and give it to him. If it is very wet or cold they will arrest him so he can have a dry night in the cells and breakfast. Knowing his story it is impossible to feel anything other than sympathy for him. At the end of the High Street as it separated into smaller roads we passed the shop where I had found evidence for the abduction of Brian James. It rankles that I have not solved that case but at least it led to me gliding by on this machine with my arms around this lovely man. There is no need to hold on as he is riding so slowly but that does not stop me.

I thought again. I have to tell him.

He turned right and we passed over the new bridge,

then right again and we went along my road. I looked wistfully at my house, the bedroom windows reflecting the full moon. I must ask Luke to sleep with me there soon. I do not know why I haven't. I feel myself holding back. At the end of my road he turned right again and I expected to go over the old bridge and back to his house. Instead, before crossing the bridge, he surprised me with another sharp right turn. We went up the wheelchair ramp, across the pavement and then he rode along the riverside path that I train on. I quietly said, there is no need to shout on this machine, 'you are breaking the law.'

'No I am not. They put the motorbike ramp there so that I can ride down here.' I gave him an exasperated squeeze; there is clearly no point in pointing out that it a wheelchair ramp. He knows. We reached the end of the new bridge for the second time having made a full circle. Again I expected him to turn, this time left, towards his house. We went right again up to the roundabout then left on the main road to Castletown. I have driven along it many times as our station also covers Castletown. Within a mile we will be between fields.

He is not bothering to indicate this evening as there is nothing else driving about so I was taken aback when he turned left onto a small road. I had assumed that he would take the main road. He followed this for a short while and then silently pulled to a halt alongside the last lamppost beyond the last house of a row. There are fields on both sides now. Turning to me he said, 'do you know this road.'

'No, I have never even noticed it before.'

'It is the original road between Castletown and the city but is now hardly used since the new road, as it is still called, was built fifty years ago. It is a beautiful rural road now with more dog walkers than vehicles. It would be good for your training runs.' That is an excellent idea. 'Do you see ahead where the road narrows there is a thatched cottage with a red door?'

I peered along the road. With the moonlight shining on it I can just about make out the house in the distance. 'It looks like an old Toll House.'

'That is exactly what it is. Further, it is precisely a quarter of a mile from here.' He paused and he then asked, 'I guess that you are good at counting seconds in your head.' Behind the reflecting visor I cannot see his face but I can tell that he is smiling. 'Start counting them as soon as I move off.'

I had not understood his obtuse, previous question but now the full meaning hit me. I screamed, 'no, don't,' and grasped him with my arms as he turned the power full on.

I felt as if I had been kicked in the back.

The acceleration is unbelievable, it is terrifying. The bike bucked and Luke fought to hold it down and straight. Then it seemed to settle itself and he accelerated even harder. The wind howled in my ears and buffeted me. I screamed and screamed as the fields flashed by then went to a blur. Still he accelerated and the bike settled as if it is needing this. The wind still ripped at my sides but the bucking ceased. It feels as if we have taken off, we are no longer feeling the road. It is exhilarating and utterly terrifying. I think I am still screaming but I cannot hear it.

Finally I saw the cottage flick by me and I gave thanks that we had made it. I started to relax again and I felt that I can now breathe normally.

I waited for him to brake.

He did not.

He kept the power full on. The engine noise changed from a hum to the whine of a jet plane. The continuing acceleration feels as if we are riding a jet engine. The wind is so now fast that I can feel my cheeks vibrating. He let out a loud "whoop."

Then I thanked the god I do not believe in as he finally braked hard.

He is braking very hard, there must be a problem. I felt three times my weight as the deceleration crushed me into his back. I felt the ABS kick in, bloody hell, I did not even know motorbikes had ABS. The braking is fierce but we must still be doing forty. I glanced alongside his left arm and screamed again. Directly in front is a massive stone wall. The road leads to a gate in the wall but there is a solid oak double door which is closed, blocking the gateway. Luke must have expected it to be open and for us to ride through. There is no possibility of stopping.

We are going to hit the gate.

I braced myself for the impact but the bike flipped hard down leaning precipitously to its right side. We are so far over it feels as if my knee is going to hit the road. As we turned I can now see that there is a ninety degree junction to the right which I had missed as I looked down his left side. We are going around at a dizzying speed and angle but so far the bike is holding the road.

My head had been catapulted to his right and now I looked down that side. I screamed more as we are now heading directly at trees. Again there is no hope of stopping.

The bike flipped ninety degrees now on to its left side. Now it is my left knee that is in danger of hitting the tarmac. We are half turning, half sliding, around a sharp left bend. The road has gone through a tight double bend, almost a chicane.

We exited the bend and Luke straightened up the bike, now braking gently. I can see a low wall and pull in on the left ahead. He is obviously heading for that.

The instant the bike came to a standstill I jumped off the back and I spun to berate him for riding so fast. I did not, I could not. My legs are like jelly and I staggered backwards to lean against the wall. He slipped off his helmet and he stepped towards me grinning like a little boy. I took a swing at him but my arm barely moved. He easily held it and stepped in close then he unclipped and slipped off my helmet. After a while I managed to croak, 'you bastard.' Infuriatingly he simply laughed. My legs stopped shaking and I felt some power return to my body. Then I started laughing with him.

He said, 'you have to admit that was good.'

'No.'

'Yes it was and you know it. Did you manage to count the seconds as well as screaming for the whole time?'

I nodded, 'eleven.' He looked irritatingly pleased at that. 'So that was a standing start quarter of a mile in eleven seconds. Is that superbike performance?'

'No, not superbike, but it is pretty good.'

I made a mental note to never, ever sit on a superbike. I asked, 'why did you keep accelerating after the Toll House? Was it just to frighten me on those bends?'

'As if! No, I wanted to push it up to 100. I do it with ease on my own and I wanted to try it two up.'

'Are you completely crazy? You did 100 on a small road at night.'

'We did a 100 on a quiet road that I could see in the moonlight was empty.'

I am not going to win this one so I tried another attack. 'Did you not see those bloody bends?'

He gave a pretend frown, 'do you mean those curves

around the old mill?' I glared at him which amused him yet more and he took as a "yes." 'I know them very well. I take them faster when I am on my own but I did not want to frighten you.'

I gave him a playful tap on the shoulder and collapsed into his arms. Past his shoulder I saw fields stretching away. Then I realised, I cannot see any water. I pushed back, looked at him and asked, 'what mill?'

'That's why I brought you here. Turn around.'

I turned around and collapsed against the wall as my breath was taken from me for the second time this night. It is so indescribably beautiful. On the other side of the wall is a grassy bank, probably three meters wide. Then there is the river. I did not appreciate that we had re-joined the river. It is totally different from outside my house where it flows straight through the city. Here it is wide and slow. A little downstream it makes a sharp curve away from where we are standing and beyond us on the apex of the curve, is a tumbledown mill. The road must both lead to the mill and to carry on around it, past where we are standing, and then on towards Castletown. There is a long curved weir roughly one hundred meters downstream at the bend in the river. The water, held back by the weir, remains high after the recent rains and is lapping at the bank in front of me. But it is the water itself that is enchanting. In the silvery moonlight it is slowly flowing by as if it is not water but mercury. As it is so full it is sliding over the weir in a glassy curve. There are only a few white horses where it is breaking at the base. Now I can hear a soft gurgling from them.

I am transfixed. Luke is behind me and I leaned back against him. Neither of us spoke. We looked towards the river, together.

After a minute or two Luke stepped away and taking my hand led me to a small gap in the low wall. On the grassy bank he turned to me and said, 'let's go for a swim.'

'I haven't got my swim...........' I was intending to say swimsuit but, just in time, I realised that would be very silly. We both quickly slipped off all of our clothes and stepped into the water. It is cool but not cold. It is delicious after the heat of the recent days. The sandy bank below the mercury under our feet is steep and we were immediately waist deep and together we both dove under then came up, surfacing side by side. I am unable to speak. Words are superfluous in this enchanted river. Still side by side we silently swam a slow, languid breast stroke towards the weir. As I moved through the sparkling stream the cool made me feel more comfortable than I have for days. The water flowed over my shoulders and down my back. It caressed my breasts and my thighs and then flowed deliciously between my legs. I felt the soft fresh touch of it all over my skin. I swam to where I could feel a gentle tug as it speeded up to tumble over the weir. Then I turned away and swam towards the left bank. I dove down again; it is deep, at least three meters, probably more.

As I surfaced I heard Luke softly call, 'Rebecca.' He had turned towards the opposite bank but had not gone far. He is standing in the water ten meters from the edge of the weir and twenty from the bank. I thought, "standing?" I swam towards him and stood myself.　　　　There is a sandy mound under the water. He said, 'there is an eddy around here and this is the very centre. Silt is deposited as the water stills.' Luke is comfortable with his shoulders out of the water. For me in standing on the bottom the water is lapping at my chin. I put my hands around his neck and I pulled myself up wrapping me legs around him. I am half floating, half hanging on, arms around him.

I have to tell him.

I plucked up courage and looked into his eyes. I can see he is troubled, he is wrestling with something. Oh shit,

I can't tell him now. I pulled him closer and nuzzled into his neck. Then I thought that I cannot go on making excuses, prevaricating. There will never be a good time. Not being able to face him, still pressed against his neck, I started.

'There is something I have to tell you.' We both pushed back looking and laughing at each other. We had both spoken at exactly the same time and used precisely the same words.

'Ladies first.'

I wanted to say, "no, you first." I wanted to say, "it was nothing." I wanted to say, "I am no lady." I am in a public place, naked and wrapped around him after all. I must say it.

'Luke.'

He waited.

'Luke.' He still waited but now he has an even more troubled expression. He can see it is difficult for me. He can see that it is serious.

Holding his gaze I mustered all of my courage. 'Luke, I love you.'

He looks stunned. Oh god, what have I done.

He cannot speak. Please let me take the words back.

Then he roared with laughter. Smiling, laughing, kissing me, holding me; he could not form a reply. Not exactly what I had expected. On the other hand I had had no idea what to expect.

He stammered. 'Rebecca. Rebecca, oh Rebecca.' What is going on? Eventually he calmed and deliberately returned my eye contact. 'Rebecca. That is exactly what I was going to say to you. I love you'

I can't believe it. Now I understand why he laughed. I am laughing as well. I am holding him, kissing him. I am crying with joy.

We said to each other over and over again, "I love you, I love you." We had inadvertently stepped to the edge of the underwater mound formed by the eddy and the current gently took us. It lifted us and slowly twirled us around. The water took us in a slow circle and gently spun us at the same time as we kissed in the moonlight. It was as if the water was making us dance together.

Eventually the river settled us back in the still centre and Luke's feet found the bottom. He stood there with me still wrapped around him. We fell silent and I held him. I felt myself glowing with happiness. Then he pulled away a little and looked at me with his little boy cheeky grin saying, 'I suppose that means we are in love.' I nodded "yes." This is clearly going somewhere but I do not see where. 'People in love make love don't they.' Now I see; I like the direction. 'So perhaps we should make love for the first time. Let us see if it is any different. Presumably until now we have only been bonking.'

I bit his shoulder and he gave a pretend "ouch." It is my turn to tease him. 'Well, let's try. I am willing to experiment with anything for a little improvement on what went before.'

He smiled again at that. At least I think he did. We have both been smiling since our mutual confession so it is difficult to interpret whether or not it is a new one or the previous one continuing. My eyes said "yes " to him and I pulled away and went to swim to the bank. I can't wait to get home. I urgently want to make love with him.

He pulled me back to him and pushed my arms back around his neck. He shook his head and said, 'not on the bank. Here.'

He is not joking. I hadn't been swimming to the bank. I was going to his home and expecting to make love there. Bloody hell, he means here, now, in the water.

He gave me a very quick kiss but then pulled back so that we could continue looking into each other's eyes. He slipped his hands down under my bum and pulled me towards him and rubbed me against him. He said nothing more but he did not take his eyes off me.

Very soon we were both ready. I am more than ready, I will scream if he does not enter me soon. He took one hand off my bum. Then he held his cock and guided it into me. The fresh water has washed away my natural lubrication and it felt a little odd, almost uncomfortable, as he entered me. Initially it did not slide as easily as usual. Then he was in and I found that I am pouring. I flowed over him and wrapped around him as the river flowed and wrapped around us both. The eddy twirled us languidly as we made love in the moonlight. We made love, I kept repeating it to myself; we are making love. We have never "bonked" as he had teased. I could see then that he did not mean it. We connected at our first dinner. From the start it was more than bonking. We have made love before, I know it. But this time we are making love having admitted it.

Afterwards we swam silently back to the bank. He pulled himself up the bank and then turned around and held my hand to help me up the steep slope. As he did the water dripped off his body and hair which look even darker in this light. It looked like molten silver dripping off him in the moonlight. I went to lie down on the grass but he put his arm around me and held me up. 'Not there, lie over here next to me. There is a moon shadow from that tree. If we lie in it for a few minutes our eyes will adjust and we can see the Milky Way more vividly.'

We lay on our backs in the still warm soft grass, just our fingertips touching. I can immediately see the Milky Way but as my eyes adapt it appeared brighter and brighter. More stars can now be seen. I have never seen anything like it before. I have seen the Milky Way many times but not with this intensity. Five things have taken my breath away this night. The bike ride, the river in the moonlight, making love in the water and now this. I would give up them all for the fifth, Luke saying he loves me.

After twenty or so minutes, when I was quite dry, I heard a distant noise and Luke sat up and spoke, 'there is a car coming. Better get dressed.'

He quickly slipped on his clothes and stood nonchalantly leaning against the wall. I cannot find my knickers. The car is slowing and I can see its lights pointing one way then the other as it negotiated the double bend. Sod my knickers, I quickly pulled on my blouse and slacks, stepped into my sandals and I then stood alongside him at the wall. Luke then said, 'it is your colleagues, a police car.'

Oh crap, I moved sideways a little so that I am partly hidden by a bush. There is no reason for them to stop. I have not broken any law. More accurately I have stopped breaking the law on lewd acts in public. There is no concern but I prefer to keep this evening to be kept private.

They slowed and then they stopped. I heard the double thwack of both doors opening and closing. Bugger. I cannot see them at present but in a second they will emerge from being in line with the bush. Here they come. I can now see who it is. Richie is walking purposefully towards Luke's motorbike and he has not seen me. 'Good morning sir.' That shocked me but of course it is morning. 'Is this your motorbike?'

Jenny has spotted me and said quietly, 'Richie.' Either he did not hear or he ignored her. She repeated but now louder and with some urgency, 'Richie.'

He spun around reaching for his baton clearly thinking from her tone that there is danger. When he spotted me his face contorted through several emotions in a second. Surprise, disbelief, and bewilderment all flicked across his rugged features but he settled on a degree of embarrassment. He looked back at Luke, who he had seen at the party, and recognition dawned.

I said with a big smile, 'good morning to you both.'

They replied with a relieved, 'good morning ma'am.' I am not going to insist on "Rebecca" this morning.

They hesitated, clearly they had wanted to question Luke but now felt they either cannot or should not continue. Then I saw Richie's face light up.

He turned back to Luke and said, 'bloody hell Luke.' I thought ten out of ten for remembering Luke's name; you have only met him once. 'Is that a Livewire?' Luke in pride and Richie in wonderment strode over to the bike and within seconds all I can hear is snippets such as 'low end torque" and "power bands" coming back. Knowing Richie is a biker I had expected that as soon as he identified the bike.

Jenny sidled over to me saying, 'do you mind if I join you? They will be talking about their toys for ages.' I patted the wall next to me and she leaned on it. 'This is beautiful here isn't it ma'am.' I nodded and we looked across the water together. Then she looked at the bank and a wide, cheeky smile came to her. An area of the grass has clearly been flattened by two bodies, and there are my panties, right where my feet would have been. 'It looks as if someone has been making out here ma'am.' She was delighted to think that she had caught me out. If only she knew.

I laughed, 'it's not what it looks like Jenny. We went for a swim and we were lying there to dry off.' She looks disappointed.

If only I could have left it there. If only I could have applied my training to my response. I know that if in an interview you leave a space in the interrogation the suspect will as often as not hang themselves with a giveaway comment or look. I fought it but I lost. My eyes turned to where we had made love in the water and I felt my face soften and glow with love.

Jenny spotted it immediately. 'Oh no. Oh ma'am.' I saw her lean heavily on the wall. The realisation had the same effect on her knees as the bike ride had on mine. 'There, in the water. Oh how beautiful. How romantic. You lucky sod, if you don't mind me saying so ma'am.'

We heard the men coming back towards us. Jenny and I looked and the moonlight caught Luke in profile. He looks even more like a Greek god than when I first saw him. Jenny trembled again and said softly, 'Oh my.' She managed to largely compose herself as they joined us but Richie still gave her a searching look. She whispered to me, 'your secret is safe with me ma'am.'

'Thanks Jenny.' She started to walk to the car to re-join Richie but turned back and again whispering said, 'my Steve will still be in bed when I get back off shift. He won't know what hit him.' She gave a conspiratorial wink and went to the car. I remember Steve, he is a quiet, gentle, good looking man. They should have a good morning.

Richie opened the car door but to my surprise he did not get in. He turned back and approached Luke again. He is trying to look serious but failing. 'One more thing sir.' So, back to "sir," he is up to something. 'We stopped here when we saw your bike in order to question you. We were in the Toll House down the road beforehand as the old lady there thought there may be a prowler. While we were looking around a motorbike went past, must have been doing a hundred or more. We could not get away as the woman needed reassurance, we would not have caught it anyway.' He gave a theatrical pause, 'you didn't see any other bike did you?'

Luke shook his head also failing to hide his amusement. He knows he is being teased.

'Never mind. It was odd though as the bike was nearly silent. All we could hear was the woman on the back screaming. At least we know that it could not possibly be you.'

'Of course not officer.' Luke is entering into the spirit of the exchange now.

'No, it was definitely not you. That would be quite impossible. DS Fletcher would not ride with someone speeding and she most certainly would not scream; would you ma'am?'

'Of course not Richie.' Everyone was trying and failing to look serious.

'We will be off then.' With that they got in and drove off.

We put on the helmets and got back on the bike. Before moving off I reached forward and slid my hand down Luke's trousers and cradled his balls. He said, 'that's nice.'

'Be careful not to misread what I am doing. If you exceed thirty on the way back I will squeeze. If you exceed forty I will squeeze hard. If you exceed fifty I will rip them off.' He laughed. I squeezed hard and he yelped and doubled over the handle bars. 'For your information, that was a thirty squeeze.'

We rode home at twenty-nine miles an hour.

The morning is now lightening and it is sublime slipping through the city with nothing other than a faint hum and tyre swish. I leaned against his back and looked at the brilliant sunrise as the still deserted streets quietly passed by. I feel so happy and fulfilled. I have a new job, I have been promoted beyond my dreams, the station is humming with enthusiasm since the raid and the new blood. All this is good. It is also secondary. The main reason is that I am in love. Before today I had not even dared to think that Luke may love me in return. He does. I am in love. We are in love.

We came to some lights and to my surprise Luke stopped. He has looked around carefully but not stopped for any other road signs as there is still no traffic. He said, 'you had better move your hand. There is another police car coming up behind.'

Oh crap, there are only two patrols out tonight. We have seen them both. I deliberately left my hand in place. The car pulled alongside and stopped at the lights. Their window is down and I could hear them guffawing. It is Bruce and Kevin. Though my head is on Luke's back and my face is turned towards them with the reflecting visor they cannot see it is me. Bruce shouted out of the window, 'I can see it is true what they say about biker girls, sir.' More guffaws. I half stood on the footrest. I put my other hand down his trousers and on his balls and gripped him with my knees shaking him from side to side. They exploded with laughter. The lights changed, I let go and sat back while we moved off. As they pulled ahead of us Bruce waved his handcuffs out of the window and they both cheered. If only they knew.

Luke put the bike away, made coffee and heated up some frozen croissant. We took it all out into the square and sat at the base of the statue. That is all three of us, Toby insisted on coming and having his own croissant. We heard a car drive quickly out of the rear of the station and speed down the road. Looking up Luke said, 'isn't that the police officer who stopped at the river?'

'Jenny, yes.'

'She is in a heck of a hurry.'

'She told me that she has something to do before her husband, Steve, goes to work.' He can tell from my tone that I know more but he let it pass.

Finally, reluctantly, we had to admit that the night was over and we had to go back in. We both have to prepare for the day ahead and I have to go home first. I do have to prepare for work but I doubt that I will achieve much today other than strolling around dreamily. Hand in hand we walked back into the house.

As I was leaving Samantha came in chattering, 'wow, another hot one last night. Thankfully the forecast is for..............' She stopped dead, looking at us for the first time. 'Oh thank god for that. It has been bugging me for ages. I wanted to prod my useless brother to say it but I thought it best not to interfere. Now you finally have we can all relax.'

I tried to give her a "what are you talking about" look but I think I know.

She was obviously teasing us and she was not going to clarify what she is talking about. Knowing he is being wound up Luke capitulated and in a pretend-exasperated tone asked, 'what do you think we have said.' As the words came out I saw realisation dawn on his face.

'You have finally told each other that you love each other, haven't you. It is written all over your cherubic faces.' She gave us each a kiss and a hug. 'Come on Toby.' With that they both walked out. Sam and Toby are both looking very relieved.

CHAPTER 23:
LUKE: MISTAKES

At least this one will be easy. As we wait I thought of Rebecca, I should be with her, not here. It is now only three nights before Sam and I fly to the States but I have to undertake two more of these before I leave. Though this is again breaking one of our rules, the one saying not to do too many corrections in quick succession so we do not draw attention to ourselves, again it is necessary. I dare not postpone these two until I get back. There are signs that they are escalating so I need to escalate in response. Not only is this demanding, undertaking two all-nighters within three days, it is risky but I have no choice. If I postpone them until our return these poor women could be badly injured, if not killed.

At least my lectures for the States and my responsibilities here are all sorted. Rebecca has also been so busy; I have missed not seeing her all the time, but at least I have been able to get on top of my university duties. It was the correct decision for her not to come with us. From my point of view it would have been wonderful to have her in the hall when I give the keynote lecture and I would love her to meet Jacob. In reality though she is correct, she needs to be here whilst the station settles down. She has done an amazing job in the last few months and in another few weeks she should have more free time. She had jumped at my idea of going to Paris for a long weekend next month. She immediately said, "Paris with the one I love, what could be better?" That is exactly what I had thought. We are so in tune.

I wish that Sam and I were back in accord. Our rows are getting more frequent and repetitive. It is the same every time. She wants to reduce the corrections. In fact I think she wants to cease. I cannot understand her. In addition to her own experience everything we look at shows what misery these women suffer. She is so wrong. I am so surprised at her. We must continue.

As he has still not left the building I tried a little small talk with Sam, hoping to heal the rift. 'I am very surprised by this one. It will make matters easier and safer for us but he is oddly atypical.' She simply nodded but I felt her relax a little. Thomas Castle is at sixty one not only the oldest we have dealt with so far he is also the smallest. At roughly five foot five inches tall and slightly built he will be easy to subdue. He is a lady's hairdresser and has a soft, effete manner to go with the stereotype. I will never cease to be amazed at what goes on behind closed doors and how different even the mildest people can be there. He looks like a wimp but he is a vicious pig. The hospital records show that he has regularly assaulted his wife for years.

'Shouldn't be long now.' Again Sam only nodded but she did squeeze my arm. That may have been at least a climb down, possibly even an apology. The collection point is ideal, a dead end screened passageway from the back door of his salon. The only nuisance is that his leaving time varies and so we have to wait. No one has yet passed us so we have not drawn suspicion.

The rear door opened. 'Here he comes.' I stepped out of the van as he passed. Our well-oiled pirouette was faultlessly executed and fifteen minutes later he was on the ducking stool and Sam was leaving.

His treatment was also atypical. He hardly moaned and except when I branded his cock he did not cry out. He went limp from the start and lay there non-reactive. When I told him to stop abusing his wife or he would be in for more he only then showed some response and tried to shake his head. He seems to be trying to deny it. Tough luck Tommy, Sam has seen your records.

Early the next morning I dropped him off not far from his house where there is a secluded lay-by. I hadn't even needed to Taser him, he remained flaccid. I was a little worried leaving him non-responsive on the grass. I went back to him and turned him into the recovery position. He is breathing but lying quite still.

....

.

This next evening is a very different and more dangerous proposition. Patrick Reagan is a big man and only forty. He may work as an estate agent but he looks like a scaffolder. He is our main worry this week, both from our safety and that of his wife. She has been in and out of the refuge for weeks and all there are pleading for her to stay. He is getting more drunken and violent and all in the refuge feel it is only a matter of time before she is badly injured. This is why we decided that he had to be dealt with before we left for America. Even the recently reluctant Sam was in favour on this occasion. His wife will not leave him as he controls the whereabouts of the children. She cannot get them away from him.

The situation is, like last night, ideal. Another deserted passage behind the agency where I managed to Taser him as he went to his car. These rear service entrances behind rows of shops are a great advantage for this work.

Then the difficulties started. He is much bigger and heavier than me and manhandling him into the van was difficult and time consuming. Before I had the straps secure he was beginning to come round. I Tasered him again then immediately gave a hefty shot of Ketamine. I tightly secured the straps and added more of them than usual for additional security.

In spite of the extra precautions he was beginning to stir as I took him out of the van at the farm. I had to give him yet another injection. Sam is becoming concerned about the amount he is receiving and the risk of side effects, even death, but there is no choice. We are committed and we cannot allow him to wake outside of the building.

Finally I had him secured on the ducking frame, again with several extra straps. He is a brute of a man and already overcoming the drug. Within minutes he is fighting his bonds and roaring. With the gag in place he cannot make more than a splutter but it is clear that his shouting would be shaking the old warehouse were it not for that.

I quickly got on with the job and submerged him for longer than usual on the first occasion. I need to take control of this. As soon as his head left the water he was fighting his bonds and trying to shout again. I submerged him again and again over hours, rapidly increasing the duration but still he came out fighting. It is exhausting. I cannot break him.

In the middle of the night his writhing mouth forced the gag free. He bellowed, 'that fucking bitch has put you up to this. I will fucking kill her.' So he has heard what I have been saying. He understands I am trying to stop him abusing her but not that she is unaware of this. I am going to have to do more than usual with this one. I must not leave him in any doubt that he must stop his abuse.

In the early hours I became desperately tired. This being the second night in a row and having such a battle with him is taking its toll. At around three am, after I submerged him I closed my eyes for a few seconds respite.

I jerked awake. I must have drifted off to sleep but

thankfully only for a moment. Even so I rapidly lifted him out of the tank so that he can breathe again. Hopefully a near death experience will finally subdue him.

Instantly I can see that he is quite dead. I swung him from over the pool and when he was at the side I listened for breathing. None. Then I slipped off his gag and pressed his eyes and grasped and twisted his nipples and ears so hard that I felt there is a danger of ripping them off. There was no reaction. He is dead. I left him lying there for ten minutes watching for breathing and then repeated the painful stimuli. I cannot risk this one pretending and then overpowering me. Again, none, there is no doubt that he is dead.

I must have dozed off for longer than I was aware of.

My first reaction was "oh shit." Then I thought it through. It is quite possible that I would have succeeded in correcting him and so his wife would have been in more danger, not less. Sam will not be happy but, even so, perhaps this is the better outcome.

I wheeled him out to the pre-dug graves left over from Clive's research. I cannot lift him. I rolled him over the edge and he hit the bottom with a dull thump. The sky is lightening but I cannot make out his body in the depth of the pit. From somewhere I found the energy and I filled it in. I put in a good layer of Clive's composting mix first and then finished off with earth. Then I moved one of the small trees, one of the cuttings that is now three feet tall. I planted this on top and then I surrounded it by the old sewerage residue compost which should be full of degraded DNA. Even if forensic tests are done on the soil the presence of human DNA will be unremarkable.

I cut some turfs from the nearby field and patted them down alongside the tree. Within days the mound will look like all of the others. No one will realise that it is a fresh grave.

I rested for a while and then it was time to call Sam to collect me. During the tense drive home I prattled on saying that this is possibly the better outcome in this case.

All she would say was, 'we should not kill. We must stop.'

I fumed. In spite of what he has already done, in spite of his threats she still refuses to acknowledge that this was essential. If anything I think we should undertake more corrections and if they are very violent we should deal with them as I have just done with Reagan, as I did with Robin. We should completely remove any risk for other women, as I did for Sam. I can see there is no point in discussing it with her this morning. I am too tired to discuss it tactfully and she is not hearing, her intellect is being blocked by fear and doubt.

I will go home and get some rest. Tonight I am seeing Rebecca. Tomorrow we fly to America. I will speak to Sam again on the 'plane. As we have club seats together we can whisper without fear of being overheard. People may think we are lovers but we are used to that.

CHAPTER 24: REBECCA: REALISATION

I kicked back from my desk, the wheeled chair sliding easily on the thin hard carpet. I leaned back and I happily looked around the room. It is sparsely and cheaply furnished, as is usual in police stations, but it is mine. I love it. Friday morning, I guess many in the city are looking forward to the weekend. As Luke is away there is a cloud for me but, even so, I am looking forward to coming into work tomorrow and training on Sunday. I love both, or should I say all three.

I am not only enjoying having my own office for the first time, but, to my surprise, I am also enjoying the administration. I insist on mixing admin with continuing to undertake detective work. I will not become a desk jockey. The Chief Constable supported this and to everyone's surprise I have been allowed a secretary to help so that I can do both. She is excellent and she is already developing her role and becoming more of a manager. We both enjoy it when I delegate to her.

In addition to station command, and continuing plain-clothes detective work, at least once a week I go on patrol dressed as a WPC. I have to keep my hair hidden under the cap. Though my face has become known, as the local newspapers will not leave me alone since the raid, I am not usually recognised in such a uniform unless people spot my blond curls. When on patrol I always take the subordinate role to the usually male PC or Sergeant I am with. It required a lot of persuasion for them to accept this but now they have become accustomed to it, or at least to go along with the role reversal. It is good for us all.

I glanced at the clock. Luke is starting to cross the Atlantic. I hope that he is alright. He was so tired yesterday. I think he has been overdoing it combining both his Professorial work with, on both Tuesday and Wednesday, undertaking two consecutive overnight moth collections. No wonder he is exhausted. I left at ten last night. He wanted me to stay but he could hardly keep his eyes open. After we made love I got up, dressed and kissed him goodbye. I think he was asleep before I left the room. I so wish that I was on the 'plane with him but it is still too soon to leave here even though the new detectives are settling in so well.

A knock came at the door and I called them in. I am pleased to see that it is Julian. When I am out and about as a detective I often go with Julian or Barbara. I work especially well with both of them. Though, as Julian and Barbara are now officially an item, they never work together. 'Mornin' boss.' I have tried to get everyone to call me Rebecca. Some do but most cannot and so I compromise on "boss." Julian deliberately uses boss unless he wants to tease me when he reverts to "ma'am." 'We have just received an unusual 'phone call from Mary Roberts, the Nursing Sister in A and E. They have an odd case in that they feel is a result of an assault, one Thomas Castle. Just letting you know that I am popping over.'

Immediately I said, 'I'll come along; I need a break from the office.' I have the distinct impression that is what he had wanted. He enjoys working with me as much as I do with him.

As I got up from the desk I had a sudden concern. Marcus may be there. I have not spoken to him since the evening we were interrupted by his wife. When Julian was admitted Marcus was around but I only saw him across the department and we did not have the opportunity to speak together. They were very busy, mainly from the injuries sustained by the criminals during our raid. Meadows and Coyle had been the most badly hurt but they were not the only ones injured. Some of the arrests had not been gentle, especially of the creeps controlling the girls. I would like to see Marcus but I hope that he will not feel awkward. I doubt that he will. He probably has someone else now and, as I have also. So, what happened is definitely in the past.

We walked into A and E and bumped into the drab, dumpy, but highly effective Mary. 'Hi Julian, I see that you have brought the boss with you.' Julian is a regular here so I am not surprised that she knows him. I am surprised she recognised me, I would not think that she would have time to read the local rags, and I have not spent much time in the department since we were investigating the assault on the little boy. 'Perfect timing, we are just about to start a departmental meeting and Mr. Castle is first on the agenda.'

She ushered us into the same room as before and again they are all sitting around, including Marcus. He looked up, saw me, and to my delight gave a wide welcoming smile. He stood and came over to me. At first I was completely thrown as I thought he was going to give me a kiss. He saw my reaction, guessed its cause, and his grin widened. He held out his hand and shook mine but he spoke to Julian unknowingly echoing Mary, 'hi Julian, I see you have brought the boss.'

Then he turned to the others and said, 'you all know Julian well both as a patient and as an invaluable police presence here. No doubt, as her 'photo is on the notice board in the coffee room, you will also recognise that today we are graced with the presence of Detective Superintendent Rebecca Fletcher.'

They all smiled as I thought, "what the bloody hell is my 'photo doing in the coffee room." Again Marcus picked up on this and continued, now speaking to me, 'the incoming junior nurses are encouraged to see you as a role model. The rest of us throw darts.' They all laughed but then the atmosphere soured as Windbag came in scowling and muttering, "bloody coppers again."

Marcus suggested that one of the junior doctors, Sue is all he called her, presented the case as she had examined Mr. Castle. He stressed that as Julian and I are not medical or nursing practitioners she should only mention medical details that would be pertinent to any investigation.

She blushed but spoke calmly. 'Mr Castle is a sixty one year old man who has his own business as a ladies hairdresser. He has been happily married for more than thirty years. Other than a psychiatric disorder some years ago he was, until this week, fit and well. He was initially brought in on Wednesday morning, two days ago, by ambulance. He had been found lying semi-conscious on a grass verge in a secluded road. On arrival he resisted examination and shouted, "no more, go away." He refused to answer any questions. I could see he was moving all limbs so he had not had a stroke. He did not appear intoxicated. He had obviously been incontinent and therefore I thought that he may have had a fit. We identified him from his wallet and called his wife. As soon as she arrived he recovered somewhat. Then he insisted on getting up and leaving immediately with her. She wanted him to stay but he would not and I had no opportunity either to talk with her or to examine him properly.'

Sue paused and Marcus indicated she is doing well and should continue. 'Mrs Castle called an ambulance this morning and came in with him. She is very concerned as his condition has deteriorated. She reported that at home, initially, he refused to say what had happened and indeed he barely spoke at all. Today he is much worse. He is now turning away from everybody and is in a mute stupor. He stares at the wall and he will not or cannot properly speak. He is muttering something incomprehensible. Mrs Castle reports that on awakening this morning, before he deteriorated further, he said that he had been attacked. On examination he looks completely normal other than an unusual burn on his penis. I have a 'photo of it here.' She reached into his file.

Before she could show it the door opened and in came two more. Marcus said, 'ah, good. You have assessed him.' Turning to Julian and me he said, 'this is Colonel Jenny Hill.' He indicated a tall, skinny, serious looking woman. 'She is seconded here for a six month respite from her usual work as an A and E consultant in military hospitals. Jenny and I were junior doctors together in Afghanistan.' He then turned to a slight, kindly looking coloured man, 'and this is one of our excellent psychiatrists who we simply call Dr. Aayansh. That is his given name. We use that as most of us cannot pronounce his Siri Lankan family name.'

Aayansh smiled and said, 'that's OK Dr. Reech.' All laughed except Windbag who harrumphed, "get on with it."

Marcus ignored him and said, 'we are uncertain what is wrong with him Aayansh but we suspect a stress induced psychiatric emergency. What do you think?'

'I agree. He is atypical but I consider that he has developed catatonia. I understand from his wife ....' He hesitated, and looking at Julian's uniform he added, 'I feel that I need to reveal some medical details but I consider that is ethical as these may be relevant to a police investigation. His wife tells me that he has a history of a bipolar disorder but he has been well for some time. She also told me that before becoming mute he said that he had suffered some form of trauma. Jenny, er Dr Hill, has also told me she suspects severe traumatic stress. The combination of the two can produce such an unusual psychiatric state particularly in one who may be vulnerable due to suffering from other psychiatric disorders. I have given a low dose of an intramuscular sedative. I hope that will be enough to calm him sufficiently to talk without putting him to sleep. I will go back and see if I can now speak with him and then I will return to report to you.' He quickly left the room.

Marcus turned to the military consultant and asked, 'Jenny, what do you think?'

'Unfortunately I have seen far too many such cases.' She turned towards Julian and me to tell us what she thinks but she is being kind to the others. It is clear that they are mystified. 'I have worked in several conflict zones, both in the local hospitals and I have treated civilians in our military hospitals.' She turned back to address the whole room. 'It is obvious that he has been tortured.'

All of us froze and looked at her in horror. Tortured, surely that cannot be correct? How can a competent, law-abiding, harmless adult be tortured in our society?

Windbag exploded, 'don't be daft woman. Other than a little burn on his cock there is not a mark on him.'

Jenny turned a look on Windbag which made even him quail. After a long disparaging stare she said only one word, 'waterboarding.'

The room was totally silent for a long time. We were all obviously thinking the same thing, "waterboarding, in our gentle city? It sounds horrible and unbelievable. Yet it seems to be true." Even Windbag looks upset.

Marcus recovered first. 'So we have a catatonic state precipitated in a vulnerable individual by torture. That is a first for me.' He looks astonished, they all do. After another pause, as we all came to terms with this, Marcus said, 'Sue, let's have a look at the 'photo of the burn.'

Sue held up the 'photo and in unison two of the junior looking nurses blurted, 'I have seen something like that before.' They then sat back embarrassed at having spoken out.

Marcus said, 'excellent, that is why we have these meetings, to call on the experience of all of us.' He had done a good job in reassuring them and their colour faded. 'Racheal, you go first. Where have you seen it before?'

'Dr Rice, my brother is a leather craftsman and he likes to decorate some of his work. He brands it at different temperatures and for different durations and that looks like some of the branded "R's" he has done for me. As it is the first letter of my name he puts it on items he makes for me.' The unpleasant Windbag muttered under his breath, "nonsense." Racheal reached into her pocket and took out her leather purse with an "R" branded on the side. It is identical.

We all immediately sat back dumbfounded. Clearly we are all again thinking the same. That someone is torturing, branding and waterboarding apparently innocent people, here, where we live.

Marcus calmly spoke yet I can see that even he is ruffled. 'I see there is no doubt that you are absolutely correct Racheal.' Even he could not resist a critical look at Windbag. 'Now, Christine, where have you seen it before?'

'Here, in this department Dr Rice. I can't remember the date but we can easily look it up as it was the morning after Julian was brought in. A man was here with an identical burn pattern but it looked deeper. He said that he had been welding and dropped something red hot on it. I asked Dr Wynn-Davis who was looking after him if that was likely to be true, it sounded odd to me. Dr Wynn-Davis said that it must be otherwise the man would not have said so.' The poor girl's demeanour showed that his comments had not been kind to her. Christine hesitated, plucked up her courage, then continued without looking towards Windbag, 'there was something else that was strange. He kept turning to his wife saying "I am so, so sorry. I will never touch you again." I had no idea what he meant. Thinking about it later I wondered if he had been hitting her but why would he apologise for it whilst his burn was being dressed.'

We all sat back. None of us yet know how to put all of this together.

Eventually Sister Roberts stood and said, 'let's break for a coffee while Aayansh assesses Mr Castle and I will look up this other burn victim's name. Let's see if we can throw light on Christine's observations.' As she left she turned to Christine and Sue saying, 'well done you two.' They beamed.

Over coffee I was mortified to see that my 'photo is indeed on the wall. It is the one that was in the newspaper taken from the media briefing after the raid. It is not just a press clipping, someone has ordered a reprint. Underneath is written, I suspect by Sister Roberts, "to all junior nurses, if she can do it so can you." I moved away from it but Julian smiled and winked at me. The bastard is winding me up yet again. I love him for it.

I wondered how to deal with Marcus but he settled the issue by coming up to me. 'Hi Rebecca, I was hoping to see you again.' He gestured to me that we should move a little away from the others and he whispered. 'Are we good?'

'Of course we are and I am delighted to see you.' He looks exhausted. 'If you don't mind me saying you look tired. Are things tricky at home?'

'Home, no, the divorce has been difficult due to her being vicious but the lawyers are finally nearing the end.' He took a breath and nodded at Windbag. 'It is here. Thankfully he retires in a month and we have a wonderful replacement so all should get better then. For the moment, I am having to do everything.' He gave one of his lovely cheeky grins, 'his replacement is a woman of colour and Windbag predicts that the department will fall apart. I think it will flourish.'

Before we could continue Aayansh and Sister Roberts came back in as if on a mission. We all can see that they have much to say and so we hurried to the meeting room and we resumed our seats.

Aayansh kicked off. 'I was able to have a chat with Mr Castle, after he had relaxed and before he went to sleep. Jenny had previously told me that she suspected torture so that was my first question. Mr Castle confirmed this. He was abducted, trussed up and repeatedly submerged through the night. Whilst this was being done he was told many times that he must stop beating his wife or there will be more. He was burnt on his penis and he was then told that if he ever hit Mrs Castle again it will be cut off. He was told that the burn would brand an "R" on his penis meant to remind him of the threat, "R" for "remember" apparently. Both he and Mrs Castle deny any abuse whatsoever and she said that he has always been a gentle, loving husband.' Looking at us he added, 'I am sorry to say that he is now fast asleep and I do not think he should be questioned until he has recovered a little, at least a couple of days.' I nodded and thought, bugger, but understandable.

Having the torture confirmed sobered us all. Sister Roberts continued but with an expression warning us that it will get yet worse. 'I have tracked down the man that Christine thought had a similar burn. I managed to speak to him and his wife on the 'phone. He is adamant that he will not speak to the police and he does not want his name used. He is clearly terrified. He reports that he was abducted and bundled into a van and driven away locked in a box of some sort. He was bound, gagged and drugged so he is uncertain of the details. One thing he was clear on though was that there were at least two of them, one was a woman, and he heard them laughing and singing during the journey.'

Can it get worse? One of them is a woman and both they both party while taking a man to be tortured.

She continued, 'he admits to previous domestic abuse but he says he has now been able to stop.' She tried to make the atmosphere a little easier, 'I can't think why.' There were more grimaces than sniggers. Looking at her expression I fear there is still more to come.

'I also looked up Mrs Castle's records. She was here five years ago with an ingrowing toenail so she is on the system. The records show that she was also here a month ago with a severe beating following domestic abuse. On the same day the examining doctor recorded that there had been many such previous episodes. However they also state that her two year old child was with her. As Mrs Castle is sixty four I do not think that is likely. It appears that the examining doctor incorrectly filed a report in the wrong records.' She glared at Windbag. She did not have to say and no one asked who that examining doctor was. We all know.

Julian and I looked at each other aghast as the realisation that has been growing all through the meeting is now inescapable. It is plain that in our beautiful, quaint, provincial city we have a team undertaking multiple abductions and torture. Their victims all seem to be men involved in, or at least in one case wrongly accused of, domestic abuse. The criminals may consider themselves to be vigilantes on a mission to stop abuse but that does not excuse any of it, especially targeting the wrong man. Due process is required for a good reason.

I spoke to a very subdued room. 'Thank you all. It is

clear that we have at least a pair of, or possibly a group of, serial criminals. We will go away and open an investigation. Dr Rice and Sister Roberts, would it be possible for your team to review the records of the last two years to see if there is anything similar? I say two years as we have a couple of unsolved cases over that period that may be related.' Julian caught my eye and nodded. We are both thinking of Robin Newnam and Brian James.

Both immediately said in unison, 'we will get on with it today.'

'Again I thank you all but particularly Sister Roberts, Rachael, and Christine whose observation and detective skills put us to shame.' They all blushed but are clearly delighted to receive such a compliment. Perhaps the fact that it came from one feted on their own notice board is a reason it was so appreciated. They certainly deserve it.

Julian and I made our exit. We could not speak. We drove in silence to my office. As we went in Barbara was nearby. Seeing our expressions she came in and worriedly asked, 'what is it?' We told her. Repeating it made it seem even worse. Barbara joined us in our mortified silence.

After a few minutes I finally roused myself and started. 'OK, I have a few ideas on how to proceed but do you have any suggestions?'

Julian said, 'why don't I go down to the womens'refuge and sound them out. There may be more men who have been attacked and the women at the refuge will probably be aware or at least suspicious. Let's face it, there are almost certainly more. They may have heard whispers.'

'Yes, I was thinking that. No, Barbara should go.'

Julian replied with a hands up supplicant gesture, 'I know, not sexist, just sensitive policing.'

'No, she is a much better copper.' I tried to look serious but failed. Even so Barbara smiled and gave him a "told you so look." He looked delighted for her. 'Julian, would you please look up the known recent cases of domestic abuse and call to see them. Perhaps you can find some who are prepared to talk and go on the record. I will set up a task force and call the Chief Constable. I will also set up a media briefing for tomorrow morning. As it is at short notice and on a Saturday hopefully many will not want to come. We can quickly undertake what is expected without being dragged into a brouhaha.'

Having a plan helped us to recover and we all stood determinedly to get on with it. We did not get far. Peter, the desk sergeant, knocked and came in. He was taken aback to see us all together and looking so serious. We quickly filled him in and asked him to arrange a station meeting in the late afternoon. Friday afternoon is not the best timing but that cannot be helped.

We stood again to go but Peter said, now looking even more serious, 'you had better sit down while I tell you why I came in.' Yes, I had quite forgotten. 'I think I can add another case straight away.' Julian, Barbara and I exchanged "oh shit" looks. 'I came to tell you that Fiona Reagan is waiting downstairs and she is almost hysterical with worry. We regularly get called to her house as her husband beats her. He is Patrick Reagan the estate agent. He is a vicious bastard. She won't leave him. She says that it is because of the children but I think that she still loves him. Anyway, he is missing. It is only for a couple of days but that is apparently completely out of character. She actually came in on Thursday. As he had then only been missing overnight she was then reasonably told to wait a little longer as so many turn up. Now she is beside herself with worry and says that she will not leave until we investigate. Actually, I think she is correct to be concerned. He has never done this before and he has missed several important work meetings both yesterday and earlier this morning. Apparently that is also completely unlike him.'

Before we could respond my 'phone rang. It must be the hospital, I had told the reception desk to put them straight through when they called. I answered, it was Marcus. He skipped all pleasantries and told me his findings. As he spoke the others looked at me with increasing concern as they read my expression. In my shell-shocked state I had not thought to put it on speaker.

He rang off and I looked at them. 'They have discovered three more similar burns over the last eighteen months and they have called them. The patients or their partners reported exactly the same story of domestic abuse and torture and none of the men will speak to us. All were extremely fearful and Mary Roberts is trying to persuade one to go back to A and E for assessment; she suspects that he has PTSD. So now we have five burns and and three missing men in a two year period. All eight either have a history of domestic abuse or were incorrectly recorded as having so in the hospital records. There are clearly links to both Casualty and to domestic abuse.'

Peter said, 'and that is only the start of the investigation.' His words hung in the air.

I went with Peter to speak to Fiona Reagan and the others carried on as planned.

....

On an appropriately drizzly Saturday morning I walked to the Park Hotel ballroom for the Media briefing at ten am. This is becoming a habit. We moved it here as my speculation that the media would not attend in large numbers on a Saturday was quite wrong. They put two and two together and the chatter flew between them. We have been inundated, even two national TV stations are coming.

I thought the Chief Constable would present it. At my suggestion of a meeting she simply said it was an excellent idea and that she looked forward to seeing me on the TV. So, I am in the spotlight again.

I was uncertain whether or not to invite the victims' wives but the Chief firmly said I should. Fiona and Mrs Castle, who asked me to call her Jane, were very keen to attend and make their points. I telephoned the A and E department. Marcus was out but I spoke to Sister Roberts and I suggested that some members may like to come as they had been so instrumental in the discovery of the cases being linked. I specifically asked if she, Rachael and Christine would come. She assured me she will be here and she thought the others would be as well.

At ten prompt we started again. I found before that not only does wearing my full uniform give me confidence but looking directly at the camera and pretending to talk to an individual helped. Beforehand it was Luke. As he is currently asleep several thousand miles away this time I decided to tell Dad the story. In fact I am. I know he and Mum are watching. I spoke not to the camera but to his calm, listening face. I spoke in the same tone and volume as if we were opposite each other at the kitchen table. The camera disappeared and I told Dad what we had discovered. At times I could not help glancing at the huge screen to the side and seeing what the hundreds of thousands of viewers are seeing, my head and shoulders. I clenched my bum and looked back at "Dad" and carried on without faltering.

As the full horror unfolded the room firstly went quiet, a first for a press briefing. Then looks of disbelief and distress came to all their faces. When I told them that we have in our midst at least two, possibly more, criminals who for at least two years have been abducting and torturing men they sat stock still, slack jawed. To my left, at the front, there is a coterie of the red top gutter press. At the start their self-important braying together had reminded me of the Troop. Now, even they are quiet.

I finished my presentation and said that before answering questions I would like to present the women married to the two latest victims, one definite victim, one missing. The journalists nearly fell off their collective chairs. They had not expected that. I called Jane and Fiona to the podium and to my relief the screen finally changed from a "head and shoulders" shot of me to them walking calmly up though I remain on screen, now full length.

I introduced Jane first. She spoke directly into the camera as I had. However she is very different. She is raging with anger and there is no doubt that she is speaking to whoever abducted her husband. 'A disgusting pervert has abducted and tortured my lovely husband. He was drugged, water boarded and branded. During this ordeal he was repeatedly told that he had beaten me.' She hesitated and glared into the camera with a terrifying ferocity. I hope we catch the perpetrators before she does, I do not want to arrest her for murder. 'That is a filthy lie. My husband is a kind, gentle, loving man. We have in nearly forty years hardly had a cross word, let alone him threatening me. He has never ever struck me. Not only have you behaved like an animal, you have attacked the wrong man.' Even the hardened reporters are open mouthed.

Jane stepped away and I quickly took her place. 'Before I introduce the next lady I would like to add something more to my summary. What I told you before and what Jane has just said is certain. This additional information about to be presented is provisional and we will investigate it further. A man is missing but as yet we are not sure of the circumstances. We have good reason to believe that there are at least two people involved in the crimes. One is a woman and they sang and laughed during at least one of the abductions.' I did not think it possible but the medias' jaws fell further open and their horrified looks intensified.'

I looked questioningly at Fiona. I am worried; she is barely holding it together. She nodded back that she still wants to speak. She came to the microphone but cannot yet look up, her eyes are on the lectern. She started to shudder and I went to her but she shrugged me away. Finally she looked up at the camera. It zoomed in and her distraught face filled the screen. She must be filling many living rooms in the land. 'I know he is dead. I know that you have killed him.' Everyone held their breath including me. This is not what we had discussed. Tears now streamed down her face. 'Patrick would never not come home to me and the children. He would never miss work meetings without a 'phone call to explain. That is unless he is dead.' A sob burst out. Again she shooed me away. I am concerned that I have misjudged this. It is too much for her.

Yet again she gathered herself. 'Yes he beat me. I forgave him. If you knew what he had suffered as a child you would at least understand. I forgave him and I still love him. You may not agree but that is my choice. You killed him for your own gratification, not for me.' Again she had to pause as her face contorted. This time I knew not to approach. 'Please let me have his body. Please let me see him one more time.' Now her knees started to buckle. I moved in quickly to hold her and Jane joined me. Jane whispered that she had her and together they stumbled back to their seats in the silent auditorium. Silent that is except for Fiona's crying and the muffled sobs of many present, not all women.

I let them take their seats. Then I started clapping. The whole room stood and applauded their bravery and joined in their grief and anger.

When it was quiet again I said, 'strictly speaking we

have, at present, to list Patrick Reagan's absence as missing, not as murder. Obviously though, I, and I am sure most of the room, give great weight to Fiona's opinion.' As I paused there were a few muttered here, here's. 'Now, I am happy to take any of your questions.'

There followed a ten minute session of responsible, pertinent and informed questions. Some lead to valuable comments and suggestions that I mentally noted. This is how it should be, an intelligent interrelationship with the press and through them with the public.

I knew that it would not last. I had noticed the gutter press troop getting restless. They do not like it going well for the police. One of them finally put his hand up and I reluctantly acknowledged him. 'Aren't you missing something?' He spoke to me while condescendingly sneering at the whole room. Obviously he considers that it is not just us wooden tops who are substandard; he considers that his colleagues are as well. 'This has been going on for at least two years. You must have been asleep on the job to have missed it before.' He looked around with a supercilious air but did not get the support from the room in general that he had obviously thought due. Only a couple of the troop around him nodded and smirked.

For some reason I thought of the Military Consultant, Jenny Hill. I copied her expression and I turned it on him. He initially looked haughty but as I held his gaze I saw him become uneasy. Then I made my decision. I will factually answer his question. Then I will let rip.

'You seem confused by the time scale. Allow me to reiterate it in simpler language that you may grasp. I apologise if some of my previous words were too long for you to understand.' The responsible majority sat up sharply and they look engrossed by the anticipation of a fight. They are obviously delighted by the put down of one determined to undermine their own reputation. They will not be disappointed. I tried not to think of this spat being aired nationwide. 'Until yesterday we in the police only knew of two disappearances separated by two years with only the fact they were both abusing their wives to link them. That is not much of a coincidence as such abuse is so common. In spite of this tenuous link we had noted it and we were keeping a look out for more. Until yesterday no one in the A and E Department had seen more than one case each so they could not have made a link. Yesterday morning a very astute A and E Consultant, Dr Rice, called us in to see a gentleman, Mr Castle whom you have just heard about, whose extremely unusual symptoms he thought may be due to an assault. In the Departmental meeting that followed it transpired that not only was this the case but that he had been tortured. During this meeting two sharp-eyed junior nurses made connections with cases they had recently, individually, seen. This lead to an investigation worthy of Sherlock Holmes by the Nursing Sister and the full extent of the crimes was only then known for the first time. Please concentrate and try to remember that this is less than twenty-four hours ago. An hour after that meeting, when I and other officers had already commenced planning an investigation, Fiona came to the station concerned about her husband and was talking to me within ten minutes of her arrival. Some of my officers have already interviewed people and discovered what may be more cases.'

I paused and glared at him. He is beginning to look hot under the collar. 'So, in summary; this came to light yesterday. Already we have already formed a squad, initiated an investigation, we have discovered yet more cases and briefed you.'

I paused again. He clearly thinks that I am finished. He is about to learn that I have not yet even started my main points, should I say offensive. I see on the screen that I still have my "Jenny Hill" expression, good. 'Perhaps as you stare through that instrument so loved by the less responsible press, the retrospectoscope, you could examine a couple of other points for me?'

Now he is really rattled and I suspect fearful. His supposed friends are slowly backing away. 'Please peer through it now and tell me what else we could have done.'

Again I waited. The rest of the room is delighted. The decent journalists obviously cannot stand this lot either. 'Nothing is your answer. You cannot think of anything more we could have done. So why did you criticise us?' He is speechless for the first time. 'Now, perhaps, you could turn it on yourself. You are often in A and E, you see all the crime reports. Did you spot the pattern?'

He muttered, 'not my job.' He waved his hands dismissively and went to turn away.

I thundered, 'you asked me a question. You should wait for the full answer. I have not finished.' There were claps for me and jeers towards him from across the room. 'While we are holding your retrospectoscope,' I heavily emphasised the "your," 'let us turn it on some of your own scribbling.' Now the others are openly laughing at him. 'Some weeks ago you published an article adversely commenting on the number of female detectives that I appointed. You predicted a collapse in morale and case resolution in our station. Are you now going to print a correction pointing out that you were entirely wrong and that the reverse has occurred?'

He tried to stare me down but soon backed away. I then turned to address the whole of the room and spoke more softly. 'I admire most of the press and I consider it essential that we fully brief you, hence today's meeting. In fact I enjoy seeing you and our investigations profit from our mutual cooperation. In addition, if there is any hint of us not meeting very high standards, or if there is any complaint, I not only agree to you holding our feet to the fire, I insist on it. I assure you of my complete co-operation. I will undertake all in my power to support a free press.'

They started to clap, I held up my hand to show that there is more. 'But, there is always a but.' That brought smiles along with raised eyebrows. 'This has only come from one quarter so far,' I looked at the fool I had just savaged and they all know from where, 'but I have to say this to all of you so that it is clear it is a warning , not a threat. If anyone ever again publishes articles such as the recent one referring to the breasts and legs of the new officers reporting to me, all co-operation will be withdrawn from that person. They will be totally excluded from a meeting such as this or from any of the information coming from us.'

Everyone, except one that is, clapped, especially the women.

I thought it is time to start to wrap up the meeting. Now in a congenial tone I restarted. 'There are three matters I would like to comment briefly on before we close. Firstly, I told you of the stunning professionalism and detective work by three of the nurses. They are in fact here.' The three of them looked at me both delighted and horrified. They have guessed what is coming. 'Please stand so that people can see who cracked this case.' They awkwardly stood looking embarrassed. Wild cheering and clapping broke out, initially from the rear but soon the whole room joined in. I looked to see who had started it. Marcus, I had not spotted him before. All three are now broadly smiling and playing up to it with mock curtsies. The screen to the side shows the camera is now zoomed onto their shining faces.

It quietened and I was able to continue as they sat. 'Secondly, I have made a note of the three excellent suggestions that came from the floor today.' I indicated the journalists responsible and now I spoke to them, 'I commit myself to exploring these further with you and producing a public, written response within a month. If I am late I will fine myself fifty pounds for every week's delay which will be payable to a charity of your choice.' That went down very well. I will have to get on with it though or it will be expensive and I already have more than enough to do.

'Finally, I wish to address the culprits.' Again I looked straight at the camera but now I am not addressing Luke or Dad. I put back on what I will now call my "Jenny face" and started. 'You are all not only criminal and immoral but, having tortured the wrong man, you are obviously stupid as well. Your actions are unlawful, disproportionate and not following due process. Here such actions, as in all countries other than a few nasty dictatorships, they are regarded as an abuse of human rights. Your actions are vile. We will do our utmost to stop you and, one way or another, I am sure that the excellent squad I have assembled will succeed.'

There was another round of applause, now muted by the gravity of what we have been discussing. People started to file out. Marcus waved and tapped his watch showing he has to go. Julian came over to me along with several of the new detective recruits and several PCs and WPCs, all in civilian dress. They all looked at me with what seemed to be adoration. Julian astonished me. He leaned forward, grabbed my hand and then kissed my cheek, that's a first. 'Bloody hell boss, even by your standards that was amazing.' All the others looked on in agreement. I felt proud.

Then I came down to earth with a bang. 'Thanks everyone but god only knows what the Chief Constable is going to say.' At exactly that moment my 'phone pinged as a text came in. I had been turning it on as they spoke to me. I looked at them and they heard the apprehension in my voice. 'It's her.' Their brows creased with concern at the rapid communication and then relaxed as I broke into a smile.

Julian said, 'stop bloody grinning and tell us.'

Reading it aloud I answered, 'bloody marvellous. I have always wanted to stick it to them but in my job I have to be so fucking PC.'

Julian scoffed, 'you are making that up. She would never use the F word.' I held up the screen to him. 'Well, fuck me.' I have never heard him use it before either. However, as Billy Connolly has so rightly said, sometimes it is the only one that will suffice.

....

On Sunday evening I staggered in to my home at ten PM. I feel absolutely shattered. I have been working flat out since Friday morning. I have exchanged a few e mails with Luke. He is having a quiet time with Sam and Jacob before his conference starting tomorrow. At least he is catching up on his rest. He looked shattered before he left. He is unaware of what has happened here and I have not told him. He needs to concentrate on rest and his lecture. Now it is me who is whacked. I know that about now they are going for Sunday lunch in a Californian vineyard. How I wish I could now be with him, hand in hand, having made love this morning. I can't wait to show him the recording of yesterday's media circus.

That was yesterday. It is said that a day is a long time in politics. I did not think I was a politician but the briefing has unleashed a political storm.

None of us, not a single person in the station nor the Chief Constable, predicted the reaction to my media briefing. To say we have been wrong footed is an underestimate. We had thought there would be some blow-back from the press. That was completely wrong. The decent ones were singing our praises, the red top troop were uncharacteristically quiet.

Of all places the challenge came from the Women's

Refuge. Their beef is, and I concede they have a point, that we have immediately formed a squad to catch the people torturing abusers but we have not formed a squad to stop the men torturing their wives. Brutus had done nothing for years. One of my first tasks was to divert more effort into such work. But, another bloody but, I could have, should have, done more.

I have already had several face to face meetings with Amber Watkins, the refuge CEO. In fact we have had four meetings in less than twenty four hours and near constant texts. I had never spoken to her before. I know that I have only been in place for a short while with multiple other things to get on top of. However, I am a woman, I should have been pro-active. Amber is a sincere and reasonable woman. There is another but. She, indeed the whole refuge, now have the bit between their teeth. They are not condoning the abductors' actions but they are using them to draw attention to their own plight.

The social media sites have been swamped. The press and the refuge are swarming over each other. Then tonight, at dusk, a candle lit procession with the moniker, "reclaim the home." I thought that was a superb play on the "reclaim the streets" movement. There was a strong police presence in two ways. The refuge representatives are peaceful but we feared rowdies trying to disrupt them. With a strong police escort and with many women officers in uniform marching with them, including me, it all went well. In retrospect, though I had dared not risk it, I thought that there would not be any trouble. Fiona's distraught face has been all over the media and on the front page of all the Sundays. Though she was pleading for her husband, or at least his body, to be returned, she has become a mascot for beaten women. Not even the most hardened and idiotic rowdies would dare turn up and barrack a procession with her in. They would be lynched. There seems to be a groundswell of opinion that at first glance appears contradictory; catch the tortures; stop the abusers.

At least I have an idea of how to respond. Earlier today, I floated it by the Chief who was immediately strongly supportive. She said that she will try to speak to the Minister today.

Oh god what am I into. Not only the bloody Minister again but the Chief is calling her over a weekend.

CHAPTER 25 LUKE: CALIFORNIA

I lounged back in my spacious seat, only an hour to touchdown. Club class may be an indulgence but it is worth every penny, especially on this long journey after such a fraught week. Rather than being exhausted after the transatlantic flight I now feel refreshed and I am so looking forward both to the conference and, especially, to seeing Jacob. Recently, for the first time in our lives, the three of us have not been together for over twelve months. He was in the UK for a while during Sam's initial rehab but since then, with Sam's continuing treatment and Jacob and I being so busy we have not been able to meet. Boy, do we have a lot to catch up on.

I am now wide awake and I feel tremendous. I did not want Rebecca to leave on Thursday night but she was correct, I was exhausted after my two consecutive nights awake. I slept like a log until Sam woke me at ten on Friday morning when it was time to leave for our flight. I have slept for six hours on the 'plane and now I feel as if I have caught up.

For the hundredth time I thought again that I did not want Rebecca to go on Thursday. She was lying in my arms as I dozed. I felt disappointed as she slipped out of the bed, dressed, kissed me and quietly left; but I then fell deeply asleep. Rebecca, Rebecca, Rebecca, I have to pinch myself to check that I am not dreaming. Not only am I with a woman as wonderful as her but we are in love. She loves me, I love her. It is unbelievable. I so wish that she could have been alongside me now. I want her with me. I want Jacob to meet her in the flesh, not only on zoom. I have to be realistic. She has been working extremely hard during the last few months. All the responsibility for the station and the new team is falling on her. Finally, it appears that work is coming under control for her. I hope that she is having a quiet weekend. She said that she was looking forward to catching up on training and domestic work. I looked at my watch; it is ten am on Saturday morning for her. With luck she is only now rising after a lie in, as I had yesterday.

I looked across at the other wonderful woman in my life. Sam is still asleep in the window seat next to me. She looks calmer now after our talk in the airport. The last couple of days have been the worst ever between us. The strains have been growing for weeks. They came to a head two days ago, during the early hours of Thursday morning, when she collected me after I had buried Reagan. Then, immediately, she again started arguing that we should stop the treatments. She said, as I already knew, that she is now unhappy about the ducking and persuasion and she had already wanted us to stop that anyway. She felt that the death of Reagan was the final straw. She tried to insist that we must immediately cease.

I had been so tired. My judgment was clouded. Instead of answering her reasonably I exploded and we had our first ever full blown slanging match. I could not then, and I cannot now, understand her. She says it is time to back off. Can she not see it is our duty to continue? She of all people, after what she has suffered, after what she has seen both in casualty and in the refuge; she should be able to appreciate our obligation to continue this mission. I then thought that she should understand that we must continue. I still do. However I should have reacted more constructively.

I had hardly seen her during the day on Thursday, in the evening I was with Rebecca. We had remained silent in the taxi to the airport so, in effect, we had not spoken properly since our row in the van during the early hours of Thursday morning. I had a little sleep during Thursday and we both had packing and work to do. It was neither deliberate nor sulky that we did not discuss anything during the day. Our silence in the taxi to the airport was just a tired quietness, it had not been antagonistic. We had, as always, begun softening towards one another again.

Finally we had checked in and found ourselves a quiet corner in the club lounge. We hugged, said sorry, and then we properly discussed the whole thing, like adults. We both spoke calmly. We both spoke with logic and passion. We were then, and we still are, convinced that our own conclusion is correct. The problem is that we have diametrically opposing views.

Sam thinks that not only have we done enough but that we have gone too far. She insists that we should immediately and completely cease.

I think that there is so much misery and need all around us that we must continue and hopefully Increase. I did not say, but I am sure Sam knows anyway, that I desperately hope in time we can get Rebecca involved as well and do even more. When we return from the States I will start by discussing the problem of domestic abuse with her. Later I will gradually move to the public being justified in taking action. If she responds, as I expect, that she considers it necessary, then I will come clean and ask her to join us. It will be a risk but if I take it slowly I am sure all will be well. Even if she does not join us I am sure she will not condemn us. At least, as we are in love, she will not arrest me.

That was all for the future. We had to address the here and now, how are Sam and I going to reconcile our differences?

Sam made a brilliant suggestion which I immediately agreed to. She picked up on my own suggestion of some weeks ago which I admit that I had forgotten. We have not yet told Jacob about the increase our mission and that we have accomplished far more than he is aware of. We did not want to keep anything from him but previously we both felt that it would be better to discuss such a major topic in person. Sam said that we should tell him about it all, including the deaths, at the first opportunity. She proposed that then we ask Jacob for his opinion, not to arbitrate, but to tell us what he thinks. Does he think that we should escalate, row back or, I reluctantly agreed to this option being on the table, stop? We will then merge Jacob's conclusion with the one of ours that is closest to his and progress that way.

Jacob knows that we disposed of Robin and he agreed with us that had been essential. We all knew that unless he was stopped Sam would again be injured and probably killed. Who dies, Robin or Sam? It was a "no brainer." He was less enthusiastic about, but still supportive of, what was then only a vague suggestion, treatments of other offenders. He was aware of the possibility that some more may need to be disposed of, not simply persuaded, to protect us. He agreed with our rules for this but clearly thought they were theoretical and would not be needed. I assume that he guesses that we have done a few but not the number we have, now in the twenties. He does not know about the two further deaths, James and now Reagan. Those I definitely wanted to discuss with him face to face. We both love and trust Jacob. There is no doubt that he is a deep and clear thinker as well as a man of action. We will both be happy with his recommendation. I do admit to myself, though I suspect Sam thinks it also, that he is likely to be closer to my view.

We drove through the Californian sun to lunch in a vineyard that Jacob knows. The orange trees slipped lazily by then we started to climb in the mountains towards the winery. During the drive I mused on what we had to discuss with Jacob about the treatments. We had chosen not to do so yesterday as it would spoil the excitement of our overdue reunion. Sam and I agreed we will speak to him after lunch today.

I thought of Rebecca. It is now Sunday night for her. We have exchanged several emails. I thought of 'phoning but she may be getting an early night. She has not mentioned work in her emails so I think she must have finally had a relaxing day. I was in the rear seats of the car and turned from the window to look at my lovely siblings in front. I had subconsciously realised that they had gone quiet. I found the reason is that Sam has turned to look at me, actually that should be smirk at me. Jacob is grinning at me in the mirror.

'What.'

They screamed with laughter. Jacob said to Sam, 'I wonder what he is thinking of?' For some reason they both found this hysterically funny and they roared together.

Sam said, 'shall we guess?'

Together they shouted, 'Rebecca.' That was followed by yet more laughter.

Jacob then said, 'bloody hell sis. Look, he is blushing.' Again this was found most amusing. Then to me, more seriously, 'Luke, I can't wait to meet this woman. On the zooms we have had and from the media briefing she gave after the raid, that I caught on the net, she looks gorgeous and seems very professional.'

Sam interrupted, 'I have to admit that in the flesh she looks even better and in action she is ruthlessly proficient. She is like bloody superwoman. I hate her.' Jacob smiled at

Sam. He knows what she really thinks.

Lunch was sublime. We sat outside under a canopy of vine with dappled light across the crisp white tablecloth. The vineyard basked in the sun and stretched away up the slope in front of us. Beyond the vines misty blue-grey peaks interlocked in the distance and birds of prey circled in the turquoise sky. The food and wine were sublime. I had a perfectly grilled marinated chicken, a herby salsa, along with a delicious salad with multiple ingredients that I did not even know the name of but they all exploded with differing, lovely tastes. There was a crisp chardonnay from the grapes before us. The coffee was strong and deliciously bitter. The waiters and all of the other guests were slim. Were it not for the accents I would have thought that I was in France. There were no quadruple burgers heaped with chips being consumed by fatties here.

I asked Jacob, 'why is it that this place is so different from the usual America? It appears so European.'

'A lot of rich execs from Silicon Valley who have worked in Europe come here.'

Sam chipped in, 'like you that is.'

Jacob smiled, then his face went more serious, 'I think this is a good time to discuss whatever it is you wish to raise with me.' Sam and I looked at each other. Nothing, simply nothing gets past our perceptive half-brother. Like Sam, he is incisively intuitive. He is the perfect person to ask.

Sam indicated that I should speak. We leaned forward so that we could discuss it privately. I gave a report of what we have been doing along with what I hope was an accurate and fair description of the differing positions that Sam and I hold. Certainly she nodded in agreement with everything I said about her feelings. Jacob listened with his usual concentration and in silence. At times he smiled, at times he looked serious. On occasions he looked horrified. By the end I had no idea what he was thinking.

Finally I finished. Jacob sat back and looked dumbfounded. 'Well, I did not expect that.' He paused, looked at the mountains and then reluctantly back at us. 'My chief concern is that whatever I say, I will fall out with one of you.'

Sam reached quickly across, grabbed his hand and, looking at him intently, said, 'no Jacob, absolutely not. Luke and I have not fallen out over this and nor will we. We do not want you to arbitrate. We want your opinion and we will then compare it with ours and follow the best possible compromise. It is likely that neither of us will be entirely in agreement with you and the two of us are certainly poles apart. However Luke and I will not fall out either with each other or with you over this. We want your opinion to help us. I hope that between the three of us we are able to ascertain the best way forward.'

'Jacob, I agree completely with what Sam has said. Let's face it; there is no way any of us will ever fall out.'

We sat quietly as we all processed what has been said. I had amazed myself. What I said at the end is so true yet I have never before expressed it even to myself. We are so close. With one dad and three mothers between us we are genetically not as close as most brothers and sisters. In spite of this, possibly because of this, we are rock solid together.

Eventually Jacob spoke. 'I am completely reassured that we will not fall out. I would not arbitrate but I am happy to give my own opinion for you to use as you wish. It is a very complex problem. I need to consider the morality, the legality, what is best for you and what is best for the community. I need to think on it. You are here for the week; let's not mention it again until the day before you leave. I will answer you then.'

I sat back relieved. That is an excellent response and what I had hoped for.

Jacob restarted, 'the central question is that, is what you are doing merely vengeance or is it retribution or restitution? Whichever it is; I can immediately see that you are missing something important so I will be at least suggesting some alteration.' Sam and I looked at him with respect and anticipation. 'You are missing prevention. Surely that is the most important? If all that you undertake is clandestine then this wider effect will not apply. I appreciate the need to keep your activity under the radar, even so, you are missing an opportunity.'

My little brother never fails to impress and surprise me.

CHAPTER 26
REBECCA: THE MILES PORTON SHOW

The limo driver held the door for me as I slipped in whilst thinking, "this is a first." Then I remembered; it is actually a second. I can count Max Caruthers and his chauffeur, John, driving me back from the cell as a ride in a limo, if not a conventional one. Today's driver introduced himself as Mick and he said that he had been asked to collect Ms Watkins as well, but, not to worry, we will be at the studio on time. I thought, "no Mick, that is not my worry. If I ask nicely can you make us late, say an hour late so that I will arrive when it is over?" I slid onto the vast soft seat and I immediately found an unexpected advantage in a limo. My uniform will not get creased. I had it tailored a couple of weeks ago and I spent much of this afternoon ironing it, regretting that I had not had sufficient warning which would have enabled me to arrange for a professional pressing. Though I mostly wear my track suits at work I have to admit that I feel good in my uniform. I want to be seen as a policewoman and I am proud to be a senior one. I would only ever admit it to myself but the dark blue compliments my light blond hair and the fitted jacket and skirt show my figure in a good light.

I need to look my professional best and to summon all of my confidence for the coming evening. The Chief

Constable had 'phoned me first thing this morning. I now think, ironically of course, "what a wonderful start to a Monday morning." She was very chirpy and bright as she told me there is something I need to do this evening. Great, I then thought, I wondered how I was going to fill my time. Little did I know than that a mountain of paperwork along with the start of a major investigation would be the least of today's problems. She was delighted to tell me that I am to appear on the Miles Porton TV chat show. 'You know,' she had said with a flirty laugh, 'your favourite presenter, the one who was ridiculed by us in the media briefing and you later publically savaged him in the discussion.' She was laughing but also warning me to watch my back. She told me who the three co-panellists were to be. Thankfully, Amber Watkins from the refuge is one, we had bonded well during the march last night. There is another I prefer not to think of and final one that I have never heard of.

I tried to argue that it would be better for her to represent the force. She firmly and quickly replied, she had anticipated my plea and that there were two problems with such a suggestion. Firstly they had asked specifically for me as I was on last night's news. Secondly, she would have volunteered me anyway. Thanks. The only good news was that she had secured some seats for other officers in the audience, but only four, apparently Amber had already commandeered a huge number for her people.

I wanted to talk to her about the other events over the weekend. Not the realisation of serial criminals at work, nor the media briefing and the march. I tried to ask her about Julian's computer development and the new idea that I had floated but unfortunately there was not time. She only said that there was to be yet another media briefing regarding those on Tuesday but, not to worry, she will undertake that as I am so busy. Great, she has bagged the easy and good one.

I thought of Luke, it is five pm for me, early morning for him. He will be having an early breakfast at the conference, his first day. I wish that I was there, with him. I wish that he was here, next to me now. He would encourage me and give me the strength to face, in a short two hours' time, the odious creep who is no doubt out for revenge. That sleaze ball Miles Porton will certainly attack me for the trick played on him at my first media briefing when the DCI made it seem as if he was me. Then, I tore into him later. Finally, when I arranged for last Saturday's briefing at ten am he would have been on his radio show and so could not come. The other papers and presenters scooped him. It was completely unintentional, I was not to blame, I simply had not thought of him. If I had I would have made double sure that it was when he was not available.

As we approached a leafy lane on the outskirts Mick said, 'we will be at Ms Watkins's in two minutes.' I thanked him and then I thought, "bloody hell, this looks posh." For some reason I had imagined her in a city centre Victorian terrace, like me I suppose. I had never met her before Saturday when she introduced herself after the briefing. With the emails and texts we have exchanged all over the weekend, seeing her on the march yesterday evening and our meeting earlier today, in a mere three days I feel that we have become friends.

Mick drove up the long drive to the largest house in a manicured road of big, discreet properties. Before he could get out to knock on the front door or to hold the car door for her, Amber came out, strode over and stepped into the car. I heard Mick softly inhale. She looks lovely. She is expensively dressed in a dark power suit witha long double ring of heavy pearls and she is immaculately groomed. She is tall, taller than me, heavy set but not fat and she has strong features. I sense that there are two sides to her. Over the weekend I found her to be a sensitive, gentle soul. For the march she had dressed for that role in a comfortable jumper and loose jeans. I previously suspected, and her walk and appearance tonight is confirming it, that she is also a formidable woman. Not one to cross. As she said hello she leaned across and kissed me on the cheek. I am pleased to find that she feels as close me as I do with her. I said, 'Amber, you look great, and your house is superb.'

'Why thank you, for both compliments. And you look very sexy. That uniform really suits you. I am not sure if it is meant to make you look sexy but it does.'

'Thank you as well; with what we are facing I think a little pre show mutual admiration will help. Porton will not be on our side.'

To my surprise Mick chipped in, 'yea, everyone at the studio can't stand him and his nasty carping.' Amber and I looked at each other a little taken aback. 'I saw you two ladies on the TV news, yu' no, the footage from the march yesterday. We are all looking forward to you shreddin' 'im.' We laughed conspiratorially with him. 'Sorry, I should not speak but I had to tell you how all of us behind the scenes people admire what you are doing and what we think of Miles Plonker. You will be fine but if you need a stiffener that mahogany box in front of you is a drinks cabinet'. We grinned at each other, both realising that Porton is nicknamed Plonker. It suits him perfectly.

Open mouthed we leaned forward looking like naughty schoolgirls and lifted the heavy, inlaid lid. It is full. Gin, whisky, champagne, and there are delicate, cut glass flutes and tumblers. I said, 'thanks Mick but I dare not go on TV plastered.'

Amber said, 'nor me but can we drain it on the way home?' He smiled and nodded.

Changing the subject I asked Amber, 'that is a

beautiful house. Have you been there long?' Meaning of course, "are you married and what does he do?" We have not yet talked about personal issues.

'Fifteen years, ten with the shit and five perfect ones on my own.' That told me so much in one short sentence. 'Even better, it is now all mine. When I divorced him, as he was then in prison for beating me, I took him to the cleaners.' I saw in the mirror that Mick's eyebrows had shot up. He is no doubt thinking the same as me, "how can such a strong looking woman be abused?" 'I would not wish it on anyone, not even him, but better still for me he is now crippled with MS which came on whilst he was at, what was then, Her Majesty's pleasure. So I am not in fear of being attacked again as so many of the women in the refuge are.' With that we fell to chatting about domestic abuse for the remainder of the journey. Beforehand, as a police officer, as an empathic woman, I had thought that I was up to speed on the subject. By the time we arrived both I, and the earwigging Mick, were nearly in tears. It hardened my resolve.

I desperately wish that I could tell Amber what the Chief Constable is going to announce tomorrow. I cannot. It would leak. She would have to tell some of the other women who would have to tell others and so on. If I were her in that situation I could not keep it to myself. I barely can now.

We were ushered into an ante-room to meet our co-panellists. Amber knew their names but had not met them. On entering she looked over and quietly asked me, 'who is that tall, gorgeous one?' When I had Googled him this afternoon I thought he was good looking but in the flesh even more so. I led her over an introduced her to the one I know and then both of us introduced ourselves to the other. 'Good evening Dr Wynn-Davis, good to see you again. This is Amber Watkins from the women's refuge.' Amber shook his hand with clear distaste. He ignored mine and scowled.

Clearly it is not only Porton I have to be wary of tonight. Turning to the other I said proffering my hand, 'you must be Professor Liam Dicks, the Professor of Philosophy who will make sure that we do not commit any thinking errors this evening.'

He is handsome. He looks studious, that is not surprising for a Professor of Philosophy I suppose. There is a melancholic, wistful air about him. I was about to introduce myself when he said, 'and you are the famous Detective. Please call me Liam.' I said to call me Rebecca as he turned to shake Amber's hand. 'Ms Watkins, I recognise you from the weekend's news. May I call you Amber?' I saw a surge of mutual attraction hit them both as they held hands together for longer than usual. I know that it is possible to generate a static charge from rubbing amber. He received a shock just taking her hand, so did she. Amber managed to splutter "of course" and called him Liam. I saw Amber look at his left hand, so did I. Bugger, she will miss out, he is married.

Windbag clearly was having nothing to do with this informality and would only be happy with Doctor Wynn-Davis, or sir, or best of all, god.

Another man came over and introduced himself as Richard Jones the producer. He is charming but when he mentioned his husband Windbag looked down his nose and stomped off to the bar. I was enjoying chatting to Richard and, probably intentionally, his banal chatter was calming me.

Amber and the Prof had stepped a little away and seem to be getting on very well. I hope that she has seen his ring. I half heard their conversation turning to the tonight's subject of domestic abuse. Windbag came back with a drink, only one for himself of course, and rudely pushed past Richard to join them.

A conversation ensued and I heard the Prof say

that it was necessary to understand that most of the abusers had been abused themselves. Windbag chipped in with a comment about the men always being blamed. I already know that Amber is understandably very cross that insufficient criminal proceedings are being brought against abusers. I can see that the attitude of these two is riling her and Liam is diminishing in her eyes. Her anger may be heightened by already being nervous regarding tonight. Though she is clearly very attracted to the Prof this is too much. He made another short comment that I did not catch and I saw Amber switch instantly from her previous almost simpering to near incendiary. Thankfully at that moment Richard looked at his watch and shouted that it was time to go in. Amber was separated from the rest of us by the crew rushing in. I could not get to her to calm her down but nor could she get to Windbag and the Prof to resume her onslaught. This, along with Plonker who is no doubt out for revenge, does not bode well for this evening's show which, even worse, is going out live at prime time.

I stepped into the studio and my heart sank. It is terrifying. On the TV it looks cosy. In reality I now see that it is vast with the set in the middle and multitudes of staff scurrying around offstage. There is a triangular set. The front seats for the audience form one side with a gap in the middle marked "camera only.". The panel sits along two sides. Porton, or as I will now think of him after Mick's comment, Plonker, sits in grandeur behind a vast desk at the apex of the set and front on to the auditorium. Either side of him are the chairs for the panel, no desks for us. We are in pairs side on to the audience.

The auditorium itself slopes steeply up and curves around in a parabola. The mid-point of the triangle formed by the set is the focus of the parabolic audience arena. The part that Plonker obviously enjoys most is the beginning and end of his shows. He steps with full pomp and circumstance up to this central point of the triangle, literally at the focus of the audience's gaze. From there he gives his opening and closing five minute tirades.

With a tremble I estimated that there must be at least two hundred seats. It feels as if there are as many cameras.

The audience is filing in and as the seats fill so does my apprehension. Four of my new, lovely, female detectives have made the trip and are sitting at the front giving me smiles and thumbs up. They can see I am becoming terrified. To the rear on the right there is a large group of women who came in together. They are carrying placards and won the fight with the staff, insisting on keeping them. I recognise many of them from the march and they look like trouble. Top left I spotted a well-dressed couple coming in hand in hand. As they stepped under a light I saw to my astonishment that it is the Chief Constable and the Commander. They are either out of the closet or they do not think they will be recognised. Of course neither of them is in uniform so I will have no support from that quarter if there are any unpleasant questions.

Plonker is sitting in his chair behind his desk, ignoring his panel and barking at the staff. A make-up girl is putting vast amounts of slap on his face which, now close to him for the first time, I can see that he desperately needs. He is wearing several heavy rings which are glinting in the floodlights. His very being shrieks vanity and avarice. He is being constantly rude to the make-up artist and eventually openly shouted at her and she scurried away in tears. This is a repeat of what happened at the media briefing. He is clearly always the same. No wonder the crew hate him. After she composed herself she came down to me, looked at me and said, 'with your lovely complexion you don't need any.'

'Thank you for the compliment, it means a lot coming from a professional such as you.' This acknowledgement of her work coming after the treatment she has just received obviously went down as well as it was intended. 'Any way I am surprised that you have any left after filling in all of Plonker's cracks.' She laughed loudly, I am not sure at what I said or finding that I know the nickname. I nodded across the stage, 'he is known as Windbag. You will also need a lot for him and do take a long handled brush to get all the dandruff off his jacket.'

Laughing again she squeezed my shoulder saying, 'I can't wait to see this show. You are going to be tremendous.' I hope that she is correct. I certainly feel stronger after that exchange.

Richard came over as men started moving chairs, 'OK Rebecca, his highness wants you over on his right on your own. Amanda is going to be between the two men opposite you.' I looked across and saw that Amber is still fuming. I am being set up and a confrontation on the opposite side is brewing.

'Richard, I strongly recommend that you do not put Amber between them. There may be a row. I would like to swop with her or for her to re-join me here.'

'Sorry Rebecca, I agree with you but I have to follow Plon... Mr Porton's behest.' He saw me grin at his near slip. He realised that I know what he had been about to say. With a shrug he added, 'what sir wants, sir gets.'

I stood and walked past an astonished and now concerned Richard and I had the temerity to approach sir's desk. A tall skinny camera woman is adjusting her shots on a preening Plonker. Behind her green hair, nose piercings, dungarees and boots, I can see a sexy, competent, professional. Plonker is shouting at her as he had at the make-up artist. I repeated my concerns and advice to him. He rudely waved me away with a dismissive, 'it is my show.'

I can do no more. As I turned, with a violent feeling

of a presupposition of disaster, I saw Amber sitting between the two men. She is close to them and at the same time she is brooding apart. Reluctantly I went across to my seat, on my own. It implies that I am in the naughty corner. So, there is a belligerent host, a pompous consultant, a professor who does not realise that he is in a minefield and a fuming, outspoken woman. Actually two, after Plonker's behaviour towards me and to his staff I am fuming as well.

I decided to calm myself in the same way that I prepare for a taekwondo tournament. I sat still, balanced and upright. I performed a mindful breathing exercise. As always it worked perfectly. The anger has dissipated and I am now serene. Too late I realise that I had also inadvertently prepared myself to attack which is what I mostly employ it for.

The red light came on. The show started.

Plonker ponderously came around his desk and strutted across the floor. He stood at the focal point of the audience parabola, at the middle of the set. The applause was muted to say the least and I spotted him bristle at that. The camera operated by the green haired woman was propelled to directly in front of him. The wide wall screens, out of the camera field, filled with a head and shoulders shot of him. Then followed from Plonker a five minute, ill informed, biased wittering on domestic abuse and how to deal with it. He obviously does not have a clue but he clearly considers himself to be an expert. Amber stifled a laugh as members of her group at the rear, to his right, cat-called his worst comments. He tried to ignore them but they are getting louder and he wisely said that it was time to start the debate. By that he meant that he could not deal with the heckling and he wanted an excuse to avoid it.

He finally managed a coherent couple of sentences in closing, 'we are here to debate the policing of domestic abuse.

Is it sufficient, or are vigilantes needed?'

It started very, very badly. He turned to me and he said, 'firstly I ask DI Beccy Fowler to give the girls point of view.' He gave a false laugh and added, 'I suppose in these PC times I should ask for the woman's point of view.'

The auditorium was silent. The only laugh had been his.

I turned to face him. I deliberately hesitated and at the same time I gave him my "Jenny Hill" look. The camera had switched to one behind him. On the screen above and further to his rear, out of shot and his view, I can see that it is focused on my face. No wonder he is looking concerned, I am frightening myself. 'I am Detective Superintendent Rebecca Fletcher and I am her to give the police's view. My gender has nothing to do with this debate.' My tone had been deliberately harsh. You could hear a pin drop.

He faltered, recovered and then as I had expected decided that attack was the best defence. That is only true if you are in a good position and competent to attack. 'Well, you are wearing a skirt. Surely you can speak as a woman as well.'

Perfect, he has stepped on a bear trap right at the beginning.

'And you are wearing trousers. Does that entitle you to speak as if "you wear the trousers?" Do you consider that mere gender entitles any one to treat another person in a different manner or for their opinions to carry more or less weight?' There were shrieks and cheers from Amber's group. Clapping broke out all around the auditorium.

Before he could recover I thought that I must immediately continue. This is a now a fight. At least that is one arena where I have more experience than him. Though he is a prat he is more seasoned in debate than I am. He will win if I allow him to recover and reply. I sharply continued, speaking over him as his mouth opened. 'I deliberately used the word entitle twice in my questions to you. That is the nub of the matter. In the police we can only act after a crime has been committed. Then the woman, it is not always a woman but in the cases we are discussing tonight all have been, the woman will have already been harmed, always psychologically, often physically. A major contributing factor in this is a pervasive male thought pattern that engenders a feeling of entitlement towards women, including the presumed entitlement to use violence.' I managed to avoid adding, "such a thought pattern as we have just been forced to listen to from you."

I had to breathe and he took the opportunity to interrupt. He sneered, 'you are a police officer. Surely it is beyond your remit to talk about psychology.'

Every repost that he is attempting simply deepens the hole that he does not yet fully realise he is in.

'You are completely wrong.' I managed to bite my tongue and not to say "as usual." I deliberately paused, hoping that he would deliver yet more ammunition to me. For once he wisely kept his own counsel and I was forced to continue. However, there were smirks all around, the occasional whoop, and he is now a puce colour. 'Not only do I see the psychological effects every day but also I have a Doctorate in forensic psychology. I practiced as such before joining the police.' The surprised audience are tittering and I can see the set staff holding their mouths to stifle laughs. He is clearly astonished and wrong-footed.

He decided he had had enough and tried to sidestep me. 'Well, let's ask Ms,' he heavily stressed the Ms, 'Amber Watkinson who is the manager of a refuge. Perhaps she can give a gir..... woman's perspective?'

Amber bristled and said, 'most people call me Amber but you may call me Ms Watkins. I do not know a Watkinson.'

Thank god the camera is now on her not me. I cannot suppress a wide grin and many in the audience are again laughing. 'As the CEO of a charity that deals with domestic abuse, and in addition maintains a women's refuge, I agree with DS Fletcher.' In return she heavily stressed the DS and the sarcasm was not lost. 'As a woman, but presently wearing trousers, perhaps I will be allowed to give a gender neutral point of view?' Most in the auditorium, including the staff, are now smirking or openly laughing. That is all except Plonker and, I see now, also Windbag. They do not like the current direction. Amber continued, 'Society simply does not take domestic violence seriously. I have been in close contact with Rebecca, that is DS Fletcher,' she did not add, "only for three days." I silently gave thanks for that, 'and I know that we have her full support............'

To the fury of the audience Plonker interrupted again. 'Well, clearly the women,' the bastard deliberately pronounced it as wimmin, 'are in cahoots. Perhaps we can get another perspective. Professor Dicks, you are a Professor of Philosophy, what is the morality of the vigilante behaviour which the ladies are encouraging.'

Amber and I shouted simultaneously, 'we said no such thing.'

'By implication.' Before we could interject again he spoke loudly, 'Professor please continue.'

Liam Dicks looked at Amber with a mixture of concern and apology. He is clearly uncomfortable with being used as an excuse to shut her up. Though exasperated she indicated that he should speak.

He sat back and gave a reasoned philosophical analysis discussing the differences between vengeance, retaliation, retribution, restitution and restoration. He addressed the rights of both parties stressing that the abuser has rights as well. He was allowed to continue uninterrupted, that is not interrupted by Plonker. Amber was getting increasingly restless. She is clearly in agreement with the shouted interruptions from her group. Cries of "what about the women," and, "how are you going to stop the beatings," grew more frequent and louder. Plonker is of no help. His patronising comments to "calm down" are making matters worse. After a while I realised that he is deliberately inflaming them.

Dicks made an excellent philosophical analysis but that is a grave error in this tense context. He is a great speaker and an excellent philosopher but he would be a useless policeman. Then it became even more dangerous. He changed tack and commenced a perfectly accurate discussion on the origins of male violence. He suggested that we should be more understanding as so many of the perpetrators had been victims themselves. That is a perfectly valid point, relevant but not the most appropriate in the present circumstances. He is clearly completely unaware that the mood of the whole room is as if tectonic plates that are grinding together are about to split apart, an earthquake is starting. Amber is at the epicentre.

Then I saw Amber look with concern up at her group. I followed her gaze and to my horror I spotted several standing and moving to the isle. Amber interrupted, clearly trying to calm them, 'Professor, if you are an apologist for such behaviour are you not letting down the thousands of men who suffered violence as children yet do not beat their wives. They are undoubtedly the majority. Should you not condemn the minority even if in the past they had been victims?'

Dicks started to reply, 'Yes, I did not mean to be an apologist, merely..........' He stopped abruptly as he followed her gaze and looked up at the audience. Amber had failed. More than thirty of her group had left their seats and are streaming down the aisles, waving placards like weapons.

They are intent on a stage invasion.

I caught the eyes of my detectives at the front and I waved my hand across in the direction of the end of the set. Thankfully they immediately understood and they leapt to their feet and turned to face the audience, standing in a too widely spaced line across the bottom end of the slope of seats. They stood firm and held out their warrant cards. The female detectives in the station, in fact most of the men as well but less stylishly, have copied my designer track suit style. They looked well but practically dressed, well-groomed and, confident. No wonder Twitter had developed the moniker for them which had been taken up by all of the Sunday papers yesterday. It was appropriate, they look magnificent.

It is hopeless. They are out-numbered eight to one.

As the women swarmed down towards them, Felicity, who is one of the central pair of detectives, stepped not backwards but forwards into the fray. Felicity, what a name that is for her? She looks more like one of the Valkyries than a Felicity. She opened her arms wide and instead of attempting to repel the women she hugged the first two. All of the others stopped dead in astonishment.

Felicity spoke to the women in a voice loud enough for all of them to hear, loud enough for me to hear as I am on the same side of the auditorium, but thankfully not loud enough to be detected by the microphones. 'Please don't invade the set. I have a better idea.' That is a request not an order. Good thinking but will it work? 'Rebecca will do a much better job of shredding those prats than I could or your stage invasion will. Let's go back to your seats and enjoy her routing them.' Knowing smiles broke out amongst the women and encouraging nods from the people sitting near enough to have heard. They all walked back to the rear seats, including Felicity who is still arm in arm with the ringleaders.

Clapping started at the rear. I looked up and in doing so I spotted the Chief Constable returning to her seat. She is still holding her warrant card out. She had been on her way to support. The clapping was coming from the Commander, as a male he had wisely kept sitting and out of the way. A man in the line would have had the opposite effect. All of the audience joined in and they started clapping and cheering. Plonker looks disappointed.

I breathed a sigh of relief, excitement over. The thin blue line had held, even though none of them are wearing blue. The cameras which had followed the stampede returned to focus on us all on the set.

The clapping died away and Porton is preparing to speak. I spoke first stopping him and he glared at me, 'Mr Porton,,' I winced, not because of Porton but because my face again filled the side screens, 'you are on record for criticising the police, calling us heavy handed, in fact you have also used the word brutal. Would you like to comment on how the "Armani Army" have just saved your show if not your skin? There are a mere seven police officers in the room and yet we, mainly the four "wimmin," I could not resist pronouncing it in that manner, 'at the front, prevented a stage invasion by an understandably infuriated group who outnumbered them eight to one. Now you have some facts to hand, do you wish to amend your opinion?'

He glared again but he was unable to respond as jeers and catcalls directed at him drowned him out. When they settled he chose to move on even though there were continued calls of "answer the question." After several attempts he finally made himself heard, 'we have not yet had the benefit of Dr Wynn-Davis's opinion. Let us hear the medical view. Dr Wynn-Davis.'

Windbag scowled at me, then at Amber and then at the women to the rear of the audience. He is clearly not happy with how the evening is progressing. He puffed himself up and he started in his usual condescending manner. 'We need to be clear about one thing, that these women,' he looked down his nose as he said women and clearly directed it towards the ones present, 'need to realise that men and women are different. Men may, at times, act and respond differently.' My heart sank. So far he has not actually said anything wrong but I fear where he is heading. He is going to precipitate another charge and if so it will be unstoppable. 'Today's women seem to want it both ways. They want strong men yet they want to be treated as if the men they are with are eunuchs.' The howls started at the rear. Please shut up you old fool. Amber has gone from having calmed down through being merely cross back to being incandescent. 'If you are with a strong man and you do something silly and antagonise him, what do you expect? A little slap is understandable.'

The howls turned to shouts and through them I can hear Felicity pleading for calm. The women started to get to their feet again. There is no hope this time Felicity.

Everyone was suddenly silenced as Amber sprang to her feet and whirled around to face the two men. Her movement was aggressive. She towered over them. The men instinctively moved to the edge of their seats and looked simultaneously precarious and apprehensive. The audience immediately fell silent, gripped by what is unfolding. Amber swung her right arm back and up.

Oh no, please don't.

I started to stand but there is no way I can be there in time. Amber swung and slapped Windbag squarely on the cheek. It was not a hard blow but with the surprise and him being unbalanced anyway he crashed full length on the floor.

With her arm now across her chest she turned to look at Professor Dicks. I can see what is coming. I am now already half way across the stage but I still will not make it. He is still on the edge of his chair, unbalanced, looking at her with amazement but not moving. Her backhand slap caught him across the cheek. He also toppled of the chair and similarly ended up full length on the floor.

I reached Amber a split second too late. I put my hand to her shoulder to restrain her but it was now drooping, soft. There will be no more attacks from her, I think, I hope. She spoke softly to me, 'please let me speak Rebecca.'

'No more slaps.'

'Of course.' I kept my hand on her, just in case.

The men had staggered to their knees but as she turned to address them they froze in that position. She spoke softly but clearly. The audience was silent, still, spellbound. The microphones picked up her words and all can hear her.

'That is what it is like to be slapped. That is what I had to face at home every night for ten years until my ex-husband was finally arrested. That is what many of the women here with me have to face every night. Some will return home from here to receive the same this evening. While you are tucked up in your little jim-jams sipping your cocoa they will be suffering something similar to that. The differences for them are that it will be harder; it will be a fist; it will be in their own home; there will not be a police officer in the room; it will not be on this one occasion but all the time. What would you think if that happened to you?'

She turned to Windbag. 'What would you think of that Dr Windbag?' Bloody hell, she has not heard that before, at least not form me. She has immediately come to the same understanding and obvious nickname. 'Would you find it so perfectly understandable then?' He could not hold her gaze.

She then turned to the Professor. 'And what do you think Professor Limp Dick?' The play on his name raised a few sniggers. His reaction is different. He held her gaze resolutely. 'Would you discuss the erudite permutations with your attacker?'

Amber's shoulders slumped and she looks lost. She is finished. She is not going to attack either of them again. I started to lead her away with the intention of swopping seats with her. A call came from behind us. 'You asked me a perfectly reasonable question. Please allow me the opportunity to reply.' We turned back to face the Professor as he staggered to his feet holding on to the chair for support. Windbag took the opportunity to do the same.

Dicks continued, 'Ms Watkins, would you please accept my fulsome apology? I deserved that slap. I can see that it was meant as instructive, not as an assault. I wish it was allowable for me to do the same with some of my students.' Amber gave a winning smile and many in the audience tittered. Is this evening going to get any odder? He apologised to her. Surely that is backwards. He continued, 'I thought that I was here to discuss the philosophy of the issues. I am, I was correct to raise all the points I did. I do not retract any of them. They were factually correct. However I was wrong in that I only addressed the philosophy. There is a place for all the hot air and there is a place to stop theorising. Even Ivory Tower academics need to concede that there is also a time to step into the real world and make a useful comment, hopefully to contribute to a good decision leading to the better course of action. I correctly undertook the former and I failed to address the later. Your passion and fully understandable instructive action has shown me my error. I am sorry. Will you forgive me?'

Cheers of support rang out. Amber stepped forward. I let her go, the threat has dissipated. She said "of course" but given the cheering only the Prof and I could hear her. She shook his hand. He pulled her towards him and he embraced her. She overcame her shock and quickly kissed him on the cheek in exactly the spot she had so recently struck.

I moved in again to lead her away but he held on to her hand and turned to address Windbag while still holding her. He is not finished. 'My late wife was a general practitioner.' So, like Julian, he is another handsome professional who is a widower. The loss of his wife explains his bereft air. 'Through her I met many other medical practitioners. I have never heard any of them spout such misogynistic bilge such as that which we have heard tonight from Dr Wynn-Davis. I assure the audience that his antiquated opinions do not reflect those of the majority of his profession.'

Windbag went the colour of a beetroot. He looks as if he is going to pass out. I hope that one of my team is good at CPR; I am useless at all first aid. I could not see his reaction as I lead Amber to my previous seat. I then returned to take her original one as the audience applauded.

As I sat back, now between the two men, Windbag found his voice. He turned to face me and went on the offensive. 'Do your job why don't you? That woman assaulted me. You should arrest her.' I completely ignored him and I serenely looked at the audience. I saw the camera had now again focussed on my face. I am getting quite good at acting the emotions to suit the point I am making. My Jenny Hill look stops everyone. Now I look as if I am in a spa.

Plonker joined in the attack. 'Well, it is your turn to answer the question. Are you going to arrest Ms Watkins?'

'No.'

When he finally realised that I am not going to elaborate he said, 'why not. There was an assault. It is your duty to arrest her.'

I now tried a condescending schoolmarm look. The camera has cut from him back to me. It is working. 'If you had been watching you would have seen me do my job.' He spluttered but I talked over him. 'I assessed the situation and in order to control it I put myself in harm's way in the centre, as the other officers did earlier. I acted in the same way that so many police do every day. Mostly, the only thanks they get is the condemnation heaped on them by carping commentators.' Now there are two beetroot coloured men on stage. 'I judge that there is no current further risk but I am continuing to monitor the situation.'

He barked, 'so there is no way that you are going to arrest this assailant.' He rudely jerked his thumb at Amber.

'No, that is not the case. There are two circumstances in which I will consider an arrest.' That drew hisses from the rear but a look of intrigue from Amber. She has correctly read that I have laid a trap.

'Plonker stepped on another mine, 'well, tell us. What are they?'

'The first is if the Crown Prosecution Service direct me to then I will arrest Ms Watkins. I have no doubt that they will want to review the footage of tonight's show with me tomorrow.' I did not say that I also have no doubt they will quietly direct me to thank Amber. 'If they instruct that I arrest Ms Watkins then I will recommend to them that we also arrest you, Mr Porton.' I so nearly slipped and said "Mr Plonker."

'What for, I have done nothing wrong?'

'You could be charged with aiding and abetting. Prior to the show I attempted to undertake the most satisfying aspect of police work, prevention. I had spotted the risk of conflict in the seating plan that you were insisting upon. I drew this to your attention. You brushed me aside in a manner suggesting that you were encouraging a situation that could lead to an assault. In fact this may be easily proven. The cameras were being tested at the time I gave this advice and it may have been recorded.' The woman with the green hair gave a big grin and a thumbs up. She is behind Plonker but the audience can see her and a cheer rocked the seats. There is no way such a charge would stick but it would be fun to try.

Now we have three men on the set the colour of beetroot. The Prof is beetroot coloured with an internal struggle as he fights to maintain composure. He is shaking next to me as he tries to suppress his laughter. Amber is in tears of mirth.

When it had a calmed I continued. They have all obviously forgotten that there is a second reason. 'The other reason I would arrest her is to give her publicity for the wonderful work she undertakes and the much needed campaign she runs. I am sure the charge would either not stick or that she would only receive a minor caution. Professor Dicks has said himself that it was an instructive slap, not an assault.' He vigorously nodded in agreement while at the same time beaming across the set to Amber. She blushed and tried to cover her delight. I continued, 'the righteous furore any such arrest would undoubtedly unleash would bring much welcome publicity to her essential, yet often unrecognised, work. I am certain that the opinion of the majority of people would be favourable to her and I can live with the adverse comments that would be made about me.'

Then followed a few minutes of meaningless bluster from Plonker. He is trying to rescue his position by throwing Windbag to the dogs. I realised that he is going to do all in his power to stop Amber and I speaking again. Good, I have made my points.

I looked across the audience and caught the Chief's eye. She started waving frantically at me. When she had my attention she started gesticulating. With one hand she is mimicking a camera rolling and with the other a mouth open and closing. Next to her the Bear is waving, his hands are in front of him turned palms up and he is pumping them up and down. He seems to want me to stand. They seem to want me to speak to the camera. I have absolutely no idea what they want me to say.

Richard came around out of camera shot and held up five fingers to Plonker and, at the same time, pointed to the audience focal point with his other hand. I guess that we are five minutes from the end and it is time for Plonker's strutting wind up.

Plonker started to stand but a button of his jacket caught on his chair. He leaned to free it and as he did so it struck me what the Chief and the Bear want me to do.

I sat up and said loudly, 'I wish to make an announcement.'

Plonker froze and looked horrified, clearly thinking "how dare that woman speak in when I am about to give the country the benefit of my wisdom." Richard looks delighted, he frantically waved at me to stand. As I did so he even more wildly indicated I should go to the front to where Plonker stands for his summation.

I quickly strode across the set. As I moved I spotted that Plonker has freed himself but it is clear I will be in his spot before him. All he can do is to sit down again. I have literally upstaged him.

I saw on the side screen a camera to the left had tracked me walking across the stage. As I did so the green haired woman, who is driving an enormous camera on an electrically powered stand, raced around in front of the audience and took up position directly before me. As I started to speak a red light situated on top of her camera flicked on and my head and shoulders shot filled the screen on the wall and no doubt the screens in peoples' homes.

I instantaneously froze, aware that there are two hundred people here but hundreds of thousands watch this show at home. I used my technique to calm me and to help direct my attention. Who to address now? Amber, I will speak to Amber. She is behind me but she will see me looking at her from the screen. I will speak to her in the same manner we spoke in the limo on the way here. I will speak softly, calmly, but with total candour.

I started; my initial freezing had been so brief that I hope that it had appeared as a deliberation. 'I wish to make an announcement regarding the handling of domestic abuse and vigilante abductors in the station that I am responsible for. The Chief Constable will give full details in her media briefing scheduled for tomorrow at ten am. She has indicated that I give an outline tonight.' God, I hope that is correct. I glanced at her and both she and the Bear were giving me thumbs up.

'You are already aware that last Friday, within hours of the actions of serial abductors and possibly murderers being discovered I formed a specific team to hunt them down. This was in response to the need that had arisen.

Over the weekend, in consultation with the Chief Constable, in response to the need that the actions of Ms Watkins and her group have drawn attention to, the remit for this team has been modified.' The screen briefly changed to a shot of Amber's face from another camera. She is transfixed. Then it cut back to me.

'As I said before I regard prevention to be the pinnacle of best police practice. With regard to domestic abuse the various programmes, including anger management, alcohol restriction, the various step schemes and other programmes to alter gender entitlement ideas only occasionally work.

I am not criticising them. I support them. I am merely acknowledging that they unfortunately only have a limited effect.

Further I echo what Ms. Watkins said earlier. I would criticise the comments of some who apologise for these violent people, mainly men, by saying they were abused themselves. This is indeed correct but in concentrating on this we are letting down the majority of people who were themselves abused who control themselves and do not resort to violence.' The camera flicked to the Prof who is, thankfully, vigorously nodding. Then, yet again it is back on me.

'Given these limitations it is essential that we have a strong police and criminal justice response to such vicious crimes.' Applause started, I held up my hand. 'Thank you but please allow me to finish. I have several more points to make and our time is limited.

The remit of the new team has been extended and it will now include a zero tolerance programme for domestic abuse. This team will continue indefinitely, even after the abductors currently being hunted have been brought to justice.' I can see people starting to stand to applaud. I held up my hand. 'Please, bear with me, there are two more points.

Firstly, over the weekend the Chief Constable has been in contact with the Home Office and she has secured additional funding for this and a promise that, if our pilot scheme is successful, this will be rolled out across the country.' I had to hold up my hand again.

'Finally, when I tell you this please remember that this has all happened over only a forty eight hour time period. One of our PCs, who is a computer wizard, has developed an app to assist this work. This will be offered, free of charge, to any man or woman who has complained to us of abuse. The user does not need to make a call. If they are being threatened then all they need do is to tap on the app in a secret sequence coded to them. The app will send a distress call to the station with GPS location of the 'phone along with the name, address and description of both the victim and the suspected assailant. As well as alerting the desk sergeant a call will automatically be sent to the patrol car that the programme has detected to be the closest to the scene. The alerted officers will not stop until they have confirmed that the fearful person is safe. They have the authority to force entry if necessary.'

I drew breath for my conclusion, yet again having to hold up my hand to request to be allowed to finish. None of the people in the room can believe that there is yet more, that includes me. 'The action of the abusers is criminal. The abductors, possibly murderers, may invoke some distorted thinking in an attempt to justify their actions. Professor Dicks has shown their thinking errors. Our criminal justice system considers them common criminals. The European Council of Human Rights considers that such actions breach human rights. These people and their actions are vile. I will do all in my power to stop them.'

Richard had moved to stand next to the camera and waved at me. He held up ten fingers and started folding them over. That must mean there are ten seconds left.

'That is all. Thank you.' As the audience erupted I became aware that someone has moved next to me. I turned expecting to see a furious Plonker. It is Amber with tears of gratitude flowing down her face. She threw her arms around me. Out of the corner of my eye I saw Richard gesticulating for us to turn towards the camera. We turned to do so and I saw on the screen a full length shot of us embracing. The camera zoomed in to our faces, both smiling, Amber in tears. Richard is now down to three fingers. He held up his hand for us to remain motionless as he counted them down.

As his pinky folded over the red camera light and the

"on air" lights above the doors flicked off. The large wall screen went blank. Richard rushed forward and threw his arms around us saying, 'thank you, thank you, thank you, for the best show I have ever done.'

The camera woman joined in. In spite of the green hair and unusual clothing, I see that close up that she is gorgeous. She looks like a goddess. She said to Amber and me, 'you were wonderful.' She stopped embracing us to shake our hands saying, 'I'm Gemma, I am honoured to meet you.'

I asked her something that was bothering me. 'Gemma, have I got you in trouble mentioning that you were filming when I advised Mr. Porton to alter the seating?'

'Not at all. You have helped. He has been trying to get rid of me for ages, he would prefer a man. If he tries now a tribunal will skin him.'

Richard spoke, 'Gemma, have you?'

'Of course.' She held up a tablet and flicked through three still 'photos. There was one of me speaking to Plonker and him looking beetroot coloured, another of Amber standing over the men lying at her feet and lastly, Amber and I arm in arm smiling at the camera at the end. Looking at me she added, 'I have a group e mail list of all the major news feeds in the country. These photos along with a synopsis of the show have already gone to all of them and have been uploaded to our website with a full recording of the show.'

The Prof came up and joined us standing close to Amber and giving her a hug. The four detectives now also joined us and we all chatted. Jane said, 'you said seven police in the audience, who are the other two?'

Her timing was perfect. They all looked as I indicated behind them. The Chief and the Bear were coming to join us. I said, 'you know our Chief Constable.' Richard, Amber and Gemma's eyes widened, 'and this is Commander.........'

As I said Commander their mouths dropped and I thought that the detectives were going to bob a curtsey. The Bear interrupted me and stepping forward and embracing them said, 'tonight I am Rupert, not Commander Lightman. I am also very proud. You were wonderful. You too Laser, or should I say Tibs now?' All the police laughed and the others looked mystified at my nicknames.

Many of the audience had left. Plonker and Windbag had run as soon as the cameras had flicked off. There are only us, a few audience obviously known to the stage crew and the crew themselves. Even so it is at least thirty people. Richard clapped his hands for attention. 'As the visitors do not know let me explain the usual arrangement here. This set is mostly used for comedy shows. The reason the audience laugh like drains at the weak jokes in that show is that through there,' he pointed to double doors in the side wall, 'there is a free bar where we get them drunk beforehand.' Knowing sniggers went between the crew. 'Let us go there now. Plonker is paying from his budget although he will not know that until the end of the year.' Yet another cheer went up and we streamed through the doors.

The drinks flowed and everyone wanted to speak to me. That is almost everyone. I noted as the evening wore on that Amber and the Prof were sitting quietly to one side wrapped in each other's' attention.

To another side, in an equally quite area, sat Felicity and Gemma. I know Felicity is gay. At her interview she had said that she thought I should know and did I have any problem with it. I could have lost my job if I gave any indication that it was a factor but thankfully that is most certainly not the case. When I replied "does she have any problem with the fact I am not" she smiled. When I added that she faces the same sanctions as everyone else, no shagging in the station house, she guffawed so loudly it confirmed that she would be offered the post. I was standing close to Felicity and Gemma when the other three came over saying it was time to go for their train. They need to be back to prepare for duty tomorrow.

I chipped in, 'you were all brilliant tonight. Take the day off tomorrow in recognition of that.' They all smiled but Gemma leaned forward and whispered in Felicity's ear.

Felicity looked at her colleagues and said, 'you carry on, I will see you on Wednesday.'

They walked off laughing and saying, 'woo hoo, lucky girl.'

Gemma called, 'which one?'

They shouted back, 'both of you.'

Two relationships seem to have sprung up tonight. There must be something in this fevered atmosphere of the studio. I know that through it all I was and I still am aching for Luke. If he were here I would want to find a quiet area but not for only a chat. He will be starting his first day of conference about now. I will not tell him what has been going on for me until I have watched the footage of his keynote speech. He made me promise not to look at it on line but to wait for his return. I do not want to detract from what will be his undoubted success.

It is getting late. I finally spotted Mick at the bar where he is drinking only water. I indicated five minutes and he gave a thumbs up. Reluctantly I went to tell Amber it was time to leave. She may not be happy with that. She is still with the Prof. They are now arm in arm staring into each other's eyes and they have obviously been kissing. She spotted me coming. To the Prof she said, 'her comes mum.' To me she said, 'I know, I'm coming. Give me a minute.' Then she leaned across and fell into a passionate kiss with the Prof. I quietly exited and went to wait with Mick. Much more than a minute later she joined us.

We walked to the car but we were unable to speak as well-wishers stopped us every few yards. As he held the car door open Mick said, 'I was watching on the screen in the bar. You were bloody marvellous.' We thanked him and got in.

As soon as we hit the plush seats both of us unwound and fell back laughing. Eventually as the car softly moved off I turned to her and said, 'bloody hell Amber, I thought you were going to put your tongue down the Prof's throat at the end.'

'You weren't looking closely enough.'

'You didn't?'

'Well, only a little.' We clasped each other laughing again.

'Are you going to see him again?'

'Of course.'

'Are you going to sexually abuse him?'

'Of course.' We are now shaking so much we can barely speak.

'Will he want me to arrest you after all?'

'Of course not.'

After a couple of moments silence I ventured, 'not the best start was it, calling him limp dick.'

With a completely straight face she replied, 'I will soon sort that out.'

We collapsed laughing again. From the front Mick, weeping with laughter, said, 'will you two shut up. I am having difficulty driving.'

After another pause Amber asked, 'you are not wearing a ring. Do you have a significant other?' Blushing I nodded yes. She looked at me very carefully. 'You are in love aren't you?' After another nod she squeezed my hand and said, 'lucky girl.' Then she looked thoughtful and added, 'he is not with you tonight though. He is not married is he?'

'Oh no, he is in the States at a conference.'

'An international business man, more luck.'

'Not a business conference, a science one. He is a Professor of Earth Sciences.'

She dropped my hand and whirled to face me, 'tell me you are not shagging Luke Cape.' She saw the answer in my face. I realised she must have met Luke through Sam. 'You lucky sod. Every woman I know, including me, wants to shag him.'

CHAPTER 27 LUKE: UNRAVELLED

The taxi meandered up the hillside. It passed under a canopy of interlacing trees and between manicured gardens. Beyond white boundary fences I can glimpse impressive white villas; all with their panoramic views over the choked city. Fine homes, all spaced out and spacious whilst shimmering in the Californian sun. Behind me, I can see through the side window as the car twisted and turned as it rose higher and higher, is the demanding but vibrant metropolis that I am leaving for the last time of this visit.

I love it here. I will return, soon, maybe permanently. Ahead of me is Jacob's elegant hilltop home. In there are my lovely half-brother and half-sister along with the promise of dinner. We will all be together again on his terrace; unfortunately for the last time for this trip. We will no doubt discuss the job offer that I have received and what to do, whether to accept or not. Samantha is doing her best to appear neutral. She does not want to influence me but she is failing to hide her excitement. She wants to come to live here.

I thought back two days to the surreal hours after my keynote lecture. My presentation was good. Without bragging I can say, dispassionately, that it was very good as I am not taking sole credit for its success. Partly I had been extremely lucky in my research with an unexpected, serendipitous finding. Partly I had worked like hell assembling an excellent team of post grads and developing my discovery with them. I had tried to play down to the other delegates my part in the original observation. The Chair of the Session had responded by quoting Louis Pasteur, "in the fields of observation chance favours only the prepared mind." Judging from the applause given to me at the end the whole auditorium agreed.

After the plenary session and my keynote presentation all of us on the council retired to the Chancellor's palatial office. I thought for celebratory drinks. I thought that the reason for the attendance of the University Chancellor, who is from an unconnected department, was to honour the Earth Sciences Faculty for hosting an international meeting. I had noticed hints beforehand. I had thought that I may be approached on the subject today, our final day. I had not expected a job offer there and then, two days before the close. Nor had I expected the breadth and depth of the position. I half expected the specification, if indeed it came at all, to be as a professor and hopefully, just maybe, with tenure. To be offered both that and to be vice-chair of the department surpassed my wildest dreams. Though I am currently the chair of my present faculty the Californian department is twice the size and it has six times the budget. If I accept my professional kudos and influence will be much greater here to say nothing of the extended research possibilities. I caught myself thinking, "will." There is one matter outstanding which will have a major impact on my decision. I would perhaps be more accurate in thinking, "may."

My possible, hopefully, new colleagues are a delightful collection of caricatures as would be expected in a university in California. Along with two camp men, an elegant lesbian with boots, dungarees and green hair, one Hispanic whose brother runs a drug cartel and another who is a transvestite; there are two huge African-Americans with ripped muscles and backwards pointing baseball caps. I must tell Rebecca about the woman with green hair. To my surprise I find her elegant and alluring. I am sure Rebecca would as well if she ever saw anything like that in a professional woman. My, dare I say "my," my new colleagues do have one thing in common. They are all foremost scientists and highly respected in our field. They also each have a wicked sense of humour. I played to this. During my reply, after the job offer, I asked if I was to be the token straight white guy in keeping with Californian university political correctness. I bit my tongue thinking that it may be too edgy to make such comments until they know me better. Thankfully they all laughed. There I go again. I should think, "if in future they get to know me better." Mercifully the Chancellor insisted that I did not respond formally until I had returned to the U.K. and I have discussed it with my colleagues and family. I need to reply within two weeks. The faculty were disappointed not to hear my decision there and then but his insistence is helpful to me, it gives me time to talk to Rebecca. I do not want to give her a fait accompli. I had no need to discuss it with Sam and Jacob. I knew what they would say.

At least I had thought that I knew what they would say. I had seen that underneath they were wildly enthusiastic but they were trying to hide it. They only said, "oh, that's nice. You will have to think about that." My lovely siblings were trying not to pressurise me. They knew that I would want to consider and to talk to Rebecca. Their love, concern and diplomacy backfired; it made me want even more for us all to be together again.

That is the one difficulty that keeps coming to my mind as I near Jacob's beautiful home. What about Rebecca; can I persuade her to come? If not I will be torn. I would love to move to here and I know Sam would as well. All three of us half-siblings, who are closer than most full brothers and sisters, very much wish to be reunited. I would guess that Rebecca's amazing skills and C.V. would be transferable and that she would find policing here a satisfying challenge. But, will she consider it? Though it is early in our relationship we have become so close that I do not think I could leave her. After all, we are now officially in love. Can I turn down one of the best jobs in my field for her? The answer is abundantly clear, yes; but I do not want to. I hope that I do not have to choose.

As soon as I stepped through Jacob's front door I realised that there is something seriously wrong. The house is ominously quiet. Usually there is the noise of them cooking and chatting together with music playing in the background. This evening there is not a sound. I quickly moved through and, with a shock, found them sitting rigidly next to each other on the long leather sofa. Sam has obviously been crying. Jacob is cradling his smartphone, looking at it as if it is poisonous. My first though is that there is something wrong with Dad or one of our Mums. 'What is it, is someone ill?'

Sam shook her head and replied, 'no, not in the family though Jacob and I do feel very sick with what we have found on the net. Come and sit down. You need to see it though I don't want you to.' She patted the seat next to her. Putting her arm around me, as I sat whilst feeling mystified, she half sobbed, 'you have to see this but it will hurt you my darling brother.'

Jacob said, 'I will put it on the big screen so we can all see it better. Though I am not sure any of us want to.' He played with his 'phone and the window blinds closed blotting out the blue sky and the sunlit valley. Then the painting taking up much of the opposite wall slide sideways into its recess revealing the twelve by nine foot screen behind. The screen blinked into life and then displayed what is showing on Jacob's smartphone.

I looked and my heart clenched. There are three files

listed; Rebecca media briefing, Rebecca media briefing 2 and Rebecca T.V. The last two are new. The first is the footage on the net from Rebecca presenting the results of the raid on the corrupt officers. We had already watched that together. Shaken I stammered, 'is something wrong with Rebecca.'

Sam clenched my hand and said, 'no. Quite the opposite. She is showing just how wonderful she is. That is the problem.'

My head is now reeling. How can that be a problem?

Jacob said, 'I was searching on the net to see if could find any footage of Rebecca in a Taekwondo contest for us to look at. Sam and I were talking about her, Sam singing her praises that is. She said that you have never seen Rebecca fight other than when she smashed the yobbo's knee. That is what I sought. Thankfully, and unfortunately, I found this instead. You need to see this before you see her again. Luke, it will not be easy viewing for you.'

If there is nothing wrong with her, if it is showing how wonderful she is; then how can it be difficult for me? I was then hit with an awful realisation. Rebecca must have found and publicised something relating to our treatments. With mounting trepidation I looked at the screen again.

Jacob clicked on the "Rebecca media briefing 2" file. A close up showing only her head and shoulders filled the massive screen. It is several times life size. She is in uniform, looking beautiful, looking straight at the viewer. It is as if she is looking straight at me. She is also deadly serious and commencing a presentation. Her demeanour screams both focussed professionalism and that she is about to impart something unpleasant to hear. As she spoke the camera zoomed out. Now I can see that she is on a podium in the Park Hotel. The ballroom is full of reporters and other cameras. It is clearly another media briefing. There are three other senior police officers, sitting at a desk, behind her and to the side. There are two women sitting a little separately from most of the audience. They are clearly emotional. One is visibly upset and the other is fuming with anger. I have not seen them before and I have no idea how they relate to the police or this event.

Rebecca had intimated that something good had happened at work. She wanted to postpone discussing it until I returned. She wanted to see the footage of my lecture and then, only after she had heard of what she described as "my undoubted success," for us to discuss her work. I went along with this. Though I had been eager to hear what had occurred and to tell her about my job offer; I wanted that discussion to be face to face and at the same time. I felt that I could not complain about her delaying telling me something if I am doing the same. This presentation must be what she was going to tell me about. But why are Sam and Jacob so upset? Rebecca was obviously pleased by the events though she does look resolute now.

She started to speak. She is using her devastating technique of speaking directly to someone behind the camera. Even on my T.V. it would be gripping but here, with Jacob's large screen and Rebecca appearing greater than life size, it feels as if she is in the room and addressing solely me. As her narrative unfolded all the other noises that had been coming from off camera, from the audience in the ballroom, fell away. It is clear that all there were spellbound.

I am not spellbound. I am shattered. It is clear that the police have not only become aware of but have also linked many of the men that Sam and I have treated. I realise that I thought "police." I should have thought, my girlfriend, the woman I love. It is also clear from her presentation that she considers, no not considers, she obviously strongly feels that my actions are distasteful.

With a curl of her lip she revealed that she knows that

there is more than one perpetrator, that one is a woman. I looked at Sam with horror; I cannot cope with the idea that she may be found to be implicated. Sam is in tears, they are silently running down her cheek and she is not attempting to wipe them away. Jacob is looking at me searchingly, almost disapproving. He knows what we have been doing, why is he now on his high horse? I raised my eyebrow at him and he gesticulated at the screen, something serious is coming.

Rebecca continued, with horrified incredulity at its apparent callousness, she said that the abductors had been singing together when they had taken one man, some weeks previously. She added that she had never before come across such a despicable lack of insight or empathy. From the out of sight audience I heard cries of condemnation.

Jacob paused the video. Unfortunately it stopped at a point where Rebecca is frozen, looking straight at me with an expression of repugnance. I cannot take my eyes from hers. She is looking at me. I heard Jacob calling my name. I looked at him. He is staring at me and said, 'well.' He has asked me a question. He realised that I had not heard it. 'Luke, I cannot believe that. Please tell me that you were not singing. In his drugged state perhaps the man was hallucinating.' He caught my expression and his own hardened.

Sam chipped in, 'no Jacob. Well, that is yes and no. We were singing but not in delight or celebration. We were nearly hysterical. We had him in the back of the van. There were police cars everywhere. We had been stopped twice. The van had been opened and inspected once. Thankfully that was only briefly and they did not spot the hidden compartment. It was terror that we were feeling, not celebration. It was a release of emotion.'

Jacob looks mollified but still suspicious. Then, as if this had not been bad enough, he said, 'brace yourself Luke. You are about to see the worst. In fact, I am sorry to say, the two most upsetting things.'

I don't think I can take anymore.

He pressed play and Rebecca's voice continued. She said that it was considered that these abductions were undertaken as vigilante attacks on men suspected of domestic violence. "Vigilante," "attack" and "suspected;" what on earth is she saying. They are guilty. It is retribution where the criminal justice system has failed.

She paused and then said, 'A little over a week ago Mr. Thomas Castle was abducted. He was driven to a place where he was tortured for hours. If they considered this to be payment for abuse then they could not have been more wrong. They are wrong both to abduct anyone at all for any reason and to consider Mr Castle to be an abusive man. They abducted the wrong man. It is clear beyond doubt that Mr. Castle has never abused his wife nor anyone else.' Cries of "shame" came from off camera. 'We suspect that he was thought to have been a culprit due to a misfiling of some records. We do not wish to say where this occurred for operational reasons.'

I groaned and slumped forward with my head in my hands. Jacob paused the playback again. Sam held my hand. After a while she squeezed it saying, 'it gets worse but we must go on. It is our duty.'

It can't possibly get worse. The wrong man; it must be the bloody hospital cocking up the filing. I should have realised though, he was so different. The hospital made mistakes but I am culpable.

Jacob tapped play and yet again Rebecca's lovely face and voice filled the room. 'The two most recent cases from last week are Mr Castle who we have discussed and a Mr Patrick Reagan who is currently missing. We consider that he may have similarly been abducted. Mrs. Castle and Mrs

Reagan, the wives of the victims now wish to address you.' A muttering of surprise went around the room. I felt a deep foreboding. I do not want to face Mrs Castle and what on earth is Mrs Reagan going to say; he was most definitely a vicious bastard.

Mrs Castle spoke first. She unleashed her anger. She detailed what a gentle, kind man her husband is. She emphasised with absolute clarity that she had never even been shouted at, let alone abused. There is no doubt from her presentation that she is telling the truth and that she despises the attackers. That is she despises me. Her rage at me shows the deep love she has for him and the depth of my error. I have tortured not only an innocent man but a good man. Now I have to live with that. Yes, Sam is the one who drove the van but of late it has been me who has been driving this work. Sam has been pleading to desist, or at least to reduce it.

Can it get worse? From the expressions on Jacob and Sam's faces I can see the answer to that; yes.

Fiona Reagan stepped to the podium and looked resolutely into the camera. Then she quivered. Then she broke down. Rebecca stepped forward to help her but Mrs Reagan gently pushed her away thanking her and saying she will be alright. She most certainly does not look alright. The camera zoomed in tight on her now distraught face, her tears, like Sam's, are streaming down unchecked. I have never before seen such anguish on a face as I now see on Mrs Reagan. Even the cheap, voyeuristic, supposed news close ups of refugees from bombed out cities do not look as wretched.

Then, gathering herself, she let rip. She let rip at me. With her face being much more than life size on Jacob's screen, though I am thousands of miles away, though this recording is now days old; it feels as if she is flaying me right now. She detailed that, yes, she had been beaten, often, and sometimes badly. However she had chosen to stay and chosen to forgive him. Mrs Reagan emphasised that it was her choice to do so and that I had no fucking right to interfere. The BBC missed bleeping out the F word. Possible they missed, possibly they let it through as it emphasised her passion, her hatred of me, as no other would have. She understood why he beat her and felt that his attackers, me that is, would have understood as well if we had bothered to ask him. She explained how she knows that he is dead. She pleaded for his body to be returned so that she can see him and then mourn him. Shaking and now gripping the lectern, barely able to stand, weeping uncontrollably, she pleaded again and again for his body to be returned so that she can say good bye and mourn him. She concluded with, 'I love him, whatever he did.'

Then, near to collapse, she finally allowed Rebecca to lead her away.

Rebecca spoke again and detailed the squad formed to hunt the abductors, hunt me that is. No one watching her conclusion could doubt her resolve and competence. Anyone involved and seeing this would have fear in their heart. I certainly do.

Jacob stopped the playback and the screen returned to the list of the three files. I slumped forward with my head in my hands. I felt ashamed, fearful, appalled at what I had done but most of all horrified by what the woman I love had said about me.

After a while Jacob softly said, 'the final recording is not so bad. Why don't we watch that as well and then discuss them together?'

As I nodded in agreement Sam said, 'except for one bit it is easier.' My bowels clenched at the "one bit." What is to come now?

Jacob played the final file. I marvelled at the skill and poise of Rebecca, how she handled herself, how she destroyed the professional pundit and rescued the woman from the refuge. At times it was almost fun to watch but all the while Sam's words, "except for one bit," tormented me. The analysis by the philosopher was presented as a dispassionate overview. That is what had angered the woman from the refuge and her supporters. However, I thought it clear that he did not support what I am doing and he considers it to be vigilantism. I don't care. As he said himself he changed his mind when faced with the reality when he received a blow. He would support me if he had held Sam in the hospital.

Then it came, right at the very end. Rebecca looked into the camera and said that she was addressing the abductors. She called them vile and vowed to do all possible to bring them to justice. She called me vile. The woman I love despises my actions and has publically vowed to catch me.

Jacob closed the file and switched off the screen. The bright painting slid back in front of the foreboding blank screen but did not cover the images. The blinds softly whirred as they opened and the brilliant Californian sun streamed back into the room. A soft warm breeze came through the partly open windows. Fresh air and sunlight are said to be the best disinfectant but they are not working. I feel grubby and contaminated.

Again we sat in silence, me with my head back in my hands. Again after a few minutes of agony Jacob spoke. 'A week ago, when you arrived, you asked for my opinion on your activities. I was, and in fact still would be, reticent about giving it as I would feel as if I would be arbitrating. I would not have been happy with that. Thankfully I do not have to face that now as these events we have just witnessed have made such a discussion irrelevant.'

I took my head out of my hands and looked at him wondering what on earth can he mean? I see that Sam is doing the same.

Jacob caught our expressions and said, 'surely you can see what I am going to say.' We looked blank and he, whilst shaking his head, continued, 'you have to stop. Whatever the needs and the ethics for what you are doing you have made mistakes. An extremely competent detective has formed a no doubt crack squad to hunt you. They already have leads. Who knows, they may have more that they have not disclosed to the media yet as they do not want to show their hand. You must stop. You are no bloody use to the cause if you are in prison.' Turning to me he added, 'Luke, even if you are happy to take the risk you must stop for Sam's sake. She has suffered enough at the hands of Robin without having to go to prison resulting from that as well.'

I slid down to the floor and curled up. I feel as if I am unravelling. My mission, my retribution for Sam, my love with Rebecca; they all held me close and wrapped around me until an hour ago. Now they are all unwinding and falling away.

Sam came over and held me. She started to speak but I interrupted her. 'Don't worry Sam. I know that Jacob is correct. No more.' She held me closer and I can feel her shaking with silent sobs. I am rigid. My head is filled with what I have just heard, "vigilante," "despicable," "doing it for themselves, not for me." Worse is Rebecca looking into my eyes and saying "vile."

Jacob came over and held us both. We were in a knot on the floor as we so often were as children. That had been a happy playing knot. This is a togetherness born of despair.

Jacob said, 'sorry Luke but there is more.' Sam and I sat up. Sam looks astonished, she did not know that there is more to come.

All three of us faced each other cross legged on the floor. I have now regained my composure. Whatever happens the three of us are together. Looking intently at me he said, 'you have to return Reagan's body. You owe it to Fiona Reagan. Allow her to mourn.'

Sam and I shuddered at the thought of digging up a corpse. I do not know how quickly Clive's composting technique works, how decomposed the remains will be. That is not something I want to do. I said what I had to. 'Of course Jacob; I will do that as soon as I return.' I looked at Sam, 'on my own.'

CHAPTER 28
REBECCA: THE
MORTUARY

During my drive to the mortuary two thoughts kept whirling around in my mind. Well, in reality there is only one; Luke. There is something seriously amiss but so far I have no idea what it is. His flight back from California arrived on Saturday afternoon but for some mysterious reason he could not see me until yesterday lunchtime, nearly twenty-four hours later. When I did finally meet him he was exhausted, both physically and mentally burnt out. His appearance and demeanour were similar to how he had been a little over a week ago, before he left. That was explainable by his excessive work and two moth collections during the preceding few days. I don't know why he is exhausted now. He has clearly had a successful conference and on the occasions we spoke on the 'phone, whilst he was away, he was animated. I know that he is jet-lagged but this is far more than that. Something has upset him again since his return. Presumably it is related to whatever was troubling him before he left. I am terrified that he may be having second thoughts about our relationship.

I had been disappointed that he had seen my T.V. appearances whilst he was away. I had hoped to see his lecture first of all. I would have preferred to view both my TV appearances and his lecture with us sitting together.

I was surprised that he did not wish to show me his lecture yesterday afternoon. Even more than that I was disappointed, even hurt, by his lacklustre response regarding mine when he told me he had seen them. Talk of being damned by faint praise; it felt like a slap in the face. I caught myself. That selfishness is unlike me and I need to focus on the fact that his response was unlike him. I must forget it. Something is preventing him from being himself. I must focus on finding out what is wrong with him and to try to help. I must not selfishly criticise.

I had been equally surprised not to have seen Sam yesterday. It was obvious that she was in as windows and doors were opening and closing in her part of the building. She may well have wanted to allow us time together but even so; normally she puts her head in to say "hello." I have a good relationship, now a friendship, with her also. Maybe she is keeping out of Luke's way. They may have had a major rift and that is the underlying problem with Luke. Maybe she has also been affected by whatever is troubling Luke.

We had made love in the afternoon. At the time I had cruelly thought that we "finally" made love. Again he was not exactly overenthusiastic. He had hardly pounced on me, tearing my clothes off and my initial advances were rebuffed. It is not a recurrence of his initial problem. It seems to be associated with him being so tired and preoccupied, even upset. All in all, physically and emotionally, it was not the homecoming that I had been expecting.

I had planned to stay the night but by late afternoon I was beginning to think that I should go home. I had been so desperate to see him but not like that, not with the almost strained atmosphere. To my surprise I had been beginning to think that I should leave him to recover alone and then to tackle whatever is going on when he was refreshed. I had expected us to be tightly wrapped together, not me planning for us to be apart.

Events interceded. At five pm I received an apologetic call from the station, they had not wanted to disturb me on a Sunday off. I suspect that word had gone around that Luke had returned. Little did they know? The call was so important that I assured them that it was absolutely correct to contact me, whatever the circumstances.

Patrick Reagan's body had been discovered.

I told Luke that I had to go and that I would see him the next evening; that is today. He said that he was sorry I had to leave. He looked as if he meant it which made me feel a tiny bit better. He also acknowledged, without prompting, that he was not himself and he apologised for that. He promised to talk to me this evening. After a grim afternoon I had left feeling a little easier.

As I pulled into the Mortuary car park I forced myself to stop thinking of Luke and to concentrate on the case. I must address the professional issue, the one that I am supposed to be thinking of when at work, instead of being consumed by thoughts of Luke. I had telephoned Professor Fisher, the Pathologist, first thing this morning and I had asked, in fact I had pleaded, that he performs the post mortem asap. I nearly fell over when he said that he would do it today. I know how backed up his department is. He is obviously bending over backwards to help. I do not usually attend the actual PM. I find that coppers simply get in the way, some faint. What we really need is the report which I receive immediately via email anyway. This time I had asked his assistant to text me when the Prof was nearing completion. I wanted to see him and thank him face to face.

I smiled to myself; I think it is my first smile since seeing Luke and being so concerned about him. I have seen three Profs in a couple of weeks; that is a first for me and surely something to smile about. Liam Dicks was one. I know

Amber has spent the weekend with him. She had called to tell me how they had passed the time. It was much the same as what I had hoped for with Luke. At least one of us is fulfilled. Then Luke, I sometimes forget that he is a Professor. And now I am seeing the helpful Prof Ron Fisher.

As I entered the Mortuary I was met by the cold and the smell. The combination of antiseptic and putrefaction is pervasive. Once the sickly-sweet, cloying stench of decomposing human flesh is known it is never forgotten.

A memory flashed into my mind. Years ago, sitting in his home when he was still alive, I recalled my grandfather talking of his World War Two experiences. He had been in the first wave of the D-Day Landings. Having fought his way off the beaches some time later he was crossing the killing fields of the Falaise Gap. As he then told me that it was impossible to walk there without stepping on body parts I had noticed his nose wrinkling. All those years later he could still remember what I am smelling now.

The Mortuary Assistant approached. I have not seen him before. He is known throughout the nick as "the weasel." One glance told me why. He is small, skinny and has a tiny pointy face with a twitchy nose. With a nasal, squeaky voice he effusively welcomed me. I immediately felt guilty at thinking of him as a weasel; he is utterly charming.

He ushered me in to see the Prof who is still in the dissection room completing his report. I have met him before and I have always found him to be charming as well. He is also short, like the weasel, but there the similarity ends. He has a relaxed, chubby face with old-fashioned mutton-chop whiskers. His deep-base booming voice always comes as a surprise from such a small man. The old yellowing, once-white, rubber apron is tight around his paunch and overhangs his white wellies; unfortunately not covering the stains of god knows what. The floor is wet where the weasel has recently finished washing away the split body fluids and morsels of flesh. In the old fashioned drain set into the centre of the floor I caught sight of a flap of discoloured skin, a clot of congealed blood and a sickly yellow fluid, the origin of which I preferred not to dwell on. The Prof stood amongst this as if it is an everyday event. Of course, for him, it is.

He smiled at the assistant and said, 'thank you Wesley.' So, that is another reason why he has been nicknamed "weasel."

The Prof turned to me, beaming, he continued, 'Rebecca, it is as always a pleasure to see you.' Relieved, I saw that he is not going to shake my hand. As lovely as he is I would have difficulty in touching him knowing what he delves into each day. I could not help thinking of what his wife feels when, or if, she cuddles up to him in bed each night. Is she able to detect the traces of the odours of rotting remains in his hair? I forced myself to snap out of these unhelpful thoughts. I have to focus on how kind and competent he is.

'The pleasure is all mine, Professor. Before we start may I say how grateful we all at the station are for you undertaking this PM so quickly? We all know how busy your department is.'

His face turned to a thunderous frown. I was taken aback until I saw the twinkles at the edges. He is putting it on. 'Rebecca, it is not for you or the station. I watched your media briefing with my wife and daughters. If they found out that I had not dropped everything to help you they would have me there,' he nodded towards his dissection table, 'forthwith.' His tried to prevent it but his twinkles deepened. He is obviously doing this expedited PM for me as well and he is pleased that this has been acknowledged. Then, again deliberately deepening his faux-frown, he added, 'may I also remind you, Detective Superintendent Fletcher, that I have previously said that you should address me as Ron. If you call me Prof I will call you ma'am. It has come to my ears how much you prefer that title and in return you offer the user of the said title, "ma'am," the most enticing delights.'

Is nothing sacred in our station, how did he hear of that? Even so, I could not help but grin at what he said and his deliberately outdated construction. He saw this and could no longer retain his act. He grinned at me. I had never thought that a PM could be fun. This part is anyway but I am trying to forget what is to come.

Whilst I thought that I will find it difficult to address such an eminent man by his forename I realised that I do chastise my staff for having difficulty in calling me Rebecca. I am developing double standards. He turned to the "weasel" and said, 'you call me Ron, don't you Wesley?'

With a deadly serious face Wesley replied, 'oh no m'lord, never.'

The Prof smiled again and gave an exasperated shrug. I still have difficulty with such levity while standing only feet away from a murdered corpse. Then lapsing into sadness he continued, 'after seeing that poor Mrs. Reagan's face at your briefing I want to do all I can to help. She is coming in soon to see the body. I have tried to dissuade her. It is not a pretty sight.'

With this he pulled back the sheet covering Reagan.

I gasped in shock, not in horror. I have seen plenty of dead bodies in all stages of decomposition before, yet another does not bother me. It is the surprise at his appearance that caught me off-guard. 'Bloody Hell Professor, his decomposition appears very advanced.' Reagan had been a big man but I had already noted that the white sheet that had covered him also revealed that he was larger than I had anticipated. Now the sheet is pulled down to his waist I can see that the corpse is grossly bloated. The skin has changed colour and whorls of red, magenta and black are contrasted by the silver of the stainless steel table he rests on and the harsh white of the tiles of the floor and walls.

I involuntarily jumped as a sharp metallic crash came behind me and eerily echoed around the cold unforgiving walls. Wesley muttered a soft oath and then more clearly, 'sorry.' He had dropped a bone saw on to a steel trolley. Better that sudden clatter than the rasp of it cutting through dead limbs.

The Prof had not appeared to notice the noise or what I had said and he is still closely scrutinising the body. Like me he is obviously mystified. 'As you can see, Rebecca, his decomposition is very advanced for one whom we know for certain was still alive only ten days ago. As Mrs. Reagan is coming Wesley has secured his jaw shut so that you cannot see that his teeth are falling out.' The Prof pulled back the sheet a little more, 'however you may observe, his nails have come loose also.'

My first thought blurted out, 'Fiona Reagan is coming to see.......this.' It is no longer a "him."

'I have tried but she is insisting. I cannot stop her. At least she will have her sister with her and the children are not coming.'

Changing back to my role I asked, 'how can this have happened Professor, this advanced decay?'

Either he did not notice me calling him Professor or he chose to ignore it. 'The initial cause of death was probably drowning though with the amount of liquefaction of the tissues even that is uncertain. It is presumably murder. However, it would be difficult to drown such a large man with no other injuries being sustained from incapacitating him and there is no evidence of any other damage other than the decomposition.'

I chipped in, 'that would fit with a waterboarding either going wrong or deliberately being extended. We know that others have been strapped to a movable arm using soft restraints after being drugged. Then they were plunged in and out of water, possibly in a tank. He would have been secured and drowned without any other injury.'

He looked at me with horror. 'Is that what has been done to the others?'

'Yes.' There is nothing else that I can add.

'You are chasing very sick people, best of luck with that.' He looked back at the distorted shape on the table. 'As to why the body decomposition is so advanced I can only guess. I suspect that the body has been stored somewhere hot such as a boiler room or near a furnace. Further, there is no insect invasion so the body has been in an airtight bag or area.' He pulled the sheet over Reagan again. That was helpful. Whilst I have no difficulty in seeing a decomposed body it is distracting. I want to concentrate on solving this conundrum. He continued, 'there is precious little to go on. As you know the body was naked and wrapped in a tarpaulin, the sort that you can buy in any of the DIY stores. I suspect that the body had been washed before being dumped by the roadside as there was almost nothing else to be seen. We did find two small items but they may be contaminants. I do not imagine they will help.'

He walked across to his desk and held up two clear plastic evidence bags. He selected one and then he passed it to me. 'I believe this to be a single dog hair though judging by the length and thickness the beast would be nearer to a wolf than to a Yorkshire terrier. I have not seen a dog hair such as this before. I suspect it is a contaminant as it is solitary and if the assailant is a dog owner I would have expected more hairs. On the other hand whoever is doing this has washed the body and presumably they took other precautions to avoid leaving evidence, so, it may be relevant.'

Whilst he was musing out loud in this fashion, I can that see he is intrigued by this case. He nonchalantly passed the evidence bag to me. Innocently I held it up to the light to look at this hair myself. I doubt a single hair will be much use but at this stage I will grasp at any straw.

I felt my knees buckle.

I grasped the edge of the desk for support. Thankfully the Prof is examining the other evidence bag and Wesley is cleaning the body remnants from the drain in preparation for Fiona Reagan's imminent arrival. They had not seen the effect this hair had had on me.

I have seen a dog hair such as this before. In fact, I have seen one identical to this. Sitting in Luke's house, Toby's head on my lap, I had been stroking him whilst listening to Luke and Sam tease each other. It was a gentle, innocent Sunday afternoon. Now it is here, in these Gothic surroundings. One of Toby's hairs had snagged on my nail and I held up my hand to pull it free. The hair in this bag is exactly the same as the one that dangled from my finger on that lovely afternoon.

I half heard the Prof talking about an unusual grass or herb that appeared to be half dried and half rotted. He was holding out the other bag. I forced my knees to lock and I took the bag and, tearing my eyes away from the hair, I looked at it. It looked like composted grass or herb but not like Dad's garden compost. I have seen this before as well. I have run my hand through compost such as this at Luke's research farm. It looks identical to the old, stored Alfalfa.

The room is now starting to spin.

I clenched and relaxed my calves repeatedly. I am desperate not to faint. I tried to think. It is impossible that Luke is responsible for Reagan being on the table feet away from me. He cannot have undertaken all the other abductions, torture and disappearances. Luke is not like that. He is not capable of such deeds. There must be another explanation. I am trying to tie my bubbling thoughts together. Surely there are myriad other possibilities.

With relief the obvious alternative interpretation hit me and I found focus again. My stupidity in thinking that it may be Luke who is culpable, and not one of the more likely scenarios, was probably due to the injudicious comments by Julian and the Met team lurking in my subconscious. It must be coincidence. This must be one of those obfuscating false clues that lead the irrational to conspiracy theories, religion and miscarriages of justice. The more I think of it the clearer it is. Toby must have brothers and sisters and as he was born locally they are likely to be in this area. Many people use garden compost. The owner of a large dog is likely to have a garden. The coincidence of the combination a Toby-like hair and composted Alfalfa being found together is, on rational analysis, not unlikely. As Julian and Luks discussed at the party, it is a Prosecutor's Fallacy.

With relief I felt strong again. The apparently spinning room stabilised.

As a hopefully good detective though, it is my duty to explore all alternatives, even ridiculous ones, such as Luke being involved. I asked the Prof, 'is it possible that the body was stored in a compost heap giving the accelerated decay and this evidence?' I held up the bag which contained the minute sliver of composted material. I tried to make it an innocent, innocuous question but I held my breath as I waited for his answer.

He immediately replied, 'no, Rebecca. I see where you are going but a compost heap would not be hot enough to have done this to him.'

Now I breathed again and my heart finally calmed as

I thought, "good work. I can tell Julian to shut up about Luke and we can develop these slim leads."

Then the Prof, who had been thinking further on my question, added, 'a household garden compost heap that is. It is possible that he was kept in an industrial compost heap such as those used by local authorities. Good thinking, Rebecca. Yes, yes, that would do it. Yes, look at those. A hot compost would cause the accelerated decay and keep out the insects, especially if the body was buried in it.'

As he spoke I remembered Luke talking about Clive's research and the efficiency of his technique using higher temperatures. It hit me like an express train. The thought was physical, a blow.

It is Luke.

There was a woman heard by one of the victims. It must be Luke and Sam. The man who heard the singing was abducted on the night of our raid on the Langley Pub. Luke was out and about with Sam supposedly collecting moths. The moths are a front. It is them.

I heard worried voices and hands are firmly but kindly holding me by the elbow. Wesley and Prof Fisher guided me to a chair and made me sit. Wesley held up my feet and the Prof made me lie back against him. I felt the room come back into view. I must have nearly fainted. I have never ever before fainted, not even when I was shot.

As they fussed around me I heard a bell ring. Wesley said, 'bugger, that must be Mrs Reagan. She is early. I will tell her we will be a few minutes.'

I recovered and while thinking, Luke, Luke, Luke, I managed to say, 'I am sorry. I am not feeling well today. I will go home. I will be alright now. Thank you so much.' I have to get out. I cannot sit next to the Prof and not tell him that he has just solved the case.

Somewhat apprehensively the Prof said, 'well, you have regained your colour. Let us see you stand.'

I found that I can stand. I thanked them again and I headed for the door nodding at Wesley who was returning from speaking to Fiona. I went out and as soon as I turned the corner in the corridor and I was hidden from sight I slumped against the wall. I feel numb.

Voices echoed down the corridor. Firstly Wesley's, shrill but laden with concern, 'I hope Rebecca will be alright. Not nice in here today is it Ron. I am not surprised it got to her.' So he was not fooled by my excuse.

The Prof spoke, 'no Wesley, I think you are wrong. Rebecca could walk across the Somme battlefield and not turn a hair. She is not well. I hope that she is not going down with something serious. The public need her on this case.'

No Prof, I am not the one for this investigation.

Wesley said that he would bring in the widow. I heard doors open and close twice. I heard footsteps drag across the floor as I remained slumped against the sickly yellow wall. I can still smell Reagan, even down this corridor. How will Fiona cope with seeing him in his current state? He was a shit but she loved him.

Then came a piercing shriek followed by choking sobs. They clearly came from Fiona. I have met her. She has leaned on me. I should go back in. I should help.

I cannot. I ran for the car.

Throwing myself into the driver's seat I realised that I had subconsciously come to the decision to see Luke right now. I revved the engine, put it into reverse and the tyres squealed as I reversed out of the parking slot. I crunched the gears into first but before screaming out of the car park I came to my senses. I must not continue in this state. If I do my driving will be fast and erratic. Being in an unmarked police car means that I will not collect any penalty points but I will be dangerous. I have seen enough death today.

Slowly, carefully, I drove forward back into the bay that I have just left. I switched off the engine.

I flicked the keys into the back seat so that I need to get out to retrieve them, so that I will not do anything more without an enforced pause. I looked at my watch and I determined not to start the car for at least ten minutes. I will go to see Luke but not until I have calmed down and decided what I am going to do and say. Do I arrest him or do I ignore the evidence which will then be lost as no one else can make that connection? If I do not arrest him what should I say to him?

What should I say to myself? In theory love conquers all but I do not see how this can be overcome. I cannot dither. I have to arrest him.

What on earth will he say to me when I confront him? Will he try to invoke our relationship and will he plead for me to ignore the evidence? I slumped across the steering wheel. Whatever the answer to the last conundrum the inevitable outcome showed its all too obvious head. Our relationship is over within just under three weeks of us confessing undying love to each other.

Forcing myself to stop feeling sorry for myself, there will be plenty of time for that, I sat back and did what I always do when faced with apparently insurmountable difficulties. With my eyes open, defocussed, seeing nothing, I observed my breathing and I allowed it to slow. My Taekwondo training immediately kicked in. My mind calmed and my body softened. Then, and only then, my mind cleared and I was able to start to think through my questions. The whirling automatic thoughts and images slowed and faded. They did not go but now I can see past them. Hopefully an answer will present itself as I cannot think of any way to fashion one.

My mind was blank for several minutes but at least it remained calm and open.

Finally a usable idea came to me. If I think of Luke I will be overwhelmed with bias and emotion. Any decision made in this way is likely to be second best at least, more likely flat out wrong. Sam is also involved. I guess that she is in the van during any abduction and it was her voice that had been heard. I suspect that she is not involved in the waterboarding as she has said, I now realise that she has in fact pointedly told me, that after the so-called moth collections she drops off Luke and goes to the hospital or refuge. They may consider that an alibi but any half-decent investigation will blow it apart. If I arrest Luke then I will have to also arrest Sam. I am invested with Sam. I like her, a lot. However I do not love her as I do Luke.

So, my dilemma is, what should I do to or for Sam? This is easier.

Then another idea came to mind. I should ask myself, what would Claudia or the Bear or the Met team do? I can get a second opinion. Obviously I cannot actually ask them but I know them well enough to predict accurately their responses.

The obvious answer is that we should all immediately and unquestioningly decide to arrest the pair of them. That is the clear, truthful answer that follows our wonderful criminal justice system.

That is also only one of the possible truths.

There is a strong suspicion in my mind that they would think that but they would not undertake it. I feel that there is a likelihood that they would turn a blind eye. I remember that when Julian told the Met Team that Luke was a suspect, when we first all convened in Julian's flat, that Tom had replied, "I would like to catch him but to give him a medal, not to arrest him." I then thought back to Liam when I knew him as only Professor Dicks and Amber thought of him as Limp Dick. A simple slap showed him that philosophical truths are not always practical ones. He publically stated this, undermining his whole raison-d'etre, in front of the TV cameras.

I only have to face my mirror.

I cannot do it to Sam. She has already suffered so much. If her husband had not been disposed of; I thought to myself, drop the euphemisms you prat; if he had not been murdered; then it is very likely she would have been seriously injured again if not killed. It feels as if she was punished before the deed, as an appetiser rather than just desert or, to strain my metaphor, dessert. Luke suffered then as well. He is an empathic man; for a murderer and a torturer that is. In some ways, whilst Sam was unconscious with the probability of brain injury of unknown extent, he suffered more. No one knew then that she would make a near full recovery. Even so it has taken years of gruelling treatment during which they have both suffered, her physically, him having to watch and not to be able to help.

I cannot bring myself to arrest Sam. Inevitably that leads me to the inescapable conclusion that I am not able to arrest Luke. "Not able to," I am full of excuses and euphemisms today.

The question I should ask myself is; "am I not going to arrest them because that is a just way to proceed or because I love Luke?" I dare not ask myself that. I may find it difficult to live with the answer. The deeper question that follows is; "is this my decision to make?" As I believe in the rule of law the answer is inescapable. I dare not ask myself that question either.

I looked at my watch. I have now been sitting here for half an hour. So in a little more than thirty minutes I have failed to do my duty as a human being and to look after Fiona Reagan and I have decided not to do my duty as a police officer. This is not a day to be proud of. On cue the door to the mortuary opened and out stepped Fiona. She is no longer sobbing but she can barely walk. Another woman who looks like a younger, less careworn version of her is holding her, helping to walk. I remembered that Fiona has a sister, this must be her. I remembered that the sister is eight years older, today she looks eight years younger. The effects of Fiona's grief and distress are only too apparent. Like a spineless excuse for a woman, which is what this revelation has made me, I slide down in my seat so they would not see me. As they drove off I started the car.

Now feeling calm and determined I drove through town keeping rigidly within the speed limit, driving courteously, smiling at the aggressive business men and distracted mothers as they cut in front of me. I was courteous as I inwardly marvelled at how they remain preoccupied with their personal, intimate dramas and at how they manage to ignore the mad hypocrite passing by. In truth that is how I always drive. I have no need to bolster a flagging ego with aggressive driving. That may change after today.

If I had driven immediately after leaving the Mortuary I would have probably roared up and parked in Luke's drive. Instead I calmly parked in the station. I carefully locked the car and I strolled back out of the rear gate, around the corner, and up to his front door.

I swung the elegant brass hoop and knocked on the door. Without intending to I had given the "I am a police officer and I expect you to open the door now" knock, not my usual knock saying, " I am here my darling." Whatever, a gentle tug on the bell pull would not suffice today.

The door opened. It is Sam. She looks terrible. Though it is only ten days since I last saw her, like Fiona Reagan, she looks years older. If anything she looks even worse than Luke did yesterday. Luke had told me that the three of them had watched my TV footage together. They will have seen the effect of their activities on Mrs Castle and Mrs Reagan, the anger and the distress. They will have been aware of their errors and the resulting effects. Though they may be murderers and torturers I feel sure that their intention was to do good and to help abused women. To have made such catastrophic errors with such awful consequences would have devastated them. Partly I wanted to hug her; instead I gave her a long hard look and I remained silent.

Sam registered my expression and without speaking she turned and directed me towards the kitchen-diner. As we walked along the short corridor, which today seems a mile long, Luke's voice called out, 'who is banging so loudly on our door Sam?'

I went into the room first. Luke stood up quickly and stepped towards me with his arms out to hold me. He said, 'darling, this is wonderful, I did not expect you until later.' As he said this I saw him register my expression and doubt come into his face.

'Don't touch me.' I stood back.

As he froze in horror Sam stepped around me and with a shaky whisper she said, 'Luke, Rebecca knows.'

He recoiled. He still looked horrified but other expressions now compete on his handsome face. There is now also relief, I have seen this so often when I have confronted criminals and they realise the game is up. In addition I can see hope. Surely he is not thinking that I will join them. I supressed my guilty secret, it had crossed my mind. Only briefly but it had been there. I have seen too many women failed by the system I uphold not to have fantasised about doing the same.

I took control of the situation and more importantly of myself. Still silent, since coming through the front door I have said nothing other than "don't touch me." I pointed to the chairs around the dining table and we all sat. They sat together with me facing them across the table. Sam looks as if she is on the verge of crying. Luke is now ashen. His usually handsome face is contorted in anguish.

I started. 'This afternoon I have attended the Mortuary and I have discussed the results of Patrick Reagan's post mortem with Professor Fisher, the pathologist. He uncovered two items of evidence that link the body with this house and the farm where you compost pigs. It is now clear that it is not only pigs that you have dealt with in this way.' They are staring at me in terror. 'So far I am the only one who knows of the connection. If I do not reveal it then there is no one else who has the knowledge required to join the dots.'

Realising the implications of this Luke looked at me with hope again and Sam with pleading in her eyes. Sam shakily whispered, 'what are you going to do Rebecca?'

Before I could reply Luke said, 'don't be silly Sam. All this, the treatments we have been undertaking are only known by the three of us. There is no need to do anything.'

I exploded. 'Treatments, what the fuck are you saying? It was torture and murder.'

They jerked back in surprise. They obviously thought that I was going to hit one of them. I had managed to restrain myself from punching Luke. He half stood and I can see that he is going to reach out to me. 'Don't you dare touch me. Don't ever touch me again.' I remembered what I had speculated as to what Mrs Fisher thought and smelt as she lies in bed with the Prof. 'Yesterday you dug up a rotting, stinking corpse. You handled it. He is large; you must have held him close to manoeuvre him. Then hours later you held me. How dare you.'

'But Rebecca, I love you. We are in love.'

'How can it be love when you have lied to me from the start?'

'I have never lied to you.' He said this with a knowing nod, as if this is sufficient to excuse everything.

'Don't give me that nit-picking pedantic crap. You have wilfully misled me. You have shown me things but only revealed half of their purpose. You have hidden facts in plain sight.' I saw him flinch at this; that must have been his intention. 'Those have been deceitful lies of omission. No worthwhile relationship can ever be built on such foundations. It cannot have been love. It must have been a fantasy. Yes I did think that I loved you but I am sure I will be able to overcome that. The Luke I loved was not the real Luke.' Previously I had not articulated these points even to myself. They had spilt out but now I see them I can tell that they are unmistakably correct.

Sam is now softly crying. Luke is slumped back in his chair disbelieving and distraught.

Hardly lifting his head Luke hesitatingly said, 'Rebecca, we had already decided to stop. After seeing your TV appearances we realised that we must do so.' I looked at him in disbelief. This had been said as if it was sufficient to absolve them. Mistaking my stunned silence for acquiescence he continued a little more strongly, 'I wanted to tell you something else yesterday but I was too upset. I have been offered a post in California. I was going to ask you to come out there with me, with us. We can put all this behind us and start afresh.'

He lifted his head and finally he looked at me. Too late he realised the true meaning of me not speaking.

As he quailed before my thunderous look I spoke. My voice is hardly audible but it came as a snarl. 'How gracious it is of you to make such a wonderful offer to me. You want me to leave my senior post that I love. You want me to travel to another continent, to retrain, to start again as a lower rank, all so that I can be with a murderer who has deceived me. Let me think about it.'

For a second or so I could not continue. They both sat mute and motionless in shock, probably from my tone, in fear as well.

Then I shouted at him. 'You say you are upset. How very tiresome for you. This afternoon I have had to listen to Patrick Reagan's wife scream in anguish. That is what upset means, not this confession of half-baked second thoughts. I have come to know her, by the way, whilst hunting for her husband's killer. Her name is Fiona. She is a lovely person. If you had bothered to ask her rather than playing accuser, judge, jury and executioner, then you would have found out that she loved him and that she wanted to be with him. In your conceit you thought that you knew better. It is said that the way to hell is paved with good intentions. The difficulty is that it is Fiona who is in hell not you two.'

Sam is sitting still but fat tears are rolling unheeded down her cheeks. Luke's recovery has disappeared and he is again ashen and slumped. Both now cannot look at me and they are staring at the dining table.

We sat in silence for what felt like hours but it was probably only a couple of minutes. We all processed what I had said, including me. All that I have told them so far was unplanned. At least it was not consciously planned.

Then I started to say what I had initially intended

to say. Looking firstly at Luke I spoke softly but firmly, not lovingly as in better times, 'I suspect that you have been the main actor in these crimes.' He winced at the word crimes and went to speak but Sam wisely put a restraining hand on his leg and he slumped back again. 'However a woman was kinvolved in at least one and that is presumably Sam. If I arrest you then I have to arrest her as well. I think that she has directly suffered enough at the hands of an abuser and should not be imprisoned because of any resulting criminal, vile and misguided actions. However wrong I suspect they were well-intentioned and you were both led to them by what you had suffered.'

Now looking at Sam I continued, 'you have both been arrogant and stupid in considering yourself above the law but I believe that you both thought you were doing good. I cannot send you, Sam, to prison for that. You have suffered enough already.' I looked back at Luke and I felt my love draining away in response to my realisation of his deception of me. What I have planned to say is not my decision to make. I am acting in a similar fashion to them taking the law into my own hands. Yet I cannot undertake my duty. I cannot arrest them. At least, now, I am certain that this is a decision that would be carried by my thoughts of Sam alone. My withering love for Luke is not relevant. However criminal and biased my decision is, love is not at the root of it. I can face that. I can sleep knowing that. At least I hope that I can.

'I am going to file the evidence without comment. I am not going to arrest you. As no one else has the necessary knowledge to link the evidence to you then it is most unlikely that you will be arrested by any other officer.

There are two caveats. If you have left any other clues then they may lead others to you. If I hear of any other similar case then I will immediately arrest you. It will not be me politely knocking on your door. You have seen us in action. A squad will burst through your door in the early hours.

Of course you need to hope that there are no copycats, or, if there are, there is sufficient difference in what they do to make it clear that it was not you.'

Luke went to speak. 'Do not say a word. Do not move. Do not speak. The only possible thing you could achieve by doing so is that I change my mind and arrest you right now. I am leaving now. I hope that I will never see either of you again. If by chance we do meet then we are strangers. We will not speak.'

I stood and walked calmly out of their house. I felt eerily collected and attentive. I strolled around the corner feeling the low, warm sun on my back. As I went through the rear entrance to the station I stood aside to allow a squad car to pass. We cheerily waved at each other. In spite of all this normality I am not feeling normal. I am detached. I am watching someone else who looks just like me enter the main corridor of the station.

I approached the front desk. Behind reception, as usual, Peter was in his Desk Sergeant's office. Julian is with him, probably awaiting my return and for an update on the case. No doubt they are wondering what has delayed me. I handed in the car keys to the always cheerful receptionist, Tim. Even he seemed to be poised, expectant. No one spoke but they all seem to be shouting, "what was found boss? Were there any clues?"

Julian spoke, 'good to see you boss.' His meaning is clear, "at last." 'The task force are in the briefing room ready for you.'

I cannot face them today. I can see that yet again, is that the third or fourth time today, that I am going to fail to undertake my duty. It is certainly the first day in my career that this has occurred even once.

'Thanks Julian and give my regards to them but ask them to stand down. We will have a full briefing at nine in the morning.' Julian, Peter and Tim looked at me in total disbelief. 'The PM was unhelpful other than that he appears to have been kept in a warm environment.' I handed over the evidence bags. I tried not to look at them and I tried to keep my voice neutral. This is where and when, for the first time ever, that I suppress evidence and I deliberately subvert justice. 'These were found on the body. One is a dog hair and the other some composted material. Prof Fisher thinks they may be contaminants.' All I have to do now is to face myself in the mirror when I return home.

Not only have I interfered with a case I have lied to two colleagues who I trust and respect. How can I ask them to trust and respect me in the future?

Without saying a word, still with all of them wearing astonished expressions, Peter took the specimens, signed the log and put them ready to be taken to the evidence room.

I cannot simply walk off. That will appear suspicious. 'Julian, please advise the team that as I said we will have a full discussion in the morning but my instincts tell me that we will not have any more abductions. The body is badly decomposed. It must have been gruesome handling it. I presume that the culprits saw Fiona Reagan on the TV and were overcome with remorse. Because of this I think they will now stop. Obviously we will keep the investigation open but unless any new case comes to light we can now focus primarily on our other remit of preventing domestic abuse.'

That was a mistake. I can see from Julian's expression that he has gone from feeling disbelief to knowing that I am hiding something. My error was in saying, "my instincts tell me." Julian knows full well that I scoff at the idea of "instincts" or the "copper's nose." They are excuses for prejudice and lead to miscarriages of justice. He knows I have no truck with anything other than the scientific method.

It is too late to take it back now.

I simply said, 'good bye. See you all in the morning.' Then I made another mistake. I walked towards the back door, my usual route home which takes me past Luke's door. I cannot ever go that way again.

I turned on my heel and I tried to appear nonchalant as I left through the front door. That is something I have not done since my first week. Peter's jaw has dropped to his chest, Tim is confused.

Julian's expression has changed. He knows. He also knows that he cannot tell anyone, he would be laughed out of the station. I know that he will not tell anyone anyway, not even Barbara. If anything I now feel worse having put him in that position, even more so as I will never be able to even discuss it with him let alone thank him. He gave me an almost imperceptible nod. It is clear that he is telling me that he knows and that he is happy to keep it to himself. I flashed a look of thanks and respect back to him. We then softly smiled in our complicity. Thank god, at least I still have him. Even better, the others have not spotted our silent exchange.

I walked back along the old main road route. I remain eerily calm and alert. As I approached the new bridge I can see, up the tatty road to my right, Brian James's fishing shop which now has a "sold" sign over the broken shopfront. Only last week I spotted Susan James in the supermarket with her children. She was looking better fed, better dressed and radiant. The children looked carefree, not cowed as before. I presume Brian James is nourishing one of the cherry trees. He is no loss to society. Even Fiona may feel life is more rewarding when she gets over her loss. That is if it is possible to get over seeing your husband as she did only a couple of hours ago. Sam is safer and no doubt happier with the removal of her husband. I guess that he is under the larger cherry tree to one side.

I paused as I walked over the bridge and watched the river slide by. I must stop thinking that way. I am falling into the trap of excusing them. On the other hand have I not done the same today? Have I not acted as judge and jury? Perhaps the scale of my misdemeanour is less. Perhaps as I am a police officer it is more? Whatever, the difference in my culpability is only in scale, not in guilt. I am no better.

At last I arrived home. I kicked of my shoes and I lay down on the sofa. At last I can cry. The tears silently flowed. I cried for Fiona Reagan. I cried for Mr and Mrs Castle. I cried for Luke and Sam. I cried for the loss of my love.

Finally, much later, I stopped crying and I sat up. I realise that I have not cried for what I have done, for the cover up. Though so very wrong it inescapably feels right.

CHAPTER 29:
REBECCA: ONE YEAR

It is so unlike me to look backwards. Usually I am focussed only on what is to come. So, as I leaned on the wall in front of the war memorial, as I looked over the gentle river slipping by; it came as a shock to find myself musing on the last year. Today is three hundred and sixty five days from when I first walked from my house, thirty yards or so behind me, to my first day in my then new post in the station, half a mile in front of me. From here I cannot see the station but I can see the spires of the tall, elegant church overlooking the green enclosed by the square. That shows me exactly where the station is. The rear entrance is just beyond those spires. Now I can say not simply 'the station,' but, 'my station;' meaning that it is my very welcome responsibility. Feeling good, resting here after a morning run which, as usual took me alongside the river and across both road bridges, I paused a while. I allowed my mind to wander. That is something else uncharacteristic of me. That is something else which marks this anniversary.

It has undoubtedly been an incredible year. The time from when I first started feels simultaneously as if it is both one month and one decade. So much has happened and yet the time seems to have gone so quickly. Einstein showed that time dilates when you move quickly. He was referring to physical dilation and he overlooked the psychological dilation that I am feeling this morning. When, at school, and I first read of his conclusions, I did not understand his use of 'dilation.' He meant that it slows down. Now I do understand it. This year has held more than a normal year so the usual span must have enlarged. If the year is considered to be a vessel containing events then it has dilated. He must be rolling in his grave to hear my deliberate misuse of his theory.

Whatever, it has been a hell of a year. When I first stepped out to cross the river a year ago not even in my wildest dreams would I have thought that within that year I would have been promoted to DS. Then I had been struggling to keep my equanimity at, what I then thought, being moved sideways and overlooked for promotion. Today I can smile at the subterfuge of Peter and Claudia though, I have to admit, I was then hurt and demoralised.

Looking to my right, upstream, I can see the new bridge that I crossed on that day. I did not then know the way across the footbridge in front of me, through the city, past the church, traversing the square and in through the rear gate. I did not know what I would meet that day. I had yet to appreciate the disgusting behaviour of Brutus and the sycophantic troop. I had yet to meet Julian. The coming momentous events were unknown.

A flash of light, reflected from a glass door opening and closing at the far end of the Market Square, caught my eye. It is too far away to see but I know from its position that it came from the Culture Café. That reflection made me reflect on Marcus and our wonderful dinner followed by the disastrous interruption by his wife immediately afterwards. He is a good and interesting man to say nothing of being very sexy. He is not affected by the frequent medical consultant demeanour of a contrasting combination of being effete and pompous at the same time. Old Windbag is an example of that, being simultaneously conceited and pathetic. He must be due to leave about now. That will be a relief for the whole team.

Not only is Marcus clearly excellent at his job he, and his team, have been a great help with mine. Without them we would not have been able to discover the connections leading to the realisation that there was a serial abductor team operating in our city. Though that has led me to a personal difficulty it has also most likely saved me from a total disaster in the future. Even if the identity of the abductors is not publically known the squad's work has stopped the crimes, though they do not realise that yet. The related publicity has led to Julian's app, along with heightened awareness, effectively switching off domestic abuse in this gentle city. That is for the present anyway. No doubt we will need to maintain constantly our vigilance.

Yes Marcus is a successful and handsome man. I have seen that most of the women in his department have the hots for him. I hope that he has found happiness with one of them. I wonder what would have happened if his wife had not interrupted us. I wonder what I would be doing now. I wonder. I smiled to myself as I thought of what the scene would have been if she had come in ten minutes later.

The elephant in the room, that is metaphorically in the room as I am outside, that I have so far managed to ignore, tapped me on the shoulder and spoke to me. I did not realise that elephants can speak. Well, this morning, I find that metaphorical ones can. It said only one word but it said that word forcefully; Luke. It is nearly three months since I last saw him.

I had cried all night after confronting him, after telling him that I had found out he and Sam are the culprits. The next day I had to face the team with red puffy eyes and it was clear that I was exhausted. I must have looked as if I had been crying all night. I must have looked as if I had been doing what I had been doing. Paradoxically, my previously not seen before, dishevelled and vulnerable state helped. My inexplicable and out of character announcement confirming what I had said to Julian, that on a gut feeling we were effectively stopping hunting the abductors, went unchallenged. No one pointed out that before I have said, many times, that guts produce shit and feelings coming from them should be considered just that. I have always said that we follow the scientific method in any station that I run. We do not have a "copper's nose." Until it was the only excuse that I could think of that is.

I am sure that behind my back there were mutterings about my distraught demeanour and my daft decision but they said nothing to my face. That was not out of fear, as it would have been with Brutus. It was out of consideration and I love them all even more for that. They are with me even when I am wrong.

After that awful night and the following dismal day I went home and slept for twelve hours straight. I awoke feeling recharged. My love for Luke had gone. No, I had realised that it had never existed. As it had been built on sand and lies it must have been a delusion, not love. I do not miss him but I do miss being in love, that is I miss falsely thinking that I was in love. Before Luke I was alone. Now I am lonely. Since my break up of two, no, now three years ago, I have made my home, my whole life, a sanctuary. I have excluded men from both. Even Luke hardly came into my house, just my heart. Now that I have realised the error of that and that it is better to be open and welcoming there is no one to welcome in. I have thought of internet dating but I suspect my job would put off many, at least many of the men I seem to attract such as criminals and husbands. I do not want to start a relationship as a catfish. That would mean behaving in the same manner as Luke had. Perhaps something, someone will turn up; perhaps not.

It has been made a little easier by not seeing Luke, not even a glimpse across a crowded room. That is not surprising because even when we were together I never saw him in the street or in the shops. Our schedules and activities do not overlap. I found out that seeing him in the park while exercising was simply his construction. From when I first interviewed him he was interested in getting to know me and he engineered to bump into me as if on accident. He certainly will not now, at least I think and I hope that he will not. I would prefer to walk through the city and across the green in front of his house when going to the station but I do not as that would risk seeing him. The main road route that I have returned to is not as attractive but that is a small price to pay.

Deliberately, not wanting to pick at that sore, I went back to thinking of work, especially Brutus and the Coyle family. All are on remand whilst the forensic accountants rip apart their empire. They have no hope of bail as they are flight risks. The accountants have already tracked down other overseas properties and there may be more. They will remain in prison until the trial and then for a long, long time after. The extensive list of charges already made will no doubt be extended before they get to court. Brutus had to have one of his testicles removed after my kick. I kick myself for not kicking him harder and taking off both. Coyle has had multiple operations to his limbs, especially his leg. Simon's charge, which trapped him in the car door as he was about to shoot at us again, did not break his leg; it shattered it. He has to walk with a frame and He will probably never walk normally again.

Still thinking of my work, probably trying to keep my mind off the elephant which no doubt I will find next to me if I look back that way, I glanced behind towards the war memorial. I remembered my confrontation with Denny and his pair of cronies. Resulting from my kick to his knee Denny has also required multiple operations and still cannot walk properly. After the arrests of all three were made public several very young women, some still girls, came forward with allegations of being raped by them. They had been too frightened to speak out before. Unfortunately there is no longer any forensic evidence. One girl had been impregnated but had an abortion so the DNA was lost. However, they independently gave horrible but believable, more importantly corroborating, testimonies. They were also able to describe a couple of tattoos and a birth mark. The three are all still on remand with multiple, well evidenced rape charges against them as well as the assault on me plus drugs charges. They will go to prison for a long time as well as Brutus and the Coyles.

Two groups of serial criminals arrested during my first year. I think that I can allow the team and myself a pat on the back. In thinking this I realise that I am more proud of the reduction in domestic abuse that the new squad has achieved. I managed to avoid thinking of the two serial criminals that I had turned a blind eye to. That is not my proudest moment but even after considerable reflection I do not wish to alter it.

Something heavy and powerful butted my shoulder and at the same time something long, thick and hard, yet cushioned, whacked across the back of my legs.

I was not frightened. I had not heard him approach but I instantly realised who, or more accurately, what it is. I turned my head and looked at the fierce, penetrating eyes and the heavy, vicious looking jaw.

Toby.

He stood on his hind legs with his forelegs on the wall next to me and his head at the height of my shoulder. I said, 'Toby,' and hugged his powerful shaggy neck. His tail now beat harder and faster against the back of my knees and he pushed himself forcefully against me. I struggled to keep from being knocked over. I hung on to him, partly for a hug, partly to keep balance. It is so good to see him. I had not realised how much I missed his uncomplicated devotion.

Then a chill of realisation cut through my delight. If Toby is here, then, so is either Luke, or Sam, or both of them. I cannot face seeing them, not at any time, especially not in my current, uncharacteristic, self-indulgent moping.

I quickly turned to look down the path leading from the riverside walk to here, dreading what I would see.

A woman is hurrying towards me. I do not know her. She is early thirties, slim, attractive if badly dressed. Her trousers are too short and she is wearing a sweater that is too big. She is carrying a baby and has another child, who I guess is four years old, by the hand. She looks Caucasian yet foreign, perhaps she is Eastern European. To my delight I can see that she is also carrying in her free hand Toby's lead. This must be Vera, Luke and Sam's housekeeper who also looks after Toby whilst they are away. I never met her as I was always at work when she came into Luke's house. Perhaps they are not here after all.

As she approached I saw from her demeanour that she recognised me. She started to slow down and she looked relived. 'Oh Rebecca, I am so glad it is you. Toby frightens so many people. He must have detected your trail from the river. He took off and ran up to here.' She can see that I am surprised and that I do not understand how she knows me and that I do not know her. 'I am Vera. I know you from seeing your photo in Luke's bedroom when I worked for him. Of course I saw you on the TV as well.'

As we exchanged pleasantries Toby pushed away from me and took a protective stance next to the four year old who threw his hands, I can now see it is a boy, around Toby's neck. Toby may have wanted to see me but it is clear that his love and duties are lavished on this young lad.

We chatted about the lovely view, her children and her husband. After a while I thought that sufficient time had passed to allow me to ask the question that had been burning into me from one of her first sentences. 'You said that you no longer work for Luke and Sam. Have you taken another job?' I hoped that the underlying real question that I wanted the answer to is not too obvious, "what is going on there?"

Vera did not look suspicious. I do not think that she has deduced my real meaning but she does look askance. Then she looked troubled and this immediately morphed into worry. So, there is something amiss. 'Sorry Rebecca, I assumed that you knew.' Knew what for god's sake? 'Toby is living with me now. Luke and Sam have left. They emigrated to America a couple of weeks ago. It was all decided and done very quickly.'

I felt my jaw drop and I leaned back against the wall. Vera misread this and quickly added, 'I am sorry if I have upset you. I did not mean to be so blunt. I knew that you and Luke broke up but I assumed that you would know.'

"Broke up;" that is one way of putting it. 'No Vera, do not worry. I am surprised but not upset. I haven't seen Luke for weeks and I had no intention of seeing him again.' Vera gave me a, "you let a good man slip away from you, what a fool you are," look. If only she knew.

As I processed the news and overcame my shock I firstly thought that it should not have come as a surprise at all. Perhaps the speed of them going is unusual but I knew about the job offer and that they were both keen to go even before my discovery. They were probably desperate to leave after being rumbled. On reflection it is definitely the best possible outcome. There is no chance that I will bump into either of them. There will not be any more abductions or torture, not here anyway and I suspect non in America either.

I felt my face relax and I even smiled a little.

Thankfully Vera did not spot this. Though I do not know her I do not want anyone to think of me as a callous bitch when they are unaware of the reasons making this good news for me. She was looking down at the child. Toby is standing tall and square like one of the soldiers at Buckingham Palace. His coat even resembles their hats. He is rigidly at attention, jealously guarding his new family. He is obviously loved by them and very happy in his new home. The child has grabbed the scruff of Toby's neck and is struggling to get on to his back. Toby is stock still, resolutely ignoring the resulting pulls, pinches, kicks and knees. Eventually he mounted Toby and then slumped forward across his back putting his arms around Toby's neck. They just about reached and he was able to hold on. The child said, 'I'm tired. Take me home Toby.' Without hesitation Toby trotted off in the direction they had come from ignoring me completely, not even a backwards glance.

Vera looked at me apologetically and she said with a resigned shrug, 'it looks as if it has been decided that we are going home.'

I reached forward and squeezed her hand, 'thanks for telling me Vera. I was surprised not upset. I hope they are happy in America and Toby obviously is with you.' She smiled with relief and followed them down the path.

I turned back to look over the river and the city beyond. As I did so, matching my mood, the sun came out and the scene exploded into beauty and life. I felt a surge of freedom and optimism flow through me. Though I miss our love I do not miss Luke. It has been a nagging concern that either I would bump into them or that there would be another abduction. Even if it was likely to be a copycat, unless I was certain of that, I would have to arrest them. I did not want to put Sam through that and I would have some hard questions to face myself as to why I had not arrested them before. In spite of all that they did I do still care for them and I am hopeful that they will be happy in the US. I did not want to arrest Luke either. Yes, he deliberately deceived me throughout our relationship. Though that meant I could no longer see him I can also understand why he had to. It was wrong of him to take me to the farm but that was a miscalculation, not malicious. In also came back to bite him very hard on the bum.

Though lonely I was not unhappy earlier today. Now though, I feel freer, lighter, better still. Another good point is that I can resume walking through the city to work. In fact, though it is supposedly a day off, I will go to the station this morning. I like to put my head in even when I am not on duty and there are a couple of hours of paperwork waiting. If I get that out of the way today then tomorrow I can put on a WPC uniform and go on one of my much loved foot patrols. I turned and jogged up to my house to shower and change.

The stroll over the foot bridge, across the Market square and the initial climb up the narrow cobbled street had been delightful. As I approached the top with the Cathedral-like church to my right the street opened out but the memories crowded in. I involuntarily slowed. I found walking more difficult. I found even breathing more difficult. I forced my leaden feet to take me on.

Mistakenly, alongside the church, I glanced to my left and the first bolt hit me. I had not thought about the entrance to the little alley; the one with the tall mossy wall to one side and the iron fencing to the other; the one with the memories attached. Along there is where we had walked back from the restaurant. The entrance is where he had held me and kissed me. I had been prepared for the recollections that I will face on the green but this had stealthily crept up on me and struck, literally, from left field. I pushed on past, along the street which now shimmers with a ghostly distortion as if it is a mirage.

By the time I reached the square I was composed again. From the outset I had known, and I have mentally prepared for, what I will face here. Quickly, forcing my mind blank, I stepped out across the green. At the centre I deliberately, as planned, stopped next to the statue. I looked at its beautiful, gentle face. She seems to be saying that, "all will be well."

Deliberately I looked at Luke's house, what had been Luke's house. Mentally, I opened the gates and I allowed the memories flood out. I want to be able to walk this way every working day. I have to face them down now. I took them in order. At least I deliberated on them in order. They hit me all together, in one go. Firstly I thought on sitting here on my first day, after first meeting Sam and Luke. Tomorrow, that will be one year ago. I had been blinded by falling for him. Julian had been correct. I can never tell Julian that but I am sure he knows. What would have happened if I had not been distracted by my attraction for Luke?

Secondly, I can see myself looking out of the bedroom window; the very one that I am now facing. At times I looked out after having made love; at other times I was about to get back into bed and make love then. I can see myself on the other side of that very window, lying in bed, looking at it filled with sharp segments of light.

The third memory, the hardest, was the last time that we sat right here, next to the statue. We were watching the early sun rise having just confessed our love after the swim in the river.

These memories have been frequent during the last weeks. They have not tormented me. They hurt but in a deep warm place and in an obtuse manner that I almost I enjoyed. Before today they did not get easier, I simply became used to them. I sense that from now they will fade.

A deliberate scrape of a foot and a gentle cough from behind, a soft female cough, snapped me out of my reverie. This is the second time today that I have been so lost in thought that I have been unaware of being approached from behind. The first time it was Toby. I turned around to see who it is this time.

I was stunned. An astonishingly beautiful woman of around my age was standing still, watching me, a soft smile playing on her lips. She is my height, my age, my build and, like me she is wearing an Armani tracksuit. There the resemblance ends. Her skin is like ebony, her hair is cropped tight and jet black. It is her eyes that are arresting. Her eyes are like bright coals. She is smiling, her eyes are warm and soft, but, even so, they are penetrating. She has a bewitching quality, a thoughtful air; and there, now I see, a quick smile.

We looked at each other. I felt admiration come into my face and, to my further shock; I saw recognition come to hers. I have not seen her before. I would not forget her. For the second time today I have been recognised by someone I have not met. She spoke; her voice came as a warm, deep mix of the USA and the Caribbean. 'Hi, sorry to disturb your thoughts but you are staring at my house.'

I looked quickly at the house, god knows why, it has hardly moved, and then back to her. There is only intrigue in her expression, no suspicion or malice. With a shake of my head and a light laugh I said, 'sorry, sorry, I did not mean to stare. I used to know the people who lived there. I found out today that they have emigrated. I was thinking of past times.'

Now she is clearly more intrigued. Which of them did I know; why did I not know until today they were leaving; those questions must be going through her mind? Feeling a little vulnerable I decided to deflect the conversation. 'I am on my way to the police station. I work there.' I am babbling like a teenager who has been caught shoplifting.

She gave a gentle nod. She knows. How does she know who I am and what I do? She held out her hand and we shook. She said, 'I am Elakshi Clarke, please call me Elakshi. I am delighted to meet you.'

As I held her hand I started to say, 'I am ....'

She interrupted with a laugh, 'I know exactly who you are. May I call you Rebecca or should it be DS Fletcher?'

Now it is my turn to look intrigued. Initially I feared that Luke may have left something identifying me in the house. Then I realised that he is a considerate man, for a murderer that is. No, he would not do that and even if he did this good woman would be more tactful. She gave me a teasing smile and I relented, 'OK, go on. Tell me how you know who I am.'

'Firstly I saw you on TV, both the media briefing regarding the serial abductors and the debate on the Miles Porton show. No reasonable person, especially not a woman, could forget you after your presentations then.' I felt myself colour a little at this compliment which was especially powerful as it came from a woman who is clearly professional and sincere. 'Secondly your photo is in the coffee room at work and Marcus has told me all about you.'

The realisation hit me. 'You are the new A and E Consultant.' She nodded as I thought, "I hope Marcus has not told her everything." I continued, 'I knew that Windbag was leaving, I did not know that he had already left.' Picking up on my own slip I quickly added, 'that is, I meant to say, Dr Wynn-Davis.'

She shook her head and smiling replied, 'Windbag is far more accurate. I have no idea how Marcus put up with him. When the woman on the Porton show knocked him to the floor my wife and I cheered. It was a good job that it was her there and not us. We would have killed him along with Porton as well. The one she called Limp Dick, we roared with laughter at that, initially came across as a Limp Dick but he exonerated himself and they seemed to get on well. If you ever see her please give her my regards.'

'Actually, I do see her. We have a drink together every couple of weeks. Her name is Amber and given your work I am sure that she would like to make contact. She has started a Domestic Abuse Liaison project. I know that Marcus is on their What's App group as well.' Hearing me mention Marcus like that caused her to look carefully at me. I quickly added, 'Amber told me that he is and I am certain that she would appreciate you also being a member.' It is now well known and certainly not a secret so I added, 'Amber and Limp Dick, more correctly Liam Dicks, are now an item.'

Elakshi looked thoughtful at this and continued, 'sometimes an unusual start can be auspicious. I met my wife, Simone, when she reversed into my car on a supermarket car park. That reminds me, I am sorry but I have to go, I have some computer supplies for her. I popped out to get them. Then I have to go on duty myself. She works from home in the fortified annex that was Samantha's house. She undertakes top secret computer security work for a City firm and the protection is necessary for her. Her mysterious boss, who she has never even met, insists on it.'

When we based the task force at Julian's apartment I had noticed the high level of physical, as well as cyber, security there. I had an idea, 'does she by any chance work for JCCS ?'

She looked astonished, 'yes, most people have never heard of them. How do you know them?'

'I know the owner. If Simone is interested I may be able to arrange an introduction. That is if she can keep his other role a secret. He is not elusive and I know that he meets his people whenever he can. He simply prefers to keep the different aspects of his life separate. He is actually a wonderful person, one of my favourites.'

'Wow, of course. She would love that, thank you.' She paused then continued, 'thinking back to Samantha it was through meeting her in the department, when I came for orientation before taking up this position, that I found out this house was coming on the market. It is perfect for Simone and I. Us being able to move quickly suited them as well. Marcus has told me what happened with her ex-husband and why she lived in such a fortress. I am sure they will be happier in a new country.'

If only Elakshi knew what she was saying. I managed a stifled, 'let's hope so.' We shook hands but before she left I asked, 'your name, Elakshi, I have not heard it before. It is beautiful.'

'Why, thank you again. It is Caribbean. It means bright eyes.'

Not only does she have such a lovely name but it is so apt for her. As she walked away I called out, 'and please give my regards to Marcus. I have not spoken him since he and his team, your team now as well of course, uncovered the serial abductions.'

As she walked to the house she turned and with a wide, knowing grin, said over her shoulder, 'I will be sure to tell him that I have met his heroine.' With that, leaving me bemused and feeling more than a little pleased, she was gone.

I strode past the house, Elakshi and Simone's house, to the back door of the station. Knowing Luke has left and having met one of the women who now live there adds to my sense of release. The day seems yet more brighter and freer. I have a good feeling that I will get to know Elakshi. I will certainly meet her professionally and hopefully socially as well. I have no doubt that she will be interesting and that Simone will be as well. Someday I may be invited into their home. I will defer accepting that until they have had the chance to put their own stamp on in. I will wait until all traces of Luke have vanished.

As I reached the rear door of the station it opened and out stepped Julian. He did a double take seeing me. No doubt that is due to me not having used this entrance recently. He has probably also spotted my ear to ear grin, something else less frequent of late. 'Hi Julian.' I had to stop myself from kissing him. I feel like kissing everyone at present.

His double take and surprise morphed into an uncertainty. It is not my cheery grin that has disturbed him. There is something else that he finds troubling.

'Hi boss.' Not Rebecca, I gave him a "tell me all look." 'Sorry, I do not want to intrude on your private life.' He hesitated as I thought, "you don't Julian. You have kindly refrained from mentioning Luke or that I am using the front entrance since the day of the post mortem. He knows on that day there was more than a PM." 'As you are coming in this way you must have found out what I have been mulling over. I have been wrestling with myself about telling you, whether I should and if so how. I have seen two people coming and going from Sam and Luke's house. They are clearly new owners and so Luke and Sam must have left. Sorry Rebecca, it is none of my business. I feel bad for not telling you before as well as for talking about it now.'

I squeezed his arm and, to his surprise, I now did give him a peck on the cheek. As always he is so kind and considerate. 'Julian, you are not interfering. Thank you for looking out for me.' He looks so relieved. 'In fact I only found out by chance an hour ago. Walking here today I met one of the new owners. Before I tell you something I have found out I need to ask you something to identify the one I have not seen. I met a gorgeous ebony coloured woman, she is called Elakshi. What does the other look like?'

'Another woman as I guess you already know. They are clearly a couple. The other is also coloured but a coffee colour. She is equally beautiful but not as strikingly black as the one you met.'

'Well, the other is Simone and she is a computer securities expert who works from home.' I can see from his expression that he recognises the name. 'You may know the company, JCCS.'

He smiled and said, 'she is a recent addition but excellent. I have not met her as she previously worked from Scotland and I was away when she was interviewed. I knew that she had moved but I did not know that it was to here.'

'I told Elakshi that I knew you but did not say how or what you do here. She said that Simone is keen to meet you.'

'I will call round tight now.'

'In uniform?'

'Yes, in uniform.' He hesitated again but at least this time he is smiling. 'Rebecca, you are looking great. The whole station will be relieved. You have looked so troubled of late but it has now all fallen away from you. He gave me a tight bear hug which took my breath away and then he turned and jauntily walked across the car park, past his car, and on out of the back gate. He is obviously going to give Simone a shock.

I stood for a while thinking of Julian. I now feel selfish that, during my maudlin moping in front of the war memorial, I thought only of the changes in my life over the last year. I should also consider the changes for those around me.

Julian was, similarly to the manner in which I keep people away from my own home, very private. He did not talk about his grief over the loss of his first wife. He kept his differing roles in the police and in his firm separate, the two groups of people around him being ignorant of each other. Now he is on his way to "come out" to the securities firm. Perhaps he will then reveal all to his colleagues here. Barbara knows, but she has been sworn to secrecy and can only discuss it with me. The Met team know but were sworn to secrecy. Then, of course, there is the new relationship between Julian and Barbara. It has been transformative for both of them. Barbara has even physically changed and with a combination of that and her superb performance in the raid she has made great strides professionally. This is clearly resulting from a new confidence she feels.

Then there is everyone else in the station. Their boss has changed. I hope for the better but it is still a change that requires adjustment. The gender balance has radically altered. There is not only me but now there is also the Armani Army. I have yet to find any misogynist in the station; that is since Brutus and the Troop left; but even so it must be quite a change for the men.

I stepped into the station and walked to reception. Tim and Peter similarly did a double take and then broke into wide smiles as they chorused 'hello.' Whether it is me coming in the back way again or my beaming smile, which is beginning to ache, I am not sure which caused their reaction. Yes I am, it is both. I told them that I will be in my office for a couple of hours and I skipped up the stairs.

I raced through the paper work and after only an hour and a half I was finishing up and preparing to leave. To my surprise the 'phone rang. Tim usually does not put calls through on my day off; he diverts them to the duty DI.

I answered and he rather diffidently said, 'Boss, sorry to trouble you on a day off but I thought that you would want to take this call yourself. I know that this man has been closely involved with previous cases.' I thought, "Tim, you are prevaricating. I will not shout about being disturbed today but please get on and tell me who it is." Tim spoke. Maybe he is telepathic, more likely he was just about to tell me anyway. 'It is Doctor Rice for you.'

'Tim, you did very well contacting me. Please put him straight through.' The 'phone clicked and I can hear breathing and traffic on the other end. Marcus obviously does not know that he has been transferred. 'Hi Marcus, this is a lovely surprise.'

'Rebecca, I am sorry to disturb you. Thanks for taking my call.' The lovely Marcus, he is as self-effacing as ever. Of course I will always take your calls you daft bugger. He continued before I could tease him, 'Elakshi said that you met this morning.'

Marcus then gushed on in a most uncharacteristic manner. He told me about Elakshi, how wonderful she is, how well the department is already going, etcetera, et-bloody-cetera. In fact he spouted everything except whatever it is that he has called about.

Eventually I interrupted him and I said in a gentle teasing tone, 'OK Marcus, OK. It is great to speak to you. I am delighted to hear what you have been telling me. I want you to tell me more. However, I am intrigued to find out what it is that you have actually called me for.'

He burst out laughing, 'oh god, I forgot that you are a brilliant detective.' No need for any such skills here Marcus. It is blindingly obvious that you want to tell me something but that you are finding it difficult to start. 'There is something I want to show you, not tell you. I am in the city on some errands. May I come to the station and see you?'

'No.' I could not help ribbing him further. I paused until I could hear his disappointed intake of breath. Only then did I put him out of his misery. 'I have a better idea. I was just about to leave. Why don't we meet in the city and have a coffee and a general catch up, as well as seeing your mysterious offering. Say, fifteen minutes?'

'That would be great.' The relief in his voice was so profound that I felt guilty for teasing him. 'Where shall we meet?'

I could not miss such an opportunity to rib him again. 'The Culture Café of course.' He laughed out loud and rang off. Clearly he agrees that not only we meet there but that it is a risqué place for us to do so.

Twelve minutes later I stepped in. He was already there, waiting. He is at the same table and in the same seat as when we first met there. Many tables are vacant; he is playing me at my own game. He stood, we kissed on the cheek and I looked at him. 'Marcus, you looked good before. Now you look great. Obviously Windbag leaving and Elakshi starting has made life much easier for you.'

'It is not just that.'

He is clearly not going to elaborate but before I could press him the waitress came to take our order. He then prevaricated again. As I was about to insist that he told me what is going on, before I could demand that he shows me the mysterious object, the waitress brought our coffee and cakes. The moment was lost. We were quiet for a while as we enjoyed our food and drink. Then he started to talk about Elakshi again. I silenced him with a squeeze on his arm. He can see what I am going to say and he looks almost frightened. 'Marcus, it is wonderful chatting with you but it is now time to tell me why it is that you wanted us to meet? Also please show me what you want me to see, my curiosity is killing me.'

Now he looks terrified. He did not speak but he took

an envelope out of his pocket and handed it to me. He did not want to let it go. I had to pull it out of his fingers. His address is typewritten and it is franked, not stamped. The envelope is of top quality stiff paper yet only contains two A4 sheets. I took them out. The top one was a covering letter from a solicitor simply saying the document that he had discussed with Marcus is enclosed. I thought that he was going to snatch them back as I slid the other sheet to the front in order to read it.

The heading told me all, "Decree Absolute." I scanned the rest which was just giving confirmatory details of his divorce. I put the documents back into the envelope without looking at him. Then I put it on the table between us. Finally I looked up at him. He now looks as if he is going to faint. He started to stammer something but I squeezed his arm again to stop him speaking. I cannot think what to say but my face must show that I am delighted for him. He saw that and he started to relax. At last I managed both to move and to speak. I leaned across and lightly, briefly, kissed him, but this time on the lips. As I did so I whispered, 'thank god that is over for you. No wonder you look so good.' The smile and the look of relief that he returned lit up an already bright day.

We stayed chatting for an hour having yet more coffee. We discussed the difficulties of his divorce, his work, my work, the media briefing and the TV show. As we went on, speaking openly and frankly, enjoying the company, I became aware of another elephant next to me; the second one today. I can see that Marcus is aware of it as well. The subject that we are skating around is behind everything we say and do not say. Neither of us seems prepare to address it.

Eventually we felt that we had to leave. We walked out shoulder to shoulder, when we were outside I took his arm and we walked into the square arm, in arm. I realised that he does not know my situation. He has studiously not asked and as we have spoken about everything else I overlooked to tell him. Not exactly overlooked; he felt he could not ask and I felt that I could not blurt it out.

I am the only one who can break this deadlock. He is in an impossible situation.

I stopped and turned to him. Taken unawares he looked at me with intrigue. 'I feel that I should answer the two questions that you have not been in a position to ask me even though you wish to know the answers.'

Muttering, 'bloody detectives,' he shook his head.

'Firstly, I am unattached. There was someone for a while but that is now well and truly over.' Now a look of optimism came over him. 'Secondly,' intrigue replaced the optimism, he is uncertain of what the second question is, 'yes, I would love to join you for dinner.'

Laughing out loud, yet again he said, 'am I so transparent?'

'No, I am just so hopeful.'

He laughed again and asked, 'same place as before, Friday seven thirty?' I nodded "yes." 'I should warn you, I was in there with my aunt, the one who raised me, a few weeks ago and the Maitre de is still going on about the "bellissimo" lady. It led to a grilling from her. I had to tell her some and that things did not progress. She was mystified as to why not but I did not answer that for her.'

'Wise move.'

'I guess that you would like to meet there as before.'

I had not thought of this. Remembering my earlier resolutions and how only today I had determined to not push people away, I realised that this is an earlier than expected opportunity to act on this. 'No, I would be very pleased if you would come to collect me. Come a little early, I can show you my house and we can have a drink.' I told him where I lived. He already knew roughly whereabouts but not which house.

He gave me a little hug and the briefest, deliberately un-presumptuous, kiss, again on the lips as he said, 'I will come at seven. I am so looking forward to it.'

We turned to walk away in our opposite directions. I felt that I did not want us to part but I do have Friday to look forward to. After a couple of steps an idea exploded in my mind. Before I could do the sensible thing, before I could think, before I could stop myself, I turned and I called to him. 'Marcus.' He stopped and turned. 'When you come on Friday you can leave your overnight bag at my house ready for when we get back. It will be easier than taking it to the restaurant.'

He looked shocked and delighted simultaneously. He stepped forward and held me and kissed me again, this time it was no longer chaste. As he pulled away he looked straight into my eyes and softly said, 'unfinished business.'

'Yes, I so much enjoyed the start we made before. On Friday we will not be disturbed.'

THE END

Printed in Great Britain
by Amazon

22090584R00297